# Path of the Lion

## Rising Kingdom

## Part Two: The Throne

## K.T. Brown

Published by Lions Footprints Ent.

# Introducing the Multiworld

In literature, we are accustomed to journeys that navigate through continents or even galaxies. But what if the journey itself were a tapestry woven from different realities? The multiworld genre is a key idea in speculative fiction. It breaks the limits of one universe and explores new possibilities.

The multiworld narrative is a broad story. It unfolds in various connected realities. It goes beyond a single hero and one setting. Instead, it offers many voices, each a hero in their own way. It also showcases various worlds, each with its own unique identity.

At its core, a multiworld story is defined by three key elements:

- **Multiple Worlds:** Each reality has its own natural laws, history, and challenges. These aren't just different kingdoms or planets. They are separate universes, each with its own logic.

- **Diverse Cultures:** With each world comes a new culture. The story explores these societies. It looks at their unique traditions, social structures, and philosophies. This lets us compare what it means to be human or something else in various contexts.

- **Multiple Protagonists:** The story doesn't focus on one hero. Instead, it features a group of main characters. Each character lives in their own world. Their stories come together to create a larger tale that includes all the realities. In *The Path of the Chosen series*, one story centers on Moses Ezenwa, a Nubarian prince set to save his kingdom. Another follows Peter Tucker, a young warrior in a cyberpunk city in Atlantica striving to better himself in the martial arts. Lastly, there's Donavon Ahoka, a warrior from the Hawk Clan with hopes of one day becoming a grand master. No matter the distance or culture, their stories link through a shared fate. They must face a single multiversal threat: the Shadow Lord.

Multiworld literature offers an immersive experience. It invites readers to explore not just one new world, but an entire multiverse. By weaving these different stories together, it forms an epic tale. This narrative is as rich and limitless as our imagination.

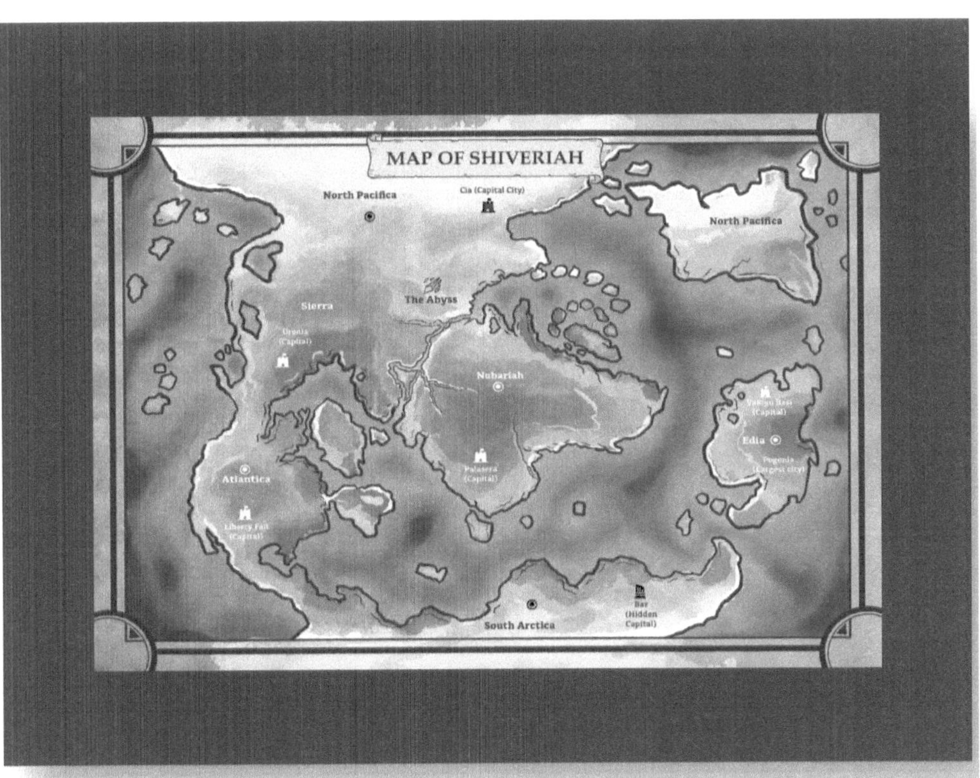

MAP OF SHIVERIAH
North Pacifica
Cia (Capital City)
North Pacifica
Sierra
The Abyss
Utopia (Capital)
Nubariah
Yukiyo Rovi (Capital)
Edia
Pogenia (Largest city)
Atlantica
Palastra (Capital)
Liberty Fall (Capital)
Bar (Hidden Capital)
South Arctica

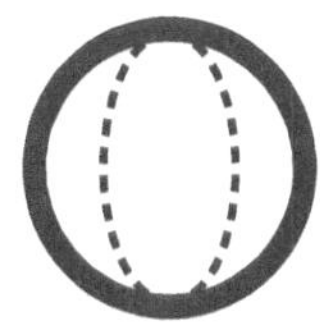

# Six Nations of Shiveria

North Pacifica

Sierra

Atlantica

South Arctica

Nubariah

Edia

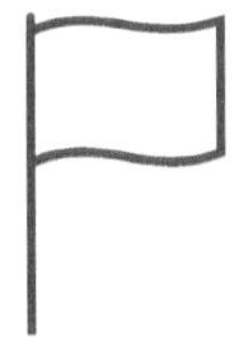

# Clans of Nubariah

Lion Clan (Ouidah Territory)

Oph-Ur Clan (Aswan Territory)

Jaguar Clan (Mombasa Territory)

Wolf Clan (Hidden within the Walswe Mountains)

Monk Clan (Genies Island between Atlantica and Nubariah)

# Contents

To my wife Desiree and my three children Hezekiah, Kyleah, and Selah.

# Chapter One

# A Dark Entity

C *ome, boy*," said a mellow voice amid burning light.

Karungu, the heir of Thuku, followed the voice entering the burning light. He wore brown beads dressed in a white kaftan that sparkled.

*"Come, boy… Come… come… I have everything you desire."*

Karungu continued to follow the burning light with a curious mind. The light blinded him in milliseconds before a room full of gold was revealed to him. It was an unlimited amount of gold with gems glistening in blends. He was mesmerized by the unlimited wealth that was placed before him. He looked up and saw the burning light return but it shifted into a bright circle. Karungu was puzzled at the mysterious light.

*"All this will be yours if you tap into your true nature and power,"* said the same voice through the light.

Karungu was still puzzled. What is his true nature? If only he knew his true power. Then another thought came up.

"My power is what I learned from my ancestors," said Karungu.

*"Yet your father became powerless. Tell me. Is that the power you desire? Or do you want more? Be free from this curse and create your own destiny. It is set all around you. Unlimited wealth, power beyond your imagination."*

Karungu stared at the gold and gemstones. The voice had a point. Karungu did not want to be held back. His mindset was to become Mombassa's greatest Chieftain. He drew to a stack of shinning gold and grabbed a handful of it enthralled by its touch.

*"Got you right where I want you,"* said the voice as it grew more sinister.

Two black tendrils with the texture of gooey ink shot from out of the burning light and grabbed Karungu by the arms. The young man gasped using his strength the pull away from the dark tendrils, but they were too strong. Another tendril shot out and wrapped itself around Karungu. He looked down and saw the pure white of his kaftan stained in black oil. He felt another tendril catch hold of his throat. He gasped for air, but the atmosphere was closed from his esophagus. Karungu was desperate. He grabbed the tendril that gripped his neck trying to break free from the tight-fisted grip. Karungu could feel his body ascending to the light. Death and Hell were calling for him. He wanted to scream but couldn't. This was it. His eyes widened as the light grew brighter.

A long-winded gasp came out of the breath of Karungu as he sat up from his comforting bed. He peered at his surroundings and patted himself. He was not in Hell. It was a sigh of relief to him as he began to turn his focus on reality.

It has been seven years since he witnessed his father turning his back on his nation for the sake of his tribe. He'll never forget that day Ouidah fell to the Shadow League which caused a chain reaction of every tribe in Nubariah to be submissive to the Shadow Lords. Karungu was only a teen groomed to be both a man and leader to take his father's place as Jaguar Clan Chieftain. Witnessing that fatal day left him in a place of hopelessness. Watching his father make deals with the Shadow Lord of abiding by the laws and codes of the Shadow League in exchange for his people's liberty was baffling. *My father is a coward*, were the thoughts he tried to hide from his visage. If he was to take his father's place someday, he knew he had to become fiercer to lead his people.

Karungu summoned a couple of servants to freshen him in his personal washroom. It was the lavish treatment he was delighted to wake up to. The servants drenched him in his royal garment of leopard-spotted fur with a kaftan underneath. A gold chain was dangled over his neck as well as a gold digital watch. Karungu was officially in his reality, the lavish lifestyle into which he was born.


Once Karungu was dressed, he entered the palace halls of Lyayo, the Capital City of Mombassa. Lyayo was known as the Chrome City since the material for each building were made of solid chrome. Karungu walked down a path that led to a series of chambers. A woman stopped him in his tracks.

"You know your father is waiting for you in the council chambers," she said.

"I am aware of what father wants," said Karungu.

He turned around and faced the woman ignoring her Bantu braids and rose-colored lipstick.

"But I need to take care of something first."

"I know I am only your father's betrothed and not your mother, but I do care for you like a son. And I do care about your relationship with him. He may have made bad decisions as Chieftain, but he does mean well about your future."

"And that's the thing. You or Father know nothing of my well-being and how I feel. But you are right about one thing, he made a lot of bad decisions. Tell him I'll be there in a few minutes."

"Please don't keep him waiting Karungu. You know he's not a man of much patience."

Karungu turned from his father's betrothed and continued down the path leading to the chambers that were lined in rows. He entered a chamber that had an altar leading to a shrine. Burning incents were leaning within golden bowls in the shrine. A man in a beige kaftan wrapped in a turban matching his outfit was on his hands and knees praying in Swahili at the shrine. *"Mkubwa Ponyeni watu wetu. Iponye nchi yetu, ili tuwe kitu kimoja."* (Great Supreme heal our people. Heal our land, so we can become one). The man stood facing Karungu.

"I see that you are troubled young man," he said.

"Chief Priest I come to you to see if you can understand this dream I had last night," said Karungu.

The Priest nodded and gestured for the Jaguar Clan Prince to sit at a table near the altar. Karungu sat across the table from the Chief Priest. For a few seconds, there was silence.

"So tell me Karungu what bothers you?"

"I had a nightmare. It was pleasant for me in the beginning, but then things grew dark. I saw a burning light that led me to an unlimited amount of wealth. But then a voice told me that I must tap into my true nature and power to receive it. I embraced it at first, but then I was taken by three tendrils that came from the burning light. I was dragged to the light then I woke up here."

The Chief Priest was silent for a moment.

"Be careful of the decisions you make Karungu. We are living in dark times. Every choice we make has an impact on the people around us. You are the heir to the throne. A crucial moment will happen, and you alone will have to make a decision that will change the rest of your life."

"I see, but you didn't explain the tendrils and the burning light."

"If you had a dream of tendrils dragging you to a burning light then you are dealing with great deception. Perhaps your own heart is deceived. I did dream myself. I was shown by the Supreme that the dark entity is returning to join the Shadow Lords for the final war yet to come. Ekwenzu is looking for a new host. That dream you had is a warning Karungu. If you are tempted by your darkest impulse, you must turn from it quickly. Every man is capable of evil. But we also are capable of righteous acts. We all have decisions to make. Be sure to choose wisely Karungu."

The Jaguar Clan Prince rose to his feet and bowed to the Chief Priest.

"Thank you for bringing me clarity Chief Priest. I better get going. My father is waiting for me."

"The pleasure is all mine," said the Chief Priest.

Karungu walked out of the chamber to get to his father as the Chief Priest returned to the altar resuming his prayer.

Karungu rushed to the war chamber to meet with his father and his council. He slammed the wooden double doors open panting for air. His father and the council members stood to their feet giving him a disgusting look. Karungu stepped forth.

"Baba, my apologies for being…"

His father raised his hand to silence him. He was impatient. Karungu could tell by his scrunching lips.

"Save it, boy," he said. "You are the heir to my throne, and you arrive fifteen minutes late to an important meeting."

"But baba I…"

"Save it. Sit. There is much to discuss."

Karungu gave his father a quick glare and sat down. It was bad enough he was being scolded like a child at the age of 23, but for him unable to explain himself or have a say was getting to him. Karungu sat at the long table. The council sat along with his father. Karungu tried his best to draw back his temper. His lips were poked. He folded his hands on the table making himself appear to be engaged in his father's words as he continued the meeting.

"As I was saying before I was interrupted, there will be some changes made for Mombassa for our people to be more safe and secure. Now recently I made a deal with Emperor Mercius that will change the course of our territory. The Emperor agrees to withdraw his warriors from monitoring our cities and villages. We will now police our own people without interferences from outsiders."

The council in the chamber was cheering. Karungu curled his lips slightly with a smile. Conceivably his father finally did something right since Nubariah's destruction and the rise of the Bronze Empire. His father continued.

"In exchange for our military and militia to get re-educated in the dark arts."

"What!" yelled one of the council members.

Karungu was in a state of shock looking around at the baffled council.

"So, you're telling me that you are now selling out your military too!" questioned the council member.

Karungu stared at his father in utter confusion. He knew there was a catch to this. His father was helpless. It was too good to be true.

"Please, settle down," his father pleaded.

"How can we settle down with this outrage! It's bad enough our people are docile and lost their way of life. But now our military?"

"They will have an advantage..."

"But how? Once one practice the dark arts, there's no coming back. You can't wield both light and dark elements. You can only wield one power and quench the other. You might be scrambling for survival your highness, but the rest of us here are suffering. The Shadow Lord will soon set you up for your grave..."

"Enough!" yelled the Chieftain. "Nubariah is gone, and we have no leader to guide us in these times. The Bronze Empire has taken over and if we rebel now, our efforts will be buried along with our bodies. Compromise is the only answer to stay in power and lead our people to a new age."

Karungu leaned back peering around the council and his father. Another council member opened his mouth to speak.

"I say we put this decision to a vote."

"This is not a democracy!" yelled the Chieftain banging his fist on the table. "We have no choice but to follow the Emperor or face death."

"We're dying anyway as a people. All favor of vetoing the military re-education initiative say "I"."

The entire council raised their hands with "I's". Karungu was hesitant glancing at his father who scowled at him, but he raised his hand saying, "I".

His father scowled.

"You don't know what you're getting your into," he said. Emperor Mercius is ruthless. He can cause a mass genocide in seconds."

"We must gain back our honor," said the council member. "Chieftain Oba died with his."

Karungu watched as his father stormed out of the chamber without a word. He felt a hand touch his shoulder.

"Your father is a good man," the council member said. "He means well for his people, but he's doing this the wrong way. Have faith in your father."

Karungu dropped his head. *Why keep making excuses for him*, he thought. Karungu stood to his feet.

"Looks like this meeting is adjourned," he said. "I will now retire back to my chambers for now."

# Chapter Two

# The Next Phase

The words of Moses' victory of becoming Ouidah's new Chieftain was spreading fast like wildfire throughout Nubariah. Will he be able to overthrow the Shadow Lord? were the questions being asked by each tribe. There were doubts of Moses overthrowing the tyrannous power of Mercius, yet the hope of many dwindled the naysayers who lost hope in their people and themselves.

Palasera, that city that became a painful memory to Moses was full of darkness that clouded his senses. He couldn't deviate the plot against him nor could he imagine it as Mercius sat on the throne with his wife Amaryllis sitting beside him. He was comforted in the custom kaftan chieftains would usually wear. A crown of gold circled his head. The scepter which was the tradi-tional chieftain's spear was hung on the wall above him. He was truly a god. Members of his dark council sat along with him in a meeting. His seven-year-old son Kulrath was by his side learning the ways of becoming a Shadow Lord to be groomed as the next emperor of the Bronze Empire.

"I must say for myself that we must end our conflict with the Outer Realms," said one of the council members. "We have everything we need. With Nubariah conquered and colonized, the Shadow League no longer has a threat. Besides, we still have our realms intact. The clans have been brought to heel. There is a reason why Lord Chashak established the Shadow Legion. I say we make peace and merge once again with the Outer Realms.

"So now we are to take the coward's way out?" questioned Mercius. "You know Lord Khonshu will not stand for such ideology. Yes, Lord Chashak has created the Shadow Legion to take over the cosmos. But you should understand that this is about power. And that is the reason the Shadow Legion will remain divided between the Inner and Outer Realms. Besides, Lord Chashak gave Khonshu the freedom to invade the Outer Realms if there is a weakness."

"Pardon me for interrupting but we will have to create a better strategy," said Amaryllis. "Maybe we could send a few spies in worlds like Drakirus or Thesatune. Use some of our slaves for their servitude as bait."

Mercius rubbed his fiery red goatee.

"That will be too risky. Besides, the Outer Realms will use our servants against us. I trust in Khonshu's efforts. The only thing I'm mainly concerned about for now is the royal family of Ouidah."

Amaryllis smirked while the dark council sat in silence.

"The family of the dead Chieftain should be the least of your concern," she said. "Remember what Lord Khonshu said. Eventually, they will be smoked out."

The door of the throne room opened gaining the dark council and Mercius' attention. A cyborg woman sauntered with its black metal body and pale face. Its grey eyes were as emotionless as the Shadow Lord's. Mercius got up to his feet in anguish.

"What now? Can't you see we are in a meeting? I should dismantle you right now!"

The cyborg kneeled to the Shadow Lord ignoring his outburst.

"My lord," it said in a woman's voice. "Apologies for intruding during your meeting. I know it is forbidden in my programming, but I have an urgent message that you must hear immediately."

Mercius gave the cyborg a cold stare and hummed.

"This must be urgent if you bypassed your programming," he said. "Proceed."

The cyborg got up to its feet as its eyes began flashing white sending images from its memory bank. Mercius and the dark council watched with intrigue.

"There have been reports all over the three territories that Ouidah has chosen the new Chieftain. The youngest son of the late Chieftain Oba, Moses Ezenwa, has defeated his older brother Ramses with a power that nearly matches the gods. Moses will soon be consecrated by Grand Guardian Amine in the small village of Dolsa where the royal family has been laying low since the Sack of Palasera."

Mercius rubbed his goatee as his wife sneered.

"Looks like this is your chance," she said.

He let out a smirk.

"Yes, it is," he said. "And it's time for the next phase. The Lion Clan truly tried to build an army under our radar and expect to attack us when we least expect it? Ngozi and that sniveling widow of Oba must be more foolish than I thought. We will move in silence. Our attack will hit them hard where they least expect it. Then the remnant of the Lion Clan will finally be destroyed. The blood of Oba's family will glisten in my hands. And their new little Chieftain will die by my hands alone."

"And the Inner Realm will have the upper hand in prestige," said Amaryllis.

"Yes, and it will be bittersweet."

***

It was only a week after Moses defeated his brother as he waited day by day to be consecrated by the Grand Guardian. Each day he passed by the market, people were greeting and congratulating him. The lady at the bakery stand gave Moses free cookies as a complimentary award. At the Academy, Moses gained the attention of every student, including the students of Level 3 in the School of Knowledge that usually gives Ramses all the attention. Moses hoped his big brother would commend him for his victory, but he was rarely seen except at home and practice where he was completely shame-faced for his failure.

"Congratulations Moses," a student would say walking past him.

"You have gained a lot of popularity, my friend," said Korah. "Good thing I'm on the winning team."

"Yeah," said Moses. "But I can't wait until the Grand Guardian consecrate me."

"When will that be?" asked Korah. "I don't remember him saying. He just disappeared again after the fight."

"I don't know. But I'm sure it will be soon."

The days went by as Moses waited as patiently as he could for the Grand Guardian's next entrance to consecrate him. But soon his patience thinned. The celebration of his victory calmed throughout the village. As the week went by things went back to normal. Moses' old life began to rise back to the surface. It's as if he never earned the title of Chieftain.

Moses groaned wiping his eyes as he laid flat in his bed. It was the day of Eke, the fourth day of rest where the markets were closed in observation of the holy day. This was the day Moses had a few extra hours of sleep before his mother would call him to get up for their weekly Odinani worship within the shrines.

"Moses!" yelled his mother. "Get up now, you've had enough rest!"

Moses rolled out of his bed ignoring the scent of fresh mint coming from a hot beverage that his mother made. Moses already knew the average meal he was about to sink his teeth into, forcing his taste buds to swallow every bite of bread sandwich consisting of the flavors of boiled eggs, omelet, Sanga sausage and bacon, canned sardines, corned beef, and mackerel in tomato sauce with the finishing touches of mint and mellow leaf tea.

He slid his feet to the closet wiping his eyes while picking his outfit for the Odinani gathering. Moses slipped on a blue kaftan with blue matching shorts. He picked out a pair of brown sandals then went to the bathroom and freshened himself. He splashed his face in cold water to get the sleep out of his eyes. He brushed his teeth and wiped his body with an oily fragrance that had the sweet scent of citrus.

Moses stepped into the kitchen while wrapping the white turban on his head and kissed his mother on the cheek as she sat silently on the table. She wore a red and rose gold linen dress with a red hair covering. Food was already provided at the table, the very same meal Moses predicted.

"Good morning mother," he said.

"Good morning my sweet," she said. "Ramses! We don't have all day to wait on you today! Your brother already beat you to the table!/"

Moses watched as Ramses dragged his feet to the kitchen. It was like his spirit drifted from his body as he looked pale wearing a tan kaftan that looked like sackcloth. He wore sandals on his bare feet with his locks dangling from his back to his forehead. It was a sad image for Moses. He began to feel guilty figuring he crushed his big brother's spirit. Moses was used to Ramses wearing one of his dazzling kaftans that would impress the women around him. Ramses' confidence was truly gone.

His mother turned her head nearly letting out a gasp.

"Why are you dressed like that?" she said. "Have you no shame at all?"

Ramses ignored her walking to the table.

"Boy don't you ignore me when I'm talking to you."

Ramses walked past her to get to his seat not responding. His facial expression was blank. He felt his arm being jerked. He wanted to react, but he knew it was his mother grabbing him. He would never harm her. He vowed to protect her and Moses before he advanced his training within the School of Combat. Ramses turned to face her. He saw the anger ignite in her eyes.

"Just because you are advanced in your training doesn't mean you can disrespect me. I am still your mother!"

Ramses jerked his arm away from her and planted himself in a chair next to her on the table. Moses could feel the tension. This was his fault. He allowed the luster to fade from Ramses. His big brother was broken. His mother slammed her hands on the table with a fury he never could fathom. Moses wanted to leave, but he felt he would be scolded next if he tried.

"Dammit child!" she shrieked. "I carried you for nine months! There is no reason for you to feel such pain! You have been in this mood all week. You haven't spoken to anyone. You have been all but disrespectful to me. You look at your brother like he has taken your life.

"Because he did mother!" replied Ramses. "Moses took everything from me!" He took my pride, my light, and most important of all my birthright."

Moses and his mother were silent. The guilt was now hanging.

"That's right mother, you might as well say I don't exist. Moses is now the firstborn. He is now the legacy to the Ezenwa name. But I forgot, you favored him over me anyway didn't you."

*Smack!* was the sound heard across the table as Ashanti's hand met Ramses' cheek in a hard impact. Moses' jaw dropped. Breakfast was over before it started. Ramses held his cheek and scowled, storming away from the table. Ashanti marched after him. Her fury was at an all-time high.

"Come back here boy!" she yelled.

Ashanti used her body weight to push Ramses to the wall. He huffed nearly letting out tears of frustration. She glared into his eyes and pointed her finger at him getting his attention.

"You listen to me and listen to me good! Your father did not sacrifice himself just so you can stoop this low. I know it's been hard, but we still got through this."

Moses could see tears streaming through her eyes. Ramses tried his best to hold back his, but the emotion he felt from his mother got the best of him.

"I know the birthright was given to your brother," she continued. "The Supreme God works in ways I can't understand. But that's why you must pray. Pray for your next journey. Offer your sacrifice in the shrines. Now you pull yourself together and honor your father's name, your ancestor's name. And put on some decent clothes."

She wiped the tears from her eyes and walked back to the table. Moses' head was down. He wiped the tears from his eyes placing his head on the palm of his hands. Ramses walked back to his room without a single glare.

Moments later the door was banging. Moses and his family finished eating their breakfast as Ashanti finished clearing the plates.

"It must be Ngozi," she said.

She rushed to the living room answering the door. Ngozi stood at the doorway with a smile and kissed her on the palm of her hand. He wore a yellow garment with kente patterns of orange blended with black, green, and white. His black suede shoes were glistening by the rays of the sun.

"Greetings your highness," he said.

"Ngozi, how many times have I told you, you don't have to call me that."

"I know, but you are the widow of the late great chief."

"Of course. Come in, I don't know why you keep acting like a stranger when you enter my home."

"I can't help but to be polite. It's in my nature."

Ashanti grinned.

"Just come in and enter."

Ngozi walked through the door and took a seat at a nearby couch.

"I'll go get the boys," Ashanti said.

"You mean men," said Ngozi.

Ashanti smiled and walked past Ngozi towards the kitchen.

"Boys, it's time to go! Ngozi's here!"

Moses got up from his chair and made his way to the living room. He saw Master Ngozi sitting on the chair with his leg crossed. It seemed like he was in deep thought. Moses bowed with his fist pumped to his chest.

"Greetings master," he said.

Ngozi turned and saw Moses.

"Greetings," he said. "You look the part."

"Thank you, master."

Ashanti walked back into the living room as if she was in some type of urgency. Moses knew it was time to go as she put on round golden earrings in her ears.

"I'm just waiting on your brother," she said.

"He's still down I'm guessing," Ngozi said.

"Yes, and it's utterly ridiculous," she said.

"Just give him some time."

"Well, today he's on his own. I've waited enough. It's time to go."

"Are you sure you do not want to wait for a few minutes?"

"I am not fooling around with that boy today. Let's go."

Moses saw his mother's hand already turning the knob to the door. Ngozi shrugged his shoulders getting up from his seat. Moses followed his mother out the door with Ngozi following. This was going to be the first Eke without Ramses. He didn't know if this was the best thing that ever happened to him or a sad moment. It was however weird.

The shrine was only a few miles away as Moses lagged behind his mother and Ngozi. His mind was in and out thinking about his consecration as Chieftain. It was the greatest accomplishment of his life, but he could feel the pressure weighing on him. Moses knew eventually he would have to face the Shadow Lord for the sake of his nation. He couldn't understand how to face him, to match his power, his strength, his impossible speed. Then Moses thought of Khonshu. He wanted to avenge his father, but he knew nothing of the potential he has of defeating him. This was getting way over his head. He was not consecrated yet. Perhaps he wasn't ready after all. He suddenly snapped out of his thoughts after hearing his mother and Ngozi giggling. Every time she's around Ngozi she seems to have a smile that sparkles like a kindling fire. Ngozi always made the best of company for her. He never failed his vow of protecting her, Moses, and his brother. Moses smiled. It brought him joy to see his mother happy.

It was moments later when Moses accompanied his mother and Ngozi to the shrine as they entered a gate of clay walls. Around them was red dirt with a structure that was painted red with white runes. The roof was decorated with piles of straw that looked like wool. Different types of artifacts surrounded the shrine. The sacred grounds.

"It's such a shame that Ramses decided to forsake the Supreme God on His day of rest," Moses heard Ashanti say to Ngozi.

Moses was silent. There was nothing he could say to justify how Ramses was acting. He only followed his mother and Ngozi to a circle of men, women, and children in colorful drapes and kaftans. Within the circle, women were dancing barefoot to the rhythm of drums.

Moses settled in a spot next to his mother along with Ngozi and a group of high-class villagers. Sitting in the center of where he sat, Moses saw a man of a shaved head with a long white beard covered in a yellow drape with multi-colors; the High Chief Priest of Ouidah.

"Greetings your highness," said a man with a white and gold kaftan and black ozo hat to Ashanti.

She replied in a calm tone while watching the women dance in the Odinani ritual. Moses watched as the women continued to step in rhythmic harmony. The man with the yellow drape stood to his feet as the drums stopped beating. The women departed as the High Chief Priest stood in the middle of the circle.

"Brothers and sisters," he said. "We are gathered here today for another day of Eke, the day our Supreme God has ordained as a day of rest. We may have lost our land to the dark ones, but we will forever have our honor as long as we do not turn from our way of life."

Moses turned his head to Ngozi remembering the similar wisdom he gave to him over the years.

"We must not turn away from our gifts," the High Chief Priest continued. "Abiama has gifted all of us with the spirit energy of T'kaf. Only a few are powerful enough to wield it. But only one is chosen for their T'kaf to allow them to become as powerful as the gods."

The High Chief Priest looked directly at Moses. In a brief moment, Moses could feel the attention he once felt a week ago.

"When one is chosen, it is not only his responsibility but his choice. There are two paths a warrior must choose. One path is Abiama's knowledge, power, and the light of Chukwu. Then there is another. The path of Ekwenzu, the traitor, the trickster, the dark one of Nubariah that follows Chashak the Dark Lord. How fate can change a man's spirit. That's why we must guard our hearts; use our power wisely and never forget our way of life or we will face the other side of chaos and destruction."

After the High Chief Priest was done preaching, everyone went to the shrine for their sacrifice and offering.

"Come, Moses," said his mother letting out her hand on the shrine steps. "We're up next after Ngozi."

Moses took her hand awaiting Ngozi's exit out of the shrine. He turned his head and saw Ramses at the corner of his eyes greeting a few of the villagers with changed clothes. He wanted to squeal to his mother of Ramses' rebellious act of showing up after the Odinani was close to the finish. It was as if he could do whatever he wanted with little to no repercussions. But then Moses thought to himself, *Whatever he does on Eke is his problem, not mine.* Moses turned back to his mother as Ngozi made his exit out of the shrine. He placed his hand on Ashanti's shoulder and whispered, "Do not get angry but your son has arrived."

"After most of the Odinani ceremony is complete? This is un-acceptable!"

Ngozi shushed her.

"Take Moses to the shrine with you. I will handle the boy my-self."

Ngozi walked away before she could speak another word. Ashanti scowled, nearly gripping Moses' hand but she kept her composure as she straightened her face.

"Come, Moses," she said. "Let us go and give our offering to our Supreme God."

Moses nodded his head as he walked side by side with his mother into the shrine. Moses looked around at the relics of Ouidah's history of kings, warriors, and deities. He could see the runes on the statues of warriors leaning on the clay walls full of white dots. He could smell a strong aroma of burning incense lingering around the shrine's interior. Moses walked side by side with his mother along the brown carpet leading to the High Chief Priest as he sat on a wooden chair. Moses saw his mother get on her knees in a calm he would only see her for moments like this. He did the same as the High Chief Priest spoke.

"What is it you ask of Abiama this day?" he asked.

"I ask that He continue to protect me and my sons. That my oldest will not be led astray."

"It is done. Now, what about the boy?"

"I'm sorry?" questioned Ashanti.

The High Chief Priest turned to Moses.

"The boy, what is it you ask for Abiama? You are our chieftain to be."

Moses leaned his head down. This is the first time he would ever bring a request to the Supreme directly.

"Moses speak," said Ashanti. "This is an honor for a child to make his request in the shrine."

Moses looked up staring into a space away from the High Chief Priest. Away from his mother. He knew he couldn't hold back the feelings that were bottled down for years. This was sacred grounds.

"I ask Abiama for justice, that my father will be avenged. I ask for peace, that my people will be free from darkness. I ask for healing, so I can finally be whole."

A streak of tears drew from Moses' eyes. He felt a hand patting and rubbing his back. Moses knew it was his mother. He saw on the corner of his eyes her eyes welling with tears. The High Chief Priest got up from the wooden chair.

"Your request is done," he said. "But for your request to happen, you must perform the act and choose how this will be done. You must perform the acts of justice. You must wage war to make peace. And you must unite the people to become whole. This is the wisdom I am passing to you on your journey."

The High Chief Priest began to speak in Igbo. "Mee ka umu gi nuru gi. Nam nditọ fo ẹkop. Abiama gozie ha. Gọzie ha na njem ha. (Let your children hear you. Let your children hear. Abiama bless them. Bless them on their journey.)

Moses saw the smoke from the incense fuming around him and his mother. It was dense. The smell of myrrh tingled his nose as he could see the smoke separating him and his mother. He couldn't see anyone. At this point, his ears were shut from the sounds around him. At this point, all he could see was his destiny.

All he could see was the throne with the shadow monster stepping in front of him.

"You will never see this day boy," it said with its iron sharp teeth snaring.

Moses gasped backing away as the monster stepped towards him.

"Long live the chief," it said.

Moses let out a cough nearly choking on the incense. The smoke was beginning to clear. His mother wrapped her arms around him. She could tell this was something he wasn't used to. The High Chief Priest sat back on his chair.

"It's okay son," she said to him. "I got you."

"I just don't know what to do," said Moses in rapid breaths. "Even the Grand Guardian is starting to see me as unworthy."

Moses felt his mother's embrace in continuance. He looked up as the High Chief Priest leaned on his chair in a troubling look.

"It's like what your master has taught you," he said to Moses directly. "You must let go."

"Come, Moses, our requests have been answered," said his mother.

She helped him to his feet as they walked out of the shrine. Moses turned around with an apologetic look to the High Chief Priest. He felt embarrassed and ashamed placing his fear over his faith in such a sacred place. He's supposed to be the new chieftain soon. But after being conquered by the vision again, he felt he wasn't worthy of carrying the title. At least not right now.

Outside, Moses followed his mother back to the sacred grounds. He watched as Ngozi walked side by side with Ramses towards him and his mother. Ramses looked apologetic. It was as if he regretted everything he said to his mother earlier that morning. Perhaps this was another one of his tricks to win his mother over like he always does, were thoughts that entered Moses' mind. He knew his brother all too well. Ramses bowed to his mother in a kind gesture which was a way to show respect to the king and queen of Nubariah.

*Oh, he's good*, thought Moses.

"Mother," said Ramses. I apologize for my actions this morning. Especially on a day like this. I have broken the sacred values of our nation by purposely missing the weekly ritual of Odinani. I'll accept whatever punishment you give me."

His mother stared at him as if he were a page to a book. Moses hoped she wouldn't let him off that easy. What he did was completely uncalled for, and if it was him, he would get severely punished for his actions. She sighed and pointed her finger at his face.

"Make sure this doesn't ever happen again," she said. Do you hear me?"

"Yes mother," Ramses said sounding innocent.

"Although your brother has won the throne, you still be the example of being his big brother. Do you understand me?"

"Yes, mother."

"Apology accepted."

*Wow just like that and no punishment*, thought Moses. *Typical*.

Ngozi walked up to Ashanti and her children.

"You don't have to worry about the boy," said Ngozi. "I straightened him out. I promise you he won't do it again. He will receive punishment this week."

Moses made a slight smile. His very dream of his brother getting punished for his actions was coming true. Finally, his days of perfection were over. Winning the throne was the best thing that has ever happened to him.

"Good," she said. "Now let's get out of here, I'm getting hungry."

Ngozi agreed as he led her, Moses, and Ramses out of the sacred grounds. While walking Moses began to feel a presence. It was a familiar presence in which its power radiated the atmosphere. He could tell Ngozi could feel it too because he stopped in his tracks. Moses' mouth was open, hearing the voice of the High Chief calling in the background.

"He's here!"

Moses could hear the confused chatter of people around him. But Moses knew exactly who the High Chief Priest was referring to, the Grand Guardian. He walked through the gate with four of his men. His majestic presence tensed the atmosphere around him. The crowd gasped and bowed to him. Moses did the same along with his mother, Ramses, and Ngozi.

"You may all rise to your feet," he said. "I am not a god, but a messenger."

Moses stood to his feet watching everyone around him arise. The Grand Guardian scanned the crowd for a moment before letting out a word.

"Our Supreme God Abiama has spoken! The new Chieftain will be consecrated!"

Moses could hear the sound of joy spreading throughout the sacred grounds. He was gracious for the Grand Guardian to show himself on the day of Eke, but he still questioned if he was ready.

Ramses could feel the rage within him. The thought of losing his birthright replayed in his mind.

"Moses Ezenwa!" called the Grand Guardian. "Step forth!"

Moses felt as if his heart shot up to his throat. He didn't know if he felt heat flashes or his nerves getting the best of him. Moses knew at that moment he would pass out before he could take a step. Then he saw Ngozi's face, feeling a grip on his shoulders.

"Listen to me," said Ngozi. "I don't know what happened to you at the shrine, but your destiny is calling you. Do not fear child. You are the bloodline of Ezenwa. The power of Chukwu is within you. Now go. I will be with you, I promise."

Moses nodded as Ngozi gestured him to step forward. His mother smiled at him nearly welling out tears of joy. His brother stared at him blankly hiding his true feelings. Moses stepped out to the open towards the Grand Guardian. He was timid, but he knew what he had to do at this moment. The Grand Guardian stared into his eyes. Moses never felt this timid before.

"I can sense your fear boy," said the Grand Guardian. "If you are to be chief, you need to put all emotions aside for a higher purpose. Perhaps you are not ready."

Moses felt as if a spark shot in him. He dropped to his knees and held the Grand Guardian's sandaled feet.

"I am ready for the trials your majesty," he said. "I promise you I am."

The Grand Guardian looked down with a look that nearly became a scowl.

"Actions are more effective than words. Get up, boy. If you are truly ready, then you will have to show me that you are ready."

Moses got up to his feet. It was as if his stomach was knotted in a double loop. But he had to face his destiny. He had to have courage. He had to conquer the demon inside.

"I promise you I will."

The Grand Guardian was silent for a moment. He stepped up to Moses rubbing his long beard.

"You have untapped power boy," he said. "And it will come out. I promise you."

There was another pause.

"You will come with me to Sahawayda for one week of training. Ngozi will accompany you as well. He is after all your mentor. If you pass the trials ahead, you will get consecrated. But if you fail, you will be stripped from the title as Chieftain and the Ezenwa name will be cut off from the kingship."

Moses shut himself from the gasps thinking of the pressure that the Grand Guardian has applied to him. Was he serious? Does he even have the authority to call such a command? Moses felt as if the world was spiraling out of control.

"You have one day to prepare," the Grand Guardian continued. "Then you will take your journey to the sacred temple. Until then."

The Grand Guardian and his men walked out of the sacred grounds leaving Moses in a nervous state. The pressure was officially applied. He could hear people around him saying, "Can he truly do that?" Then he heard the naysayers speaking, "That boy is going to fail us." Moses dropped his head and turned back to face his family. He felt a hand being placed on top of his head. Moses looked up to see Ngozi smiling down at him.

"Come, let us depart from this place," he said.

Ngozi nodded in a gesture for Ashanti and Ramses to follow him. Moses walked along Ngozi and his family in silence. He was unsure of what to make of the training and trials set by the Grand Guardian. Whatever it was he had two choices that threw weight on him. He was either to pass the trials, become Chieftain and eventually challenge the Shadow Lord for the throne. Or he was to fail himself, his nation, and most importantly his father's legacy of the Ezenwa name.

# Betrayal

As Moses was left with a dire task in Ouidah, Mercius walked side by side with his wife and son at the balcony leading to the garden of the palace. He had on a bronze army plate with a flaming short sword tucked in his holster. They were surrounded by chateau walls of gold and emerald. Below them within the garden, the shadow army was gearing for war on beasts that had bare and scaley skin. The creatures had long necks with teeth as sharp as knives. Their eyes were like the color of a flame with wings that expanded in massive width.

"Ah, isn't this a beauty to behold," said Mercius. "My army prepared to deliver what will be glorious."

"Do you have to prepare your army in my beautiful garden?" she questioned. "This area is too romantic for such barbarism."

"This area is one of the largest on the palace grounds," said Mercius. "Besides, we'll be out your hair in a moment."

Mercius walked ahead of his wife to the garden alongside his son. He stared at one of the beasts that were prepared for him on the palace grounds. He placed his hand on the creature as it responded like a servant to the master with its neck wrapped around Mercius' shoulder.

"The saakuth are Nether's most reliable creature," he said. "Especially for war."

"Are you sure a small task force is enough?" wondered Amaryllis. "We cannot underestimate our enemies. They may have gotten stronger than last time."

Mercius cuffed his hand on her cheek. His stare was loveless, but Amaryllis smirked only caring about the power they shared.

"Do not underestimate the power of dark magic, my dear," he said. "Nor the art of it."

Mercius placed an arrow with a stack of bows on the saddle and climbed on the saakuth's back extending his hand to his son. The boy looked at his father, almost in uncertainty. This would be his first mission joining his father in such a rigorous task he only heard in stories. But his father told him that he would one day become a Shadow Lord, a ruler within the ten realms of the cosmos. Kulrath took his father's hand and climbed on top of the saakuth. Mercius looked down watching one of the Nubarian handmaidens walk forward towards him with a shiny bronze helmet in her hands. The handmaiden was in a frayed grey dress; her beaded braids touched the small of her back. The Shadow Lord glared at her as she bowed in fear.

"My... lord," she said. "I... I have your... helmet..."

"Just give me the blasted helmet!" snapped Mercius. "I have a timely schedule I must complete."

Tears welled from the woman's eyes as she quivered. She extended her arm to give Mercius the helmet. His glare was continuous, almost everlasting. Mercius snatched the helmet from her hands and placed it on his head. Amaryllis glanced at the woman shaking her head in disappointment.

"Why do you serfs make things so difficult?" questioned Amaryllis. "All you had to do was simply hand the Shadow Lord his war helmet and you quiver as if you caught a fever."

The woman quivered trying to hold back her tears.

"I'm sorry your highness," the woman said.

Amaryllis stepped up to her with an intense stare.

"As you should be," she said. "Perhaps we should make an example out of you."

The woman couldn't hold back the tears. She knew what the Shadow Goddess' words meant about "making an example out of you". She was one of the many serfs that both witnessed and endeavored the torturous punishments of the Shadow Lords through their dark magic. She didn't want another fair share of mental and physical torture. The woman backed a few steps while Amaryllis pursued her.

"Enough," said Mercius. "What is your name?"

The woman was hesitant but spoke in a soft tone.

"Chideah."

Mercius glowered making her body stiff. He turned his head staring at the clouds.

"Go with the other handmaidens to prepare for supper," he said to her.

"Y...Yes my lord," said Chideah. She rushed away from the garden hoping to avoid the Shadow Lord's torture.

Amaryllis viewed her husband on the saakuth. She was impressed by his valiant appearance.

"I'm leaving you in charge of the palace," Mercius said. "Make sure the handmaidens are in order and the servants stay in their place."

"I will," she said. "Now bring our empire triumph and show our son the true power of the Shadow League."

Mercius nodded his head and nudged the saakuth to walk forward. His saakuth marched forward to reach the front of the army. The dark warriors followed suit and climbed on their saakuth in unison. The Shadow Lord nudged the creature again as it expanded its wings and floated off the ground. The saakuth soared to the clouds as Mercius created dark portals for them to enter.

It was only a day since Moses was confronted by the Grand Guardian of his next challenge. His mother decided to let him spend his final day with her before departing to Sahawayda instead of going to the academy. Moses walked alongside her in the market square savoring the moment before his departure. It was just him and her, alone. No older brother acting spoiled and snobbish of losing a title he didn't want anyway. He wished he could see Korah before leaving Dolsa. He wanted to tell him that his time was coming and he would not let his people down.

Moses saw Korah as his support system more than his brother could ever be. Perhaps he would see him later. His mother smiled at him in a glee that was foreign to him. He wanted to ask her was she feeling okay because he was used to the tough love that only a father would give him. But instead, he smiled back embracing the moment that he would cherish in his memory bank.

"Outside is beautiful isn't it son?" she asked.

Moses only nodded his head as a response embracing the warm air that touched his face. He peered around the busy market. Since it was the hours of the academy, the market square was only filled with women, who were housewives probably shopping for their households accompanied by small children and babies; the elders of the village, both men and women, who were enjoying their golden years past their prime; the guard, who were patrolling the area to ensure the village was in order with no potential threats that could harm the people.

Moses felt his mother playing softly through his hair as they continued walking down the square. She broke the temporary silence through the thin crowd.

"The sun is smiling down on us," she said. "Even amid our troubles, the Supreme Abiama still shows us the beauty of Shiveria. We still are blessed to see the birds flying in the heavens; the flowers blossoming from the ground; the waters flowing from each season's breeze."

Moses heard his mother with an understanding of the point she was making. Yet he wanted her to get to the point. What did this have to do with him and what was at stake? But instead, she paused with a near chuckle.

"You must learn how to enjoy life more Moses. You're only a boy, yet you allow depression to overcome you. You know Ngozi would tell you the same thing."

She stopped at a nearby tree to get shade. Moses followed her as they sat under the tree on top of the soft grass.

"What I'm trying to say Moses is that you will overcome this. When we were in the shrine, I could feel a spirit latching on you that for some reason holds you back from your true potential as a warrior. Trust me, that spirit was on me as well. No one took the time to tell you the history of the Ezenwa bloodline."

*Do I really have to hear another history lesson*? thought Moses.

"The Ezenwa bloodline was started by the almighty Chukwu. Legends have it that his power was second to the Supreme Abiama's. He defeated Ekwenzu the trickster to earn the throne. Chukwu was a great leader and the wisest king Nubariah has ever had. Then the Nubarian Civil War took place around the Feast of Liberation."

Moses sat up intrigued after leaning on the tree. He heard of a civil war briefly in his history lessons at the academy, but he was never taught in-depth about what the war was about. He only knew that the war took place thousands of years ago between loyalists and rebels. Then a thought suddenly struck his brain like a swift spear to the gut as Moses' eyes widened.

"Did the war start because of Ekwenzu's jealousy?" he asked.

She smiled showing the gleam of her teeth.

"You will make a wise king son," she said. "Ekwenzu was Chukwu's greatest general. His might and power were second to Chukwu. He helped bring order and security to Nubariah. That was until his pride got the best of him. He built an army behind Chukwu's back and started a rebellion against the kingdom Chukwu established. The two battled again to the death, but in the end, Chukwu and his army stood tall. Ekwenzu and his followers were banished to the outer nations."

"Wow, I never knew that. How come we never learn this in the academy?"

"Because the Grand Guardian and priests don't want anyone to follow the example of Ekwenzu. Only they and the chieftains obtain this knowledge. You know if your father was alive he would tell you this story himself."

Moses' tilted his head downshifting from excitement back to the dreaded state that feeds inside him daily.

"But he's gone," he said. "The Shadow League took his life."

His mother wrapped her arm around him in comfort.

"You know before our issue with the Shadow League our nation dealt with multiple conflicts with the Ekwenzu including your grandfather," she said.

"But I thought Ekwenzu was banished," said Moses.

"For the rest of his life he was, but his spirit began to haunt our nation, seeking whom he may use to challenge the Ezenwa rulership. Your father and I were only children when the attack happened. The Ekwenzu bombed our national buildings and held hostages just to challenge for the throne."

"And my grandfather defeated him?"

"He defeated and executed the Ekwenzu preventing a second civil war from happening. Your grandfather was a powerful man. Your father was twice as powerful. But you Moses has potential. I believe in you son. The people of Nubariah believe in you. And the Grand Guardian wouldn't issue this challenge if he knew you weren't worthy. You just have to believe in yourself."

As Moses contemplated on his mother's words, Mercius led his army within the dark warp beginning his mission to destroy the remaining family that Oba left behind. His son wrapped his arms around his father's torso watching the dark violet space that they were floating in. His stare was like his father's. Hearing the stories of how his father had shed blood over the years by vanquishing his enemies, Kulrath wanted to know the feeling of binding his enemies to his will. Mercius taught him the dark arts of the shadows since birth. Now it was his chance to shed blood himself. It was seen through his eyes that made his father proud.

Mercius called for one of his warriors riding its saakuth beside him. The dark warrior reacted in obedience to its lord.

"Have you received my coordinates?" the Shadow Lord inquired.

"Yes my lord," said the dark warrior looking at a screen on its wrist. "The exact location should be twenty-one degrees north."

"Then let us get out of the vortex."

"We'll ride behind you, my lord."

Mercius' eyes glowed as the dark space in front of him began to clear into a fair blue sky of white clouds and sun rays. The atmosphere he entered was warm and welcoming despite his dreaded demeanor. Below him and his army was the chrome city surrounded by a river.

"We have reached Mombasa, my lord," said the dark warrior. "Waiting for further orders."

Mercius stared at the peaceful city. His intentions were of malice knowing blood was going to be shed this day both innocent bystanders and warriors of his enemies. He replied to his warrior still glaring at the city below him through the clouds.

"I want you and several warriors to come with me. The other warriors I want on standby out of range until summoned."

"Yes my lord."

Mercius dragged the rope on his saakuth as the creature descended into Lyayo. Below Mercius and his militia, Chieftain Thuku sat on his throne within the Chieftain's Palace. His betrothed sat next to him on a cushion near the marble floor as they held hands staring at their children playing that he took as his own. Behind them was the beautiful view of the city through the clear glassed windows. Thuku's throne room was narrow of black columned walls with palm branches leaning on them. The marbled floor was sleek with white and black linen shaped like the path of red carpet in a glamorous setting. The ceiling was patterned with clear glassed domes that absolved the sunrays of feeling the palace's touch.

"Your highness!" called someone from down the hall.

Karungu was alert as a man in a red shuka with colorful bead necklaces rushed past him to get to his father. The man bowed to his father before frantically speaking.

"Your highness," he said. "It's the Shadow Lord. He's here."

Thuku rose from his seat, letting his betrothed go.

"Unannounced?" he questioned. "Tell me this is a false alarm."

"I'm afraid not your highness. Our head of security has picked up his signal."

Thuku rubbed his bald chin. Beads of sweat were creeping through his glands as his pulse has risen. Usually, the Shadow Lord would notify him if he was approaching his territory. Something was wrong. Thuku felt as if his sins have reached the height of his continual deal with the devil for the sake of his survival. But it couldn't be shown. He had to face what was coming for the sake of his legacy.

"Inform the head of security to have every guard surround the perimeter of the palace. If drastic measures need to take place lockdown the city."

"Yes your highness," said the man.

"I will meet with Mercius myself."

"Should I have a few guards accompany you in case?"

Thuku nodded his head as the man rushed to follow his orders. He looked at his betrothed knowing that it would possibly be his last seeing her. Thuku stared into her eyes. Her lips cringed into a worried frown despite the beauty her purple lipstick had for her cream-colored brown skin. He cuffed his hands in her cheeks pecking a kiss on her lips.

"I will be back I promise," he said.

"Please be careful love," she said. "I feel something unusual happening."

Thuku nodded his head with assurance then turned to face his son. They locked eyes for a moment as if time itself waited in patience. Thuku removed his spotted fur cloak revealing his black armor.

"Karungu, my oldest son," he said. "Come, let's not keep our guest waiting."

"Yes, father."

While Thuku and Karungu made their way out of the palace's interior to meet with the Shadow Lord, Mercius and a few of his warriors descended towards their direction. The screeches of the saakuth cried in the air alarming the people below. Mercius could sense their fear even at a high altitude. He directed his saakuth towards the upper deck of the Mombasa Palace with his warriors following close. Mercius landed his saakuth on a round platform that was above the palace grounds.

"Stay here," Mercius said to his son.

He climbed off his saakuth and sauntered towards the palace door. His warriors followed behind him lining side by side in unified steps. The palace doors opened as Thuku and Karungu stepped forth with several guards following suit with spears at hand. The head of security led the guards beside the Chieftain.

"Lord Mercius," said Thuku forcing a smile. "You have come unexpectedly. I thought the next audit was in a few weeks. My people have been following the Umbra laws as requested…"

"That's not why I'm here," said Mercius cutting his words.

Both parties were halfway to meeting each other on the deck, each warrior with weapons at hand.

"I have spared your people from hard bondage because you obeyed our laws, you kept our code. And for that, I came here to make a proposition that will make you a far superior being than before."

"And what is that my lord?" asked Thuku.

"I will transfer my power to you ushering a new age in Nubariah in exchange for the lives of Oba's family."

Chieftain Thuku felt chills around his body nearly collapsing on the titanium ground. The thought of having to kill his old friend's family was overwhelming. Becoming the new King of Nubariah was tempting but shedding the blood of his own in exchange was too much to bear. He turned his back on his nation as a result of Nubariah's downfall. Shedding the blood of his own brethren would be the biggest betrayal for him and his tribe.

"So what do you say Chieftain? Do we have a deal?"

Chieftain Thuku composed himself together clearing his throat.

"I will continue to follow your laws Lord Mercius. And I have to admit your offer is tempting, but I have to decline. You're asking me to perform a task that will not only tarnish my image but my family's legacy. I cannot allow blood to be on my hands."

"This isn't a choice alone Chieftain Thuku," said Mercius. The tone of his voice became dark. Thuku could see it in his eyes.

"If you don't accept my offer then you will die and I will force the next leadership in line to take my offer," the Shadow Lord threatened, staring Karungu in the eyes.

Thuku's guards directed their spears at Mercius and his warriors. The dark warriors had their weapons ready. Mercius gave his warriors the signal to stand down.

"So now you're threatening me?" questioned Thuku. "You must be really desperate to come to my territory unannounced and force me and my clan to take out Oba's family. I guess you heard the news that Ouidah chose their new Chieftain. Tell me Lord Mercius, do a boy scare you that bad?"

"Says the one who kissed up to the Shadow Lord for the sake of survival. You forgot mutt that I run the show. I control your freedom. I control the fate of your people. I own you. Now final offer. Take it or suffer."

Thuku turned his head scowling with gritted teeth. He could feel tears covering his eyes regretting the sins of selling out his people. He was not going to carry his sins further. He had to atone for the sake of himself, for the sake of his son. He turned to face Mercius in a weak smile.

"Oba was a dear friend of mine. You devils killed him and I be damned if you use me to do your dirty work and kill his family!"

Mercius glared at him blankly.

"So be it," he said. "Then I guess you die."

"Not without a fight!"

Thuku drew a blade and aimed it towards Mercius' chest.

*Shaa!* Mercius was baffled at the sound.

"No!" yelled the head of security running towards Thuku.

Thuku gasped looking down at the blood spot that was on his torso with an arrow pierced through it. He looked past Mercius towards his saakuth. Kulrath held the bow which was directed at him. Mercius turned to face his son. He let out a vile grin in pride of his son shedding his first blood. Thuku stumbled back as the head of security caught him in his arms.

"No stay with me your highness," he said. He clicked on his Optix from his pocket. "I need medical attention! The Chieftain is down!"

The head of security pulled the bow out in a gentle way. Thuku let out a faint grunt.

"Devil!" yelled one of the guards.

The other guards repeated raising their spears in preparation to attack the Shadow Lord and his army. The head of security got up to his feet extending his arms to halt the guards.

"Stop!" he yelled. "We can't start a war through chaos. Karungu is our second in command. He is in charge of our squadron now."

The head of security glanced at Karungu while Mercius smirked with ill intentions on his mind. Tears of rage and sorrow filled Karungu's eyes. The final moment of his father's life was set before him.

"It's your call, your highness," said the head of security. "We can fight or retreat..."

"Or you can join me and take your father's place for a golden opportunity," said Mercius.

He placed his hand under his breastplate armor. Karungu was alert expecting the same threat he gave his father. Mercius threw out his hand releasing a brown sack as it landed in front of Karungu. He looked down and saw two gold blocks in front of him.

"Don't listen to him Karungu," said the head of security. "He's only deceiving you. Remember duty over everything."

Karungu picked up the gold blocks and threw them off the deck.

"It's going to take more than a stack of gold to impress me Shadow Lord," he said. "I'm already wealthy."

"That was only a gift," said Mercius. "But I can sense deep within you your desire. You want more than just a shattered legacy that your father has made for you. Darkness is within your conflicting mind."

"Karungu, let's shut this bastard up," said the head of security.

Karungu was insulted by what the Shadow Lord said, but he knew what was said is true. His father dishonored his legacy by not fighting for his nation although the people of Mombasa stood by his side. He looked behind him at his dying father with a grieving mind. He did feel something dark within him. Blood was lingering in his thoughts like a poisonous toxin. Karungu took the electro spear off his back holster and gripped it pointing it at the Shadow Lord. The guards followed behind him in pursuit.

"You killed my father," he said. "You insulted my legacy! And you want me to join you?"

Mercius stared at him, his red eyes meeting his.

"What is your answer boy?" he questioned. "Is it a new legacy far greater than your father's or share his fate?

Karungu let out a sarcastic laugh then pointed his spear back at Mercius.

"You want to know my answer Shadow Lord!? Well..."

He lunged his spear jabbing the head of security with the sharpness of the staffed blade. The guards gasped in confusion. Mercius was in a continuous stare.

"My father died a fool," Karungu said releasing the spear from the head of security.

Karungu turned to face the men he betrayed. Power and rage filled his spirit. The shame he had of his father departed from him as he watched him take his final breath. His father's face read it all, regret.

"Traitor!" yelled one of the guards holding up his spear.

"Traitor!" another guard yelled.

Karungu threw himself at the guards, using every technique that was taught to him growing up. His movements were like gusting winds to which the guards had no time to defend themselves. One by one they were caught by the sharpening edge of Karungu's spear. The strikes were too much for them to handle. Mercius smirked watching the blood seep through the guards. One of the guards stood to his feet with a deep wound across his abdomen. He nearly stumbled aiming his spear at Karungu hoping to blind site the prince. Karungu stabbed the wounded guard in the chest planting his foot on his stomach to release the spear. He heard behind him a war cry with footsteps trailing behind him. It was as if Karungu could smell the fresh blood of his final victim. He turned with his spear swinging in the wind as the blade swiped the flesh off the guard's throat. Karungu viewed the bodies thinking about what he has done, but he eliminated any humane thought that would hold him back. There was no turning back. He walked towards the Shadow Lord, spear still in hand. The blood of his victims dripped in the chrome pavement.

"You promised to give me the throne if I would join you right?" he asked.

"Yes, I'm a man of my word," said Mercius. "The throne of Palasera belongs to a Nubarian Chieftain such as yourself. I see that now. As you can see, I am just a proxy to the throne. My legacy is incomplete, and I need help making my final mark."

"I can care less about the Ezenwas. If I help you kill the boys and the mother, will Palasera be mine?"

Mercius let out a mischievous smile.

"Yes. As long as you bow to me as your lord."

Karungu placed his spear down and got on his knees.

"I am at your service my lord," he said. "As long as you live up to your promise."

Mercius paced back and forth placing his hands behind his back.

"The throne will be yours," he said. "But the child must die first. His brother and mother must be executed. The remnant of the Ezenwa family must be wiped out. But in exchange, you must help me take the sacred temple in Sahawayda. Kill the Grand Guardian and end the old kingdom presenting a new age in Nubariah. You, the new High Chieftain of all Nubariah, and me Lord of Sahawayda."

"Sounds good my lord," said Karungu.

"We must not stall our plans. Now is the perfect time to strike. You are a strong warrior, but your inexperience will be your downfall. However, I know an alternative that will make you instantly powerful, black magic."

Karungu placed his hands on the ground gripping his spear. His twisted mind lured him into the eagerness of what his father told him was forbidden knowledge.

"Teach me," he said. "I want to be as powerful as the Shadow Lords."

Mercius paused staring at the young new Chieftain.

"I can teach you, but it takes the average mortal twenty years to master the dark arts. I would transfer some of my magic to you, but it could kill you in the process because you were not born among the shadows. But there is one power here in Nubariah that you can embrace. An ancient power that matches your desire of lust, power, the throne..."

"Ekwenzu," said Karungu. "My father used to tell me his power was forbidden."

"And soon it will be yours. You may rise young Chief."

Karungu stood to his feet placing his spear in his back holster. He looked at Mercius as he stared ahead with a changed demeanor. Karungu turned his head to see his husband's betrothed and her children with medical aid rushing behind them. He glared at her for a moment. The facial expression of her children read it all, what is happening? The medical aid rushed to his father's corpse feeling to see if he had a pulse. The medical aid gave his father's betrothed a signal that he was gone. Karungu watched as his father's betrothed broke down in tears holding his corpse.

"I'll make sure to give your father a proper burial once all this is done," said Mercius. "Now come, there is much that needs to be done."

Karungu stepped forth towards the Shadow Lord following him to get to his saakuth.

"Traitor!" he heard his father's betrothed yelling at him.

Karungu turned around to face her.

"Why did you do this?" she questioned in angry tears. "Your father taught you better than this. Where is your honor? Your pride? You betrayed your people for what?!"

"Enough!" yelled Karungu. "You talk as if you know me; as if you were there to see my father's cowardly act during the siege just to compromise with the very enemy that destroyed his nation!"

"And you are no different! At least he compromised for the sake of his people. But you are willing to sell out all of us."

"You talk as if you're my mother. She died because my father failed to protect her from her illness. And you mean nothing to me. Your words mean nothing to me. You are nothing but a woman who tried to marry my father so you and your children can escape the trash heap you came from. But I guess his failure will rub off on you peasant."

Karungu hopped on the back of Mercius' saakuth.

"Damn you, you bastard!" she yelled.

He ignored her remark.

"I want a garrison of warriors at the palace immediately," said Mercius on the Optix. "Kill all the loyalists of Thuku until they are willing to serve Chieftain Karungu."

"Yes my lord," said the voice of a dark warrior on the Optix.

Mercius commanded his saakuth to take off to the sky as the warring beast flapped its massive wings letting out a cry that echoed through the air. Karungu held on tight behind Mercius and his son as the beast soared to the clouds.

# Chapter Four

# The Journey

A day has passed as Moses packed his sack for the journey to Sahawayda after spending a final day with his mother. He felt uncomfortable going on this journey although Ngozi would be beside him. He was used to being around his mother, including his brother who was originally chosen. He felt alone as he waited in the den for the arrival of the Grand Guardian. Moses barely ate, although his mother cooked him a succulent stack of rain banana pancakes smeared in syrup. Even the sweet taste of the rain bananas mixed with the buttery syrup in the pancakes couldn't calm the nervousness Moses was feeling at the moment. The fate of his nation was in his hands. There was no turning back from destiny. He was too far deep to back away.

The door knocked rattling Moses. This is it. His mother paced towards the door ignoring Moses' movements. She opened the door as Moses watched, his chest throbbing feeling as if a lump was in his throat.

"Hello Master Ngozi," she said answering the door.

The coast was clear. Moses got up to his feet and bowed to Ngozi.

"Greetings Master Ngozi," he said.

"Greetings Moses," he said. "Are you ready for the journey?"

Moses nodded his head. Ngozi smiled, placing his hand on his head.

"I know you are nervous but relax. Take a breather. Enjoy what the Supreme has placed in the land."

"Greetings Master Ngozi," said Ramses from the entryway to the kitchen.

"Greetings Ramses," said Ngozi.

"I wish you a safe travel on your journey."

Ramses looked at Moses. Moses could still feel the tension since the challenge. The look in his eyes said it all.

"You too Moses," he said. "Try not to destroy our father's legacy."

Ramses walked towards the kitchen on his way to the backdoor. Moses was surprised Ramses spoke to him. It's been over a week since he heard from his big brother. In ways, he missed him, was going to miss him now that he had to depart from Dolsa.

"Come," said Ngozi. "The Grand Guardian should be coming soon."

Moses grabbed his sack placing it on his back. He followed Ngozi out of the house to the front yard. His mother walked alongside him. Moses had set his bag on the lawn embracing the crisp spring air.

"Moses!" screamed a familiar voice.

Moses turned and saw Korah rushing to him. He dapped him and embraced him in a hug.

"I wanted to see you yesterday," said Korah. "But between the academy and training…"

"Don't worry about it Korah," he said. "I'm not mad at you. We both were occupied."

Korah smiled nodding his head.

"Korah," said Ngozi. "Should you be on your way to the academy?"

"Master Ngozi," said Korah bowing to him. "I just wanted to give Moses my farewell."

"Understandable."

Moses could feel the atmosphere shifting. He watched the gaze on Ngozi's face with a confirmation that it was time. Ngozi stepped forward as the Grand Guardian and a few of his guards approached them from down the road. People in neighboring houses stepped out from their houses amazed by the camelops they were riding that were decked in gold and jewels. Two of the guards pulled two empty camelops beside them. The large beasts were only a façade compared to the presence Moses felt of the Grand Guardian. The Grand Guardian held his hand up stopping with a signal of halting his guards in front of Moses at the front yard. Moses gulped, the pressure he felt was coming back to him.

"Moses Ezenwa," said the Grand Guardian. "It is time."

Moses nodded his head and stepped forward to the empty camelop the Grand Guardian pointed to. *Why me*? were the thoughts he had walking toward the camelop. He was beginning to have second thoughts.

"Wait!" yelled Ngozi.

Moses propped his head up. The Grand Guardian watched in a blank stare as Ngozi stepped in front of Moses as if he was a shield. He bowed to the Grand Guardian.

"With your permission can the boy say his final goodbyes?"

Ngozi nodded at Ashanti who cracked a smile. The Grand Guardian glared for a moment. Moses couldn't tell the emotion he was feeling. His stare was only tense.

"Only for a few minutes, then we must go."

Moses was relieved for only a moment. He wished he had more time, but he had to make these few minutes count. He went to his mother and hugged her. Moses felt as if he was four years old again remembering the time when she held him in her lap singing songs that would calm him down whenever he felt distressed or aggravated. He did not want this moment to end, but she let go wiping the tear from her eye.

"I can no longer protect you my sweet," she said. "You must face this journey alone. But I must say that I am proud of you son. I know you can do it. When you return Dolsa will plan a feast dedicated to the new chieftain."

Moses let out a weak smile.

"It's okay Moses," she said. "You are young but powerful. I know you can do it. You are ready for the trials."

She kissed him on the forehead,

"I love you son. Now go. Be strong. Be courageous."

Moses wiped the tears from his eyes.

"I will Mother," he said.

He turned away moving forward. Moses spotted Korah extending his hand to him. Moses gripped his hand pulling Korah to a hug.

"I wish I could be there with you, but I will cheer you on."

"Thank you Korah," said Moses.

Moses walked past Korah towards Ngozi.

"It's time," said Ngozi gesturing Moses to the camelops.

Moses walked side by side with Ngozi. The two guards led the camelops to Moses and Ngozi. Moses stepped on the rope extension that was placed to climb on the eleven-foot animal. He climbed feeling the wooly fur of the creature. Moses watched as the Grand Guardian made a signal to move forward. The guard besides Moses grabbed the rope on Moses' camelop.

"I know you're not used to riding one of these, so I'll help steer yours," he said.

Moses nodded looking ahead at Ngozi steering his camelop in front of him comforted by his presence as he rode down the road soon to depart from the village.

***

The screeching cry of the saakuth resounded the air as it descended from the clouds to a mountain of stone with moss coverings. The mountain was near a forest where the wildlife wandered. Karungu watched as a flock of birds ascended in high numbers. He knew his soul was gone sensing the darkness that even the animals had to escape from. The dark energy of Mercius and his son poisoned the air like a sharp blade cutting fresh flesh. Now that he turned on his people, Karungu could feel the dark energy resonating within him. It was now only a matter of seconds. He saw a cave within the mountain. Karungun knew where he was at, the Forbidden Cave of the Ekwenzu. His father told him stories of how the followers of Ekwenzu would worship him and use magic to slow down the progression of the Nubarian chiefs. Karungu was told that this was the exact cave the Ekwenzu would be chosen to challenge the Chieftain. But these times were different. The Chieftain was gone. The Shadow Lords made themselves into rulers after the Chieftains failed. And now he was becoming the very thing his father told him to stay away from.

The saakuth landed a few feet away from the cave. Mercius stepped out as Karungu followed.

"Stay here," Mercius commanded his son.

Kulrath nodded as Mercius led Karungu towards the cave. As they approached the cave, Mercius paused. Karungu was puzzled as to why the Shadow Lord seemed hesitant.

"Changing your mind already Shadow Lord?" he wondered. "Are the spirits of Nubariah too much for you to handle?"

"No," Mercius said. "Do you feel that? We're being watched. They know that we're here."

"Who?"

"Follow me and listen closely."

Mercius crept his way to the cave as Karungu followed. It was silent, but Mercius could feel the thickness of air surrounding him. He knew he was being followed. He stopped again dropping his head and closing his eyes. Mercius snarled showing absolutely no patience.

"Show yourselves," he said.

People with masks and spears hastily approached them with spears in their hands. Mercius stood tall. Karungu felt nervous beats in his pulse staring at the spears that were pointed at him.

"So, do you have any idea of what we are dealing with?" inquired Mercius.

Karungu was hesitant, the words nearly stuck in his brain feeling a nervousness that brought him to shame. Mercius glared.

"Well Nubarian do you?" the Shadow Lord demanded.

Karungu took a breath while the masked people swarmed around him like sharks.

"They're the Edi, watchers and hunters that worship Ekwenzu. They probably want to know what we are doing here."

Mercius lifted his hands as if he were giving himself to them freely. The Edi continuously circled the Shadow Lord and Chieftain.

"I come in peace," he said. "I just want to introduce you all to the new Ekwenzu. The glory will finally be yours for the taking."

Although he couldn't read the emotion of their faces, Karungu could tell the Edi was confused. Their body expression told it all as they stood in place watching each other. Then they began to talk in a language that Karungu wasn't familiar with.

"What are they saying?" inquired Mercius.

"I don't know. This must be one of Nubariah's ancient languages."

The Edi paused gaining both Mercius and Karungu's attention. They began to chatter amongst each other again this time walking ahead of both Karungu and Mercius. Karungu turned to the Shadow Lord as their eyes met with confirmation. The Edi was leading them to the cave.

"After you," Mercius gestured Karungu to walk ahead of him.

Karungu nodded walking ahead of the Shadow Lord. He was cautious following the Edi to the cave. A part of him felt that this was a trap. Karungu entered the dark cave of colorful mist and torch lights. The cave was widespread. There were more Edi clustered around a fire on their hands and knees worshipping their god. Karungu became more interested than paranoid. The Edi led him to a woman with brown locs wrapped in sackcloth. Her face was painted white wearing a leather necklace with a solid clear stone in the middle. The woman scowled at him.

"Why have you brought this interloper here?" she asked.

Karungu stared waiting on one of the Edi to answer her. Then he realized she directly demanded an answer from him after scrutinizing him. Karungu turned around and realized she was talking about the Shadow Lord. He cleared his throat choosing his words carefully.

"With all respect madame, the Shadow Lord has aided me to get here," said Karungu.

"This place is not welcome for his kind," said the woman.

"Listen, witch," said Mercius. "I did you a favor by bringing the next Ekwenzu that is being given the throne. Consider yourself grateful."

"No one chooses who the next Ekwenzu is. Not even you Shadow Lord."

"Then how can I wield the power of Ekwenzu?" inquired Karungu.

The woman turned her attention back to Karungu.

"To wield the power of Ekwenzu you must be chosen," she said.

"What all will it take?"

The woman observed him again. The crystal on her necklace changed into multiple colors of blue, green, and violet.

"Only he chooses who wields his power," she said.

The woman stepped up to Karungu in observance circling him. He felt an uneasiness as if she were looking into his lost spirit.

"You are young," she said. "You are naïve and foolish. But you do remind me a little of him, ruthless, ambitious, having a lust for power."

"I am ready to wield his power," said Karungu.

"Are you now?"

The woman paused staring past Karungu. He watched in bewilderment of the woman as if something was speaking to her. Perhaps something was.

"Are you certain?" she said staring at the cavern wall.

Mercius stepped behind Karungu placing his hand on his shoulder.

"Ekwenzu is communicating with the witch doctor," he whispered to Karungu. "Watch her carefully."

Karangu watched her as she continued staring in an insane babble of Igbo.

*Bụ onye maara ihe. M ga-atụkwasị gị obi.*

"What did she say?" inquired Mercius.

"I don't know," said Karungu. "She must be speaking in Igbo. Only those of Ouidah could understand what she is speaking."

"I thought you Nubarians spoke the same language."

"Each territory of Nubariah speaks its own language. In order for us to communicate together as a nation, we must use standard language. I only know Swahili and Standard."

The woman was out of her trans, getting close to Karungu.

"Ekwenzu wants to use you as a vessel," she said. "But to go through the ritual, you must first speak with Ekwenzu himself, alone."

She stared at Mercius in a heinous look. The Shadow Lord glared at her then took a few steps back.

"That's fine," he said. "As long as the ritual is done. I'll camp outside in the meantime."

Mercius turned away making his exit out of the cave. The woman turned to Karungu. He was now left alone with the people he knew who didn't see him as a traitor but as a potential ruler.

"Come," said the woman. "There is much to do."

***

It wasn't too long when the sun went down through Moses' travel with the Grand Guardian and Master Ngozi. Traveling through the day was dreadful to him despite the majestic camelop he was riding. The thought of his title being possibly stripped away from him ate him alive. Fatigue was catching up to him after traveling through Ouidah. Moses could smell the saltwater of the Great Sea which led to the Sacred Lands of Sahawayda. The stars were glistening in the sky with a touch of galactic dust. Moses watched ahead as the Grand Guardian placed his hand up signaling to stop. He watched as everyone steered the camelops to lie in the grass plains to rest. The guard steering his and Moses' camelop followed suit as his camelop placed its body to the ground.

"We will camp here overnight and rest," said the Grand Guardian. "Tomorrow will be a long journey, so get as much rest as possible."

Moses was silent. He took his time climbing down the camelop. He saw Ngozi walking towards a ledge. He could tell he was in deep thought. Ngozi was his only comfort. Moses followed him maneuvering past the resting camelops. He watched in nervousness at the Grand Guardian who was talking and grinning to two of his guards. This was the first time he saw the Grand Guardian lift a smile. Moses felt greater comfort as he approached Ngozi at the ledge. The view was a beauty to behold. Moses gazed at the soft sand below him with the tranquil ocean swaying along with the wafting breeze.

"This is a perfect time to meditate," said Ngozi. "Remove your troubles and cast them to the Supreme."

"I try Master," said Moses. "But it's like these thoughts keep haunting me. Everything is happening so fast."

"Clear your mind, Moses. Take deep breaths. You cannot allow your thoughts to cloud your vision. Look at the sky. What do you see?"

Moses looked at the sky following Ngozi's command.

"What do you see?" asked Ngozi.

"I see stars and the night sky."

"Look closer. What do you see?"

Moses squinted his eyes.

"Dust clouds?" was the best response he could make.

"Dig deeper."

Moses gazed at the stars but was uncertain of what Ngozi was showing him beside the stars and the night sky. He was hesitant, uncertain of the next word he would say. Ngozi breathed through his nostrils, his focus remaining on the sky.

"Do you know the power Abiama has given our ancestors?" said Ngozi. "Limitless power. Look at the stars. Is there a limit of their count?"

Moses shook his head out of instinct.

"Just like the stars, we must allow our minds to reach past the limit of the invisible wall that keeps us bound. It's like placing glass past the firmament, you will remain stuck, unable to fulfill your potential. You must meditate on these things Moses. Embrace the creation of the Supreme. Listen to the sound of the ocean. Feel the wind's embrace. Look at your surroundings of the sandy beach, the flowers in the grassy plain, and harness your energy through your T'kaf. I will leave you to it to meditate."

Moses gazed at the beach with the stars as Ngozi walked back to the others.

"Ngozi come," said the Grand Guardian with cheer. "I would like for you to join us. We were just talking about some funny stories about Sahawayda back in the day."

"This is what I have to hear," said Ngozi walking towards them.

Moses could hear the men laughing. They were joking about something that had to do with Ngozi's years serving the Grand Guardian before becoming his father's spiritual advisor and part of the Council. He ignored them, however, breathing through his nostrils and closing his eyes focusing on the natural elements around him.

***

Karungu sat on the cavern floor contemplating his betrayal of the Mombasa people. The thoughts of his father treaded his mind. He was no different. Before his death, he sold out his people to the Shadow Lords but was still respected by the people. Karungu had a second thought, his thoughts lingering on Mombasa. They had to respect him, he was the new Chieftain with hopes to become the High Chieftain of Nubariah. They had no choice but to accept him.

A man in orange and black face paint with white dots stepped up to him. He wore a blue drape with straw linen.

"The witch doctor is ready for you," he said.

Karungu stood to his feet and followed the man to the center of the cave. He saw the witch doctor staring at him. There were a group of face-painted men sitting in a circle around her. Karungu's chest was thumping. He swore that he was breathing heavily.

"Sit," said the witch doctor suggesting him to come in front of her.

Karungu walked past the circle and got on his knees. He placed his hands on his thighs breathing through his nostrils.

"Now that everything is set up, we can begin," said the witch doctor. "The ritual must be done in perfect timing."

The man with the orange face paint handed her a bottle of liquor in a green bottle, at least that was what Karungu thought. The witch doctor opened the bottle and offered Karungu the bottle.

"Drink," she said.

Karungu took a sip of the liquid in the bottle. The liquid burned his throat which made him feel nauseous. This was definitely liquor. He was ready to spit it out.

"Do not spit it out," said the woman. "Chug it, quickly."

Karungu closed his eyes and swallowed the liquor feeling his eyes burn and water with tears streaming. He gasped taking short breaths placing his hands on the ground.

"Good," said the woman. "Drink more."

Damn again? were the words Karungu wanted to say. But this was the sacrifice he was willing to take. He took another quick sip. Karungu coughed nearly gagging. *The hell kind of liquor is this?* he thought.

"Good," said the witch doctor. "You almost feel the full effect of the Obeah. A few more chugs and the ritual will commence."

Karungu stared at the bottle feeling nauseated. He was close to fulfilling his goal of absolute power. Karungu closed his eyes in a tremble as he quaffed a few more chugs of the unpleasant liquor. He let out a choking cough feeling his vision blur as he placed his hands on the cavern floor. The liquor splashed on the floor causing a small puddle.

"Now we can commence," said the witch doctor.

She grabbed the liquor bottle from the cavern floor and guzzled it, draining the bottle in near emptiness. The man in the orange face paint handed her a chicken. She grabbed it by its claws. The witch doctor clutched a knife from him and gripped the chicken by the throat-slitting it in the process. She poured its blood around the circle chanting repeatedly, *Bịa gị mmụọ nke ndị a bụrụ ọnụ. Mee ka anyi laghachi na ebube.* (Come to the spirit of the cursed ones. Bring us back to glory)

Karungu gasped as his vision blurred in fading light. Darkness swallowed him. He was in a trans as a figure walked up to him in a cloud of smoke. It was the form of a male with tendrils dangling on his shoulders. His muscles seemed cut through the shadows with a long beard. His eyes glowed purple.

"So, I finally get to meet the young Chieftain of Mombasa," the figure said to him in an accent that was foreign to Karungu. "I've been watching you from a distance since you were a young boy."

Karungu gasped, his eyes widening.

"You must be…"

"Ekwenzu, the god of trickery and violence."

Ekwenzu revealed his form to Karaungu leaving him in a breathless gaze. He was shirtless, wearing only a red drape around his waistline. The tendrils appeared to be long, thick braids in his hair wearing a necklace filled with skulls. Ekwenzu carried a stick stepping in front of a delirious Karungu in a devious grin.

"Tell me. What drove you to betray your father's legacy?"

Karungu was hesitant, stuttering his words in a babble. Ekwenzu slammed the stick on the ground causing the young Chieftain to tremble.

"Answer the question boy!"

Karungu swallowed and took a short breath.

"My father sold out," he blurted.

Ekwenzu paused staring at Karungu. He felt as if he had a lump in his throat. Karungu began to regret his words as Ekwenzu continued to stare. The move he made to betray his people was disgraceful, even for a monster like Ekwenzu. The demon laughed at him.

"So you decided to follow his footsteps and join the Shadow Lord just to wield my power."

Ekwenzu stared unto Karungu in a long hiatus.

"I'll have to admit, you remind me of myself when I was in my mortal body; young, ambitious, lusting for power. But you are lost, uncertain. I see through you like a glass wall."

Ekwenzu's purple eyes glowed creating more tension for Karungu. He could see that the demon was looking into his spirit. Karungu knew at this moment his soul would either be sold or taken forever. Ekwenzu smirked.

"However, I could use you," he said. "I haven't used anyone as young and inexperienced as you since the Nubarian Civil War eons ago. Yet this is a different time. The bloodline of the Ezenwa must be destroyed by any means necessary, even if we have to line ourselves with the Shadow Lords to take what belongs to us."

Karungu placed his hands on the ground bowing to the demon.

"Then I am at your mercy," he said. "Just show me. Teach me your power."

"I do not teach anyone my secret."

Ekwenzu opened his palm. Karungu was in a highly strung gaze of the flame that ignited in the demon's hand. The witch doctor and the painted men appeared behind Ekwenzu with flames in their palms chanting repeatedly, *Nara ocheeze n'aka eze. Kọchaa ndị iro anyị* (Take the throne from the king. Curse our enemies). Karungu could feel himself riveted to the spot as Ekwenzu leaned towards him in a whisper.

"I let them experience it."

Ekwenzu and his worshippers threw the flames at him in repulsive laughter. Karungu screamed in torture feeling the flames incinerating his skin. He laid on the ground as the smokescreen began to clear. He could hear Ekwenzu's voice during his torment:

*Now we will become one power. Together we will curse our enemies and take the throne. But if you fail, you will die, and your corpse will be left to rot as feed for the maggots and vultures.*


Then the laughter stopped. There was complete silence. Ekwenzu's words faded. Karungu no longer felt the pain. His vision was normal, staring at the cavern ceiling. Karungu sat up extending his arms and looking at his hands. He wondered was this experience a delusion.

"How are you feeling?" asked the witch doctor.

"I... I don't know," said Kaungu. "What happened?"

"You were in a trans. The Obeah ritual was a success."

"So what I saw was..."

"Lord Ekwenzu through the spirit realm. And now that the ritual is complete, we are at your service."

The witch doctor and the painted men bowed. Karungu smiled in devilment as he rose to his feet. He could feel the power he was desiring watching his new servants giving praise to him.

"Hail Chieftain Karungu, our new Ekwenzu!" yelled the witch doctor. "May he live out his desire to become High Chieftain in a new era of Nubariah."

Karungu smirked raising his arms in triumph. He was a step closer to reaching absolute power. It was as if he could taste it.

***

The sun rose to turn sky blue as Moses blinked his eyes using his hand to block the rays from beaming.

"Moses we're about to move out," said Ngozi.

Moses got up from the grass watching everyone load and climb up their camelop. He never detached his sack from his.

"Let me assist you, young chief," said one of the guards.

He helped Moses climb up the camleop. Moses was grateful for the assist. He saw Ngozi climb up his camelop smiling back. The Grand Guardian was ahead of everyone giving the signal to go onward for the beach. The guard next to Moses steered his camelop as they followed the Grand Guardian and company down the ledge to the sandy beach. The beach appeared different at daylight. Moses felt soothed for the moment of the swaying clear blue waters. It reminded him of the family vacations his father used to take him, Ramses, and his mother at the private beaches. Moses always enjoyed the beaches.

Moses snapped into reality watching the Grand Guardian climb down from his camelop, his feet touching the moist sand. He examined the Grand Guardian as he raised his hands to the ocean speaking a language that was unknown to Moses, "*ahrataza ilah ma ha yam.*"

There was silence. The waves of the ocean continued to splash to the shore within the depths of the ocean. Moses heard a rumbling sound from the distance. He watched from the distance something massive sailing their way. It was not a boat. The sound grew in a roar as Moses' jaws dropped at a sight that was far from believable. He saw four islands forming a curved bridge in the ocean. The island in front was near the shore. Moses could see how the Grand Guardian was able to cross from Sahawayda to Ouidah on a camelop.

The Grand Guardian led Moses and the group towards the first island which had a dirt trail that led to a colossal hill. Moses felt his camelop tilting in the seawater following the others to the island. The water raised, touching the hem of his garment the deeper the camelop was in the ocean. Within a nanosecond, the camelop rose to the surface of the island following the others up the dirt trail. Moses was astonished, amazed by his surroundings that were surreal to his sight.

Their journey was smooth as Moses was moved up the top of the hill coming down a slope to the next island of a luscious green forest. He gazed at his surroundings of fauna. The creatures around him paused staring at Moses and the Grand Guardian's company. He could tell that the creatures knew of his character through their curious looks. Moses passed through the forest island in a peaceful stride to the last two islands of forested hills that led to the walled city.

Sahawayda was Nubariah's ancient city shaped like a wheel of gold walled columns that stretched for 9,000 miles. Within the city was a community of homes, temples, and markets where merchants sold the best quality of garments and jewelry, fresh fish from the ocean, oven-baked grains, and pastries. In the center of the city stood the Grand Temple where the Grand

Guardian was occupied as the watchman of Shiveria. Moses only dreamed of coming to this place, but not in a condition of what he is experiencing now.

After passing through the islands, Moses had touchdown on the sacred land of Sahawayda. The guard in front of Moses continued to steer his camelop as the Grand Guardian passed through the desert. Time passed away. Moses was unsure of how long they were traveling. He only knew that the sun was still present passing through the afternoon. Then there it was. The walled city was miles away standing tall in its glory. The Grand Temple, the mammoth of a building stood tall over the city awaiting the arrival of Moses. This was it. The test was waiting for Moses behind those walls. Sahawayda was either going to make or break him.

# Chapter Five

# Trials and Errors

The sunlight was bright as Karungu stepped out of the cave. He felt like a vampire, the vitamin D of the sun was becoming unfamiliar to his dark skin. He was accompanied by two masked men of the Edi. Karungu caught Mericus and his son loading up the saakuth. The Shadow Lord glared at him with his red and orange eyes as he approached.

"So I see you have done it," said Mercius. "I sensed the power entering in you."

"I have," said the young Ekwenzu. "And I now feel glorious."

"We'll be able to test that power once we get to Dolsa. But for now, let's move forward. Mombasa is waiting for their new Chieftain to arrive."

Karungu nodded his head.

"You can return to the cave with the witch doctor," he said to the Edi. "I'll take it from here."

The masked men glanced at each other muttering in their native tongue at one another. They followed the order of their new leader and rushed back to the cave. Karungu followed the Shadow Lord and climbed on top of the saakuth. Mercius clicked his heel on the creature as it screeched with its wings expanded. The saakuth flapped its wings taking off to the sky leaving the Cave of Ekwenzu behind.

***

Moses was led to Sahawayda's massive city. He could feel a massive power behind those walls. It could be the Supreme God Abiama himself if Moses could guess it. Moses along with the Grand Guardian, Ngozi, and the guards rode in silence towards the city. He was led to a bridge that crossed the gates of the city that two guards dressed in gold armor plating rolled out. Moses examined ahead of him two guards in an armor of silver approaching the Grand Guardian. They wore a tall gold helmet that only covered the top of their head and chin carrying spears made of rare stones that only the territory of Sahawayda preserved after the Shadow League stripped most of Nubariah's resources. The guards bowed to the Grand Guardian.

"Welcome back your highness," one of the guards said. "How was your journey?"

"It was very pleasant as usual," said the Grand Guardian. "There was no approach by the Shadow Lord. He's plotting something, I know it."

"Well, he will not have any success trying to invade our sacred land. And that is a promise."

The guards nodded at each other and turned towards the guards who released the bridge from the gate. The guards opened the gates revealing the vivacious city below them from a bridge they were crossing to get to the Grand Temple. It was everything Moses imagined. The brightness of the city was like a precious gemstone as clear as crystal. The city itself was made of multicolored jasper stones that looked like glass. Moses took in the view of the city crossing the ten-mile bridge. The sun was setting giving the city a more wondrous view. Moses was led down a slope. The Grand Temple stood tall awaiting him. That was the power he sensed. It was the temple the entire time. He could sense the life that radiated within the ancient temple. After reaching the edge of the slope, Moses was led through an open gate that led to the temple grounds. Surrounding him were groups of oasis trees. The Grand Temple stood tall in its stature made of purple jasper stone having an even width and height of 216 feet. The Grand Guardian stopped in place. Moses observed the sun being followed by the moon.

"This day was a long one," he said. "But we are blessed to make it. Tomorrow is the beginning of Moses' training, or I would say test. The guards will show you to your chambers. I will retire for the rest of the night."

The Grand Guardian departed with his camelop to the temple leaving the guards with Moses and Ngozi.

"Follow us," one of them said. "We will show you to your rooms."

***

Miles away from where Moses was sojourned to, the full moon was lustrous in the dead sky as the sakuuth descended to the quiet city. The people of Mombasa were in grief awaiting their new chieftain's arrival. The dark warriors were in the midst of the people, maintaining order. The royal guards were in silence, defenseless after a failed attempt to secure the palace.

Mercius landed the saakuth on the palace grounds in front of the silent crowd. Karungu climbed down from the gigantesque creature. He scanned the crowd disappointed in the reaction of his return. Karungu demanded respect, and he was going to have it one way or another.

"Aren't you going to celebrate the coming of your new chieftain?" he questioned.

There was not a word coming from anyone. Karungu stepped forward to address the crowd.

"You know this is funny, or I can say ironic. You all respected my father despite his cowardice. This man sold you out for the sake of safety? He threw you all into the flames. My father caused this to happen!"

Karungu paused feeling the tension his people felt for him. The Chieftain kept his pride. He was their leader now.

"But I will be the one to finish what he started," he continued. "My father was a man with honor. He cared a lot for his people, you all. So do I. And as your new Chieftain, I plan to bring peace, prosperity, and justice to a new Mombasa. I will continue my father's legacy and give this land celebrity as I will have the throne as the new High Chieftain of Nubariah!"

The crowd spoke amongst each other finally letting out a sound.

"You think some child the Grand Guardian chose would be a better ruler?" Karungu continued. "How could a child be able to lead an entire nation that's broken? Don't you realize the old ways don't work anymore? Chieftain Oba failed you years ago, but you still hold on to a dead man's glory? Wake up! It is time for a new era of Nubariah. The Ouidah Chieftain failed us. Power must be transferred now to the next tribe. Let it be the Jaguar Clan of Mombasa. So the line is already drawn. You're either with me or my enemy. It's your choice."

One of the guards stepped up to Karungu. The Chieftain glared at him wondering what his move was. If he was going to be the first to rebel against him, he would make an example out of him. The guard grappled his fist with his jaw clenched. He took a deep breath.

"The only reason I'm still standing here is that it's pointless to rebel," he said. "The old ways are truly dead. I am at your service your highness."

Karungu smirked as the guard kneeled before him.

"Mombasa is officially under your service!" yelled the guard to where the people heard him in the echo.

The other guards and warriors knelt. The citizens of Mombasa knelt for their new Chieftain, even the ones who didn't approve of him. They did it out of fear.

"Good," said Karungu. "Now we can move forward. Lord Mercius, I believe a burial for my father was promised."

The Shadow Lord stared icily at Karungu.

"Of course," he said. "The burial will be set up when you are ready."

"I want it done tonight. It will be a private burial only."

"As you wish Chieftain Karungu."

Karungu turned to his guards.

"Lead me to my chambers," he said. "I must prepare according."

The guard bowed to the Chieftain and led him to the palace with a handful of guards escorting him into the palace. The rest of the crowd dispersed leaving the dark warriors alone with the Shadow Lord. His son sat behind him on the saakuth.

"How many casualties were there while I was gone?" inquired Mercius.

"There was a small number that rebelled against us," said the dark warrior. "There was little resistance. We took them out leaving the others in submission."

"Good. Phase one is now complete. Let us depart for now and leave our new chieftain to mourn."

"Yes my lord."

***

The guard led Moses and Ngozi down the main hall within the grand structure. Moses was amazed by the interior of the temple. He was mesmerized by the crystalized walls that even had a shine in the dark. The marmoreal floors he walked on were smooth in texture with the ceiling up high patterned in gold. Moses was enthralled by the libraries and archives which were twice the size of his father's at the old palace. The temple had to have nine floors. The guard led Moses and Ngozi on an elevator. Was this an elevator? Moses' thoughts led him to believe that this place was surreal. He stepped on the metallic disk as it shot up after Moses was on.

"It's been a while since I've been in this place," said Ngozi.

"Not much has changed since you left," said the guard. "Although the Grand Guardian does have a new protocol since we lost Ouidah to the Shadow League. It's shameful to see Palasera tainted by the dark ones."

"We will win it back. It's only a matter of time."

Moses was silent barely listening to Ngozi and the guard's conversation. The disk stopped at the seventh level of the temple. Moses followed the guard and Ngozi to a narrow corridor with a series of rooms. He overheard Ngozi and the guard continue their conversation.

"You are always welcome back to Sahawayda," said the guard. "The Grand Guardian speaks highly of you. You would work well as our general here."

"Your offer is very tempting," said Ngozi. "But I made a promise to protect the boy. He is Nubariah's new Chieftain after all."

The guard looked down at Moses in a near scowl.

"We shall see," he said.

Moses glanced at the guard feeling uncomfortable of the guard's disbelief of his capabilities. This had to be a mistake coming here if the guard of the Grand Guardian didn't believe in him.

*Why me*? Moses thought again. The guard led Moses and Ngozi to two rooms down the corridor.

"These are your rooms," said the guard. "If you need anything our servants will be of assistance."

Ngozi thanked the guard as he departed. Moses was left alone with his master.

"I hope you get enough rest," said Ngozi. "Tomorrow may be the day of Odinani, but we are living in perilous times. Expect your training to be difficult. I doubt the Grand Guardian will be easy on you."

"What am I to expect during the Grand Guardian's training?" asked Moses.

"Knowing the Grand Guardian expect the unexpected. Good night Moses. Get all the rest you can get."

Ngozi entered one of the rooms leaving Moses to contemplate on the Grand Guardian's training that was waiting for him the next day. He entered the room throwing his sack on a bed that was before him. The bed was lavished with three soft blankets and two pillows that were made up in perfection. Moses almost felt like he was home. He hasn't seen a bed like this since the old days of Palasera. But it felt like ages since he was in that place. If he wasn't under so much pressure, Moses would've felt like royalty on his king-sized bed. Instead, he breathed heavily and jumped on the bed placing his hands behind his head. The trials were soon to begin.

***

It was at the midnight hour while Moses was laying in a restless night. Karungu with his advisors and a few guards walked alongside him while the casket of Thuku was being carried in front of them by the latest Reactive Transportation Androids (RTA). LED lights were lit around them in the darkness. There were rows of stone pillars set before them in a valley the size of sycamore trees. They walked for miles traveling through the valley of past chieftains through the foggy mist. It was the dead of silence in the atmosphere.

Thuku's tomb was at the end of the valley awaiting the arrival of his burial. The tomb itself was like a tower within its interior. It was dark, hollow with stone columns and torch-lit walls. Karungu entered the tomb with his guards and advisors in a constant stare of his father's casket. They trod down the hall, the Chief Priest awaiting to begin the ceremony. He wore a light tan cream-colored custom robe with a matching turban around his head. A bed made of stone built six feet was next to him. Karungu along with his guards and advisors gathered around the grave as the chief priest spoke:

"We are gathered this night in the celebration of the life of Chieftain Thuku. He may not have been the perfect leader, but one thing I can say is he loved his people. Even if he had to compromise to do it. I'll never forget serving our Chieftain in the golden age of Mombasa of our great nation Nubariah. Thuku not only set his tribe in order but as well as his family until his wife's dying day and soon after his. Thuku loved his son, including the children of his betrothed."

Karungu caught the Chief Priest looking at him while providing his eulogy of his father. He felt insulted, knowing the message was coming directly at him. Karungu felt insulted by the Chief Priest's message making him out to be the villain after the sacrifices his father made of selling the people out. He was going to lead his people to a new era, an era where they would be free from the Bronze Empire. He glared at the Chief Priest.

"Unfortunately, his life was taken," said the Chief Priest. "Taken way too soon before he could get remarried and unite his family as one. I do wish Halima and her children were here to attend the burial. She meant everything to Thuku."

Karungu was getting frustrated with the Chief Priest's attack of words. He knew he was not a favorite of Mombasa's interest as Chieftain, but he demanded respect. Karungu stepped up interrupting the eulogy.

"Enough of this madness!" he yelled. "You or anyone in Mombasa may not have liked the decision I made, but I demand respect instead of you mentioning peasants that don't even matter at this point! The burial is about my father. I demand some damn respect here!"

The Chief Priest paused for a moment after Karungu's abrupt comment. He then nodded his head.

"Your father Thuku was a very wise man," he said. "He always wished the same for you."

The Chief Priest cleared his throat and continued.

"With our Chieftain now laid to rest, we will honor the lineage of the Lemuanik Dynasty as the Supreme call him home to the spirit realm."

The Chief Priest stepped aside as the RTAs carried Thuku's casket into the stoned bed lowering the casket deep into the bed.

"Long live our Excellency, the Mighty Chieftain Thuku," said the Chief Priest. "May his spirit rest and live on. Ash kwa majivu. Vumbi kwa vumbi (Ash to ash. Dust to dust)."

The RTAs hovered over the stone bed as the priest began to conclude his eulogy.

"And may the heir of our late Chieftain rule at his place for the glory of our tribe and nation."

The Chief Priest, advisors, and guards bowed with grace for Karungu as he nodded his head. The respect he demanded was before him giving him satisfaction. His father was laid to rest. *Now it's my time*, Karungu thought. In his mind, Karungu would become the greatest ruler Nubariah has ever witnessed.

***

The morning sun rose on the day of Nkwo, the day of the Odinani as Moses rose from out of the bed. He was used to his mother calling him to have breakfast ready on the table rushing him and Ramses in preparation for the weekly prayer and sacrifice. However, there was silence. Moses wasn't used to this staring at the majestic room around him of colorful drapes and purple carpet. If only this was a vacation. He heard the door knock rushing out of bed to get dressed.

"I'm coming!" he yelled struggling to put on his shirt.

"Open the door Moses," said Ngozi from behind.

"Coming!"

Moses opened the door. Ngozi stepped in already dressed in his custom garment with a white turban that matched the guards of the palace.

"Boy, why aren't you dressed? The Grand Guardian is waiting.

"I'm sorry master, I overslept."

"Overslept? You overslept. Moses, you are to be Nubariah's High Chieftain and you aren't taking none of this serious."

"I am master I promise."

Ngozi stared at him hard.

"Finish getting dressed. I'll wait outside."

Ngozi stepped outside. Moses rushed getting dressed and scurried out of the room with Ngozi waiting for him in the corridor.

"Master Ngozi, I'm ready."

Ngozi nodded his head and led Moses down the corridor to the elevator. Moses saw the difference of the palace in the daytime compared to the moonlight. There was an illuminating light around the temple. It was a beauty to behold. Moses ascended on the disk standing next to Ngozi in silence. He would usually ask him questions, especially of the monumental setting. The disk stopped at the top floor of the temple. Moses could feel the great power he felt before entering the city. The power was overwhelming. It was like a chokehold. Moses was led down a long narrow hall following Ngozi close. The walls were made of marble, tall in stature. Moses reached the end of the hall, his jaws dropped of what was before him.

The room was massive in size decked in ornaments of gold and silver crystals around the wall, ceiling, and floor. Surrounding the room were eight men with silver hair past their prime in chairs circling a throne where the Grand Guardian sat.

"Young Moses Ezenwa. Step forth!" the Grand Guardian called.

Moses ambled forth towards the Grand Guardian. Ngozi remained in place. The Grand Guardian and the men stood to their staring at Moses. He entered the circle, standing in front of the throne. Moses was face to face with the Grand Guardian once again. Moses avoided the Grand Guardian's eyes knowing that he was reading him.

"I sense a lot of fear in you boy," said the Grand Guardian. "You're nervous. Scared that you will fail. You are in fear that you are not worthy of being in the presence of me and my council because of the great power you feel. And that is why your power is limited. There's a dark veil clouding your potential. You don't want to die like your father."

"He's too young for this role your majesty," said one of the men. "I don't think he can handle it."

"I wouldn't count him out just yet," said a second man. "You see the potential he has, what he did to the oldest boy of Oba."

"It's true, but the Shadow Lord is a challenge far greater," said the Grand Guardian. "How can he take back Palasera and he allows his demon to conquer his mind?"

"With all respect, your majesty, haven't Abiama showed you the vision of how powerful this boy is?" questioned Ngozi walking up to him. "Isn't he is the one who will defeat the Shadow Legion?"

"Perhaps his failure will be his downfall."

"I am ready for the trials your majesty," said Moses.

Moses was afraid, there was no hiding the emotions he was carrying. Especially with the Grand Guardian. Moses was in fear of sharing his father's fate. The nightmares were a constant reminder. But had a duty. He had to save his people from oppression. Moses had to prove the Grand Guardian wrong.

The Grand Guardian stared at him for a moment. To Moses, it felt like hours although it was only a few seconds. The Grand Guardian leaned towards Moses rubbing his beard.

"We'll see," he said. "Because your test begins immediately."

***

Karungu strolled down the corridor towards the throne as the new Chieftain of Mombasa after burying his father hours before daylight. He was dressed in his father's garment standing proud despite the sin he was carrying. Karungu's pride took over as he was greeted by his royal subjects.

"Greetings your highness," were the words Karungu was hearing in a constant.

Karungu stuck his head high staring at the throne that was before him. *This is it*, he thought. The power he desired was before him. Karungu felt immortal as he took his first seat on the throne that belonged to his father and the chieftains before him ignoring the taint that was within him. He rubbed the smoothness of the armrest feeling the comfort of the soft fabric that comforted him. Karungu was interrupted by a guard as he bowed to him before the throne with a spear in hand.

"Your highness," he said. "Lord Mercius would like an audience with you."

"Ah yes," said Karungu. "Bring him in."

The guards opened the double doors as Mercius entered the throne room with his son following his shadow. Karungu stood stalking the Shadow Lord as he approached.

"Lord Mercius," said Karungu. "In what do I give you the pleasure of this fine day?"

"To focus on the task at hand," said the Shadow Lord.

"Of course. Guards, you can leave us."

Karungu waved his guards away to leave him and the Shadow Lord alone. The guards walked away making their exit on their Chieftain's command. Karungu took a seat on his throne as Mercius and his son stood in a gaping stare.

"So, about Oba's family," said Karungu his demeanor going dark. "They're located in the small village of Dolsa in Ouidah."

"That is information I've already obtained," said Mercius. "Now is the time to strike. We must raise an army to take out the village when they least expect it."

"That will be a challenge. Dolsa may be a small village, but there is heavy resistance there. Defeating Oba's family will be difficult."

Mercius stalked the young Chieftain.

"Not if we create a diversion," he said. "Tell me young Ekwenzu, how loyal are your servants?"

"They don't trust me," said Karungu. "But they are loyal to their nation and their chieftain."

"Good. Then I'm sure you have some warriors that the widow of Oba can trust who are naïve themselves."

"I believe I do."

"Then I want you to use a group of warriors to warn the widow of an attack. She will trust them and lead the people out of the village along with her children. My warriors will take out their army while you capture the widow and children."

"I thought you were going to kill them."

Mercius smirked.

"I will hold a public execution for Nubariah and the rest of the nations of Shiveria to witness the final demise of the Ezenwa bloodline," the Shadow Lord said. "Then the throne is yours as Nubariah's new High Chieftain."

"Sounds good my lord."

"We must act quickly. The more time elapses, the more the boy gets stronger. We must catch him at his weakest state."

"I will make sure their capture becomes a success."

Mercius nodded and nudged his son to make their exit out of the throne room. Karungu was in a blank stare, a small part of him wondering what he has done feeling like he dishonored his family's legacy. Yet the Ekwenzu in him thought otherwise; he was to become High Chieftain creating a new legacy far greater than his ancestors.

***

It felt like an eternity as Moses trekked down the desert plain. The turban on his head was drenched in sweat as the sun beamed from above. Dirt particles swarmed him like a bee sting, his face and arms irritated. The city was far from his site with all being left is a sea of sand and dust. Moses was on a brink of passing out getting tempted by the consistent mirages of lakes and ponds. Despite the illusions, Moses was determined not to fail, not himself or his people that were counting on him as the Grand Guardian and Ngozi rode their camelops in front of him.

"Your highness, can we take a break?" asked Moses. "I've been walking this desert for hours."

The Grand Guardian was silent for a moment before his response, his camelop still treading.

"It's only been three hours," he said. "You must keep going."

"But I'm thirsty and it's hot."

"So now your mind is connected to your animal flesh?"

"What are you talking about? How is this training and you are trying to kill me so?"

The Grand Guardian stopped the camlop. Ngozi followed, remaining silent. The Grand Guardian turned his camelop to face Moses. He scowled as Moses backed away in angst twitching his fingers.

"Tell me, boy, what makes a difference between now and a few hours ago?"

Moses thought for a moment. He felt like the sun frizzled his brain. His mind was lost. The thought Moses wanted was not there. It couldn't regardless because of the Grand Guardian's intimidating glare. Moses only stared with a thoughtless expression to the Grand Guardian. He didn't budge, however, waiting on the boy's response even if it took him an eternity.

"Moses, answer him," said Ngozi.

Moses was too fatigued to answer the Grand Guardian. He was impatient at this point since exiting out of the city.

"I don't know," he whispered.

The Grand Guardian leaned his camelop closer to hear him correctly.

"Ugh!" yelled Moses stomping his feet.

Ngozi shook his head. The Grand Guardian's expression lightened.

"You have a lot of energy for one who is dying of thirst," he said. "Tell me young Ezenwa, are you more frustrated than tired?"

"What is the point of this training?" questioned Moses. "I thought I was staying in the temple."

"You are impatient. And that is why you fail."

Moses paused. The word failure was like a plague to him.

"My apologies your highness," said Moses. "I let my thirst and frustration get the best of me."

The Grand Guardian waved his hand and shook his head.

"No more excuses," he said. "You must face reality. For the first three hours, you didn't think of food and drink. Your mind was focused, sharp. But then you allowed your mind to tread on your body's wants, giving in to your frail thoughts."

"How am I supposed to focus without food or water?"

"You are not supposed to think. Only operate. Yes, your body will give out, but when you tap into your T'kaf, it will give you a rejuvenation.  Consider this an atonement from the true test yet to come."

Moses paused for a moment dwelling in his thoughts.

"What am I supposed to do to obtain that power?"

The Grand Guardian straightened his camelop and glanced at Moses through the sun's glare.

"You must not let your emotions overtake you. Allow the Supreme to take over your spirit."

The Grand Guardian turned his camelop away from Moses and continued moving forward. Ngozi followed in silence. Moses thought for a moment of what will it take to reach the next level.

He wanted to be as powerful as his father was. However, it was a long shot. Moses kept trekking forward, focused on the task. No food or drink was the dread Moses felt he had no choice but to face.

# Revelation

While Moses was training with the Grand Guardian, Ashanti took a stroll through the village around the busy crowd of students coming home from the Academy. She passed by the village square pondering her thoughts of her late husband. Although she was past the stage of grieving, the image of her husband's last breath could not escape her. Ashanti thanked the Supreme for keeping her and her sons alive. Her mother's intuition almost got the best of her since she was separated from her baby boy. Three days have passed since Moses departed from her. Her mind was conflicting. Ashanti knew Nubariah was at stake and Moses was its final hope. Yet she was worried about her baby like any other mother although Ngozi was with him. Her mind continuously fluttered while the villagers were greeting her as their majesty.

Ashanti passed through the village to get to the Academy. Her mind focused on the task as she made her way to the School of Combat. Ashanti entered through double doors as a few gentlemen greeted her in the lobby.

"How may I assist your highness?" one of them said.

"I'm here to check on the progress of my son," she said.

"See for yourself, he's right in the training room."

She thanked the gentleman and walked through the door to the training grounds. There were only a few warriors of various ages training along with their assigned masters. She strolled through the training grounds and spotted Ramses in front of Master Amazu holding a long wooden stick.

"Remember young one, focus only on my movements," Amazu said.

The two stood still for a moment staring each other in the eyes. Amazu got into a stance pointing the stick at Ramses' face as he held his guard. He thrust the stick, but Ramses dodged the strike like a rapid wind. He felt his chest throbbing holding his guard. Amazu shoved the stick at him again after pausing for a few seconds then with multiple blows that were swift like cheetah speed. Ramses dodged each of them barely catching his breath. Amazu set the stick beside him and gave Ramses a blank stare. Ramses was feeling anxious, scarcely holding his guard trying to hold back his fear. A fear he thought he never had. He watched as Amazu twirled the stick around his body in rapidity. Ramses gulped with short breaths trying to predict Amazu's next move. He twirled the stick above his head and bewildered Ramses with a front kicked him leaving him falling to the ground. He held his chest in agony taking short breaths.

"You see, you have done it again," said Amazu. "You allowed your shame to get the best of you consistently."

Ramses groaned while rubbing his chest.

"I'm sorry Master Amazu," he said. "I won't let it happen again. I promise."

"No. You have nothing to prove to me. There is much potential in you Ramses, but since you lost your birthright to your brother, you are holding back your true potential as a warrior. I see a lot of anger, fear, and hatred trying to cloud your judgment. You must learn to let it go. Then you will reach the next level of generating your T'kaf."

Amazu helped Ramses to his feet as his mother approached them.

"I saw the shame in him too Amazu. What did I tell you about holding back?"

Ramses cut his eyes looking away from his mother. She nudged his cheek and propped it up to meet her eyes.

"Answer me, boy."

"I don't know," he said.

She stared at him for a few seconds reading him.

"Quit thinking that you are nothing," she said. "The right of the throne may not be for you, but you cannot let that hold you back for a long time. You are a warrior, a protector. Do you understand me?"

Ramses nodded his head.

"Good. And I'm sorry for intervening in your session Amazu. You may continue."

"Actually, I'm done for today," he said in a big smile. "But I promise you he will grow into a great warrior. I see it within him."

"I know. He has some of his father's features. So does Moses. I hope he's doing well in his training with Ngozi. Destiny will transpire soon. I know a change is coming, even for my son."

***

In the lower level of the temple, Moses meditated on top of a voluminous boulder on his knees and hands pressed on his thighs within a cavern scenery. His training was brutal for the past few days having to journey for hours in the desert. Water became rare to Moses. The mirages were getting worse. The hours became lengthier from morning to evening. Moses barely rested, and he could feel it. But he was determined to reach the next level of gaining his T'kaf.

Ngozi watched Moses from across the cavern along with the Grand Guardian.

"Stay focused," said the Grand Guardian. "Your emotions cannot be spared. Let go of the hurt. Let go of the pain. Embrace the warrior within you. Embrace your inner lion."

Moses was focused on his words in an entirety. He was not going to hold himself back any longer. Moses was determined to feel the power from within. His body suddenly flickered in a golden glow. Moses had a tingling feeling inside of him. Around him were pebbles levitating from the ground with a rumbling quake.

"That's it!" yelled the Grand Guardian.

Then the image of his father's death appeared in his mind. He could see the demon once. The glow faded. Gravity took hold of the pebbles forcing them to the ground. Moses gasped in a deep breath. Ngozi shook his head with the feeling of disappointment then turned to the Grand Guardian.

"So, what do you think your highness?" he asked. "Does he stand a chance?"

The Grand Guardian rubbed his white wooly beard letting out a groan.

"I think the boy has potential."

The old man let out a grin then turned his attention to Moses.

"You truly are Oba's boy, are you?" he said. "I can feel him in you. The spirit of the lion is roaring within you. But right now, it is faint. A warrior must always focus his energy with effort instead of allowing his mind and emotions to channel him. Until you learn to let go of your rage, passion, or despair, then will you be ready to let out the lion within you. Tomorrow will be your final test. In order to pass, you must defeat the demon within you that haunts your dream. But if you fail, there will be no turning back. Do you understand?"

"Yes your majesty," said Moses.

The old man turned from him and walked away in silence. Ngozi sauntered towards Moses placing a hand on his shoulder.

"I'm sorry I failed you, master," Moses said dropping his head. "I tried every method you taught me."

"Save your pity Moses," Ngozi said with sincerity. "You have succeeded in your training these past three days more than you have realized. You have reached a level that most warriors couldn't reach until the peak of their adulthood. Be proud of it."

"But what if I fail master? How am I supposed to defeat something that I can't touch?"

"Don't speak with that madness boy. Have you learned anything throughout this journey? Moses, you are more ready than you could ever imagine. Now clear your mind and join me for supper."

Ngozi helped Moses to his feet. They walked side by side out of the cavern to get to the temple's surface.

***

While Moses was in continuance of his training, Chieftain Karungu sat alone in his private chamber drinking shots of waragi deep in his thoughts. His new reign as Chieftain was bittersweet. It was as if his very soul was conflicting. Karungu gained the power he desired. He was the heir to the throne of Mombasa and gained it after the death of his father. He wanted more. Karungu had to become the ruler of Nubariah. Yet this was wrong. His soul being brought by the devil was consistently playing in his head. The constant thought forced him to swallow the white liquor just for the thoughts to exit his brain. On the surface, he wanted to destroy Moses and Ramses, but taking action was a fear he had. Throughout his life, his father taught him about the morality of brotherhood and to respect his fellow man. It was hard for him to have a cold state like the Shadow Lord. Karungu needed to break out of his morality, but how.

"Karungu," said a faint voice in his head.

He took another shot of the waragi.

"Karungu!" the voice yelled.

He spilled the bottle as it crashed on the floor. Karungu nearly fell out of his chair. The voice in his head was clear to him, Ekwenzu.

"Where are you?" he wondered.

Karungu's chest was beating to the point he could hear his heartbeat. Beads of sweat were trickling down from his forehead as Ekwenzu's voice responded.

"I'm in the darkest corner of your mind."

Karungu gasped as a portal opened in his mind that dragged him into a black space full of blue and green dust clouds. He was floating within the space in bewilderment.

"Where am I?" he asked.

"You are within a convergence," said Ekwenzu appearing from the dark space. "Our parted minds are joined within this space. I can now see your thoughts. Yet you still must be introduced to mine. Witness my experience."

Ekwenzu tapped Karungu's forehead with a touch of his finger. He was dragged through a warp touching a massive city built of clay. The city was familiar beyond its ancient construct. The streets were barrenly cluttered with empty barrels and trash. It looked nearly war-torn. Ekwenzu appeared beside him.

"What is this place?" questioned Karungu. "I've never seen any place so primitive, yet advanced."

"This is the city of the origin of my existence," the dark spirit said. "Adegu, Ouidah."

Karungu thought for a moment.

"Adegu... Adegu... I've never heard of such a place. Is this a lost city? It's nowhere on any databases in all three territories."

"That's because the city no longer exists."

"Is it because of what happened here? This place seems destroyed."

"No. Adegu no longer exists because of the change of rulership. Now what you see here was the beginning of a revolution. Adegu was the hub city of trade with the outer nations. We traded gold, silver, jewels, crops, fish, and various meats from livestock. Then they got greedy. The nations began to conspire against us to steal our resources and claim them as their own. They went to war with us that lasted for a hundred years. That was until I took matters into my own hands. I had the people evacuate underground while I and my soldiers trashed the city to create a diversion for our enemies."

Karungu turned and saw an army from a foreign nation march through the city. Their armor was made of animal fur. Their complexion was a mix of brown and tan having straight hair and long beards. The man leading the army rode on a horse, with a yellow flag textured with a black sun on the back.

"Was that part of their army?" he asked.

"It was," said Ekwenzu. "But that's not the best part."

The army looked through the markets and buildings finding no one present. They were perplexed. A spear descended the army like a bullet. The soldiers screamed as their leader lied in a puddle of blood.

Karungu looked up and saw a lively form of Ekwenzu on the rooftop. His hair was braided in thick locs wearing a breastplate of armor that covered his chest. Karungu could tell that Ekwenzu killed the leader of the opposing army in one swoop. Ekwenzu let out a roaring sound from the rooftop as his army appeared and demolished the remaining army with swords and spears.

"Wow," said Karungu. "You took them out with ease."

"That was a temporary victory," said Ekwenzu. "After learning that I took out one of the greatest conquerors known in Shiveria with ease, the outer nations began to fear me. So that was the perfect opportunity to confront our leaders during the time."

Ekwenzu led Karungu to another memory, this time they were in Sahawayda. The youthful Ekwenzu led a group of protesters down the street towards the Grand Temple. They were anguished over something, Karungu could tell.

"What's going on here?" the Chieftain asked.

"I led a protest to Sahawayda demanding a change of leadership," said Ekwenzu. "Our people suffered many casualties during the war and the Grand Guardian and his council did nothing about it. Then he showed up."

Karungu looked at the entrance of the temple and saw a man in a purple silk garment with a white turban wrapped around his head. A blue diamond was gleaming in the middle.

"Who is he?" wondered Karungu.

"That is Chukwu," said Ekwenzu. "The first of the Ezenwa bloodline."

"He wasn't a part of the Lion Clan? He was the Grand Guardian during your time? Then how did he end up being High Chief of Ouidah?"

"Come, let me show you the secret and lies of the Ezenwa family."

Ekwenzu led the young Chieftain to a sequence of memories. Karungu spotted a memory in front of him, Chukwu face to face with Ekwenzu inside a circle of white chalk. Both men were shirtless and barefoot. Around them was a massive crowd spectating.

"What you see here is a challenge issued by Chukwu," said Ekwenzu. "He agreed to our demands for us to have a king and knew I would be the rightful ruler to the throne. But he challenged me for it and defeated me."

Karungu turned to the next memory. The live Ekwenzu was back in Adegu, but it was different. A palace was being structured within the city.

"Chukwu became Nubariah's King renaming Adegu to Palasera," said Ekwenzu. "I was in second place as Nubariah's top general. Chukwu took everything from me. My kingship, my territory, my city. It was like a slap to the face. Then that's when I rebelled, for the sake of preserving my legacy."

Time-shifted in the memory. Karungu watched the city shift from a city of clay to a city made of silver, stone, and gems, the early stage of Palasera. He was now in an evening sky of dark clouds. Karungu watched the rebellious Ekwenzu lead his army of young soldiers to the palace.

"I convinced warriors from each territory that our nation was being dictated by Chukwu and that if he would rule, our freedom would be gone," said Ekwenzu. "Thus, the Nubarian Civil War was the result."

"Did Chukwu kill you in this battle?" asked Karungu.

"No, he wounded me then cast me and my army out. I was exiled to the outer nations. We built a village on one of the islands in the East Atlantic. We were known as the Fallen Ones. My reputation drove fear to the outer nations. I taught them some of Nubariah's secrets in exchange for them teaching me how to use dark magic. My next step was to gain immortality."

"Were you able to achieve it?"

"I'm very close," said Ekwenzu. "After my death, I convinced Chashak, the Lord of Darkness, to grant me immortality in exchange for the destruction of the Ezenwa bloodline. He gave me a spell that would last only 1,000 years to return to Nubariah. The deal he gave me was if I destroy the Ezenwas, I would be granted immortality. But if I fail, I will be damned to hell in extreme torment. But the only way I can perform the task is to use a vessel."

"How much time do you have left?"

"Only a short time."

Karungu was warped back into the dust clouds. Ekwenzu appeared in front of him.

"Throughout many generations, I used various men to go against the High Chieftain from tribal leaders to warriors," said Ekwenzu. "All of them has failed. The Shadow Lords came at the right time of ending the Ezenwa reign. And that is why you must follow the Shadow Lord. The young Ezenwa men must die to achieve that place of immortality. As long as they're alive, it is a possible chance that the throne will be taken back to the Ezenwa name."

"If they do die, then will I become immortal too?" asked the young Chieftain.

Ekwenzu gave Karungu a blank stare.

"Whoever I share my mind and spirit with will live forever if the deed is done."

"Then teach me! What must I do to end my morality? I can't take this guilt anymore."

Ekwenzu paused, staring again.

"Your heart must burn," he said in a dark demeanor.

Flames were lit around Ekwenzu's body. His eyes brightened like the flames swarming him. Ekwenzu hit Karungu with the palm of his hand to the chest. The young Chieftain felt the flame burning his chest making him stiff. His body felt like ice. He couldn't move a limb. Karungu was in an endless fall of space until he landed on the carpet, the shattered glass and puddle of waragi were wasted underneath him. He was once again in reality. The memories of Ekwenzu were now a vivid picture in his mind. They were now one. Karungu got himself up from the floor in a malignant state. He knew what must be done.

*** *

Ramses wandered out of the village to a grassy plain with a lone tree sitting at the distance. His thoughts continued pondering on the loss of his birthright. *He's not strong enough*, was the ill-thought he had for his younger brother.

Ramses walked towards a river downhill and spotted a group of young women collecting water with tall brown buckets. Ramses spotted Dayo among them wearing a long red dress with yellow patterns. Her hair was covered in a colorful wrap of yellow blended with red, orange, and green. The young women greeted him as Ramses walked towards Dayo. She looked at him in the corner of her eyes focused on her task of collecting water for the village.

"Hey Dayo," Ramses said.

"Hey Ramses," she said. "How was training today? I hope my father didn't give you more bruises."

"Actually, my bruises are not visible at this time thankfully."

They both laughed then paused for a moment.

"So... There is something I would like to ask you," said Ramses.

"Yes, what is it Ramses?"

"About... well... you and me."

There was a sign of awkwardness between the two. Dayo became uneasy. Ramses was hoping he didn't come at her too strong. He was already heartstruck knowing she was married. Now that he was at a place of vulnerability, Ramses felt he had nothing to lose. That included taking Dayo from her husband to be with her, to have her affection.

"Ramses, I told you already that I'm married."

"But to that coward Dayo. What does he do for you besides let you do all the work? The man is lazy. He does neither a man nor a woman's job."

A nerve was struck. Dayo refused for another man to insult her husband.

"Well, my husband loves me for me and not as a necessity like you warriors do."

"But I love you Dayo. You are such a beautiful woman. You need a man like me to protect you. I can be there for you both physically and mentally. Even your father believes that…"

"Stop Ramses! Just stop!"

She took a deep breath composing herself.

"Times has changed Ramses. The custom of our people has vanished just like our kingdom. Yes, if we were at a different time, we would be together. But Nubariah has changed. The customs of a warrior taking a wife are gone. Tobukwu has won me over through his loving words. My father may not like him, but he will one day be the father of my children."

Ramses let out a deep sigh.

"Fine, if that's how you feel," he said. "But if he messes up just know I'll be here for you."

Ramses stormed away to the top of the hill away from the young women. Dayo frowned but continued her task and grabbed another bucket to collect water.

***

In the palace of Mombasa, Tamu, the newly appointed head of security walked into the throne room armed with a holster to his hip. Karungu sat on his throne stalking the Head of Security as he bowed before him.

"Your highness," he said. "Have you summoned me?"

"Yes, I have," said the Chieftain. "Tamu, I have appointed you as Head of Security because I know you are an honest man who is devoted to his nation. But tell me, how devoted are you of your Chieftain?"

"I have devoted my life to serve the Chieftain of my tribe."

"That's good to hear because I truly need you at this moment. I believe the Shadow Lord is out for my life."

Tamu balled his fist clenching his fist.

"I don't mean to intrude your highness, but what happened with your meeting with the Shadow Lord?"

Karungu sat still as if time was in a frozen state. He rubbed his goatee staring away from the Head of Security.

"I'm glad you asked that question," he said. "Shadow Lord Mercius is ruthless and will annihilate anyone who stands in his way. He's trying to use me like my father. He wants me to get my hands dirty and kill the surviving Ezenwa family, using me and my people as pawns! But I refused because I'm not some toy he can play with. Now that bastard is out for my blood!"

"Then I will make sure your protection is my first priority."

"I have a personal task for you. I need for you to take a squadron of troops down to the Village of Dolsa in Ouidah to warn the former queen of the Shadow League's attack. Mercius' plans need to be thwarted. If he succeeds in killing her and the children, Mercius will come after me next. The Shadow Lord is power-hungry. He does not want any leader of Nubariah to possibly challenge him for the throne of the High Chieftain. I'm no exception."

"Well, shouldn't it be the Captain or the General to warn Queen Ashanti of a possible attack? I'm only Head of Security of the clan's palace."

"This is a special assignment I'm giving you Tamu. This is a chance to prove yourself. I'm shaking things up with the clan, and I want you to be a part of that elevation. If you can prove to me that you can lead a squadron, then I will add you into the ranks of the Jaguar Clan Army."

Tamu smirked.

"That would be a great honor, your highness," he said.

"If anyone objects of me to send you on this mission, they will hear from me. And don't worry about picking your squadron. I will assemble the warriors for you. You will leave tonight. Time must not be wasted in this matter."

"Then I will prepare for my journey, your highness."

Tamu turned and walked out of the throne room closing the door behind him. Karungu stalked the Head of Security until the doors were shut behind him. The Chieftain dug into his pocket, pulling out his Optix. He pressed the button. His facial expression darkened as he began to speak to the device.

"The first phase is complete," he said. "He fell for the bait."

A holoprojector appeared from the Optix revealing Mercius in his armor.

"Well done Lord Karungu. My army will follow them closely through the Shadows until they reach the village."

"I will follow them as well from the distance. If anyone spots me..."

"I will direct you on where to go. They will not see this assault coming."

"Then I will wait on your signal, my lord."

"Phase 2 has now commenced. Prepare yourself Lord Karungu."

Mercius disappeared from the projector ending the chat. Karungu stared at the wall allowing his pride to overshadow his morality. He was now one with Ekwenzu. The darkness within him began to give him satisfaction. He was no longer bound by his father's teachings. Karungu could finally build his own legacy, as long as the Ezenwa family were out of the way.

***

Moses laid cozy in the bed of his guest chambers. It was a silent but calm night. A voice was lingering inside him. It called his name in a whispering voice that was soothing to his ears. Moses thought it was a fascinating dream until the voice called to him, *"Wake up Moses. Wake up."*

His eyes shot open watching a figure that was the shape of a woman near the doorway gesturing him to follow her.

"Come," the mysterious woman said.

"Who are you?" questioned Moses

"I am the one who will give you the revelation of every vision you foresee."

He was uncertain to follow her, but the woman's voice was sweet in a soft calm. Moses got out of the bed and followed the woman down the dark corridor of moonlight. She led him down the corridor to the round metal disk. The mysterious woman was the first to step onto the disk, gesturing Moses to step on. He followed her and stepped on the disk. It began to descend itself to the depths of the temple. Moses stared at the woman in fascination. She was slender wearing a shiny purple dress with fluffy hair. She wore no shoes showing her brown polished toes. Her presence was strange to Moses. He studied her closely. She carried no signs of emotion. It was hard to tell if she meant him any harm or came to him for peace. But he could tell she was on a mission.

The disk-like elevator landed at the bottom of the temple. The woman led Moses out of the temple to the night air of Sahawayda. Moses followed the woman past the quiet city. He watched as the woman walked past the guards with leisure through the gate without an interaction. *How can they not see her?* he thought. *Shouldn't they say something?* Moses paused and saw the woman entering the desert plain. She turned around and gestured to him.

"Come, Abiama is with you," she said.

Moses smiled and followed the woman. He walked past the guards staring. None of them recognized his movements. The desert was a different feel for Moses in the night air. Darkness surrounded the sands of moonlight. Moses was refreshed walking through the desert plain of the night hours compared to the harsh hours of days throughout his training with the Grand Guardian. The air was warm at a near cool temp giving Moses satisfaction. The desert was endless, even for an enjoyable walk such as this. Moses followed the woman in continuation of a silent walk.

Then he was in awe seeing in front of him was an oasis that was monumental. Date palm trees swarmed an endless lake of water as bright as crystal. Moses followed the woman to a cavern in a corner of the oasis. The interior was full of illuminated gems that brightened the area. There were no animals in sight.

The woman stopped in the middle of the cavern with her back turned.

"You never told me who you are," Moses said. "And why have you led me here?"

She turned to face him letting out a smile.

"I am only an entity from the heavens," she said. "I was sent by Abiama, the Supreme Great Creator to reveal your destiny young one."

Moses' jaw dropped. He realized he was standing in front of an angel, but she had no wings. He was speechless for a moment before he spoke again.

"What is my destiny?" he asked.

"I cannot reveal it to you. It is not my place. But when the moment comes, you must let it nurture and let it grow."

Her voice echoed in the air as she formed into a bright purple orb and flew out of the cavern disappearing in the night air.

"Wait!" yelled Moses following the orb. "Where are you going! Why have you brought me here?"

Then a familiar voice called his name. Moses turned and paused. His chest was throbbing as he froze. It was his father standing in front of him.

"Father?" he questioned.

"It is me, son," he said.

Moses rushed towards him and gave him a hug squeezing him tight. It was real, there was no shadow. He did not transform into the frightened little boy. Moses was himself feeling tears streaming down of delight. He let go and beamed at his father.

"I can't believe it's you," he said. "And I can touch you."

"This is a sacred place," he said. "The spirits can contact mortals if permitted by the Supreme."

"I miss you, Father. Mother misses you. We all miss you. Nubariah has fallen and is in chaos. I wish you were here to stop the Shadow League."

"My life is no longer with me I'm afraid. I did everything to protect my people and lead our nation. But it was not my destiny to stop this tragedy."

"But I'm not ready to challenge the Shadow League and liberate our people from this nightmare. I can't even defeat the haunting demon. You were our only hope."

"No, there is hope of ending Mercius' reign and Khonshu's terror. I would've never thought you would earn the birthright and defeat your brother. But I underestimated you, Moses. You were always special."

Moses' lips curled to a weak smile. His father's words were encouraging, but he heard this countless times from various people.

"But how can I defeat them both?" he questioned. "This is happening so fast. I'm too young. I'm not strong enough."

"That is what your mind says. The Supreme Abiama has sent me to tell you that the time is drawing near. You will unleash a power that is twice as powerful as what mine ever was. It may seem impossible to you Moses, but you are the final generation of this bloodline before the cycle ends. The Supreme has placed power within you that is unimaginable. It will be of Chuckwu's ancient power connecting the beginning of the bloodline to the end. You just have to tap into it."

"Is this the destiny the woman told me about that led me here? Master Ngozi told me about this destiny as well."

"Yes. You will confront Mercius in an intense battle for Palesera. There, your destiny will be fulfilled."

"How about Khonshu? Will I be able to avenge you by defeating him?"

His father gave him a blank stare.

"You will have your chance to face Khonshu when the time comes," he said. "I have foreseen it. The battle will be fierce. And when you face him, do not fight him through rage. That could be your downfall."

"I promise you that I will take him down, Father. He will answer through his tyranny. Mercius will be first and his treacherous wife."

"I am so proud of you son. You have grown to become strong. Tell your brother to stay encouraged. I know both of you will achieve greatness."

Moses held back his tears wishing his father could come back and stay. He wanted him to unite with his mother so they could once again become a happy family.

"Do you have to go father?" he said.

"I'm afraid I have to," he said. "Remember your destiny well Moses. Never forget. I will always be with you. I love you son."

His body suddenly vanished into the night air as Moses made his exit out of the cave and gazed at the stars.

"I love you too Father, goodbye."

The moonlight began to darken. The oasis vanished from Moses' sight. His chest was like a beating drum waiting for the demon that raged terror in his mind for the past seven years. But instead, he found himself lying in his bed. What Moses felt was real, far from an ordinary dream. His spirit must've detached from his body. It was a revelation.

# Chapter Seven

# Test of Fate

It was the next morning as Ramses got out of his bed smelling tasty food following its aroma. His clothes were already prepared in his closet for another day at the Academy. Ramses entered the kitchen as his mother was preparing pap and akara with egg sauce.

"Good morning Ramses," she said. "Sit, I have breakfast ready."

He curled a weak smile without saying a word. Ramses took a seat at the table with his mouth watered in cravings ready to devour the meal his mother fixed. She placed the dishes on the table, then the food, each dish one by one. They said a prayer together to the Supreme God of all Creations then began to eat. His mother watched him as he ate, but she could tell something was wrong with him through his doleful facial expression as he dipped the akara in the pap with each bite.

"You haven't spoken to me in recent days," she said. "Is everything okay?"

Ramses paused without responding. He looked at his mother as she stared at him waiting for him to respond. He sighed.

"I still can't get over how Moses defeated me. It was like a flash then I was blacked out. His lucky victory means nothing. Moses is not ready for such a trial. Out of any of us, it should be me. I should still have the birthright. I was always meant to rule. I proved my leadership countless times here in Dolsa, yet my right as heir has been stripped from me!"

Ramses slammed his fists on the table nearly breaking it in half causing the food to jump off the plates. His mother sat in a calm without flinching. She wanted to get through to him.

"I can't control the moves the Elders of Sahawayda decides to make. Besides, the Grand Guardian has appointed this."

Ramses sighed.

"I know, it just isn't fair."

Ramses dipped the egg sauce in one of the akara and took multiple bites. His mother smiled.

"You miss your baby brother, don't you?"

Ramses let out a weak smile and shrugged. He was still angry that his younger brother who was smaller than him carrying a lot of fear won over his birthright. He was angry that the Grand Guardian issued such a challenge knowing he was going to lose. But in a way, he missed Moses. He missed giving him tough love of nuggies and punches on the arm. Ramses always loved his brother. He only wished that change wouldn't happen instantly from what he felt. But this was a change he knew he couldn't control at this point. His brother has surpassed him. Those days were past him now.

"I guess so," he said. "I can admit it doesn't feel the same without tussling him."

She laughed.

"You boys are something," she said. "Always challenging each other. But it's a good thing. I'm so proud of how strong you two have gotten."

The door knocked in three beats. Ramses and his mother were alarmed. They weren't expecting guests.

"Get dressed for the Academy," she said. "I'll see who it is."

"Are you certain mother?" asked Ramses.

"It'll be okay. It might be an inquiry of one of the market squares. Besides, if there was an actual threat, the alarm would ring."

"I'll be in my room if you need me."

Ashanti nodded her head and approached the door as Ramses went in the opposite direction to his room. Her intuition knew that something wasn't right. Ashanti had to stay guarded. She opened the door as Tamu and a few Jaguar Clan warriors stood in front of her. She was astonished. Ashanti wasn't expecting such company.

"How may I help you?" she asked.

"I know this is sudden your highness," said Tamu. "But your life is in danger. We've been sent by Chieftain Karungu to warn you of an attack planned by the Shadow League."

"I heard about Thuku's passing. You have my condolence. Now as for your new Chieftain, why didn't he have you contact my Council of Authority? We could've been warned sooner if he didn't give you the trouble of rushing here."

"My apologies your highness. Chieftain Karungu is fairly young and inexperienced."

"It seems like he picked an inexperienced council as well. I will inform Master Amazu at once."

"We better come with you, your highness. We were given orders by Lord Karungu to escort you out of the village."

"I'm sorry commander…"

"Tamu your highness."

"Well, Commander Tamu, I don't know what Chieftain Karungu does in Mombasa, but here in Ouidah, we do things differently. For me, my people come first. If you want to help, you can report to General Amazu."

Dolsa's emergency alarm rang in multiple trumpet sounds. The Shadow League has invaded. The time for action was now as Ashanti glared at Tamu and the guards behind him.

"It looks like you have your chance to prove yourself. Wait here, I need to get prepared. It looks like the war has come to us."

Ashanti turned from the Jaguar Clan guards and rushed to her room. Ramses rushed past her to the den uncertain of what to do. This was not a test. He already experienced it. Ramses never experienced a real battle. The thought of his father's dying day clouded his mind. The Sacking of Palasera drove him to fear. Ramses had to fight to prove his might of what everyone in Dolsa and all of Ouidah could see in him. He had on a light brown kaftan and sandals carrying a sack. He saw Tamu and the other guards watching him.

"What is this?" he asked. "Your attire. You must be Jaguar Clan warriors."

"And you must be Prince Ramses," said Tamu.

"I have no title as of now."

Tamu stared at him.

"You don't look dressed for what's coming," he said.

"I wasn't prepared," said Ramses.

"You always want to prepare for battle at any given time."

Ashanti rushed back into the den loading a shotgun wearing a bulletproof vest. She had a pistol and a machete in two holsters surrounding her waistline. She threw Ramses a pair of boots.

"You will need to switch shoes son," she said.

Ashanti stared at Ramses' clothes in mere disgust.

"And clothes too. We need to see what's going on?"

"Yes ma'am," said Ramses.

Ashanti turned to Tamu and his men.

"I need the five of you to come with me."

"Yes your highness," said Tamu.

After Ramses put on his combat training suit, he hurried out of the house after his mother and the Jaguar Clan warriors to the dirt road of their neighborhood until they reached the market square. Ashanti pulled out her Optix.

"Master Amazu...Master Amazu do you copy?"

There was no answer.

"Damn!" she said.

She spotted a crowd of people hovered in terror. Young men and women of various ages were in bloodied uniforms getting carried away by medical aid. She could tell they were restless by the fear in their eyes. Both parents and elders were in mourning for their children. Ramses saw familiar faces covered in blood. He saw others covered in body bags. Ramses and his mother figured this was a genocide.

Ashanti spotted Dayo and Tobukwu outside the crowd with disturbed looks. Ramses followed his mother as she called Dayo's name to get her attention.

"What's going on?" Ashanti inquired.

Tears stained her eyes as her husband wrapped his arm around her. He was barely older than her wearing a short goatee. Doya responded.

"There was an explosion in the Academy. No one saw it coming. Some of the teachers and students are dead. There are others that's crucially wounded."

Ramses was speechless. He didn't know whether to be angry or mournful. He was hoping that his friends survived.

"The bastards, they've gone too far," Ashanti said. "Ramses, stay here I'll be back. Tamu, you guys try to thin this crowd. I'll try to get ahold of General Amazu again."

She rushed through the crowd leaving Ramses with the Jaguar Clan warriors and young couple. Ashanti grabbed her Optix again with hopes of reaching Amazu.

"Amazu, do you copy? There has been an incident at the Academy. Do you copy?"

There was no answer.

She watched as the Jaguar Clan warriors surrounded the crowd hearing the plead of Tamu, "Calm down! I need everyone to calm down!"

She talked on her Optix for the third time.

"Master Amazu do you copy?! Please answer me!"

She began to wail in panic witnessing the chaos that continued to swarm the market square. She watched as the Lion Clan warriors appeared in their armor and shields. She was relieved as they thronged the crowd with commands for them to calm themselves. She spotted Amazu within the midst of the warriors and hurried towards him.

"Amazu," she said. "What happened? I almost had a dreadful thought that you were killed."

He turned towards her with a pale but enraged look on his face.

"We are being invaded," he said.

"I know, by the Shadow League. Jaguar Clan warrior Tamu warned me at my door."

Amazu glared at the warrior with suspicion.

"Why wasn't I notified about this?"

She shook her head.

"Their new Chieftain decided to send an order without communication. Tamu warned me when it was too late."

"I don't know. Something isn't right. I'll be sure to keep my eyes on that one."

"Right. But for now, we better get both shuttles and motorboats ready for evac. We'll have a few guards escort everyone out the town."

"You take care of that while I gather the warriors together for battle during Ngozi's absence. If only he was here with us."

A tremendous boom sounded from the distance. Ashanti was rattled watching the villagers around her scream in terror. Smoke clouded the sky blocking the sun. She stared in disbelief at the direction the smoke was steaming from.

"That's the direction of the port," she said. "Damn. So far for our evac."

"Then they have no choice but to escape on foot," said Amazu.

He turned his attention to the crowd to calm them down.

"Alright listen up!" he yelled. "Everyone stay calm! I need you all to listen and listen closely. We have been infiltrated and found out somehow by the Shadow League!"

The crowd gasped and screamed as Amazu threw out his hand to calm them down.

"Unfortunately, after that explosion, your escape here will be difficult. I want you all to go further South with Queen Ashanti to the coast. You will all live your lives in peace without the Shadow League or any type of raider intervening. You will have guards escort you as well, so you will not travel alone.

"And as for the warriors, you have sworn an oath to protect the people no matter what. There is no submission. There is no retreat..."

He paused with sweat trickling through the shortness of breath. Ashanti placed her hand on his back.

"Amazu... Amazu!" she yelled. "Are you okay? Speak to me!"

He nearly collapsed falling on one knee staring in space. Her voice faded from his ears for a few moments. Then his conscious thoughts returned to him as he looked into her eye with fear.

"You need to leave now," he said.

"Why?"

"The Shadow Lord is with the army. They just arrived."

She froze and backed away. Ashanti turned to the crowd shrieking.

"We need to leave now! And if anyone is still in their houses, tell them to follow us!"

She stormed away from the market square with hopes of the villagers following her. She could hear the frenzy of screams with a stampede of panicked villagers. She could hear the guards shouting, "Go with the queen, it isn't safe here! Authorized personnel only!" Ramses, Doya, and Tobukwu followed striding beside her. Tamu and his men rushed to walk alongside her. Doya stared at her father in worry. *Please don't die on me*, is what she wanted to tell him.

"Mother, what's going on?" Ramses asked.

"The Shadow League is here. There's no time to explain."

"How could the Shadow League have known we were here?" he asked.

"I don't know, but stick by me," she said. "We must fight together as a family in case of an ambush."

"But the Shadow Lord…"

"No son. You are not strong enough. And here, take this."

She unsheathed the machete and hand it to him.

"In case we are attacked by the dark warriors or any type of raider who wishes to sell us along the way, you have something to protect you beside your bare hands."

Ramses placed the machete in his back pocket feeling the sharpening of the blade rubbing the fabric of his pants.

"We will do everything in our power to protect you as well your highness," said Tamu.

"Then follow your duty and protect the villagers behind me. I will be fine."

Tamu nodded his head gesturing his men to march beside the villagers that were crowding behind them. The village guards were in the midst of the growing crowd.

Ramses glimpsed behind him seeing Korah walking alongside his mother in grief. He at least saw a familiar face that wasn't a part of the massacre. Ramses walked alongside his mother to the countryside. Although Dolsa was seeing its destruction, at least he and his mother had an opportunity for an escape before encountering an armada.

***

Moses sat at the edge of his bed meditating. This was his big day, and he was beyond anxious. His destiny was beginning to come clear. He was happy to see his father, even though it was a vivid dream. But was he truly strong enough to liberate his nation? Was he truly the heir? His youth and age overwhelmed him. Now he had to face a challenge against his demon, the very demon that haunted his sleep from the past seven years of his life. To him, this was too much of a task.

One of the temple guards entered the bedchamber with poise dressed in an all-white kaftan with a white turban.

"Moses Ezenwa," he said. "It is time."

The guard led Moses down the hall to a narrow chamber. Another disk-like elevator within the chamber illuminated in blue lighting. The two stepped on the disk as it descended to the depths of the temple. Moses could feel his stomach turn with the feeling of nausea. There was no turning back from this. The thought of his destiny replayed in his mind the further the disk took him down the depths. Anxiety struck Moses as the disk stopped at the bottom of a dark cavern. The only light he could see were lanterns lighting on the rails of an arched bridge.

The guard led Moses across the bridge leading to a narrow tunnel. Moses followed the guard through the tunnel, his pulse beating in every step. The guard stopped in place. Moses glimpsed at the chamber before him. It was a room of cavern walls made of metal with black polished floors. Ngozi was across from them with his hands behind his back. Four other guards dressed in gold were standing in each corner of the room with incense beside them. The Grand Guardian appeared and stood in the middle of the room.

The guard escorted Moses to the room.

"May Abiama blesses and keep you young Ezenwa," he said.

The guard bowed to the Grand Guardian and vanished back into the dark cavern. Moses was left face to face with the Grand Guardian.

"Moses Ezenwa son of Oba," he said. "For four days you have trained under me to gather and unlock your untapped potential. Now today you will be tested. You must face the very thing that has terrorized your mind having you respond to your emotion, hurt, and trauma. If you can defeat it, you will pass the test. But if the demon overtakes you, then you will fail and be driven by madness for the rest of your days. And your destiny will fade to dust. Do you understand?"

"Yes your majesty," said Moses giving a bow.

"Then let the challenge commence!"

The Grand Guardian walked away leaving Moses and Ngozi face to face.

"Remember Moses, focus," he said. "And let go of your toxic mind. Clear your mind."

Moses nodded his head hiding the fear he had. He could feel the rapid beats speeding in his chest.

The Grand Guardian nodded to guards. They lighted the incense and waved their hands controlling the smoke. A drum was beating in the background. Moses shut his eyes as the smoke blew around him in a hurling wind. Moses opened his eyes witnessing the smoke spreading throughout in a vast fog. Moses could not see anyone around him, not even Ngozi who was in front of him. There was utter silence. Moses walked around the room puzzled.

"Hello!" he yelled.

But there was no answer. He only heard an echo from his voice.

A voice echoed in a roaring boom echoing the chamber.

"Moses Ezenwa! It's time to meet your destiny!"

Moses looked around the room hearing his breath. His body was tense. He clenched his fists barely putting up a guard. A bulky figure appeared from behind ready to devour him. Moses could sense a dark presence behind him. The demon was present, this had to be an illusion. *Be strong*, he thought. *Be courageous. You are the son of Oba from the mighty Ezenwa bloodline. No demon or beast can defeat me.* Moses took a deep breath and turned to face the creature. He held his guard showing no signs of fear. The beast smirked and threw swift strikes. Moses reacted with instinct blocking each swing until the beast disappeared into the fog. Moses was afraid, but he knew he couldn't give up. He held his guard, this time sensing out his enemy.

***

Mercius gathered his army in a nearby valley. He was prepared to finish the remnant of the Lion Clan. A dark warrior appeared in front of him and kneeled.

"My lord their army is gathering," it said. "They know we are here."

"Good," said Mercius. "And how about the Widow and her children?"

"They are gathered together heading South."

"They're trying to escape. I'll let Lord Karungu handle them with a squadron of my warriors assisting him. I want the dead chieftain's wife and children captured for their execution. And capture as many of the villagers then send them to the nearest port to be sold. Whoever resists, kill them. The rest of you come with me. It's time to end this."

A small militia of dark warriors gathered and marched through the dark portals.

Mercius led the rest of his army to the village in preparation for battle against the Lion Clan army. His son followed behind him as they trod on foot. Mercius grabbed his Optix and spoke, "I'm sending a squadron your way. They are heading South."

Karungu's voice responded, "I will be ready for them."

Mercius led his army in silence. He was ready to devour his enemies. He stopped and glared at the distance. The village was only a few miles away. He was in a near gasp noticing an army waiting for him in the distance. The Lion Clan was already charging with Amazu leading.

"Charge!" Amazu yelled to the warriors. His fist was pumped in the air with a sword in hand.

Mercius saw the warriors from the distance lunging their spears and swords at his army. He scowled at the sight of them. They caught him off guard, but the Lion Clan army was still at a place where he wanted them. It was the perfect time to strike as he glared at his enemies with bloodlust.

"Kill them all."

The dark warriors followed his command and attacked the warriors. The two armies collided trading blows with their swords. Amazu slashed each dark warrior instantly glaring at Mercius. The Shadow Lord watched his every move folding his arms across his breast-plated chest.

* * *

The crowd expanded following Ashanti out of town to avoid the battle. There was no hesitation from anyone to leave their houses since the explosions. Ashanti led the villagers up a hill with the village out of their reach. She stopped. Ramses beside her was shocked staring at Chieftain Karungu as he stood at the top of the hill. Tamu ran to the Chieftain with the eagerness of gaining his reward for protecting the Queen of Ouidah.

"Your highness," he said bowing. "I have done the task you have asked. The queen and children are safe."

"Well done Tamu," he said. "You have proven yourself worthy."

"Chieftain Karungu," said Ashanti. "As much as I'm glad you showed your face, you have a lot to explain once we make it out of here."

Karungu smirked folding his hands.

"Actually Queen Ashanti, escape is not of the plan."

A dark portal appeared behind him. Tamu rose in shock backing away in fright. Ashanti scowled and grabbed her shotgun. Ramses clutched the machete from his back pocket and held his guard. The villagers behind them let out shrieks.

Out of the portal, a militia of dark warriors emerged.

"Your highness, how could you use me like this?" questioned Tamu.

"I knew something wasn't right about this," said Ashanti.

"Capture the villagers," ordered Karungu. "But leave the wife and child to me."

The dark warriors hovered around the villagers like sharks in the deep sea down the hill. Ramses grasped the machete scowling at Karungu. Ashanti gripped hold of her shotgun and shot one of the dark warriors with the atomic shell to its chest killing it instantly.

"Everyone run to the hills and defend yourself the best you can!" she yelled. "Guards, protect the civilians with your life!"

She fired another shot at the dark warriors as the villagers scattered in separate directions. It was pandemonium as the dark warriors captured each person they could get a hold of and dragged them away into portals. The guards fought off the dark warriors the best they could with their stun batons and electric clubs. However, they were overpowered by the dark warrior's combative skills. Ramses stood beside his mother alongside the Jaguar Clan warriors.

"When I'm done with your Chieftain, I'm coming after you," Ramses said to Tamu.

"Then you might as well take out the rest of Mombasa," said Tamu. "Karungu deceived us all."

"Let's discuss this later when we're out of here," said Ashanti.

Ramses roared running towards Karungu. He slashed each dark warrior that was in his way. The dark warriors attacked Ashanti with aggression, but she shot each one with perfect accuracy. Tamu and his warriors fought beside her in defense.

***

Moses had shut his eyes, his guard still up. He could sense the demon's dark energy, but the movements were faint. The creature was moving too swiftly. Moses felt his chest-beating again with the shortness of breath. He walked around the room on his guard in blind faith.

"I sense your vulnerability," said the creature's voice lingering in the room.

The creature appeared in front of Moses and aimed for his legs. Moses defended himself through reflexes and blocked the creature's attacks from the legs to the shoulders, to the head. Their movements were like flashes of lightning, then the creature disappeared. Instead of holding his guard, Moses decided to use a technique he learned in his training. He took a calming deep breath through the nose and clasped his hands together. He closed his eyes meditating in deep focus, this time clearing his mind. Every fear and doubt he had was let go from his mind. The anger and sorrow he once felt, he had let it go. The creature appeared like a whirlwind to the side of Moses. He was not startled. It was like time was moving in slow motion. Moses opened his eyes and dodged the creature's chop that was flung at him. He saw that his fists were glowing in static combustion. He jabbed the creature causing it to explode into the smoke that clouded the room itself. He could hear the creature's terror echoing until there was silence. The fog began to clear. The room was back to normal. The test was over.

Moses was amazed at the power he gained staring at his glowing fist. Was this part of his destiny? Perhaps he was ready for the Shadow Lord with the discovery of this newfound power. This had to be the power of Chukwu.

Ngozi was astonished standing in front of his accomplished pupil. Moses was now at the next level. He found his T'kaf. Only if his father lived to see this moment. Moses turned his head and saw the Grand Guardian smiling.

"You have passed the test Moses," he said. "You are now a step closer to reaching your destiny. Your time here is over, and Ngozi is no longer your teacher."

Moses turned back to Ngozi and hugged him.

"You have done well," said Ngozi. "And you have made your father proud."

"Thank you, master," said Moses.

"No, you heard the Grand Guardian. I am no longer your master. You have passed."

"Then what should I call you?"

"Anything you desire… your highness."

Moses thought for a second, flattered by Ngozi's words.

"How about Mazị Ngozi?"

"Yeah, it rings a bell."

***

The tide of the battle turned as the Lion Clan warriors were overpowered by the Shadow League. A garrison of dark warriors was sent through multiple portals to finish the army off. Corpse after corpse was purged by energy swords of slashes and piercings. The corpses of dark warriors lay alongside the bloody corpses of the fallen Lion Clan warriors who were Mercius' front line and sacrifice.

Amazu fought through more dark warriors to get to the Shadow Lord, who stood in the middle of the grass plain. He slashed and kicked the dark entities one by one until none stood in his way. His sword was in hand, black blood dripping on the grass. Mercius glowered.

"Shadow Lord Mercius," said Amazu. "We finally meet."

"And who are you supposed to be?" the Shadow Lord questioned.

"I am the man that will stop you."

The Shadow Lord let out a sigh.

"That's what they all say. You know, you remind me of this warrior that did the same thing you did. He challenged me to protect the Chieftain's family, but he was utterly defeated."

Mercius focused his attention on the battle, each warrior falling one by one by his army, screams echoing the air. The battle became his for the taking. Then he placed his attention back on Amazu. Mercius placed his hand on his son's shoulder.

"I have a change of heart, however," the Shadow Lord continued saying. "Join me, and I will spare the few men that you have left. I will even relieve some of the servants to you. As long as you give up your queen and the children for my ultimate sacrifice."

Amazu scowled and gripped his sword.

"You cannot buy me out Shadow Lord," he said. "I have sworn an oath to my Chief and my people. That means even if I have to die."

Mercius shook his head.

"Such a shame. We could've used the muscle, but the pathetic villagers will have to do. If you choose death, then so be it."

Mercius in a millisecond let go of his son and kicked the sword away from Amazu leaving him astonished. Mercius threw hammering strikes at Amazu while he quickly threw his arms up to block the punches. Amazu could barely handle his supernatural agility. He felt a kick to the gut as Mercius back slapped him on the nose. Amazu stammered a few steps back not knowing if this was a one-on-one or two on one battle. He held his nose and felt something warm dripping in his hand. Amazu looked and saw blood-stained in his hand.

Mercius let out a heinous laugh.

"I guess I started with too much impulse. I wasn't being fair at all. Go ahead Lion, amuse me for my entertainment. Strike me with all you have. And please don't bore me."

***

Ramses slit a few more dark warriors before reaching the top of the hill. He was face to face with Karungu, his machete was dripped in his enemies' blood. Karungu smirked, not phased or intimidated by the young and powerful warrior.

"Traitor," said Ramses. "You dishonored your father's name by joining the outsider, the oppressor. Why did you decide to sell out?"

"Ramses Ezenwa," said Karungu. "I heard of your reputation throughout Ouidah. Nubariah was rooting for you to become the new High Chieftain until your little brother stole your birthright. I guess you are left with nothing."

"Man shut the hell up."

Ramses swung his machete at Karungu's neck in full strength. The young chieftain grabbed Ramses' arm, preventing the blade from touching his skin. Karungu grinned.

"I can see why you lost," he said.

Karungu spun and unsheathed his dagger. He slashed Ramses' in the back of his legs leaving him wailing in agony.

"Because you focus too much on your strength and not your opponent's movements."

Ramses felt sharp stings on the back of his legs. His eyes watered while stumbling on his feet. Ramses was determined not to lose this fight no matter the pain he felt. He swung his machete at leg length towards Karungu. The young Chieftain hopped over the blade and plunged his at Ramses' face. Ramses reacted in an instant, raising his machete to cling with the dagger. Karungu pushed his blade aiming to drill his skull. Ramses pushed back, using all his strength to force the chieftain backward. Karungu scowled knowing he was being outpowered by his new enemy. He was struggling trying to keep his balance while being forced to back away. Karungu heard the voice of Ekwenzu in his head, *Don't be a fool. His strength is too great for you. Outmaneuver him with your speed.* Ramses pushed Karungu off his feet causing him to fall on his back. Karungu rolled to his feet holding his guard. Ramses roared ignoring the stings in his legs and aimed at the Chieftain's chest with a front kick. Karungu used his quickness to evade the kick and low kicked the wounded area of Ramses' back leg causing him to fall on the back of his head. The machete fell on the grass a few feet away from him. Ramses grunted, writhing in pain. The agony he felt was worse. Ramses could feel blood staining his legs like sweat. Karungu dragged him on his knees forcing him to watch his brethren get defeated by the dark warriors. The villagers had no escape. Ramses watched the villagers from children to women, to elders get dragged into various portals. He heard their cries. Ramses felt like he was at the palace once again watching innocent lives get taken. And he was the target.

"You see young prince, you have failed," said Karungu. "Your mother the queen has failed. The era of the Ezenwa rule is now over. And with your cursed family gone, I will lead Nubariah to a new era. An era of freedom and democracy. No more do we have to make decisions off of one family. Finally, the Ekwenzu will have the throne. And the Shadow Lord will hand me the title."

Ramses' elbowed Karungu in the stomach and targeted his jaws, ribs, and stomach with jabs. Karungu used his quickness to defend himself. Ramses used the energy he had and grabbed him by his legs using his strength to lift him from his feet. He was being overpowered by Ramses' strength once again. He was out-maneuvered. Karungu had a rapid thought tapping into the mind of Ekwenzu. He unsheathed his dagger and thrashed the back of Ramses' skull with the hilt. Ramses stumbled, dropping Karungu leaving him staggering. He could feel Ekwenzu's power flowing through him. Ramses got back to his composure clinching his fists. He thought of another way to bring down the Chieftain. Karungu smirked.

"I don't know what's so funny," said Ramses. "But I'm going knock you down from your little cheap tricks."

"This isn't one of your competitions where you have rules to incapacitate your opponent," said Karungu. "This is war, a war that you can't win. If you can't handle me in my normal stage, then you cannot handle the power of the Ekwenzu."

Karungu spread his arms while laughing in a vindictive manner. Ramses watched, astonished by the dark violet and flaming glow brightening his body. This was a power that was overbearing to him. He never fought a single being with much power. Ramses thought of how Moses knocked him out with one single punch of released T'kaf. This was far beyond the power his brother wielded. The dark power of Ekwenzu was revealed to him. Ramses swallowed his fear and scowled. He roared, attacking Karungu flexing his strength. Ramses deceived him pulling a punch then aimed for his legs with a sweep kick. Karungu backed out the way with ease and used his newfound power to shove him a few feet away. Ramses rolled through the grass landing on his stomach. He groaned, struggling to get to his feet. Karungu cackled strolling toward Ramses with his arrogance.

"You make this too easy kid," said Karungu. "I expected better from you. But it looks like your overconfidence became your weakness."

He raised his hand forcing Ramses off the ground through his dark magic. Ramses grunted feeling a tightening grip of his muscles. It felt as if he was being crushed by a boulder. Blood streamed from his nose. Grass and dirt stained his clothes. Ramses felt helpless, defenseless. He was defeated. Karungu grinned knowing the task was done. He watched Ramses' hopeless body float by his command.

"You are finished," he said. This battle is over. If it was up to me I would kill you where you stand. But the Shadow Lord wants you and your family as a sacrifice. But tell me, where is your brother? He is missing in action."

Ramses frowned, unable to move any of his body functions. He was disabled. Ramses stared into the eyes of Karungu responding to his question.

"Go… to… hell you bastard."

Ramses felt his joints tightening. He could not break out of this spell. He grunted in agony. Tear stains were squirting from his painful eyes. Karungu held his hand up, torturing the young prince through the reaction of his words.

"Don't play with me boy because I can do this all day."

"Argh!" Ramses heard from the distance.

He looked past Karungu and saw Korah fighting through a group of warriors uphill. He counterstruck each dark warrior that tried slashing him. An energy sword was in his hand. He must've stolen it from a corpse. Ramses was relieved to see a familiar face, but he wanted him to turn back. Korah could not take on Karungu's magic. He tried speaking the words, "Korah don't." But he was too weak to talk. Ramses instead gave Korah a pleading look.

"Ramses!" Korah yelled.

He ran towards Karungu, the energy sword was gripped in his hands.

"For Ouidah!" he yelled.

Karungu sneered and unsheathed his dagger.

"No…" mumbled Ramses

Karungu blocked the energy sword and used his velocity, jabbing the boy in his back with the point of the blade. The energy sword fell on the ground. Korah gave Ramses one last stare quivering with tears.

"They took my momma," he said.

Ramses watched in guilt as Korah fell face-first on the grass. His breath was released.

"No!!!!" roared Ramses.

He clenched his fist realizing he could move. Ramses' feet touched the ground as he roared, rushing towards Karungu with one more attack giving it all he had.

"Pathetic fool," said Karungu. "I'll let you join your mother for the time being."

He used his magic to grip Ramses, throwing him downhill. Karungu stared at the chaos downhill. His focus was on Ramses' mother as she reloaded her shotgun while fending off the dark warriors. She saw her son rolling at her feet. Bruises covered his face.

"Mother," Ramses murmured. "He was too strong. I failed."

"Save your strength my sweet," she said. "It's going to be okay."

"He's too powerful Mother. We can't escape. He got Korah. He's gone."

His mother wiped tear stains from her eyes. She cocked the shotgun. It was fully loaded.

"Your father died during the Siege of Palasera seven years ago by sacrificing his life so our family can survive. Tamu and I will cover you, just gather whatever strength you have left."

Ramses laid on his back writhing in pain. Karungu appeared from the top of the hill with a look of satisfaction. The dark warriors swarmed around Ashanti and the Jaguar clan warriors. She was outnumbered. All the guards were dead. The protection she had thinned. The villagers were captured. Tamu yet had to gain her trust.

"It's over Queen Ashanti," said Karungu. "You are outnumbered. Your warriors are all but slaughtered. Your people are now captives. Surrender now and I promise to spare your life and let the villagers go."

Ashanti spat in the direction of the young Chieftain. She aimed the shotgun at him glowering in disgust.

"You must think I'm a fool to just be willing to give myself up freely," she said. "If your father was still living, he would be ashamed of you."

"Don't bring my father into this. You have no clue about the things he did. I am making a move he was afraid of. And that's taking the throne willingly. You truly thought the Shadow Lord would have the Chieftain title himself? No, even he knows only a Nubarian can rule this land."

"The Shadow Lord is using you to gain power. He wants a puppet he can control for the Bronze Empire. And you're that right lapdog he can use as a proxy."

"You know nothing. And just think. I was willing to spare your lives so I could have a fair challenge for the throne. However, I think him sacrificing you would be quicker."

"I'll show you sacrifice traitor!"

Ashanti blasted the shotgun, the atomic bullet glided towards Karungu's chest. The young Ekwenzu placed his hand up stopping the bullet as it floated in midair. He used his magic to disintegrate the bullet without it exploding into pieces. He looked at Ashanti, smirking. Then he pointed his eyes to Tamu and his warriors.

"Stand down Tamu," he said. "Or I will execute you immediately."

Tamu looked at Ashanti with sincerity.

"If you want to earn my trust Tamu you will stand beside me."

Tamu looked at the swarm of warriors surrounding them. Their energy swords pointed at them in continuation. He backed away into the swarm of warriors with his hands up.

"I'm sorry your highness," he said.

The other Jaguar Clan warriors joined him.

"Cowards," she said. "You all are a bunch of sellouts. You all will pay for this!"

She pointed her shotgun at the crowd of dark warriors ready to pull the trigger. She was now the lone survivor. Her son was quivering on the ground beside her in defeat. Ashanti's hand was on the trigger she felt a chop on the back of her neck. She saw flashes. Her vision was blurred. Then there was darkness.

***

"No," said Ngozi falling on the hallway floor. "No, no, no, no, no."

"Tell me it's not true Mazį Ngozi," said Moses. "Please tell me what I'm sensing is just a coincidence."

"I'm afraid it's true. Dolsa is gone. I sense the blood of our brethren being spilled. I also sense the Shadow Lord's presence. They slaughtered our army."

"What about my mother? Ramses?"

"I don't know. All we can do is pray. We must not leave back to Dolsa. The Shadow Lord will be expecting us, and you are not ready to face him yet."

"But the Grand Guardian said I am ready."

"No," said the Grand Guardian sauntering towards them. "You are not ready to face the Shadow Lord. You have passed the test of conquering the enemy within, but the journey is not complete. Your destiny is not yet fulfilled."

"Then what must be done Grand Guardian? I cannot leave my mother behind. She needs me. My brother can't fight by himself."

"They will be able to handle themselves; but if you go back, the purpose of Nubariah's liberation will crumble to dust. You must travel to the Hidden City of Ubana in Aswan. There your journey will continue."

Ngozi was puzzled getting back to his feet.

"The City of Ubana is a hidden underground civilization," he said. "Even the Shadow League have had a hard time finding the place."

"If you use wisdom Master Ngozi you'll be able to find the city," said the Grand Guardian. "Look for the ruins in the far east of the Sheran Desert near the Abyss. There you will find what you seek."

Ngozi and Moses looked at the Grand Guardian and nodded their heads. They knew what their next destination was. But thinking of the destruction of Dolsa, the possible annihilation of Ramses and Ashanti was hard to sink in.

# Captured

Ashanti, Ashanti… Wake up."

She opened her eyes and saw Chieftain Oba extend his hand in front of her. She was in utter confusion staring at the clear blue sky feeling the warm breeze through her puffed afro. *Is this real?* she thought. *Is my husband truly alive?* It was too good to be true. She grabbed his hand feeling herself being pulled up from a blue wooden beach chair. She found herself in a paradise of soft sand and palm trees. The ocean water was clear blue swaying in calm rhythmic swooshes. She looked down at her clothing. She was no longer in her bulletproof vest. Her red shirt and black denim were replaced with a sleeveless blue sundress with beige and brown patterns. Her feet were in the soft sand.

Oba took her to a set of four straw bungalows and escorted her in one of them. She now started to wonder was this a dream or was the Shadow League successful in her assassination joining her husband.

"Are you okay my love?" Oba asked her.

She escaped from her deep thought and trembled at the sight of him. She placed both her hands on his cheeks holding back her tears.

"Is it really you?" she wondered.

"Of course it's me love. Are you sure you're okay?"

Ashanti was hesitant. Another thought crept into her mind; was this an illusion? She had to put this scenario to the test.

"I... I'm fine love," she said. "I just... I thought you were..."

"You must've had a terrible nightmare," he said. "I can tell. But that is why I have brought us here, for both meditation and relaxation. It's good to leave the palace sometimes. Tribal affairs can get really hectic sometimes."

Ashanti watched her surroundings. She saw in the other straw bungalows fishermen catching and trading fish to other islanders for food and coin. She saw images of boats sailing in the deep waters. She saw children and their families playing in the water at the shore. Ashanti turned back to Oba.

"Where are the kids?" she questioned.

"Don't worry about them. They're right over there."

He pointed in the direction of the shore not too far from the bungalow. Moses and Ramses were wrestling in the water. They were much younger than the last appearance she saw them. Then it hit her. This was neither a dream nor an illusion, she was reliving a memory. A memory of a vacation long forgotten. Oba laughed while wrapping his arm around her. She felt a comfort she hadn't felt in a long time. She wished this moment would last forever.

"The Supreme has truly blessed me with two boys who will continue my legacy. Although Ramses has the birthright, I know

Moses will become a great leader as well. They both are the future of Nubariah," Oba said. "Next week will be a triumphant one. Once the clans of Nubariah are united, we will show the clans of the outer nations that are scattered around the world that we have nothing to fear against the Shadow League."

Ashanti frowned, wishing she could change that moment in time. If only she knew the future so her husband could have escaped. Perhaps her husband would still be with her. Nubariah would've never fallen. She would still have her family. Regardless, she would've never been able to change the inevitable. The destiny of her family would have remained the same. Instead of dwelling on the painful memory, she decided to focus on this moment in time, being with her husband and children, remembering the powerful royal family they once were. She laid her head on his chest, watching the waves of the ocean. Ashanti was cozy, feeling Oba's embrace. She steadily closed her eyes and fell into a deep sleep.

The waves let out a roaring crash on the shore. The playful laughter of families ceased. The sound of fishermen and islanders faded. The touch of her husband vanished. The feelings of loneliness and despair began to settle back in. Then she heard a calling.

"Get up. Get up. Up on your feet now!"

She steadily opened her eyes and found herself being dragged by two dark warriors. Her clothes were damp in sweat with dirt residue staining her shirt and denim. She found herself at the market square of the village. Ashanti watched defenselessly of the villagers being chained with electrical cuffs and placed in holding cell pods. She heard their pleads, wishing she could fight for their freedom. The dark warriors threw her on the dirt. She saw that her wrists weren't cuffed, but she felt something on her neck. It was an electrical neck collar. She grunted, staring at the ground instead of her enemy.

"So, you finally managed to get her up," said a familiar voice.

Ashanti's eyes were on the ground staring at a pair of metallic bronze boots stepping up to her. It was Shadow Lord Mercius. She could tell 'by his voice and the energy of his presence that radiated. Ashanti refused to look up knowing that she failed Dolsa, the last resort of preserving Ouidah from oppression.

"Now that you're up your highness we can get down to business," said the Shadow Lord. "I know about your newfound Chieftain that's supposed to challenge me for the throne. That's cute. However, I rule unchallenged. Which leaves me to the question, where is your boy?"

"I will never tell you," Ashanti responded.

"I knew that would be your answer. That's why I came prepared."

The Shadow Lord pulled out a silver device containing multiple lighted buttons. He pressed a lighted red button causing the collar on Ashanti to glow with the matching color. She felt an electric shock from her neck causing her body to writhe. She wanted to scream expressing the pain of the electrical current jolting her body. But the electrical current was so excessive, she couldn't move her lips. Her eyes rolled with the thought of death taking her. She'd rather die than give her son up to be executed. Then the electric shock ceased. She gasped for air laying her head on the red dirt.

"Get her up," demanded the Shadow Lord to his warriors.

The dark warrior dragged her to her feet. Ashanti was forced to face the Shadow Lord. She looked at the ground evading his despicable eyes, but he grabbed her by the cheeks forcing her to look at him.

"We're just getting started," he said. "Now I can do this all day, or possibly days. Eventually, I will break you one way or another. The collar that you are wearing goes up to 200 milliamperes which could kill you instantly if I wanted you to. But that would take the fun away. Now queen, tell me what I need to know. Or I can continue torturing you."

Ashanti nodded off and scowled.

"I will never give up my child to…"

She felt the shock again shuddering from her neck to her spine Her head shook as she fell to the ground. Ashanti foamed out the mouth unable to catch her breath. The collar stopped; she was relieved to breathe again.

"I see where this is going," he said. "You're willing to die for your child. Well, your torture won't be easy."

Mercius stooped down staring at Ashanti as she sat up in composure.

"I will attack your heart," he said. "I will take away everyone you care about and break you into nothingness."

Ashanti glowered at him gritting her teeth.

"You will get yours Shadow Lord," she said. "And when you do I pray that you will burn in hell."

"I already experienced it," said Mercius. "My world is an extension of it."

Mercius pointed his attention to his warriors.

"Go into cellblock 280 and wait for further instruction," he said. "It's time to turn this interrogation to the next method."

"Yes my lord," the dark warriors responded.

Ashanti watched the dark warriors walk past her to the cell blocks that were lined in rows throughout the market square. She knew what was going to happen next would be detrimental as she scowled the Shadow Lord, his son standing next to him.

***

Ngozi led Moses within the massive city. The air was humid with energetic sounds of music playing in the background. People were passing by in their tunics and kaftans. There was much peace in the city with clean air that Moses hasn't felt in a while. The vehicles passing by were powered by solar energy.

Moses had tread for miles with Ngozi on foot since their departure from the Grand Temple. Throughout his venture in the city, Ngozi picked up supplies from different markets of dry foods and water, an abpatch kit with healing herbs, and material to build a camp when deciding to rest for the night in the wilderness. Ngozi also made sure to buy more weapons of bow and arrows in case of an attack.

Moses would've been delighted to venture the elegant sightings of Sahawayda. But the thought of Dolsa's destruction, his mother, and Ramses' possible destruction gave him a heavy heart. Ngozi stood next to him in optimism.

"It feels good to be in the city," said Ngozi. "It seems not too long ago since I set foot here."

Moses' head was hung. Ngozi knew what his thoughts were pondered on. He placed his hand on Moses' shoulder.

"I know your heart is heavy," said Ngozi. "So is mine. But we must keep pressing forward."

"I should've been there for them," said Moses. "Maybe things would've changed if I was there."

"You would've been captured and killed. The Shadow Lord would already have victory. All hope for Nubariah would've been lost."

"But I won't be able to live with myself if my mother and brother are gone as well."

"That's where faith comes into play. It is a reason you are here at this particular time Moses instead of Dolsa. You were not ready to face the Shadow Lord…"

"But I am now. I want to go back."

"You still aren't ready Moses."

"I have gained my T'kaf."

Ngozi paused, glancing at the clouds pondering in his thoughts.

"You may have gained your T'kaf, but you are still lacking. The Grand Guardian has seen this himself. That is why we must venture to our next destination with no delay."

"But what is it Mazi? What more must I do before my fight against the Shadow Lord?"

Ngozi turned to face Moses.

"You must build an army."

Moses was at a near gasp. It began to make sense to him. He contemplated on the thought. How was he going to raise an army? Who would join him in such a perilous time against the Shadow army? How would he find an army? Moses followed Ngozi across the street to a herd of rhinorses behind a gate. He was led inside a building next to the herd. Ngozi spotted a man carrying a stack of hay in the corner of a room. A row of stables was located within the building that was full of straw, multi-grains, boxes of hazel apricots, and buckets of water.

"May I help you sir?" asked the man.

"I'm looking to see if you are selling any of your rhinorses," Ngozi said. "Me and the boy are looking for transportation to journey across the desert plain."

"I have a few I'm selling. But answer this question, why not travel the desert plain with a cruiser? It's not my business or nothing."

"A cruiser is a machine that can break down and fail you compared to a rhinorse that is a living thing you can connect with on an intimate level."

"That is true if that's your choice. I can tell you and your son are travelers. Where are you from if you don't mind me asking?"

"To be honest with you, this is not my son. The boy standing in front of you is the High Chief elect. We traveled with the Grand Guardian from Ouidah for both his training and test."

The man's eyes were widened in revelation.

"Wait, you're the one that the Grand Guardian announced who was coming to determine if Ouidah was worthy enough for a new High Chief to overthrow the Shadow Lord? Wow, and you're much smaller than I would've expected."

"Underestimating my size is like saying a venus fly trap is harmless," said Moses. "I passed my test by the way."

The man placed his hands in the air in surrender.

"I'll let you two look at my finest rhinorses that will get you across the desert. Follow me."

Moses followed the man and Ngozi inside one of the stables.

Moses gazed at the furry horned creatures. Their hooves were like the hardness of iron along with their sharp-edged horns. Ngozi paused only a few yards from the herd watching the man gather them with hay. Moses could tell the rhinorses were alert of their presence because four hefty ones stood gazing at them.

"How much is it for two rhinorses?" asked Ngozi.

"Depending on the size and breed, I'll charge you 150,000 nubans each."

"Can we choose first?"

"Go right ahead."

The man stepped aside as Ngozi gestured Moses to follow him. Moses was hesitant, intimidated by the bulk creatures. Moses was never fond of rhinorses. They looked dangerous regardless of them being tamed.

"I know the creatures intimidate you, but they are harmless," said Ngozi. "Close your eyes."

Moses was averse to the thought of coming closer to Ngozi. He stared at the iron horns of the creatures in consistence.

"Trust me, this is another lesson I would like to teach you."

Moses did what Ngozi instructed and closed his eyes trying not to think of the herd that would possibly be on the brink of attacking them.

"Breathe," Ngozi said. "Let go as you did in the temple."

Moses took a deep breath, his eyes remained closed. He thought of how he was able to conquer the demon back in the temple and how he gained his T'kaf at that moment. Moses felt a sudden peace within himself. If he could conquer the dark thoughts within himself, a phobia of animals would be easily conquered.

"What do you feel?" Ngozi asked.

"I feel at peace now. It's like I hear nature speaking to me."

"It's called spirit meditation. The ancestors have passed this technique from generation to generation. Your father once promised to teach this method to you and your brother. What you are feeling is life consuming your body from the Supreme. You can feel the air, the waters, the grass, the trees, and the plants whispering wisdom of their years in the land; the animals react to the pure energy and willfully follows those that wield it. Can you hear it?"

Moses could hear multiple whispers in his head. It was soothing to his ears.

"Yes, I hear it. The air, the forests and plains, the rivers, lakes, and even the oceans. I can hear them all. This is amazing."

Moses opened his eyes and saw the entire herd surrounding them. It was as if they were humbled by their presence.

"It seems like all of them like you," said the man.

"The rhinorses are now in our command. They are in agreement with us to fight for the freedom of Nubariah."

"But Master Ngozi, how do you know?"

Ngozi turned to Moses with a smile.

"Through the spirit Ra'mah, the mother of wisdom. She is your guide. We are to pick only one for the ride to Ubana. Choose wisely."

Moses closed his eyes focusing on his spirit meditation. Then a calm voice called.

*Choose the chief's son. From heir to heir.*

Moses' eyes were widened.

"That sounds like the woman from the cave," he whispered.

Moses walked up to a brawny male rhinorse of horns as sharp as knives. He patted him on the head as the creature exhaled and motioned its head for Moses to pet.

What is his name? Moses asked the voice.

*His name is Roshan, son of Chief Joshi. His commitment to saving the kingdom is as much as yours.*

"Have you made your choice Moses?" asked Ngozi.

Moses nodded. He pointed at the young rhinorse.

"I choose this one," he said.

"Then that concludes our business," said Ngozi. "Here's 300,000 nubans."

Ngozi dug in his sack and pulled out a bag of gold coins. He handed the man the number of coins owed for the purchase of the rhinorses. He grabbed a bulky rhinorse placing a saddle over its back. Ngozi placed another saddle on the rhinorse that chose Moses.

"Let's ride," he said. "We have a long journey ahead of us."

Moses led his rhinorse out of the stable following Ngozi into the city.

"Have a safe journey and may the Supreme watch over you," said the man.

Moses turned his head glancing at the man. He nodded venturing into the depths of the city.

***

Ashanti glared at Mercius breathing heavily through her nose. She could not predict the Shadow Lord's next move, but she knew it was sinister. He stared at her with his head high in pride.

Ashanti wished she could find her shotgun and blast him from existence. But she knew he was too powerful for her to handle.

"Bring him in," said the Shadow Lord on his Optix.

His eyes glowed again in an illuminated red light.

Ashanti watched in sorrow of the dark warriors dragging Amazu towards her and the Shadow Lord's direction. She saw that he was badly beaten. Amazu's left eye was swollen shut in bruises. Dried blood stained the bottom of his nose and lips. Ashanti wiped the tears from her stained eyes knowing what was about to happen.

"My apologies our highness," Amazu said. "I have failed you. I did everything in my power to fend him off. Even if it had cost my life…"

Amazu felt a hard punch on his mouth by the Shadow Lord's fist causing blood to seep from his mouth touching the ground. Ashanti turned her head feeling the pain herself. This was already too much to bear.

"Enough," said the Shadow Lord. "This is not a reunion. This is more of mental torture. It was a waste of voltage and time shocking you. However, taking the people you love and care about will break you even faster. Now I know Ngozi is with the boy. Torturing him would've been a pleasure. But your second in command is just as good. So tell me what I need to know or your commander here dies."

"Tell him nothing," said Amazu. "If I die, then it will be through honor…"

Mercius back fist him in the jaw. Amazu's consciousness was almost fading.

"Shut up," the Shadow Lord demanded.

He ignited an energy sword from his holster pointing it at the fallen warrior.

"Tell me now, or he dies. Where's the boy?"

Ashanti couldn't help the tear stains draining her eyes. The very sight of Amazu getting beaten senseless for her torture was heartbreaking. Amazu was not only one of the top commanding warriors for the clan, but he was a longtime friend of hers. She tried making a sentence of pleading with Shadow Lord to grant him mercy, but instead, she let out a whisper shaking her head, "Please… please…"

The Shadow Lord looked coldly upon her.

"Very well."

Mercius struck Amazu with the energy sword piercing from his spine to his chest. Ashanti screeched watching Amazu's final moments. His hands twitched. Blood oozed out of his mouth while his arms went limp.

"I'm sorry Amazu," she wailed. "Please forgive me… Please no…"

Mercius threw Amazu's corpse to the ground, his armor clattered on the ground.

"Now you see the measures at length I will go to to get what I want," he said. "I will shed the blood of your friends, your family, and even your precious innocent villagers you failed to protect. But because I'm in a hurry, I'll speed the process."

Mercius grabbed his Optix from his holster.

"Send in the firstborn."

Ashanti's mouth gaped open hoping Mercius wasn't calling out the very person she thought of. Then there he was, Ramses.

He was still defenseless cuffed in electric chains. Bruises were over his face feeling the aftereffects of Karungu's black magic.

"No, not my son," said Ashanti. "No!"

She rose to her feet rushing towards the dark warriors who were dragging her son. Mercius watched as two dark warriors scrambled for her. Ashanti felt her instinct coming again of anger and desperation. She stomped the dark warrior who grabbed her by the arm while elbowing the other between its red eyes. Ashanti was close. She did everything a mother could do to protect her son by any means necessary. At that instant, an energy sword appeared pointing in her direction. She looked down and saw Kulrath pointing the violet-lighted blade at her. A group of dark warriors surrounded her and Ramses. She forced herself into the realization that this was a fight she couldn't handle.

"Hello again Queen Ashanti," said a familiar voice.

A pair of muscular arms wrapped around her neck. She struggled to try to defend herself, but the man was too strong for her. Ashanti was dragged to the ground on her knees. The man's face was revealed to her as Karungu, his hands pressed her shoulder preventing her to stand in resistance.

"Mom," said Ramses in a faint voice.

He was forced on the ground to his knees facing his mother. She wailed while tears gushed her eyes, her nose full of snot. The Shadow Lord was in disregard of Ashanti's sorrow and pain. He stepped behind Ramses and ignited an energy sword from his holster.

"Tell me where Moses is," said Mercius in a dark tone. "Or your son's life is mine."

Ashanti furrowed her brows. Her fear... her pain... her sorrow transferred to anger. Ashanti gritted her teeth. Her fists were pumped. Ashanti stared into the eyes of the Shadow Lord. Her demeanor was fierce.

"You may think you have the upper hand against me Shadow Lord," she said. "You may have beaten me, tortured me, but I be damned if you harm my children. You may have your dark magic, your god of darkness, but I have my God watching over me. The way you wish death on my children, a curse will come unto yours. Your days will soon be outnumbered Mercius. I promise you."

The Shadow Lord watched her in scorn pausing for a moment. Ramses was helpless on his knees. His body was not in fighting shape. For the first time in his life, he was in complete vulnerability. Ramses was almost in tears as Mercius took a step back. His emotional thought was absent.

"Very well," he said. His voice was further dark. "The boy dies."

He raised the blade ready to strike and put an end to Ramses.

"No Ramses!" cried Ashanti.

She struggled to try to break free, but Karungu's grip was like a python. The glow of the violet blade was inches away ready to taste the blood of its next victim.

"Wait!" grunted Ramses. "I know where he is!"

Mercius stopped the blade only inches away from his neck.

"I know where Moses is at," he said.

"Then get on with it!" howled the Shadow Lord. "I don't have all day!"

Ashanti wailed; her tears were far from ceasing. The thought of her oldest child having to confess the whereabouts of his brother to the enemy for the sake of his own life was a sorrowful moment for her.

"He's in Sahawayda training with the Grand Guardian," said Ramses. "You'll find him there."

"He's telling the truth, my lord," said one of the dark warriors reading a detector. "There is no deception in his voice."

"Good," said Mercius. "Prepare me a saakuth to Sahawayda. I want a squadron to come with me. The rest of you round up the villagers and send them to Palasera to be scanned and debriefed. Bury the corpses. Burn them if necessary."

Mercius trudged away from Ramses and Ashanti. Karungu followed close.

"Lord Mercius, me and my warriors will create a derision to distract the guards at the gate," said Karungu.

"No," said Mercius. "You have done the task you needed to do. Your new task is to go to Palasera to personally deliver Oba's wife and first-born son to my wife Amaryllis. I will handle the boy myself."

"If you insist Lord Mercius."

Karungu watched as the Shadow Lord strode away with a few dark warriors escorting him out of the market square. He turned back and smirked at Ramses and his mother. They were still on their knees face to face.

"I'm sorry mother," said Ramses. "I had no choice."

Ashanti was lost for words as she placed her hands on the ground. Tears patted the ground like raindrops. She was neither angry nor upset. Ashanti was hoping for her family's survival, including Moses.

***

Ngozi led Moses to the desert plain as the sun descended in the evening sky. Ngozi slowed his rhinorse. Moses did the same telling Joshi to slow himself. The rhinorses slowed to a casual walk with their hooves trailing the sand.

"Why are we slowing down Mazị Ngozi?" wondered Moses.

He shushed him putting his hand up.

"I sense a disturbance here," Ngozi said. "Someone or something is watching us."

Moses knew Ngozi wasn't lying. He sensed the same. The desert plain was barren, but someone was watching.

"What do you think is going on?" asked Moses. "Has the Shadow League found us?"

"I'm unsure," said Ngozi. "But something isn't right. Let's keep moving. But stay on your guard."

They ventured forth on their rhinorses with caution. Joshi stepped on a pebble following Ngozi's trail. With a sudden flash, a metal cage appeared from the sand trapping Moses and Joshi. the rhinorse tried to fight its way out, but the steel bars created a shock wave to stun Moses and the creature. Moses' vision began to blur immediately feeling the shock waves afflicting his body. Ngozi turned and saw Moses and his companion trapped in the cage unconscious. He hopped off his rhinorse and rushed towards them attempting to break the bars with multiple front kicks, but somehow it was reinforced. He let out a swear wondering how he could free the two. Then he heard the sound of a gun cocked and loaded behind him.

"Don't make a move or a sound," said a voice of a woman. "Matter fact let me see those hands."

Ngozi put his hands up to surrender.

"Listen, I don't want any trouble. Me and my son were just passing by."

"Yeah, on Silent Assault territory," said the woman. "Those who pass by here have to pay a toll."

"Listen, me and my son are on our way to Aswan to meet with our family. They are very concerned."

There was silence. Ngozi knew the woman was thinking despite not looking at her face.

"Aswan?" questioned the woman.

Ngozi could hear her and a few more guys laughing at him.

"Say ain't that the fire-breather territory?" she asked in sarcasm. "And he's riding on those things across the desert to through the ocean? This fool is mad."

The woman and the men behind them cackled. Ngozi remained still with his hands in the air.

"Do not underestimate the Supreme's creation," said Ngozi. "Every living being has a task that it must follow."

The woman sucked her teeth.

"Man, you don't even make sense."

"Imani look," said the voice of a young man. "The saddle looks brand new. Hell, they might have a lot of money. Especially if they brought all that in Sahawayda."

"I guess we better find out," she said. "You have something for me? Maybe a few coin for me and my partners?"

"I have nothing," said Ngozi. "And even if I did, I wouldn't give you a damn thing scoundrel."

There was a bunch of ooohhhs being yelled in the background. Ngozi heard footsteps approaching him.

"Is that so?" said Imani. "You know what turn around, right now."

Ngozi turned to face the woman. She was of mocha brown skin with thick locs tied in a ponytail. Her eyes were light brown that illuminated in the moonlight with a long scar on the right side of her face. She was wearing a militaristic forest green and black suit pointing an assault rifle at him. There were three other guys behind her. They tied up his rhinorse as it was unable to move. The woman stared at a lion emblem on Ngozi's muscle shirt.

"Well look at this boys," she said. "This man has on a shirt only the Lion Clan wears. I guess he thought we were stupid."

They sniggered gripping hold to their guns.

"It's no wonder they're headed to Aswan," said the woman. "And by the looks of things you're running from something. Afraid you will get found out by the 'shadow goons'?"

"Yeah, they got something to hide Imani," said a man with a box fade hairstyle.

"Listen Miss Imani," said Ngozi. "We mean no harm. Whatever you want, I can arrange it for you."

Imani thought hard but shook her head.

"Naw, it's you who I want. The price is high for a Lion Clan warrior, and also useful. You and your boy are coming with us. Help me take them away."

She pressed a button on her digital watch as suddenly a screen appeared from it. She pressed a holographic button as suddenly the bars of the cage were split enough for the men to fit in. Moses groaned fading in and out of consciousness. Two of the men chained up Joshi while the other placed Moses and Ngozi in cuffs. A part of Ngozi wanted to fight and run as far as he could for an escape. But he couldn't put Moses in danger. Besides, there would be more of them lurking in the shadows. He would be outnumbered and outgunned. Ngozi had to play it smart, regroup his thoughts while being captured.

Imani and her crew led Ngozi and Moses down the desert plain in their sand cruisers to their camp nearby. They were now captives. No telling what would happen next.

# Chapter Nine

# Sole Survivor

Moses stared at Ngozi realizing he was handcuffed on the back of a cruiser with one of the men holding an assault rifle sitting across from them. The sun was set leaving a tad bit of light. Moses felt as if he was riding for at least an hour. The dune began to fade away. The night sky left his surroundings dim with light although he felt dirt particles irritating his eyes and flying in his mouth. Then he felt the cruiser slowing down. Wherever they were going, the destination was close. Bright white lights were blinding him. Moses found himself at a gate leading to a camp he assumed. The cruiser came to a complete stop. Moses saw a few armed men in tactical night gear approaching the cruiser.

"Alright, out you go," said the man with the assault rifle.

The hatch opened as two of the armed men hopped aboard and grabbed him and Ngozi. Imani stood with a smirk watching the men drag the two Lion warriors out of the truck.

"Let them go," she said. She looked at both of them with her arms folded. She was at this point humorless.

"Follow me," she said.

Imani led Moses and Ngozi through the gate to a camp full of forest green tents the size of houses with four watchtowers on each corner. It was a perfectly built military base with the latest technology that can scope an entire region effortlessly. A variety of relay dishes and motion sensors were scattered on top of the tents. *It's no wonder they captured us so easily,* thought Ngozi. *It's too bad they won't use this technology for the sake of our nation.* Moses spotted men and women gathered in circles. They appeared to be training with sticks made to be spears. The crowd was cheering on as the warriors fought fiercely. *Wow, they seem mighty just to be raiders*, Moses thought.

Imani led the two to the largest tent. She placed the back of her hand to a scanner at the door as a 4D model scanned the rings on the knuckle part of her gloves.

"Welcome Imani Mohammed," said the scanner as the door opened.

Moses and Ngozi followed Imani to a metallic fleet of stairs leading down to a massive room surrounded by steel. A large monitor was on the back wall of the room with control panels below. The monitor was showing different camera angles of surrounding areas within the desert of Sahawayda. A man over six feet tall of charcoal black skin and wooly black locs stared at the screen with a few guards in reinforced armor patrolling the area. Imani took Moses and Ngozi down the stairs towards the man. Moses watched from the top of the stairs at guards stalking them like vultures moving about.

"Akim, I have brought two persons that you would be interested in," said Imani. "I saw the emblem on this one during our patrol. They are travelers, more like runaways from the Lion Clan."

Akim turned around revealing an eye patch. His face was rugged, and his beard was almost as wooly as his locs. A cigar was lighted in his mouth as he blew out smoke. Akim stepped up to Moses and Ngozi hoping to intimidate them. Moses stared at his eye patch as Akim stepped up to Ngozi looking at him blankly. Moses stood studying him. He could tell he wasn't a warrior. At least not a true warrior with honor. He was another breed. Akim inhaled and blew smoke again this time in Ngozi's face.

"I think I saw these two on camera before you captured them," Akim said. "Their Lion warriors alright. They must've fled during the massacre at Dolsa. Although these two do look familiar."

Akim looked at the Ngozi closely, then at Moses examining their facial features.

"Tell me your names."

Ngozi could sense that the man had evil intentions. Most raider camps were known for trapping and selling anyone indigenous of Nubariah who would pass by their territory. Ngozi was well known, not only in Ouidah, but all of the territories as an honorable and well-respected warrior who personally served the High Chieftain. Moses was the heir of the Chieftain. He couldn't give his name away or things would become drastic. They made it too far to be captured and given away to the Shadow Lord by raiders. Ngozi placed a hand on Moses' shoulder, signaling him to stay silent.

"My name is Okafo," said Ngozi. "And this is my son Mazzi."

Akim studied him again in suspicion.

"Okafo huh," he said rubbing his beard. "And Mazzi. Tell me, I'm curious. How were you able to escape the clutches of the Shadow Lord untouched?"

Ngozi let out a quick response.

"I didn't participate in the battle. I had to protect my son from the Shadow League's attack."

"So, you ran like a coward?"

"No! Me and my son... I fought them off and fled to the wilderness."

Akim paused inhaling more smoke from his cigar. He let out a thunderous laugh that echoed the entire room. Imani and the other men surrounding him laughed along until Akim scowled pointing his cigar at Ngozi.

"You must think you can play me like a fool," he said. "Do you think I believe the bullshit you're saying right now? I know in an attack that warriors of your tribe never leave their fellow brethren behind. They fight to defend their people at all cost while the women and children evacuate. Now tell me again 'Okafo', how were you able to escape without any harm done to you?"

Ngozi had to think fast. There was no time to evaluate any thoughts.

"Natural remedies," he said. "There are plenty of natural resources in Sahawayda."

Akim scowled at him then burst out with laughter pointing his cigar at him.

"You know what I like this man," he said. "Maybe we could possibly recruit him."

Imani smirked, knowing what he said was sarcastic. Akim placed the cigar back in his mouth and inhaled.

"I'll tell you what," he said with smoke coming from his nostrils. "I'm going to try you out. One of my men will escort you to the combat zone. If you impress me then I will recruit you to one of our ranks. If you don't, then I will sell you and your boy off to a slave dealer and let you be someone's chore. We have a deal?"

Ngozi grimaced, but he had no choice but to make a deal for him and Moses' survival.

"You got yourself a deal," he said.

One of the side doors opened catching everyone's attention. Moses stared at a man who walked through the door as if a ghost appeared to him. The man he saw was Uzoma. Uzoma stared at Moses and Ngozi in bewilderment. Akim followed their momentous gaze.

"Uzoma, you have the reports?" questioned Akim.

"I have them scanned and sent," he said.

"Very good. Now tell me this. You two seem to know each other by the looks on your faces. Tell me Uzoma, do you know these two?"

Uzoma was stiff unable to come up with words. Akim's suspicion now grew.

"Did someone cut out your tongue? I asked you a question."

Uzoma turned his gaze to Moses and Ngozi then back to Akim.

"I've known them once," he said. "It was such a long time ago I have forgotten."

"Okay," said Akim.

He nodded his head as the guards suddenly pointed their assault rifles at Uzoma.

"Hey!" yelled Ngozi.

Akim ignored him walking up to Uzoma in a smug look.

"Your memory came back to you didn't it?" questioned Akim. "I remember that day I fished you out of that river. You was good as dead. I could've sold you, made a profit. But I didn't. You looked so weak and helpless. The moment I've found you, you couldn't even remember your name, who you were, where you come from. All you remember were your skills. I made a home for you Uzoma. You and your people who survived the onslaught. I clothed you, fed you. All I'm asking for is for you to tell me the truth. Who are these people?"

Uzoma felt trickles of sweat under his armor. He felt rapid beats in his chest. His words could not trail off from his mouth. Ngozi has never seen Uzoma this vulnerable to anyone. This was a fellow warrior and friend he fought alongside for years. He refused to see him get tortured in such a way.

"Enough!" yelled Ngozi. "You want to know so bad who I am Akim?"

Uzoma shook his head in warning.

"You... you don't have to do this old friend," he said. "Let me handle this."

"No Uzoma. You were once one of the fiercest warriors the Lion Clan has ever seen. I don't know what happened to you since the Siege of Palasera, but I refuse to watch any of this any longer."

Akim turned and smirked at Ngozi.

"So now our new companion is opening up," he said.

"Don't do this to yourself," said Uzoma.

Ngozi ignored him.

"Akim, I am Fumnanya Ngozi, son of Warrior Jelan of Saha-wayda."

Akim walked towards the warrior and let out a sneer blowing smoke at his face.

"Thanks for your honesty," he said. "You can be at ease."

The armored guards let down their rifles and followed Akim's signal, pointing the rifles at Ngozi and Moses.

"I thought you looked familiar," Akim said. "Ngozi, known as 'The Master'. Your story is legendary. Who would've known I would have two of the Lion Clan's mightiest warriors here at my camp? So please tell me, why you lied the first time?"

"I had to protect me and my son."

Akim examined the two closely. Moses glared at him.

"I still want to issue the challenge. But I want it to wait till to-morrow. This has to be one of our biggest fights in the combat zone. I want to make this into a special occasion and decorate the place. It'll be like a warm welcome. The same rules apply. Now as far as it goes for your opponent, it will be yours truly Uzoma. Now get them out of here."

The guards escorted Moses and Ngozi out of the room leaving Akim alone with Imani and Uzoma. He blew more cigar smoke. His demeanor this time was grimacing.

"You know I would never hurt you Uzoma," said Akim. "But I had to know for sure who these interlopers were."

"I'm just glad you caused no harm to them."

"You better rest up. The big day is coming."

"Yes sir."

Uzoma made his exit out of the room as Imani stalked him. Akim turned his attention to her inhaling the last bit of his cigar before throwing it at his feet, burning out the ember with his foot.

"Imani, I want you to stay with me," he said. "I need your skillset to help me find out more about our newcomers."

She nodded her head and followed him to the monitor.

***

Ramses was once again cuffed in the electric chains following his mother in the portable cell block that awaited him. He was back in the dark cell within the narrow cylinder. His body continuously ached. The sores on his back, chest, and abdomen ached in perpetuation. The dark warriors closed the cell behind him. He was surprised to see Dayo and Tobukwu sharing the cell with him and his mother. He held her as she wailed "Why they took my baba". Their chains matched Ramses and his mother's.

"I'm sorry for the loss of your father Dayo," sobbed Ashanti. "I wish I could've saved him."

"No offense your highness, but save your apologies," said Tobukwu. "Your warriors failed us again. My father died in one siege and now my wife's father died in the next. Honor is officially…"

"Enough!" cried Ramses.

He turned to face Tobukwu.

"Master Amazu fought with everything he could to protect us. We all fought…"

"But we lost! Again! How long do we have to go through this over and over again? What's the point in having warriors and they can't protect us? What's the point in being a part of a nation that has fallen? What's the point of anything?"

"And that is your problem. You give up too easy. You're the type who would be willing to lick the Shadow Lord's boots if he asked you."

Tobukwu set his wife to the side and stepped up to Ramses.

"Says the person who got his ass whipped. I saw you get dragged by the traitor. And you're supposed to be the mightiest warrior in the village. I guess your balls dropped when your brother took your right as king huh lover boy."

"Tobukwu stop!" yelled Dayo. "This isn't helping!"

Ramses reached his boiling point. He refused to be insulted by a coward who was defenseless the entire battle.

"At least I fought off the dark warriors," he said. "I would be a better protector of your wife than a person like you who ran and got dragged to the ground getting chained in the process."

"You take that back," said Tobukwu.

"You have no say to give me orders coward."

Tobukwu charged at Ramses. He was ready to strike despite feeling the sores on his body. Dayo got in between the two young men looking to break up the pointless quarrel.

"Enough!" shrieked Ashanti.

Ramses took a short breath through his nostrils obeying his mother's cry. He glanced at Tobukwu as he turned back holding Dayo.

"All this arguing is getting us nowhere," said Ashanti. "We lost many people today by these bastards who attack from the shadows. And I be damned if we just let them win. Even though we're shackled and chained, we're still breathing. We need to fight back! Take action to free our nation from this oppression!"

"Or you can do nothing and die," said Karungu from outside the cell block.

Ramses and everyone around him was silent.

"What do you want traitor," said Ramses. "You already beat me with your cheap tricks. You come to finish me off while I'm wounded."

"That's not my task at all," said Karungu. "The Shadow Lord will deal with you himself."

"What does he have planned?"

Karungu grinned.

"I don't see what's so funny."

"I'm just imagining my glorious reign in a new Nubariah High Chief. Once Mercius captures your baby brother then he will publicly execute the three of you and I will be placed in the mantle as the new High Chieftain."

"You are nothing but a puppet controlled by massa."

"Say what you please prince reject, but your death will be my triumph. And finally, the Ezenwa name will be no more."

Ramses peered at Karungu. His demeanor was ferocious despite his visible pain.

"You better hope I don't make it out of this," said Ramses. "Because if I get a chance, I will kill you."

Karaungu cackled patting his leg.

"Good luck little lion. Send the package off."

The dark warriors followed Karungu's orders and pressed a code on the side of the cell block causing it to slowly rise from the ground. Ramses glared at Karungu until the cell block shuttled its way to midair. Ramses turned to face the others.

"Where are we headed?" asked Tobukwu.

"The only place I know they want us," said Ashanti. "It looks like I will be in my old home once more, but as a prisoner. Palasera, I don't know if I'm ready to go back."

"It looks like we have no choice," said Ramses.

***

Moses followed Ngozi as they were escorted by a few armed guards to a tent near the end of the camp. Moses saw within the tent rows of holding cells. The guards led him and Ngozi inside one of the cells. It was a small cell made of concrete. There were two beds bunked on top of each other.

*This room only has a pot to piss in*, thought Ngozi. The guards motioned him and Moses inside the cell.

"So this is how you treat your guests?" asked Ngozi. "As prisoners?"

"Akim usually tests his newcomers before adding them to his ranks," said one of the guards.

There were no more words exchanged as Ngozi stepped into the small cell. Moses glanced at the guards and followed his mentor inside.

"There will be food provided," said the guard. "But you will not be able to leave."

The guards shut the cell door. Moses sat on the bottom bunk bed beside Ngozi.

"Are our people so corrupt that they are willing to sell each other out just for coin?" questioned Moses.

"We are just living in a time of dishonor," said Ngozi. "Even Uzoma lost his way. It's like he can't even fend for himself."

"It's a good thing he is alive, isn't it? It was such a long time ago, but I remember the day of what we all thought was his death. I am so grateful he is still with us."

"With us or lost?"

There was silence. Moses heard footsteps down the hallway heading in their direction. He stood alert hearing the door to the cell being activated for opening. Ngozi placed his hand on Moses' shoulder giving him a nod letting him know to stay calm. He watched as Uzoma entered the cell and closed the door behind him.

"Uzoma!" yelled Moses.

He ran towards him and gave him a hug.

"It's so good to see you," said Uzoma. "I'm glad you've made it out alive. You truly look like your father."

Ngozi rose to his feet.

"Uzoma."

"Ngozi."

The two gave each other a hug in the excitement of seeing each other after being apart for a long time.

"It's good to see you once again old friend," said Uzoma.

"Same here. We thought you were dead."

"I'll admit Khonshu gave me a near-death experience. I'm just glad the Supreme preserved me."

"Tell me what happened to you Uzoma," said Moses. "How did you survive?"

Uzoma thought back seven years ago after the siege. He thought of Khonshu's words being played in his mind in a repetitive state before being blasted in midair, *Now that we don't need you, I can just dispose you*. Uzoma could remember that painful day of loss and agony that left him at his lowest point. He closed his eyes telling Moses and Ngozi the tale of his survival watching the images play in his mind.

It was on that day his body was in the smoke of bruises and a swollen eye. His nose and lips were bloody. He felt as if his body was in flames from the blast. He screamed ignoring the river and landscape of the city below him. Uzoma felt himself gliding like a rocket. If only the pain ended. Why was he being tormented? Why couldn't he die an honorable death like any other warrior?

Uzoma felt his body plunging to the river. If he was to die here then at least his body would cool down from the impact. He let out his final scream as his body crashed into the depths of the river. He was relieved to feel the river water's touch. Uzoma's suffrage would finally end as he closed his eyes ignoring the pain the Shadow Lords brought him.

Then there were voices as his vision faded in and out.

"His body is almost in full health," said the voice of a woman.

"Good," said the voice of a man. "I can't wait to see what this one is capable of."

*Am I dead*? thought Uzoma. *And if I am, who are these people?*

Uzoma's consciousness faded along with the voices leaving him a question unanswered. He woke up finding himself on a metal bed inside a dimmed room. He felt his face and felt no pain. The bruises were gone. He felt his torso. The burns were gone. Was he dead? He sat up on the bed and saw a dark bulky figure in front of him with locs.

"So, you're finally awake," said the mysterious man.

"Wh…Where am I?" questioned Uzoma. "What is this?"

"Awe don't be alarmed, newcomer. Feel right at home. If my crew didn't pull you up from that river you would've been fish food. You can actually thank me."

Uzoma thought for several seconds. The river. He was not dead. But why? After such pain he felt.

"Who are you?" he asked.

"I'm glad you asked."

The man stepped closer revealing his face and eye patch. He lit up a cigar and inhaled his first puff of smoke.

"The name is Akim, leader of the Silent Assault and you are in our camp. You been in a coma for over a month."

"For that long? And wait a minute, what is this Silent Assault you're talking about? I can't remember a thing."

"I know you have a lot of questions. I don't know who badly beat you, but they must've knocked the life out of you. That's probably why you have a bad case of amnesia. But let me catch you up to speed. The Silent Assault is a secret op that's been in Nubariah for centuries. We handle all the underground operations, whether it's assassinations, sabotage enemy lines, or even smaller things like security for any of the Chieftains for hire. But I was reported they were all dead. Including yours."

Akim reached into his pocket and pulled out an emblem of a lion.

"I found this in your pocket. I knew by this emblem that you were a warrior of the Lion Clan. But I couldn't figure out who you were. So I had my scientists run a few tests. We had to match your DNA, go into the Ouidah databases. Then I finally figured it out. Uzoma, the fierce General of the Lion Clan. The Shadow Lord put a whoopin' on ya'll. I tried to tell your chief to let us get involved. But he think I was too corrupt. He think I was trying to take over. Now he's dead. Nubariah is left with no leader scrambling to survive."

Uzoma was lost in his thoughts grasping every word Akim was saying. All he could remember was the current dragging him into the depths of the river. *Uzoma*, he thought. *So that's who I was. Who I'm supposed to be.*

"Yeah, I know all about you Uzoma. You had the Lion Clan army in order. But you failed."

Akim stared at the emblem then stuck his eyes on Uzoma.

"I heard the Shadow Lord is paying top coin of trafficking warriors and selling them. I bet you would make top dollar."

Akim balled his fist and aimed between Uzoma's eyes. His instinct clicked in his mind as he grabbed Akim's arm before the punch collided with his head. Akim smirked.

"So you didn't forget how to fight," he said. "You got a hell of a grip."

Uzoma released Akim as he sniggered. Three men appeared in the darkroom wearing black t-shirts with matching cargo pants and boots. They swarmed around Uzoma with vile intentions.

"He's all yours," said Akim.

The men charged at Uzoma in accord. The former Lion Clan General planted his feet out of instinct and dodged one of the men's punches while elbowing another man behind him. He front kicked the first man in his chest causing him to collapse a few feet. Metallic material clang on the hard cemented floor. The third man jumped aiming his boot at Uzoma's skull. He watched the man with the corner of his eye and moved out of the way with ease. Uzoma heard from behind the sound of a knife clicking. He drew an ounce of his T'kaf and punched the man in front of him in the stomach causing him to fly across the darkroom. Uzoma turned around and saw the man he elbowed charge at him with a knife. Uzoma kicked his arm causing the knife to fly and slide across the room. Uzoma used his husk body to pin him on the floor in a headlock. He stared at Akim squeezing the man's neck. Akim watched as the man struggled to break the hold. Instead of scowling, the leader smirked as the man struggled until his body went limp.

"At ease soldier," said Akim.

Uzoma ignored his words, he continued choking the man hearing him take his last few breaths. Everything started to connect in his mind, the Lion Clan, the royal family and his oath to protect them and the nation, the siege, then Shadow Lord's words before his demise, *Now that we don't need you, I can just dispose you.* Uzoma remembered everything. He gripped the man's neck almost snapping it.

"If you kill him that's fine. But I was only calling my bluff about selling you. I wanted to see what you can do."

"What kind of sick game are you playing?" he wondered.

"This is no game Uzoma. Your clan is gone, dismembered. Your Chieftain is gone. I want you to join my ranks in the Silent Assault. I mean, you a trained killer. I need someone like you to join our operations."

"I'll never join you."

"You don't have to join me. Even if I do let you go, where will you get to? Ouidah and all of Nubariah belongs to the Bronze Empire now. You have no one to protect. If you go out there you will end up getting sold and serve the Shadow Lord as a mutt. But if you join my operation, I will provide you shelter, food and raiment, resources. Just think about it Uzoma. You can either be a part of a new family or wander out there alone with nothing. What do you say?"

Uzoma glared at Akim and thought for a moment. He let the man go, his body flaccid on the floor. He walked up to Akim staring into his eyes.

"If Nubariah has fallen this much then I'm better off dead," said Uzoma.

"You're alive for a purpose Uzoma. Think about it."

Uzoma thought for a moment. *I can just dispose you*, were the words replaying in his mind. *I was thrown away like trash,* Uzoma thought. *Nubariah is lost. My king is dead. And his family, hopefully, Ngozi protected them.*

Uzoma breathed a sigh and walked away from Akim.

"I don't know what's the point in anything anymore," he said. "My purpose is gone. Nubariah is now corrupt by the Shadow League. I will stay, but don't expect me to get my hands dirty."

Uzoma left the room. Akim stared him down smiling in a malicious visage.

That was the day Uzoma's life changed. His perspective of life changed. The honor was past him, replaced by doing whatever he could to survive. He became Akim's right-hand man and top henchman, leading operations the Silent Assault was hired for. His memory transferred to another thought. Uzoma stared at his old friend and Moses. Perhaps there was hope.

"I'm sorry you went through that Uzoma," said Ngozi. "I wish I knew you were alive. We could've used you during our operation in Dolsa."

"I heard what happened there," said Uzoma. "And I'm sorry. Dolsa was hidden for so long I wish I have known. I would've been left the Silent Assault a long time ago."

"But we're united now. Moses is now the High Chieftain Elect."

"I heard. Congratulations Moses."

"Thank you Uzoma," he said.

Ngozi paused for a moment and fastened his eyes at Uzoma.

"Let me ask you Uzoma, how many clan warriors were recruited to the Silent Assault? It seems as if Akim has an interest in warriors."

"Since the fall of the territories, Akim managed to recruit numerous amounts of warriors from each territory. Half the mercenaries here are former clan warriors, including myself."

"This is perfect. If we can convert them over to our side, that will be almost enough warriors to challenge the Shadow Lord."

"I don't know if that's possible old friend. Mercius' army is way too powerful. Then there is Khonshu as well."

"Nubariah as a whole cannot take this level of oppression. The Shadow Lord's black magic and technology are too much for our people to bear. People are dying Uzoma from their potions of poison. People are either losing their minds or dying of diseases. Dolsa was a haven but now it's gone. Think about what we can do if we unite the clans under Moses our new High Chieftain."

Uzoma looked down at Moses and shook his head.

"It's not my power or authority to go against Akim's wishes. Besides, Moses is only a boy. I don't think he's ready for such a position. Besides, even the warriors would not be enough to challenge Mercius."

Uzoma turned to face the door.

"Do not underestimate Moses," said Ngozi. "He did defeat his brother for his birthright. Moses has already gained his T'kaf. We just need an army. Again Uzoma. Think about it. Would you rather take your nation back and purify it from corruption? Or would you rather work in continuation with a slave trader?"

Uzoma scowled, turning to face Ngozi.

"Again old friend, Nubariah is gone. Mercius is too powerful for anyone to take on. The old days are over Ngozi. We are living in different times. I hope you are prepared for tomorrow Ngozi. Once you join the Silent Assault, we can navigate through this world differently."

Uzoma opened the door and walked out. Moses looked at Ngozi with a look of concern.

"Uzoma has lost hope," said Moses. "He's not the same as I remembered him."

"Akim has stripped his honor," said Ngozi. "But it might be deeper than that. The trauma that Uzoma went through. I could sense it."

"What can we do to get through to him?"

"The only answer, for now, is to pray. The Supreme must guide him back. But for now, we better meditate and rest. I have a feeling that tomorrow will be a long day."

***

It's been hours since Ramses and his mother were carried through the cellblock shuttle. He stared at the night sky in silence. Everyone around him was restless. A Mombasan jet flew past the cellblock leading towards him and his company's destination. It had to be Karungu. He was the only person of Mombasa that was following through with this mission.

Then he saw it, the flashing city lights that lighted the sky reminding him of the stars above beyond the river. It reminded him of his childhood. Every night he would look out of the window just to see the lights of the city shine. However, coming back to Palasera was not a welcoming feeling. The city below him was different. He could hear torturous screams of men, women, and children. The buildings that were polished became tattered and worn down as slums with some burnt down.

"What happened here?" wondered Ramses.

"Corruption son," said Ashanti. "The Shadow League has corrupted our beautiful home."

Ramses watched helplessly at the city overhead as they made their way to the palace. The walls leading to the bridge had statues of Mercius and Ameryllis being glorified holding their baby. The lion statues on the palace walls were no longer there, instead, there was a tall statue of Mercius holding a torch in the air and the chieftain's spear in the other hand. Ramses felt his stomach-turning witnessing the changes of his old home.

Ramses felt the cellblock shuttle lower to ground level. The jet in front of him lowered to the palace grounds. Dark warriors appeared from the night sky surrounding the jet as Karungu stepped out. Ramses could tell from the distance he was grinning at him. He huffed a breath through his nostrils gripping the cage. Karungu walked towards the cage accompanied by the dark warriors. Ramses watched as Karungu entered the codes next to the cage to release the bars. The bars of the cage separated causing the cell block to open.

"Take them to the palace entrance," said Karungu.

The dark warriors grabbed Ramses by the arms and dragged him out of the cellblock. Karungu smirked at Ramses as he walked past. He could hear the sounds of the chains clinging behind him from the others. Ramses saw the majestic palace in front of him still shinning in glory. The four pillars still stood on each corner. The palace grounds were still the same of natural soft grass and palm trees. Ramses saw the marble ground leading to the entrance remembering the day he was bullying Moses with tough love before the invasion. Ramses came out of his nostalgia and saw a group of dark warriors appearing from the palace interior lined one by one in two separate lines. The dark warriors that forced Ramses and everyone behind him to the palace grounds joined the other dark warriors in the separate lines. Ashanti stood by Ramses. Karungu walked his way towards the door as the dark warriors knelt.

The door flew open revealing Amaryllis in a long sparkly yellow dress with jewels in her hair. The heels she had on her feet clanked the marble ground. She stared into the eyes of Ashanti walking past Karungu.

"I had to see for myself if what my husband said was true," she said indirectly to Karungu. "You did well young Ekwenzu. You will be greatly rewarded for this."

"Thank you, my Queen," said Karungu.

"Please, your Highness suits more for me."

"My correction, your Highness."

"You can go. Your work here is done."

"I was told I can stay here until after the execution." Amaryllis sighed.

"Fine, stay or go. But leave me with Oba's family." Amaryllis' stare continued at Ashanti.

"I want to enjoy every single moment of this."

"Then I will leave your presence at once your Highness," said Karungu.

Karungu departed glaring at Ramses. Ashanti scowled at Amaryllis facing her with no fear. Chains or not, she was not going to get intimidated.

# Ascension

So we have a chance to see each other once again Queen Ashanti," said Amaryllis. "It looks like you've been dug up from the hole you crawled into."

"It has been seven long years," said Ashanti. "You're still the witch I remember."

Amaryllis sneered turning her head to the side.

"Call me what you want Ashanti, but it doesn't change the slaughter you and your boys will receive in a few days. Once my husband captures your youngest son, the 'new high chieftain', the festivities will begin."

"You call slaying a woman and her children in front of the world a festivity? You are twisted. My people will not stand for it."

Amaryllis cackled.

"Your people are too docile and fearful of our power. No one believes in you anymore. They'll watch you die before 'standing up for their queen'. You couldn't even save them before. Your husband is dead, and soon, you and your boys will join him."

"We'll see who has the last laugh shadow witch. The Supreme will give us victory."

Amaryllis looked around in sarcasm of worry.

"I hope he doesn't come soon," she said. "Oh wait, your supreme whatever couldn't even save you the first time. What makes you think he will save you this time. The world belongs to the Shadows now. And once your execution is complete, Shiveria will know who the Shadow League is. Take them away to get processed and incarcerated."

Amaryllis stared at Tobukwu and Dayo watching him hold her tight.

"And take them away to get processed and assign them to their sect."

"Yes your Highness," said one of the dark warriors.

The dark warriors from one of the lines carried Ramses and his mother away towards the side of the palace. Ramses looked behind him at Dayo who gave him a sorrowful look.

***

Moses meditated on the bed in what was a restless night. There were no windows to view the stars. He was unsure if the sun rose or remained absent for the night. He felt as if the hours froze. He felt his T'kaf radiating through him.

"Moses," he heard a voice.

He continued to focus on his T'kaf through his body.

"Moses."

He looked up and saw Ngozi facing him.

"Someone is approaching," he said. "It is time."

Moses stood to his feet along with Ngozi. The door to their bunk opened as Imani stepped foot. Moses stalked her and two men holding assault rifles.

"So you guys are already up on your feet," she said. "That means I don't have to bark orders."

"Where are you taking us?" questioned Ngozi.

"We're taking you on a round trip around Shiveria! You'll be able to explore the different cultures in today's society outside of Nubariah..."

"Enough of your sarcasm and jokes raider. Where are you taking us?"

"I swear you take things too serious. Man, you should know where you're headed."

"Akim."

"Ding, ding, ding! Let's go."

Moses watched in silence as Imani stepped out of the bunk with the two-armed men following her. Ngozi nodded at Moses then followed Imani and the armed men.

"I have a feeling something bad will happen," Moses said to himself as he walked out the bunk.

***

While Moses was getting prepared to confront Akim, Mercius' saakuth screeched a war cry with the dark warriors following suit within the dark portal. He was thirsty for blood looking forward to finishing off his enemies for absolute power. The Inner Realm would win the War of the Shadows. He would become champion of the Shadow League. Chashak would favor him in the world of Nether.

"It is time," said Mercius.

The portal opened revealing the glorious city of Sahawaydah gleaming through the sun below him. Mercius' steered his beast below to the desert plain outside of the city. The saakuth made a smooth landing on the desert plain flapping its wings in a screech. Mercius nodded to his son reassuring him that they will have victory this day. He stepped off of his saakuth staring at the golden walls.

"Follow me close son," said Mercius.

Mercius led the way towards the city. The moment he stepped closer to the gates, he could hear trumpets echoing the city. The city guards flooded the gates with swords drawn and shields raised. They were talking in an ancient language he didn't hear in a long time. Mercius looked up and saw a few guards with bows and arrows drawn.

The Shadow Lord smirked.

"So primitive," he said stepping forward.

The guards pointed the swords at Mercius and his warriors. The dark warriors behind him drew their beamed swords. The Shadow Lord glared at the city guards. Mercius heard the sound of the gate open. The Grand Guardian appeared along with a band of guards that had on reinforced armor made of solid gold.

"State your purpose here Shadow Lord!" yelled the Grand Guardian.

"You should know what I came here for Grand Guardian," said Mercius. "Do not go in circles with me."

"You will not find what you seek here."

"I know you are hiding him. Where is he? Where is your High Chieftain elect?"

The Grand Guardian gave Mercius an intense stare. The Shadow Lord took a step back overwhelmed by the power he felt through the city gates. Mercius waited for his answer. Saha-waydah was not his fight. Not yet.

"If you want the boy, you will have to find him yourself," said the Grand Guardian. "But he is not here."

Mercius knew he wasn't lying. Moses was here, but he has left the city. He had to find the Ezenwa family's chosen king and put an end to this. Frustration began to take over as he clenched his teeth.

"I'm tired of these games Grand Guardian! Tell me where the boy is now! Or I will burn this city to the ground."

The Grand Guardian continued his hard stare at the Shadow Lord. There was a short pause.

"Even if you come with thousands of warriors here, your army would fall," said the Grand Guardian. "The Supreme God Abiama's power here is too mighty for you to handle Shadow Lord. Besides, the child of Oba is not the only child I would worry about."

The Grand Guardian looked past Mercius. The Shadow Lord saw the reflection of the Grand Guardian's brown eyes at his son Kulrath. He furrowed his brows and turned to face his son. Kulrath held his stomach placing his other hand on his mouth. The young lad spat out a black goo of blood on the desert plain. He coughed, falling to his knees.

"No!" cried Mercius.

He rushed to his son as the boy fell and lay flat on the desert sand. Mercius grabbed Kulrath and held him in his arms. His wrath boiled through his veins watching his son pass out in the heat. Mercius' fists were balled. The thought of killing Moses was the only flash he had in his mind. He glared at the Grand Guardian, his teeth clenched.

"I want my son taken back to Palasera immediately!" yelled Mercius. "Also, check every perimeter around the three territories. Have spies and drones sent out in every village and city rather it's Ouidah, Mombasa, or Aswan. It's time to finish this!"

A couple of dark warriors grabbed Kulrath and rushed him to one of the saakuth taking him back to Palasera through flight in an open portal. Mercius and the dark warriors behind him rushed back on their saakuth. Mercius steered the saakuth as the creature screeched and ascended to the air leaving the city as the trumpets ceased. He opened a portal leading himself to his next destination.

***

Moses followed Ngozi and Imani out of the tent to the campgrounds. It was daylight. The sun beamed in Moses' eyes as he used his hands to block the blinding light. The base of the Silent Assault appeared different in the day. Moses could see the desolation of dirt and metal surrounding the base. He saw vividly the electrical fences with four watchtowers on each corner surrounding the massive three-story tents. The mercenaries around them were dressed in all black with padded armor of camouflage. Some of them were carrying ammunition. Others carried only hunting knives and machetes. Moses could tell which of the mercenaries were clan warriors. A warrior from any of the clans never relied on guns because their power was too great. The trail he was walking on was a metal walkway covered in dirt. Imani led Moses and Ngozi to a crowd of mercenaries.

"Excuse us," said Imani pushing through the crowd.

Moses watched as the mercenaries cleared the way. Akim awaited amongst the crowd smoking a cigar. Standing beside him was Uzoma in a sleeveless polyester shirt. Moses saw the clearing of only red dirt swarming the mercenaries.

"Ah, my favorite troop has arrived," said Akim.

"They're all yours Chief," said Imani.

Ngozi stepped up to Akim as Moses followed with caution. He watched Imani join the band of mercenaries eager for what was about to take place. Ngozi stared at Uzoma, ignoring Akim in front of him.

"Are you certain of this Uzoma?" he asked. "You can still turn away from all this."

"You have no obligation here Ngozi," said Akim. "In my territory, I call the shots."

Akim placed the cigar in his mouth inhaling a puff of smoke pacing back and forth.

"Now here's what we're going to do. You and Uzoma will fight in hand-to-hand combat, you know like warriors do, and only one of you will come out as the victor. Now if you win, you will be recruited in my ranks. You and Uzoma will be able to work together like old times. If you lose, I will sell you off to the Shadow Lord and you'll be his personal servant while your boy here gets executed along with the rest of his what was the royal family."

Moses gulped as Akim stared at him. He nodded at a few of his men as they walked up to Moses and cuffed him. Moses felt multiple beats in his chest. *Is my journey going to end like this?* he thought. *Is all hope truly lost?*

"Let the boy go Akim!" yelled Ngozi. "I won't let you do this while I have every breath in my body!"

Moses gazed at Akim as he gestured the mercenaries to take him away. He was defenseless feeling the mercenaries drag him to the crowd. The cuffs were tightened on Moses' wrists as he looked at Ngozi with a pleading look.

"You thought you could fool me huh Ngozi," said Akim. "I did a little research on your boy here. Who would've known the heir of the late Chieftain Oba would come gracefully at my base? I knew something was familiar about him. You know, you're a horrible liar Ngozi. All that honesty and honor is catching up to you."

"Take me instead Akim," said Ngozi. "Anyone but the boy."

"I wouldn't be making much of a profit selling you. The Shadow Lord will pay me top coin for this one."

Moses watched as Akim pointed at him. His only hope of getting out of this was through Ngozi.

"The Silent Assault will no longer be a secret society," Akim continued. "We will be our own territory in our own land. So, the boy is not negotiable."

Ngozi clutched his fists. He glared at Uzoma as he looked at the ground in shame.

"What you going to do Ngozi?" questioned Akim. "Are you going to strike me? You're planning your own escape. You can try but look around you. There are soldiers of top military training along with warriors of all three clans you have to get through. If you try to run, you have electrical fences activated that will fry you in an extra crisp with four watchtowers in each corner of the base filled with sharpshooters. Just face it Ngozi, you have no choice. So, here's what you're going to do. You're going to fight

Uzoma and if you win by knocking him out, you will join my ranks, free from the Shadow Lord's persecution. But if you lose, you'll most likely wake up in a cellblock ready to get placed in a long life of servitude."

Ngozi felt powerless. His only thought was figuring a way to take Moses and escape from the base. But Akim was right. There were too many armed soldiers and warriors to go up against. He knew he wasn't bluffing about the electrical fences and the high voltage. He peered at the watchtowers of armed guards in reinforced armor carrying sniper rifles. Ngozi watched as Akim went to the crowd next to Moses. He smirked as Imani and a few soldiers commanded the crowd to back away to give Ngozi and Uzoma some room. Ngozi glared at Akim as he inhaled another puff of smoke gazing at Ngozi.

"You may be a warrior," Akim said. "But me, I'm a gangster. I'm far from the honorary. I do what it takes to survive."

He raised his hand in the air.

The crowd of mercenaries cheered as Ngozi turned his attention to Uzoma. There was a long pause. Uzoma looked at the crowd and back to Ngozi. Ngozi peered at Moses, staring at his pleading gaze. He had no choice but to fight. The only escape Ngozi had was his faith. Somehow the Supreme will get him out of this situation. Ngozi clenched his fists holding his guard. He watched as Uzoma pumped his fists. He turned to Akim ignoring Ngozi.

"Enough of this!" yelled Uzoma.

The crowd fell silent. Akim took a puff of his cigar in an angry inhale.

"I served you Akim for seven years doing your chores. But this has gone too far! I will not participate nor be a part of the trafficking of the High Chieftain elect."

Uzoma turned to Ngozi with a smile. He nodded at Uzoma with approval. There was yet hope.

Akim scowled.

"Don't be a fool Uzoma," he said. "I took you in when you had nothing. If it wasn't for me, you would be working in the mines or in the fields of the palace grounds. You better reconsider. This is your only warning."

Uzoma shook his head. His seven years working for Akim was a nightmare. Although he wasn't forced to traffic innocent villagers and townsmen, Uzoma was involved in the decimation of rebellions the Shadow League paid to end before it would happen, to getting paid by bureaucrats within the outer nations to assassinate rebel leaders that were considered tyrants. His mind was made up. Uzoma was not going to stand for this. He remembered his first duty, why he sacrificed himself in the first place. Uzoma had to protect Moses, protect his king's legacy.

"I'm the one that chose to stay Akim," said Uzoma. "But now I want out."

Uzoma stood next to Ngozi standing his ground.

Akim nodded in assurance.

"Then I will sell you both," he said. "I knew you were weak Uzoma. Both of you have false hope that this boy will save your nation from the Shadow Lord. You two and your blind faith."

Ngozi had a thought in his head after hearing Akim's harsh words, smirking while watching him.

"Akim," he said stepping up. "Why won't you test it out your-self?"

"Excuse me?" questioned Akim.

"If Moses is truly hopeless of becoming the new high chief-tain, then why won't you prove it? You and Moses, in hand-to-hand combat."

Akim and the crowd behind him burst into laughter. Moses stood in utter astonishment while feeling humiliated as Akim pointed down at him.

"This little man? Boy Ngozi, I have to hand it to you that you have jokes."

Moses peered at Imani as she walked up to him. She grabbed his arm feeling the muscles Moses had.

"I have to admit, little man got a little something," she said cackling.

Moses watched the crowd's laughter in degradation. He turned his attention towards Ngozi and Uzoma who were stand-ing in a sober demeanor.

"I meant what I said Akim," said Ngozi. "Let's raise the stakes. If you can knock Moses down incapacitating him, then you can deliver him to the Shadow Lord and sell me and Uzoma. How-ever, if you lose, then Moses will take over the Silent Assault Territory."

The crowd gasped, "What! He's insane. Is he serious?"

"You didn't hear me the first time," said Akim. "You have no obligation. You three will leave me now."

"So does that mean you're a coward?" questioned Ngozi. "C'mon Akim, what's all that talk about being a gangster? You truly are a bluff hiding behind your men."

Akim looked around him at some of his mercenaries grinning at Ngozi's comment.

"Ooooh, I think he's calling you out chief," said Imani. "I know you aren't going to take that."

Akim flicked the cigar to the ground and let out the ember with his foot. He marched toward Ngozi and Uzoma.

"Challenge accepted," he said. "Uncuff the boy. I'm going to make an example out of him."

Moses felt the cuffs loosening from him. He was free for the moment. The soldier gestured him to Akim. Moses was never in a fight like this before. He wanted to think of this as another test, but he knew this was real. No more illusions. No more battling demons. He was squared off with a man who was the size of a giant compared to him. He stared at Akim's bulky muscles. Even Ramses was puny compared to Akim. Moses gulped, he wasn't ready for this challenge, but he had no choice. His destiny was to defeat the Shadow Lord and save his family.

Akim stepped up to him.

"Alright little man," he said. "I hope you don't take this beaten personally. Just think of it as a chastisement. As a matter of fact, I'll be fair and let you get the first punch."

Akim knelt mocking Moses as he pointed to his cheek. Moses watched in the crowd at Ngozi nodding his head. Moses took a deep breath calming his mind. He clenched his fist and released a jab to Akim's jaw. His T'kaf ignited, causing Akim to slide and roll several yards from where he was standing.

The crowd fell silent, astonished by what they saw before them.

"Damn!" yelled Imani.

Akim rubbed his jaw in anguish. He spat out blood checking to see if a tooth was loose. He rose to his feet, the tone on his face darkened.

"That was a lucky jab," he said. "Let's see how well you can defend yourself boy."

Akim ran to Moses, his fists pumped. Moses held his guard planting his feet. He was focused, sensing every move Akim was making. Moses could see that Akim was going to throw two straight punches and a knee strike. It was as if time slowed down. Moses evaded the punches and used his T'kaf to hold back Akim's knee strike. It was aimed at his skull. Moses' palm was guided of his T'kaf. He guided his T'kaf and used it to sweep kick Akim as he fell on his head in the hard red dirt.

Moses heard the crowd whoop. He looked at his hands in amazement. He realized that his T'kaf was his third strength. The Grand Guardian's training has unlocked his potential. Moses backed away as Akim sat up rubbing the back of his head. He scowled at Moses rising to his feet.

"Give me a rod, the long one," Akim said to one of the soldiers.

Moses watched the soldier rush past the crowd.

"You're going to get it now boy," he said.

"Woo...ho...hooo!" yelled Imani. "Chief is coming out with the big guns now!"

Moses watched as the soldier brought Akim a steel bar that was a few inches taller than him. He spun it around testing it before using it. Moses focused, keeping his guard steady.

"You got this Moses," he heard Uzoma saying.

Akim looked at the bar and rushed Moses with a swing to his shoulder. Moses sensed his movement and eluded the heavy rod. He moved in circles fending off the swing of Akim's metal rod. Moses leaped from the rod touching his ankles. Akim swung the rod at the top of Moses' head. His T'kaf guided his arms, using them to block the rod from a fatal blow. Akim pulled a knife out of his pocket and rapidly slashed Moses' leg before he could retaliate. Moses screamed, writhing with his teeth clenched. Uzoma was ready to charge at Akim but Ngozi stopped him in his tracks. He gave Uzoma an assuring look.

The crowd booed at Akim as he stood in pride with the bloody knife in his hand.

"Man c'mon Chief, that was fowl," said Imani.

Akim ignored the boos pointing his knife at Moses. He was holding his leg, tears streaming from his eyes.

"I'm going to cripple you boy, permanently," he said.

Akim swung the knife at Moses' stomach. He ignored the sting he felt on his leg and focused on the knife Akim was holding. Moses used instinct, flipping backward. The knife in Akim's hand flew in midair from his grip. The knife landed in Moses' hand as he gripped the point away from Akim. He reached his holster and pulled out his gun.

"He got a gun!" yelled Imani backing away.

"That's it, I'm stepping in," said Uzoma.

Ngozi placed his hand on his chest.

"Wait," he said. "Trust me, he got this. You see how he mastered his T'kaf."

Uzoma relaxed glaring at Akim.

"I hope you're right," he said.

"Let's see you dodge this bullet," said Akim.

He pulled the trigger, the bullet firing to Moses' head. Moses closed his eyes channeling his T'kaf. He felt the power flowing through him. The crowd around him was amazed by the golden glow his body was forming. Moses opened his eyes staring at the bullet that was gliding at him. He swung the knife using his T'kaf to slice the bullet in half. He threw the knife at Akim's leg piercing his skin. He hollered holding his leg collapsing to the ground on the knee where the knife was sunk in his leg. Akim took short breaths while pulling the knife out of his leg.

Moses sauntered towards him. He opened his palm forming a ball of energy from his T'kaf. Akim panted with a scowl.

"Go on, finish this," he said. "Give in to your false hope and bask around you what is temporary. The Shadow Lord will destroy you regardless. You will fail just like your father. The hope of returning Nubariah back to where it was is dead. So it doesn't matter what you do to me here, just know you will get but so far."

Moses clenched his teeth and glowered. He felt insulted. Akim had no right to talk about his father. But then he knew that Akim was manipulating him, playing with his mind which was the last resort. Ngozi appeared beside Moses, placing a hand on his shoulder.

"Akim is defeated," said Ngozi. "You have a choice now. As high chieftain, you must be the judge rather that person is executed, imprisoned, or exiled. With Akim here, you decide his fate. But choose wisely."

Moses saw the crowd hovering over him and Ngozi awaiting his decision. The energy ball was still within the palm of his hand.

He lifted his palm ready to complete his execution. He watched Akim closing his eyes as if he knew death was inevitable for him. It was a gangster's way to die was what Moses thought to himself. He shook his head closing his palm as the energy ball quenched.

"I will not execute him," Moses said. "Death to him would be too quick, although you can never escape the punishments within the afterlife. Instead, I here banish you. You will pay for all the crimes you have committed against humanity. You will know what it will be like to suffer getting hunted down by predators; how it feels to have to fight and survive by fighting your way out of raiders and dark warriors that wish to make a profit out of you so you can be enslaved as a mutt by the Shadow League. Let's see how a gangster truly survives without hiding behind an army of mercs."

Akim watched the crowd of mercenaries around him.

"Are you all just going to stand there?" he questioned. "Get the intruders."

He watched, feeling fear for the first time in his profession as a mercenary at his army not bulging. Akim could see that his army turned against him.

"Well, you did agree to the stakes," said Imani. "Looks like you lost Akim. So do us a favor and scram. You're a disgrace to us all."

The mercenaries agreed which triggered Akim. He clenched his teeth and hobbled to his feet. He pointed at Moses, Ngozi, and Uzoma.

"Don't think this is over," he said backing away. "If the Shadow Lord don't kill you, I'm going to get you three. Don't think that this is over."

"Get out! Go! Get out of here!" yelled the mercenaries.

Akim ran from the base in a limp. Blood was trailing with each step he took pacing forth until he reached the main gates.

The mercenaries hovered around Moses. They whispered among each other. Perhaps all hope was not lost.

"It is now your time Moses," said Ngozi. "You have gained your army. Now speak to them. Give them the promise that they long waited for."

Ngozi stepped back with a smile of "I'm proud of you". Moses looked around him at the faces of warriors, soldiers. It was his time. It was his time to raise an army to take back Nubariah from the Shadow Lord's tyranny. Moses began to embrace the moment.

"For a long time, I thought Nubariah was lost forever after witnessing the death of my father," he said to the crowd. "I lived in fear and in doubt. I thought that was the way to live. The enemy came and took my dignity. The Shadow Lord took away all of our dignity. We were once a people with morals. Why not come back to the origins of who we once were instead of becoming what has been initiated through our oppression? We can do this, together. And if you stand with me, I promise that we will once again have honor!"

Moses pumped his fist in the air. Parts of the mercenary army sucked their teeth and dispersed letting out the sounds of "Aww please! What honor? I'm out!" Moses placed his head down. He failed to win the hearts of the mercenaries. He failed altogether. Ngozi placed his hand on his shoulder.

"You did well Moses, you should be proud," said Ngozi.

"I feel as if I failed Mazi," he said. "You saw what the mercs did. They mocked me. Even after I defeated their leader."

"Not all hope is lost, look."

Moses peered up. His eyes widened at the sight of all the warriors standing in front of him with a band of soldiers that remained. It was a little over half the camp that remained accepting Moses' leadership.

"Not everyone will fight in your army Moses," said Ngozi. "But you will have enough."

"I see what you mean."

"I have to admit Ngozi, you did it again," said Uzoma. "I don't remember Oba mastering his T'kaf so young. Moses must be a different breed."

"He may have the power of Chukwu within him," said Ngozi.

"You sure he fit that prophesy? Is he truly the last of the bloodline before the transition of guardianship?"

"He just might be."

Imani stepped up to Moses interfering with their conversation.

"I have to hand it to you little man, you gained my respect," she said. "But next time, if you try to win these mercs over, try to give them a promise of liquor and cigar smoke."

"I assume you'll be leaving too raider," said Ngozi.

"First off, call me by my name please which is Imani. Second, I never said I was leaving. I actually plan on joining you. I never cared about the Shadow Lord anyway."

"Well welcome to the resistance Imani."

"So now that we're reunited, I guess I have my position as general back," said Uzoma.

"Of course Uzoma," said Ngozi. "The position never left you. The Supreme has brought you back into the position you were called for."

Imani cut her eyes.

"Man I swear your philosophy bores me," she said. "Do you ever loosen up?"

Ngozi and Uzoma laughed. Moses grinned alongside them.

"You just have to have a chance to get to know me," said Ngozi. "I'm not as bad as you think."

"Ngozi has a fun side to him when he wants to," said Uzoma.

"Well I have to see it for myself," said Imani.

"We'll have to do that later," said Moses. "We must focus on the task."

Everyone around Moses fell silent focusing on the next task at hand.

"So what is the next task?" questioned Uzoma. "Where were you guys headed before ending up here?"

Imani raised her hand.

"Oooh, I know this one," she said. "Can I say it?"

Moses looked at Ngozi as he nodded with a wink.

"If you can remember," said Moses.

"You guys were planning something in Aswan right?"

"Aswan?" questioned Uzoma. "Why go there?"

"Because it has the answer we seek," said Ngozi. "Like how Dolsa was, Ubana is another hidden city I heard that is below ground which the Shadow Lord has not touched. If we can convince Princess Nadiyya to rally her army with us, then we should have enough soldiers to take down Mercius' army."

"I don't know," said Imani. "It sounds like a longshot. Even if they join our army, will it be enough to battle the Bronze Empire?"

Moses looked at the ground in uncertainty. He couldn't promise Imani anything, even if he did have the answer of what fate would lie of his army. Moses only knew his mission, to defeat the Shadow Lord one-on-one in a fate to determine Nubariah's future.

He took a deep breath and said, "Soon to find out. We will leave out tomorrow morning. I hope you all get some rest for the journey."

# Chapter Eleven

# Ubana

Ramses was in a deep sleep uncertain of the time of day he was in. There was an uncertainty of where he was. He was unsure where he was at. He only remembered the beating and torture he took from his new foe, the traitor, the new Ekwenzu. His memory jogged from place to place with images of Moses unleashing the lethal blow that caused him his birthright to Karungu's betrayal and dark magic. He couldn't shake off Karaungu's words; *You make this too easy kid. I expected better from you. But it looks like your overconfidence became your weakness.* Ramses couldn't get the images out of his head. He couldn't get the words "defeated" out of his brain. Ramses couldn't get over the power he lost. He lost the opportunity to find love, the power his father gave him as heir, the battle he lost by a man who threw away his honor. Ramses felt as if he was sinking to the depths of the waters. Then he felt the waters drain from him.

Ramses opened his eyes finding himself naked inside an empty wet pod. There were wires and cords attached to the areas of his body where the bruises were. The pain was gone. He couldn't feel the aches. He looked at his arms, touched his face. The bruises were no longer there. A machine beeped in front of him with a 3D model x ray of what appeared to be his body.

"The healing process is complete," he heard the machine say.

He saw ash grey hands pulling the cords from him and dragging him to his feet.

"On your feet," he heard a dark voice say to him.

He glanced at the red eyes of three dark warriors in the room.

"It's time to get you processed," the dark warrior said. "But first you are required to wear the attire of the special prisoner."

"Oh, so I'm special huh," said Ramses.

"Special prisoner is another word for ones going into execution," said another dark warrior.

The dark warriors showed Ramses a white prison suit with a round collar. Ramses squinted as the dark warriors dressed him. It was as if he was an animal getting cleaned up after getting captured from the wild. He slipped on white shoes to cover his bare feet as one of the dark warriors cuffed him.

"Now that's a good mutt obeying with no resistance," said the dark warrior.

Ramses scowled but there was nothing he could do. He was a prisoner overpowered by a multitude of guards and warriors of the Shadow Lord. Ramses had to wait for the right time, the right moment of an escape. He couldn't die. Not like this.

The dark warriors laughed. One of them shoved Ramses.

"Let's go," it said.

Ramses was led out the chamber he remembered as a child. It was the medical chamber but adapted with foreign technology that the Shadow Lord incorporated. The dark warriors led him down the palace corridor. It still contained the yellow patterned walls and red-carpet floors he remembered. Ramses felt like home away from home. The palace no longer belonged to him. He was a prisoner of his own home.

Ramses was led to a chamber he was familiar with. He recognized the brown patterns around a steel door. The dark warriors opened the door revealing the oratory shrine which was once his father's private chamber of prayer. Ramses looked around the room at all the Ouidah Chieftains painted on the walls. It was still there but tainted. Ramses peered ahead of a droid with human like features. Its face was smooth with eyes the color of coal. It had the body of a male with circuits flashing from its neck to its ankles. Ramses never seen such a droid such as this. It was playing with a holoprojector, at least he thought.

"We brought another one for processing," said the dark warrior to the droid.

Ramses saw the droid dismantled the holoprojector and turned its attention to the dark warriors. By looking at the droid up close, he could see its lanky, chrome body peering at him with a stone look. The size of the drone was intimidating. It had the size of a warrior. He had to prepare for anything at this moment.

"Very good," said the droid. "Bring him here so I can begin the processing registration."

"Do you have to say that every time we bring a captive?" questioned the dark warrior.

"It is my duty to both inform and perform my programming according to the directions of Lord Mercius.

The dark warrior sighed. It kicked Ramses on his back as he collapsed to the floor. The chain clattered on the floor.

"Here, get this over with and call us when you're done," the dark warrior said.

Ramses remained on his stomach hearing the dark warriors' footsteps out of the chamber. The door shut as Ramses made his way up staring at the droid.

"Newcomer, welcome to Section Zone 008," said the droid. "I am Jin-0220, an android processor. You can call me Jin for short. I know this is a hard process of losing your freedoms, but I promise you in Lord Mercius' society you will get taken care of with accommodations."

"So what will you do to me?" questioned Ramses.

"My only duty is to read your neuro senses to determine your role within the serf class. Once the process is complete, you will be directed of where you will stay as well as your as-signed task which will be permanent. I promise you that the processing stage will not take long. Are there any questions be-fore we begin?"

Ramses glared at the droid.

"Let's just get this over with," he said.

The droid's eyes flashed a silver light.

"Initiating scan," it said.

Ramses closed his eyes turning his head from the flashing lights of the droid. He froze feeling sharp tingles inside his head. Ramses grunted, feeling as if his brain was freezing.

"Scan complete," said the droid. "Tracking data."

The pain ceased as Ramses gained back his composure. His conscious was clear as he stared at a holoprojector in front of him. It was scanning for information. Then his face popped up with words next to him that was familiar. He heard the android speak while reading

"Ramses Ezenwa. Age 14. Once the heir to the late Chieftain Oba until birthright was lost to younger brother Moses Ezenwa. Records inform that you are a special prisoner who you will be sentenced to death. Date and time of public execution will be determined by Lord Mercius. You will report to holding cell 8-11-124 until further instruction. That completes your processing. A guard will escort you out."

"You mean guards," said one of the dark warriors barging through the steel door.

Two of the warriors grabbed hold of Ramses.

"Let's go," said the dark warrior.

Ramses walked along the dark warriors staring at the paintings. It was a sign of hope reminding him who he was and what he was fighting for. Ramses may have lost his birthright, but it doesn't change the fact that he was born royalty. He took one final look at the oratory shrine before the dark warriors slammed the door shut.

***

Within the main tent of what was the Silent Assault base, Moses stared at the monitor hoping to figure out the location of Ubana. The chamber seemed empty without Akim's sharpshooters guarding the top of the steps. The majority of them abandoned the base. Ngozi and Uzoma were beside him looking at a map of the Aswan Territory in front of them.

"Finding this city may be difficult," said Ngozi. "But we will find it."

"All I can do is trust in your wisdom mazį," said Moses. "Because even if we download the schematics of Aswan's latest map, it will still be difficult to find."

"Perhaps you could compare the modern to the ancient map," said Uzoma. "Ubana was a city dismantled over 200 years ago. After the siege we all know that Queen Nadiyya rebuilt the city as refuge where the Shadow Lord won't be able to locate or track it. Perhaps the city is located under the ruins of the old city."

Ngozi placed his hand on his beard thinking for a moment.

"You could be right Uzoma. Yet you could be wrong. You are only driving a hypothetic answer. The Queen might have thought outside the box and placed the city in a remote location."

The door opened revealing Imani stepping through the door.

"You called for me Chief?" she asked.

"Imani, good you're here," said Moses. "There is much we have to discuss before our journey tomorrow."

"Okay, shoot."

"Let us catch you up to speed Imani," said Ngozi. "So we all know at this point that Queen Nadiyya has hidden Ubana underground. Uzoma made a possible theory that the city is located under the ruins of the original city within the Aswan Sand Drifts. But it could be a possibility that the city could be located in a remote area in the Sand Drifts. Perhaps you could take a shot at this."

Ngozi directed Imani to the monitor of the Aswan Territory map. She gazed at the map in deep thought.

"Have you ever thought of coding a message?" she asked.

"It's too risky," said Ngozi. "The Shadow Lord may trace it."

"Not with shadow tracing," said Uzoma. "The Silent Assault has a coding system that's untraceable to any network. It's a reason why this organization remained a secret for so long."

"Well, that will work to our advantage," said Moses. "Imani, can you code Queen Nadiyya a message of our arrival tomorrow noon?"

"I'm on it," she said.

Imani rushed to the monitor typing in codes. Moses turned his attention to Uzoma.

"General, you were in a lot of foreign missions, correct?" he asked.

"I have," said Uzoma.

"What type of airships do you have?"

"There are a variety. But since our missions were dark operations, we only have the smaller ones that fit up to ten people."

"That's all that we need. If we go to Ubana with an army, then we will be found out by Mercius."

"That's a good idea Moses," said Ngozi.

Moses peered at Imani who was typing a few last words on the monitor.

"Alright I just code messaged the Queen," she said. "She said come to the old ruins around the noon time."

"Looks like your hypothetic answer became a reality Uzoma," said Ngozi.

"Now that we have the answers we seek, you guys have to have an assigned role," said Moses. "We need to keep our mission in order. Ngozi, you were always my spiritual guide and master. I want you to be my Spiritual Advisor like you were to my father."

"Of course, your highness," said Ngozi.

"Uzoma, you are still my General which once we finalize our army, I want you to command the fleet once we battle the Shadow League."

"I will abide by your will your highness," said Uzoma.

"And Imani," said Moses. "I'm sure Akim didn't chose you as his right hand just for show."

"Trust me, besides my jokes, I'm very lethal when it comes to battle," she said.

"Good, then you will be my muscle."

Imani nodded her head with approval.

"It's settled," said Moses. "We will meet at the hangar tomorrow morning for departure. Get you all some rest. This will be a long journey."

***

While Moses planned his journey, Karungu sat in the wine cellar guzzling red wine. He drowned in his sorrows despite the power that was given to him. He was consistently suppressing his spirit allowing Ekwenzu to take full control of his being. His father was gone, Karungu accepted it. His honor was far gone replacing it with survival.

Karungu, he could hear Ekwenzu's voice in his head.

He dropped the wine glass on the floor leaving a puddle of wine on the floor with sharded glass. Karungu fell on the floor on his hands and knees quivering.

"What is it you want from me?" he questioned.

*"Don't be a fool Karungu. You know exactly what I want."*

"I did your bidding. What more do you want from me?"

*Power! Unlimited power. You truly think by the Shadow Lord handing you the title as Chieftain is satisfying? No. How do you think I remained here for thousands of years?*

Karungu's chest was beating with beads of sweat dripping. He couldn't give the dark entity an answer. He was too terrified.

*Manipulation. In order to gain power, you must be stronger than both your allies and enemies. All the Shadow Lord will use you for is proxy for his empire. Yet what is standing in his way of achieving that goal is Moses Ezenwa. They will fight to the death. One will die and the other weakened. When that moment comes then you must strike.*

"How do I do that?"

*Strike when they are distracted.*

He heard a shriek from the palace hall. Karungu rushed to his feet nearly slipping in the puddle of wine. He peaked outside the hallway. Amaryllis was mourning walking aside a medical transport. Karungu spotted a guard securing the hall as the transport passed by.

"What happened?" he asked the guard.

"It's the Shadow Lord's son Kulrath. It's reported he passed out in the Desert of Sahawayda. He has been transported to the medical facility."

Karungu rushed past the guard to get to the transport.

"Stand back patron," said a guard assisting with the transport.

"I just want to make sure Queen Amaryllis is okay," said Karungu.

The guard ignored him as Karungu dashed towards Amaryllis. He glanced at Kulrath's enervated body.

"I'm sorry about what happened to your son my Queen," Karungu said.

"Get away from me mutt!" she yelled. "I don't need your sympathy!"

The guards brushed Karaungu away as he watched the transport float by.

*"You know what you must do,"* said the voice of Ekwenzu running through Karungu's head.

Karungu's expression grew dark as he pumped his fists, walking the opposite direction.

***

Moses made his way to the hangar along with his militia who all met at the set of dawn. He saw that his team was well equipped. He gazed at Ngozi who wore spare clothing of the Silent Assault. The black padded cargo pants matched his sleeveless polyester shirt. Ngozi's sword was holstered on his back. Moses saw Imani padded in black with silver linen. She had two pistols in her holster. He gazed at her wrists of two rings. One of the rings had a cylinder that appeared like a cannon. The other ring seemed like a communicator different from the optix Moses was used to. Then Moses gazed at Uzoma. He wore matching cargo pants similar to Ngozi. He had on a black armored plating on his chest. Uzoma had his sword sheathed in a holster on his hip.

"I have to say we look good," said Imani.

"I feel like I'm in a combination of a black op mission and a mission ordered by Chieftain Oba like the old days," said Uzoma.

"It's just like the old days," said Ngozi. "And thanks for the outfit too. It fits quite perfect."

"Of course."

"Uzoma," said Moses. "So which of these air ships you are preferring to?"

"Right this way," said Uzoma.

Uzoma led Moses further down the hangar. Moses turned his head with each step staring at rows of airships the size of lifeboats. Droid mechanics were making repairs of what was necessary for the ships. Moses saw how amazing of a site this was. These could work to his advantage. Uzoma stopped towards the end of the hangar as Moses beamed his eyes at an airship the size of a long sailboat. The structure of the ship was the shape of a blimp with wings on each side. The ship was silver with white patterns.

"This is definitely enough for a militia," said Moses.

"Well boys," said Imani. "Let's get this show on the road."

Uzoma nodded and led Moses to the airship along with the rest. The airship made a steaming sound of a ramp descending from the ship. Moses followed Uzoma up the ramp getting inside the airship. Within the airship Moses saw the cockpit to the left of where he was standing. To the right he saw two rows of seats on each side of the airship with two steps.

"So you want to fly the ship?" Moses heard Uzoma asking Imani.

"Just because I was Akim's right hand doesn't mean I was assigned to fly," she said. "You were on them missions right? I thought you were going to fly this thing."

"I never flew either."

"Damn, I guess we're stuck."

Moses turned around shaking his head. He watched as Ngozi intervened.

"One of us will have to fly the airship," he said. "It certainly cannot be me or Moses because none of us flew an airship before. Uzoma, during your missions, have you ever watched the pilot fly the ship?"

"No, I always sat comfortably in my seat and gazed at the clouds."

"For a big guy you sure are delicate," said Imani.

Ngozi turned to Imani.

"How about you Imani?" he asked. "You were once Akim's right hand. I'm pretty sure you know your ins and outs. Who usually pilots these airships?"

"Well, I believe all our pilots are gone," she said. "Our second-best option is to have a droid fly the ship, but I don't trust them things. Once a destination is locked, they have a one-track mind with no common sense."

"What other choice do we have?"

Imani paused in split seconds.

"You know what, I think I'm going to fly this bad boy."

Imani rushed to the cockpit. Uzoma smirked while shaking his head.

"That woman is something," he said. "I'll watch over her. Make sure she doesn't mess anything up."

Uzoma followed Imani to the cockpit leaving Moses alone with Ngozi.

"Are you sure you trust Imani flying the ship?" asked Moses.

"I trust in her judgment," said Ngozi. "I hope."

Moses and Ngozi stared at the empty seats in front of him.

"We better take a seat and buckle up," Ngozi said.

"I highly agree with you," said Moses.

Moses followed Ngozi to the rows of seats and buckled the seat belt. He saw Imani rushing out of the cockpit past him.

"Where are you going?" Moses questioned.

"I just realized I forgot something," she said.

He watched her as she grabbed a parachute from one of the cargo shelves. She strapped it on her back and made her way back to the cockpit.

"Just in case," she said.

Moses looked at Ngozi puzzled.

"She's not serious, is she?" he wondered.

"I think she's very serious," said Ngozi.

"I'm starting to second guess your judgment."

He felt the airship move.

"We better strap in," said Ngozi.

Moses agreed as he buckled himself as quickly as he could.

The crew was ready to take off into the wondering clouds. That was until the ship bumped into the ceiling of the hangar. Moses gritted his teeth. He wanted to get Imani out of the pilot's seat immediately.

*"My bad ya'll,"* he heard her say through the intercom.

"You're supposed to steer it first!" Moses heard Uzoma yelling.

"I know, just relax man," she responded.

"I have a feeling this is going to be the shortest long flight any of us experienced," said Ngozi.

"Tell me about it," said Moses placing his hand on his forehead.

Moses felt the airship lower in a steady movement. A prayer was in his head hoping the ship wouldn't crash. He felt a bump. The airship must've come back on ground level. Moses exhaled his breath feeling relief that the ship didn't wreck. He became thankful that Uzoma was the co-pilot regardless of him having less experience. Moses felt the airship move on ground level until they were out of the hangar. Once they were out in the open, Moses felt the airship takeoff in midair.

*"Good morning gentlemen,"* was the sound of Imani's voice on the intercom. *"Thank you for choosing the Silent Assault Airship. I am your pilot Imani. Today's flight will take us to the Aswan Territory of the mysterious city of Ubana. Our flight will be approximately thirty minutes. Be sure to buckle up for safety and be mindful of all safety precautions before we land. Again, thank you for choosing the Silent Assault Airship and I hope you have a nice flight."*

The intercom fell silent as Moses grinned.

"Wow, Imani should've been a flight attendant," said Ngozi.

*"Appreciate it Ngozi,"* Imani said on the intercom. *"That meant a lot to me man."*

Ngozi chuckled as the airship soared into maximum speed.

Once the airship flew at a stable speed, Moses unbuckled his seat and walked down the steps. Surrounding him were glassed windows showing the view of the clouds. It was a peaceful and quiet view as he closed his eyes in meditation. He channeled his T'kaf. He could feel the power surging within him. Visions began to flash his inner thoughts. Moses surpassed the nightmares of his father's death, but another fear crept into his mind.

Moses could visualize the burning village. He saw the bloodstains puddling the ground with bodies piled up from a slaughter. Moses saw his friend Korah among the bodies, his lifeless eyes telling him the pain and torment he went through. Tears welled up in his eyes. Was Korah truly gone? What about his mother? Ramses? He then saw the dark warriors drag someone away from the bodies to a prison. He saw his mother and brother on their knees. They were alive but injured with cuts and bruises. His mother was screaming in torment with tears of lamentation staring at the bodies. Ramses' face had no expression. The look on his face showed how hopeless he was. Then there he was. Approaching Moses was Mercius. His demeanor was dark. Moses held his guard ready to defend himself. A hand touched him as he was dragged out of the vision to reality as Ngozi got his attention.

"We're almost here," he said. "We better get to our seats."

Moses followed Ngozi up the steps and strapped himself in the seat. He could hear the ramblings of Uzoma and Imani.

"That's not how to lower the ship!" yelled Uzoma. "You'll kill us all!"

"Man, I got this!" yelled an agitated Imani.

Ngozi pointed his attention to Moses.

"You might want to check on your crew," he said.

Moses nodded and unbuckled his seat feeling a slight tilt on the airship. He wobbled keeping his balance making his way to the cockpit. There he spotted Imani and Uzoma fretting amongst each other.

"Are you guys okay back here?" asked Moses.

"Tell that to your General," said Imani.

"Hey, you volunteered yourself to fly the ship knowing that you are unsure of what to do," said Uzoma.

"At least we made it here," said Imani. "What's your excuse Mr. 'I gaze at the clouds'?"

Moses placed his hand up before they began to quarrel again. He yelled at them both gaining their attention.

"Imani, your job is to make sure we land safely," said Moses. "And Uzoma, you are the co-pilot, so guide her into landing at our destination."

"Gotcha chief," said Imani.

"Will do," said Uzoma.

Moses watched out the window of the cockpit.

"Making landing now according to the coordinates," said Imani.

Moses felt the airship tilt descending from the clouds. He viewed the ground below of sand dunes blanketing the surface.

"Alright Imani, you got this," she was saying to herself. "The airbag is your last resort, but you got this."

Moses could feel the airship descending in a steady balance.

"I believe in you Imani," said Uzoma. "The same lever you pulled up to take off in the air is the same lever you pull down for landing."

"Right."

Imani pulled the lever toward her in a leery way. The ship, in a slow descend, began to touchdown within the dunes of the desert. Moses could see the sand brushing off the dunes in a desert wasteland. The airship made a safe landing on the sand, the ruins of the ancient city were above them.

"Well, these are the coordinates Queen Nadiyya has given me," said Imani.

"We better move with caution," said Uzoma. "No telling what we will find within these dunes."

"I agree with Uzoma," said Moses. "We better be cautious."

Imani released the fleet of steps revealing the scorching sandy desert below. Ngozi entered the cockpit with enthusiasm.

"I hope you guys are ready," he said. "Moses, lead the way."

Moses nodded and walked towards the ramp leading to the desert. His crew followed behind feeling the stroke of the sand in a mixture of the dry sand on his face. Below him were four hooded figures in front of him.

"I take it that you are Imani," said the voice of a woman among the hooded people.

Moses looked at the woman in front of him. Her skin was like caramel as he stared at her face. Her hazel eyes were focused on Imani who walked behind him.

"It depends," Imani said. "Are you Queen Nadiyya?"

"Her majesty is secure within the city," the woman said. "I have been given orders to escort you all within the city to meet with her concerning diplomatic matters."

"Then please lead the way," said Moses.

The woman nodded to two hooded people who had the appearance of men. The men approached Moses and his crew.

"To enter the city your weapons must be confiscated," said one of the men in a baritone voice.

"Oh, hell no!" yelled Imani. "I need to keep my heat packed."

"Imani at ease," said Moses. "We can't jeopardize this mission by refuting their policies. Let them have your weapons."

"Listen chief. I know you're new at this Chieftain role, but I don't think it's wise for you to compromise your crew of having their weapons stripped in unknown territory."

"I know it's risky, but this is our only chance to build our army against the Shadow League."

Imani sighed while rolling her eyes.

"Alright, well you're the boss. I hope your 'compromise' is worth it."

Moses nodded at the woman. The men searched Moses and found nothing, not even a knife.

"Get off me!" Moses heard Imani from behind. "I can give you my weapons on my own without you touching me!"

The men came back to the woman, the weapons were in their grasp.

"Come with us," said the woman.

Moses nodded and followed the woman and men up the dune. He could feel the intense heat similar to his training with the Grand Guardian within the desert plain of Sahawayda. Moses made his way uphill, his crew was close behind him. He saw the ruins of the city covered in sand. It looked war-torn of broken columns and partial buildings that still had residues of ash. The ruins of the city appeared to have buildings on top of buildings with steps. But the roofs were gone which explained the piles of ash grey bricks piled in front of them. The burning of the city was far from recent. The original Ubana was destroyed hundreds of years ago according to what Moses remembered in his history class at the Academy.

The woman and her company led Moses and his crew to a large structure at the top of the ancient city. The structure like all the other buildings only had partial walls. Moses could see the rest of the dunes from where he was walking. The woman led Moses and his crew to the center of the structure where a ray of the sun pointed towards their direction.

"Be sure to stay in a thirty feet proximity," said the woman.

Moses nodded feeling the presence of Ngozi, Uzoma, and Imani standing near them. The woman pulled out a sapphire crystal from her pocket and pointed it to the sunray. The ray transformed into the color of the crystal as a blue circle formed around them. Moses could feel the ground move, feeling himself sink below.

"Oh, we sinking," said Imani.

The woman and the men grinned amongst each other.

"Is there something funny?" questioned Imani.

"Look, said Ngozi.

Moses peered at the underground city below them. The city was a wonder to behold. It was floating above an abyss through gravity pulls. There were three layers of the city formed in rings. The outer layer of the city was separated by the other two inner layers which were connected by a bridge. Each layer of the city had towers indicating the lavish lifestyle the people in the city were living. Swarming around the city were small airships hovering. Sunrays gave the city its light.

Moses could see that they were being pulled towards the center of the city. He descended lower and lower until he could see the buildings towering over him. The ground where he was standing stopped. An illuminating light of turquoise flashed beneath him. The woman stepped up to a fleet of steps.
The men accompanied by her followed suit.

"This way," she said.

Moses and his crew followed her.

"I hope there are no more surprises," said Imani.

Moses walked up the steps staring at a flash of white dots flowing in a narrow path.

"Try to keep your balance," said the woman. "A lot of our visitors fall when dragged on the grav-pull."

"Well count me out," said Imani. "I'm not stepping on that thing."

"You have no other choice."

Uzoma slapped Imani on the back.

"C'mon Imani," he said. "I'm sure it won't be that bad."

Moses watched as the grav-pull yanked the woman and the men to the city. He looked at the grav-pull in near hesitance. Ngozi placed his hand on Moses' shoulder.

"Remember," he said.

"Focus," said Moses.

Moses took a breath and placed his foot on the grav-pull. It felt like solid glass as the grav-pull snatched him, his body dragged across a narrow pane. He remembered the lesson that Ngozi gave him. *Focus.* Moses postured his body, keeping his balance as he reached the edge of the grav-pull. Moses felt his body being drawn from the grav-pull. He gazed at a massive building in front of him crystalized in sapphire and jade. There was a fleet of steps leading to the building. He saw the woman and the three men walk towards the building.

Behind Moses, Ngozi took a few steps behind him. He seemed to ease his way off the grav-pull. He heard Uzoma laughing from behind. He turned around giggling at Imani on Uzoma's back with her eyes closed.

"Is it over?" she wondered. "Please tell me it's over."

"Relax Imani it's over," said Uzoma. "And get off my back, I'm not carrying you across the city."

"It looks like we have to go to that building," said Moses.

"Wow, it's beautiful," said Imani.

"Lead the way," said Ngozi.

Moses led his crew towards the building. He observed the city of neighboring buildings that illuminated the city. Moses followed the woman and the men to the fleet of steps towards the building's entrance. A woman of dark brown skin with long silk hair appeared through the entrance of the building. She wore a gold tiara on her head with a ruby at the center. She wore a gold-colored sleeveless dress with sleeves on her fore-arms with matching colors that looked like flames. Solid gold beads were decorated in her hair. Her makeup blended with her skin wearing violet lipstick. A group of guards was crowded around her with fiery-colored armor carrying spears. The woman that led Moses bowed to her, the men as well.

"I have brought them to you, your highness," said the woman.

"Well done, Makara," said the woman in the gold dress.

"You must be Queen Nadiyya," said Moses.

"That I am. I would've never thought the son of Oba would come to me so quickly. But you came on time. Welcome to Ubana. I would like to personally show you around my fortress."

# Chapter Twelve

# The Assault

Tell me where Moses is. Or your son's life is mine, was the haunted vision Ashanti couldn't shake from her mind. She couldn't get rid of the dark demeanor the Shadow Lord had towards her after Dolsa's invasion.

*The way you wish death on my children, a curse will come unto yours. Your days will soon be outnumbered Mercius. I promise you.*

*Very well. The boy dies.*

She couldn't take the tormented memories of watching her son in near death. Ashanti couldn't shake off the voices in her head:

*No Ramses!*

*Wait! I know where he is! I know where Moses is at.*

*Then get on with it! I don't have all day!*

Ashanti could see the blade at her son's neck. Tears welled in her eyes.

"Please don't tell him Ramses," she said. "Mommy will sacrifice herself to save you both."

*He's in Sahawayda training with the Grand Guardian. You'll find him there.*

Ashanti watched as the Shadow Lord and his warriors walked towards the saakuth.

"No, you're not going after my baby," she said running after them.

The Shadow Lord could not see or hear her.

"You're not going after him!"

Mercius, his son, and the dark warriors were on their saakuth, taking off as the war beast shrieked, its voice echoing the air.

Ashanti watched as the creatures took off in midair. She was powerless.

"Noooooo!" she cried, her voice resonating.


Ashanti took a long breath as she woke up in the holding cell. Ramses was lying in the cot next to her in deep sleep. She got up from her cot and stretched letting out a yawn.

"Hello Ashanti," said the voice of a woman.

She turned around and saw a woman in a sparkly blue dress with an afro.

"Who are you?" Ashanti asked. "And how did you get in here?"

"I have been sent by the Supreme to show you what must be done," said the woman.

Ashanti's eyes were widened at the woman's glow. She was a spirit, a spirit that she was familiar with.

"You must be Ra'mah," she said. "The mother spirit of wisdom. I read of you in one of the sacred scrolls."

"You are correct. Come, there is something that I need to show you."

Ra'mah held her hand out for Ashanti to take. She was uncertain as she looked around the cell. Ashanti watched the guards pass by the cell. She looked at her white jumpsuit, there was no way she could escape. Ra'mah gestured to her.

"They cannot see you," she said. "You are in your spirit state. Your body is still resting on the cot."

Ra'mah pointed towards the cot Ashanti got up from. Ashanti's eyes gaped as she watched herself in a deep sleep lying on the cot. She turned back to Ra'mah and took her hand. Ra'mah led Ashanti through a portal behind her of bright light. Flashes of light beamed her eyes as she entered an area of swarming clouds mixed with blue, orange, and pink. A bright light was in the middle of the clouds. Ashanti's eyes were in wonder of her surroundings. Rays of light flashed in each corner.

"Where have you taken me?" she asked.

"You are in the Spirit Realm between the tenth and twelfth portal," said Ra'mah. "Come, let me show you of what is yet to come."

Ra'mah led Ashanti to one of the rays of light. She entered the light seeing flares of events dashing in front of her. Ashanti could see war and bloodshed. One side was the Shadow Army, the other side was the Clans of Nubariah.

"What is this I'm seeing?" wondered Ashanti.

"You are seeing before you the Battle of Decision. The Clans of Nubariah will rise against Mercius' tyranny."

Ashanti's mindset was full of hope but despair thinking about the endangerment of her family.

"What about Moses?" she asked.

"Your son is okay."

Another event emerged in front of her. Moses was in front of an army appearing to lead them in battle. Ala turned to face Ashanti. A gleeful smile shined on her face.

"He will raise an army and battle Mercius and his army. A king will be decided. One will rise, another will fall."

"Can he do it? Can Moses defeat the Shadow Lord and end the oppression of our people?"

"He has the power to defeat the Shadow Lord. But he must find his courage to rise against adversity."

"Then all I can do is pray."

Ra'mah stepped forward extending her hand.

"Come, there is something else I must show you."

Ashanti followed Ra'mah to another ray of light walking into another flash. She entered into a hallway that was a familiar setting. The area was darkly swarmed by red lights. Ashanti was still in wonder. She traveled from light and entered in darkness. There were prison cells on each side of the cemented walls. It was the prison created by the Shadow League that was once the underground station her and her children escaped from led by Ngozi all those years ago. But she wondered why she was brought here.

"I have taken you here because this is where your fate lies," said Ra'mah. "Don't think you will be held in the cell. You will take part in the battle from the inside."

Ashanti's eyes were bulged looking around the area.

"So, the battle will be here."

"Yes, the Battle of Decision will be here in Palasera. You must sabotage the enemy. Spoil their weapons of destruction."

"Then how will I escape?"

Ra'mah stared into the eyes of Ashanti.

"When the time comes, you will find out. But for now, plan ahead."

A glow of white light overpowered the red lights of darkness. All Ashanti could see was the light flashing on her face.

Ashanti took a gasp of air as she sat up on her cot. She looked down to see if she was in her spiritual state. There wasn't a body lying below her. If she would pinch herself, she knew that it would hurt. Ra'mah was gone. All that was left was a brief silence. Ashanti watched as Ramses rose from his cot in a yawn. They locked eyes in near tension. Ramses, eyes were sorrowful as he looked to the ground.

"There's no need to feel sorry for yourself," said Ashanti. "There is much work that needs to be done."

***

Moses and his team followed Queen Nadiyya within her fortress. Makara and the men were walking alongside her. Moses looked around the fortress. The structure was similar to the Grand Temple. The floors he was walking on were made of pure citrine and topaz gemstones. The walls were covered in a mixture of fire opal and sunstone. There was a chandelier in the ceiling made of spessartine garnet which brightened the lobby and hallway they were passing through.

"You have a very beautiful fortress, your highness," said Moses.

"Thank you," said Queen Nadiyya. "Just think that it took three and a half years to build this city after Palasera's destruction. It took the help of the Grand Guardian. He sent his best engineers to design and help our people build New Ubana."

"It was wise to build the city underground to keep hidden from intruders. My mother was hoping to build her army in Dolsa, but the Shadow League found us out."

"I've heard of the attack on Dolsa. It was very unfortunate. But let me show you around."

Queen Nadiyya led Moses towards the end of the hallway. The light from the chandelier beamed from above. A fleet of stairs was flashing in front of them.

"We just passed the lobby where usually one waits for either a meeting of territorial affairs or issues that's more local," said Queen Nadiyya. "Here in Aswan, we like to put our people first."

"We had a similar system in Dolsa," said Moses. "The village was a haven for years for those who escaped from the Shadow Lord's oppression in other parts of Ouidah. We provided them with businesses, food, water, and shelter. It's good that you are aiding your people with what they need."

Nadiyya nodded walking past the fleet of stairs. Moses and his crew were led to a massive hallway with a multitude of rooms on each side.

"Over here are the guest rooms which in many cases we lend to the homeless who goes through hard times. We usually use them as rehabilitation before offering them condos to stay in. New Ubana is big on condos. That's probably why when you entered the city, you have seen a lot of tall buildings."

"That's very fascinating your highness," said Moses. "Not meaning to intrude, but I was hoping to have a negotiation with you about Nubarian affairs."

"Of course, but first let me show you one of our most prestigious rooms throughout the entire fortress, our dining room."

"I don't mean to be rude or anything," said Imani. "But what's so special about a dining room?"

Uzoma elbowed her gently on the shoulder.

"What are you doing?" he said in a whisper. "Are you trying to jeopardize our mission?"

"Don't you think this 'grand tour' is a little suspicious?" Imani responded. "Chief just mentioned the negotiation and she went around it."

"Just stay silent."

Uzoma pointed his attention to Queen Nadiyya.

"My apologies for the intrusion your majesty. Our muscle here is a little cranky."

"No worries," said Nadiyya. "Right at the end of this hall is our dining room where we have some of our finest cuisines. We would like to invite you personally to have lunch with us while we discuss the negotiation. Our chefs have already prepared the meal."

"Sounds wonderful," said Moses. "Your hospitality is truly welcoming."

Nadiyya gestured one of the men to open an orange crystal-like door in front of them. The door was opened revealing the dining room. Moses' gasped while holding on to his breath. His companions around him were silent. Nadiyya's face turned to guilt and shame. There he was, Shadow Lord Mercuis, standing with a smirk as if he was already victorious. Moses saw the food with the aroma whiffing around. He could see the fava beans and falafel sitting on a large tray with a paste of fiery tomatoes swarming the plate. He could see trays of brick oven pizzas savored with a variety of meats, cheese, and vegetables. Some of the pizzas were sweet with syrup, honey, and a sugary substance. Skewers of minced beef and lamb sat steamy on a platter. This was a meal Moses was hoping to enjoy but Mercius and his dark warriors' presence turned his stomach sour. The dark warriors had their energy swords and laser launchers drawn ready to decimate their enemies.

"So I've finally got you," Mercius said in a dark demeanor. "I'll have to admit you were hard to find. I've been searching for you for days. And now you will be in my possession. The heir of Oba will finally die by my hand!"

*How did he know we were here?* questioned Moses in his thoughts. *I can't believe I walked into this trap without sensing it.*

Imani ran towards the table and grabbed a handful of fava beans.

"You bastard!" she yelled.

She threw the fava beans at Mercius, but he used his fiery dark power to brush the food into pieces.

"There's no need for a food fight," said Mercius. "I want you to join us for lunch. Consider this your final meal before your death. I wanted it to be special."

Moses glared at Nadiyya. Her look was pleading.

"I'm sorry Chieftain Moses," she said. "The Shadow League found us before you relayed the message. He threatened to kill me and burn my city if I didn't bring you to him."

"I'm sorry as well," said Moses.

He walked past the Queen inside the dining hall locking eyes with Mercius. This was his chance to avenge his father's legacy.

* * *

"So, you're telling me that you had a vision of our escape in the middle of a battle?" questioned Ramses.

"Precisely," said Ashanti. "It wasn't revealed to me when this will take place but be prepared."

"But how will we escape if everything will be locked down?"

"It's quite simple," said Ashanti. "Someone will free us from the outside."

"But who?"

"The Supreme will give us an answer."

"Pft, the Supreme didn't even save us from being captive back in Dolsa."

"Things happen for a reason."

Ramses heard a sound in the background of multiple footsteps. Surrounding them were solid walls with a pod on the corner of the cell to use the bathroom. There was a crack in the wall. Ramses walked toward the crack and peeped his eye through the hole. He saw a young woman doing sit-ups on the floor in the neighboring cell. Her hair was in Bantu braids. Her light brown skin gleamed drenching in sweat with dirt stains on her bearskin wearing a sports bra showing her cut abs. A pair of long white prison pants covered her legs matching what Ramses was wearing with a collar around her neck. His heart was still with Dayo, but the looks of this mysterious woman began to catch his eye. She caught his eye with an intense look. Ramses' chest began beating in a constant rhythm. He didn't know if her appearance was threatening or a beauty to behold. But for some reason, he was enticed.

"Ramses, what are you doing?" questioned Ashanti.

Ramses turned around and replied, "Nothing Mother, I was distracted."

"Well, you need to get back focused. As I said, we have been brought here for a reason. We must be patient in the meantime."

Ramses sighed nearly rolling his eyes.

"Fine, we'll do it your way, Mother. For now."

Ramses sat on the cot hearing a tap on their prison door.

"Now what?" Ramses questioned. "It's mealtime already?"

"Go and see," said Ashanti.

Ramses rose from the cot and peeped from the outside through the steel bars. His eyes were lit at the sight he saw. His chest was beating like a drum.

"Dayo?" he wondered. "What are you doing here?"

"Where is your mother?" she asked in a whisper. "I need to speak to her."

"She's over here behind me."

"Who is it?" Ashanti asked.

"It's Dayo, she's here to speak with you," said Ramses.

"Tell her I'm coming."

Ramses switched places with Ashanti as she peered at Dayo through the steel bars.

"Dayo, what are you doing here?" Ashanti questioned. "You could get killed if you get caught talking to us."

"I'd rather die for my freedom than live the rest of my life like a rat," she said. "When me and my husband got processed last night, we were given assigned tasks which we will have to work for the rest of our lives. My husband is tasked as a builder constructing the master houses and I'm tasked to work in the Empress' Garden on the palace grounds. If anyone fails their task in any part of the day, they are to face three stages of torment. The first is physical where the guards will beat you. The second stage is the mental where the shadow witch casts her dark magic to attack your brain where people start hearing voices in their head telling them to do heinous things to themselves."

"What is the final stage?"

"The witch kills off your spirit to the point you are like a robot to be easily controlled."

"That's horrible how they are doing our people."

"But that's not all your highness."

Dayo held back her tears wiping her damp eyes.

"The living conditions are horrible. Me and my husband were assigned to our house which is designed like a cage. They turned our prosperous homes into slums. I was also told that they limit everything here now. We have curfews; we are limited with food and water in the markets; we are even limited to how many children we can have. I heard if women have more than the limit of children then they will kill off the babies."

Dayo's voice was shaky. She couldn't hold the tears back any longer. Ashanti was grief-stricken thinking of the horrors her people were going through. She took a short breath.

"I don't want the blood to be on my hands if you die Dayo," she said. "But imagining the terrors you are witnessing and hearing, this is a risk that's worth your life. I will share with you my vision that Ra'mah herself showed me."

"You were visited by the mother of wisdom? This vision must be prophetic."

"I was shown a battle of decision that will take place here in Palasera. My son will fight the Shadow Lord for the throne."

"Yes, so hope is coming. I just pray Moses is up to the task."

"But that's not all. I have a role in this battle myself. And that's where you come in."

"Anything your highness. I will do whatever it takes."

Ashanti paused for a moment.

"When the prison is on lockdown due to the battle, you must unlock the doors to let us loose. Once I am freed from prison, me and my son will sabotage their war efforts from the inside. It will be a perfect time of rebellion."

"I will do your bidding. Anything to fight for the freedom of our people."

"Well, your first step is to leave my presence. You must go so you don't get caught and executed for treason. You are under their regime now, not mine. You must obey them for now until the time is right. Come back tomorrow when there is time. Hide your face, do not let them see you on their hidden cameras. Do not let the droids spot you. Figure out the controls of how to unlock the prison then keep moving."

"Yes, your highness."

"Now go before the Shadow League spot you."

Without saying a word, Dayo dashed away from the prison. Ashanti turned to Ramses and nodded.

"You see how the Supreme works fast?" she asked.

"It's too risky," said Ramses. "They could catch her before the act."

"Let's just hope for the best."

As Dayo climbed her way upstairs, Karungu stepped forth from the corner of the stairs stalking her every move.

"Looks like a setup to me," he said with a malicious smirk. "So, the plot thickens."

***

Moses locked eyes on Mercius. He was more fearless than fearful. He pumped his fists stepping forth. This was not going to be his destruction. This was going to be his rise to take the throne.

"I will not be destroyed by you Shadow Lord," said Moses. "My father's legacy will be avenged."

"I don't think so," said Mercius. "Look around you boy. There is no army to back you up. All you have is a pitiful militia. I am the one in control. I am the one who has the power."

The Shadow Lord clenched his fists staring at Moses in a fiery tension.

Moses turned his head towards Makata. She winked at him with a nod. Moses was unsure of her intentions. Makata took off her cloak revealing a solid gold armor plating on her chest. She had on leather brown pants with leather boots that reached up to her thighs. She reached to her side and threw a dagger in swift motion causing one of Mercius' warriors to collapse. Moses' was speechless. The dark warrior's death was rapid.

"Guys now!" she yelled.

The men opened their cloak and pulled out the weapons belonging to Imani, Ngozi, and Uzoma, throwing them for the crew to retrieve them for battle.

"Now that's what I'm talking about!" yelled Imani cocking her pistol.

Uzoma and Ngozi clenched their swords behind Moses. He could feel their T'kaf powering behind him.

"Secure the Queen, get her out of here!" yelled Makara.

A flood of guards burst into the dining room with flaming swords and spears. They all wore fiery-colored armor. A few of the men grabbed Queen Nadiyya and took her out of the dining hall. Moses watched as Makara drew a curved blade that had a handle of rhinestones. She gave the army an intense glare.

"Prepare your arms," she said. "It's time to send the Shadow League packing."

"We're right beside you," said Ngozi.

He stood next to Makara along with Uzoma. The guards were lined side by side with Moses, his crew, and Makara. Moses' glare was at the Shadow Lord as he flashed him a malicious frown.

"So that's how they want to operate," said the Shadow Lord. "Foolish. Kill them all except the boy. I want this city burned to the abyss."

The dark warriors readied their energy blades and launchers. The army behind Moses marched towards their enemies. Imani aimed her pistol at one of the dark warriors. The dark warriors were more bloodthirsty than hesitant as they approached the army aiming for fatal blows. Then there were clashes of ember and sparks. The warriors began their strike against the dark warriors.

Amid the battle, Ngozi struck a few of the dark warriors with ease slashing them in instant strikes. Beside him, Makara and Uzoma lacerated their enemies while pummeling them with elbows and kicks. Imani pulled the trigger, bullets sailing perfect strokes to her targets.

Moses stepped up to the Shadow Lord, his eyes meeting Mercius'. The Shadow Lord followed suit, his bronze boots clacking the smooth floor.

"How cute that you have a small army fighting by your side," said Mercius in sarcasm. "But they won't be able to win against my warriors."

Moses watched around him, a few of the guards from the fortress were already being decimated by laser swords and launchers. He saw Ngozi, Uzoma, Imani, and Makara defending themselves without a scratch. There was hope.

"I'll give you a chance to surrender and I will spare Ubana. Just think about it, you'll save lives if you just surrender."

Moses scowled, his fists clenched.

"I will never surrender to you Shadow Lord," he said.

"Very well then," said Mercius. "Then I'll just have to beat you to a pulp while you watch your friends and innocent lives destroyed."

"Enough talking!" yelled Moses.

He rushed an attack towards the Shadow Lord, leaping with his fist aiming at his enemy's mouth hoping to break his teeth. Mercius was too quick, deflating Moses' attack with a movement as fast as light travel.

"Too slow," he said.

Moses charged his T'kaf, feeling the energy within him resonating through him. His movement was swifter, his strength increased. Moses knew this time he would take away the Shadow Lord's overconfidence. He let out a flurry of punches looking to break the armor of the Shadow Lord or his bones. Mercius smirked using his speed to deflect Moses' jabs. Sparks ignited from the attack and defense. Moses struggled to land a punch on the swifter opponent as he leaped to kick his enemy hoping his foot would land on the Shadow Lord's side near his rib cage. Mercius used his arm to block the kick as Moses landed on his feet using an expeditious sweep kick with hopes of catching the Shadow Lord off guard. Mercius used his supernatural speed to slide back. A concoction of flames and electric sparks tussled after the impact.

Defending himself, Ngozi stood his ground severing any dark warrior that came with an attack. Uzoma paired himself with Ngozi, standing side by side with his ally amidst the chaos.

"I got your rear," said Uzoma.

"Just like old times," said Ngozi.

"It was just like yesterday."

Ngozi smirked, piercing his enemies along with Uzoma. He peaked from the corner of his eye at Makara throwing a few daggers at the dark warriors. She ducked from a laser blade that swung at her head. The laser blade of the dark warrior had cut off a piece of her ponytail loc. Makara's stare was intense. She swung her curved blade at the warrior, decimating it causing the dark warrior to fall on one of the pizzas causing the meat to separate from the cheese and vegetables. She dashed, joining Ngozi and Uzoma.

"Not bad," said Ngozi to Makara. "Your use of the blade is like the motion of a fan."

"Likewise," said Makara.

From across the dining room, Imani shot a few bullets, hitting more targets. She aimed at a few more dark warriors that pursued her companions. Her finger pulled the trigger. *Click*, was the sound of the gun. Imani looked at her pistol, her face was sour when she unloaded the clip. It was empty.

"Damn, out of bullets," she said. "Well, I guess I have to go melee."

Imani looked at a corpse of a guard laying near her. A sword was implanted on the floor drenched in black blood. She swept it from the ground wiping the blood on the decimated dark warrior that laid beside the corpse. She dashed across the dining hall slashing a dark warrior with the blade as a guard finished the warrior off with his fiery blade. Imani slid under a table near her, slicing the leg of another dark warrior causing it to collapse on one knee. She assembled with the others, blade in hand.

"Looks like I joined the party," said Imani.

"Just in time," said Uzoma. "I see you ran out of bullets."

"That's why you always come prepared."

Imani pressed a button on her wristband, buttons lightening up in red. Uzoma beamed at her.

"I got you," said Uzoma.

Ngozi sensed the energy flowing in the room. The guards were pushing back the dark warriors, but the longer Mercius was in full power, the more dark warriors had an advantage in this fight. He watched the battle surrounding him. The guards were holding their ground, but it was a matter of time until the Shadow League would have more leverage.

"We're going to have to go into the offense," said Ngozi.

"How come?" questioned Makara. "I think we're holding our ground."

"If we don't take out the dark warriors now, they will have an advantage. I realized during the Siege of Palasera, the more the Shadow Lord fueled his warriors' power through his, the more they fought."

"So you're saying these things are being powered up and controlled like robots?"

"That's exactly what I'm saying."

"Say less," said Imani.

She kicked a dark warrior that charged at her and pointed her red flashed wrist band at it. Three bullets the size of pebbles darted out of the wrist band dropping three dark warriors instantly. Imani charged at the first dark warrior she locked eyes on and slashed it with her sword. She shot a few other dark warriors as they collapsed and jabbed another with the point of the sword. She tossed the sword to Uzoma who was near her as he butchered his enemies in multiple flashes using his T'kaf to increase his power and speed. The dark warriors were no match for his offensive technique of two swords. Uzoma charged his T'kaf and swung the blades causing a sharp wind to cut through the dark warriors as they glided to the tables. Uzoma threw the sword at Makara as she caught the hilt of the blade.

She fought through a group of dark warriors severing their bodies. She threw the curved blade, causing one of the warriors to collapse. She used the other blade to slash a few others. She grabbed the curved blade, pushing the fallen dark warrior with her foot. She ran to the nearby table and jumped on top. A dark warrior from the other side of the table pointed a launcher in her direction. Makara planted her foot on the platter of fava beans and kicked it at the warrior's eyes causing it to misfire. She back-flipped off the table and severed the heads of two dark warriors that attempted to attack her from behind.

Makara tossed the blade to Ngozi who used his T'kaf to wipe out multiple dark warriors. Ngozi could see the dark warriors' numbers were dwindling. They had the upper hand. Ngozi took advantage of the two blades he held and plunged the blades into his enemies. The dark warriors were no match for his power, strength, and speed. Ngozi let out flashes of kicks and slashes causing the warriors to fall like dominoes. He spun the blades using his T'kaf causing a visible ring to cut through his enemies. Ngozi then saw Mercius and Moses face to face. Tension was rising between the two.

"C'mon Moses," said Ngozi. "I believe in you."


The flamed sparks disappeared. Moses was once again face to face with his adversary. He put up a guard, ready for another attack. The Shadow Lord scowled, then smirked with wicked tendencies.

"I have to say that I'm slightly impressed," said the Shadow Lord. "You have skill kid, but not enough. So now that you had your turn. It's now mine."

Mercius charged his power, his speed increasing to the illusion that his body was vibrating. Moses never saw such power so frightening. He backed up a step. His chest was beating with a burn in his throat. Before Moses could gasp, the Shadow Lord disappeared with impossible speed. Moses closed his eyes, remembering his test when he had to fight his inner demon. He remembered the speed of the monster, he remembered the word, *focus*.

Moses charged his T'kaf and opened his eyes. It was as if time froze. Moses could hear his breath in echoes. He saw Mercius charging at him fist first and blocked his punch, flames were bursting out after the impact, but Moses was not impacted. Mercius was baffled. Moses could see for the first time the Shadow Lord's vulnerability. The Shadow Lord attempted to press on Moses' foot as leverage, but the young Chieftain took a step back holding his guard in a swift motion. Moses and Mercius were moving in lightspeed, the Shadow Lord throwing strikes while the young Chieftain moved in rhythms to block and deflect the punches. Warriors on both sides of the battle moved out of the way from the impact Moses and the Shadow Lord were forming. The remaining warriors in the room stopped the battle, watching the result of the fighting between the two leaders.

"They're moving so fast I can't keep up with them," said Makara.

"C'mon Moses," said Ngozi. "Remember to focus and sense out your enemy's weakness."

Moses knew he couldn't stay in defense any longer. The Shadow Lord's speed and stamina were overwhelming. He could sense how arrogant Mercius was, how no one was a match for his power. Moses focused on his opponent. The Shadow Lord was swift; his punches throbbed like a wasp's sting. There had to be an opening for a counterattack. Then he saw it. The Shadow Lord's chest was exposed. Moses swatted Mercius' punch out the way and aimed his fist at his target. His fist pounded the Shadow Lord's bronze breastplate causing it to crack like glass. Mercius gawked and slid back holding his chest.

The dark warriors and guards of the Oph-Ur Clan huddled around Moses and Mercius. Moses ignored the crowd around him staring at his fist that steamed from the impact. Mercius laughed deviously glancing at the crack of his breastplate near his heart. Moses could see a bruise through the crack.

"Well done young Ezenwa," said Mercius. "You are one of the few warriors out of all the realms that were able to give me a scratch. And it looks like we drew the attention of all the remaining warriors in the dining room. You are impressive boy, but now I have to end this."

Moses took a deep breath and held his guard. His body began to glow as he powered his T'kaf past his limit. He could feel his heartbeat from within with a blend of ringing from the ears. The room around him was vibrating, the crowd in front of him fading.

The Shadow Lord began to increase his power. His speed increased far beyond what Moses sensed previously. It was to where the illusion appeared as if his body was splitting forming two Shadow Lords. Moses' joints were weakened, overwhelmed by the power he unleashed. Mercius dashed towards his enemy. Moses' senses were gone. He had to use instinct. Moses separated his feet and crossed his arms. He saw at the last minute the Shadow Lord launching a knee strike to his head, a fatal blow. Reluctantly, Moses' arms were in the way. He felt a crunch on both arms as Moses flew to the wall. The crowd of warriors moved as Moses collided, leaving a gaping dent between him and the wall.

"Moses!" yelled Ngozi.

The Shadow Lord smirked in victory as he walked towards the injured young Chieftain.

"Finally, I get possession of my prize," he said. "I thought that last knee strike would permanently damage you. How lucky I am."

"No!" cried Ngozi. He dashed towards the Shadow Lord aiming his sword for the shoulder blade. Mercius sensed him coming, using his speed to dodge out of the way with ease.

The remaining dark warriors united behind Mercius. There were fourteen remaining. Ngozi held his guard, everyone uniting behind him. The Shadow Lord placed his hand up.

"Wait," he said. "I'll handle this."

Mercius stepped up to Ngozi eager for another challenge through his adrenaline.

"I've been waiting a long time for this moment," said Mercius. "I will finally have the chance to defeat the Lion Clan's second strongest warrior. The special skilled warrior Ngozi."

"We shall see Shadow Lord," said Ngozi.

He charged at Mercius. His sword swinging in swift strokes. Mercius used his speed to dodge each strike. He spun, aiming at the back of Ngozi's neck. He could sense the Shadow Lord's motion. Ngozi took a breath and blocked the Shadow Lord's elbow strike with the hilt of his blade. Mercius struggled as he tried to push his elbow on the hilt hoping to pierce through Ngozi's chest. Ngozi, however, used his T'kaf to push the Shadow Lord away from him.

Moses' vision faded. He could only see two shadowy figures engaging each other. He could not make out who they were. He could not sense their energy. Moses could not feel his own body except the aches on his arms. He began to fade thinking in his conscious that he failed.

Ngozi swung his sword, pointing it at the Shadow Lord. Mercius held out his arms channeling his dark power. Ngozi knew this was a perfect time to power up his T'kaf gathering his power as his body glowed with sparks channeling through his body. Two flaming swords emerged from the Shadow Lord. He was looking to decimate Ngozi. Mercius dashed towards Ngozi, flames leaving his trail. Ngozi closed his eyes, sensing the Shadow Lord's presence although his super-speed made him invisible. He used his T'kaf slashing the air causing a wave of sparks to force the Shadow Lord to defend himself. Mercius cut through the wave with the flaming swords and darted in the direction of Ngozi. He could see that the wave slowed Mercius in a split second. Ngozi took advantage of it. He moved at a speed that matched the Shadow Lord's pointing the blade. Ngozi slashed his sword at Mercius. The Shadow Lord did the same. Their swords clashed aiming for fatal blows. After the impact, Ngozi was on one side, Mercius was on the other. The sharpness of the sword Ngozi held had split into two. He smirked as he turned to face Mercius who was untouched.

"You might as well give it up Ngozi," said Mercius. "Your sword is an example of how I can dismantle you."

Ngozi looked around the dining room at all the warriors that were in the room. He smirked.

"I wouldn't be so confident of victory Shadow Lord," he said. "I would pay attention to your numbers if I were you."

Mercius watched all the guards surrounding the room, pointing their swords and spears at him and his warriors. A garrison of clan guards rushed into the room cornering Mercius. For the first time, Mercius lost the battle. He clenched his jaw and fists. His warriors surrounded him for protection from the palace guards.

"You may think you have victory today, but you will see my wrath," said Mercius. "When I get done slaughtering you and the rest of Oba's family, I will come back to Ubana in full force. And when I do, I will burn this city to the abyss. I will kill off your proxy queen. I will make sure that all blood will be shed. I will destroy the Aswan Territory as a whole..."

"Man, you're just big mad your warriors got dealt with, shut up," said Imani.

Mercius' mouth curled in a twitch. He glared at Imani grunting aloud. His eyes glowed as a portal appeared below him and his warriors. Without a sound, Mercius and his warriors descended the portal until they disappeared with the portal closing behind them.

Everyone in the room cheered. Ngozi looked around the room with a bright smile. There was a sign of hope. He saw Makara walking towards him.

"I have to hand it to you Ngozi," she said. "We couldn't have done this without your help."

"Trust me, I only do this to serve my nation and future king," said Ngozi. "But the war isn't over just yet. We're just getting started."

"Man, we make a hell of a team, don't we?" said Imani slapping Ngozi on the back.

Ngozi closed his eyes feeling the sting from Imani's slap.

"Yes we do," said Ngozi. "But man, you hit hard."

"Man, stop being a wuss man. You come from chopping heads to crying off a back slap? I'm done with you Ngozi. But you did good. You did good."

Uzoma held an unconscious Moses in his arms approaching Ngozi. His mood changed in an instant rushing towards Moses.

"How is he?" asked Ngozi.

"He took a lot of damage, but he will live to fight again."

"That's good news."

Ngozi pointed his attention to Makara.

"Makara, where is your medical facility?"

Makara walked past Ngozi to get to Uzoma, examining Moses.

"We have our private medical chamber in the fortress near the master bedroom," she said. "Looking at the bruises Moses have on his arms, the high-pressure tank should heal him instantly."

"Good," said Ngozi. "While we're at it we can finally talk with the Queen of joining our resistance. After today I don't think there will be any doubts."

Makara locked eyes with Ngozi letting out a smile.

"You read my mind."

# Chapter Thirteen

# Reflection of the Dark Times

While Moses was incapacitated, Dayo walked towards one of the palace walls carrying a jug of water. Her husband was among the men digging ditches around the walls. The guards were overseeing their work. Stun batons were in their hands and holsters. The sight of their black armor was intimidating. Dayo approached the men stopped by the shadow guards.

"Halt right there mutt," said one of the guards. "You are not assigned to work in this sector. State your business here."

"I would like to give my husband some water," said Dayo. "Perhaps the others would like some water as well."

"Only authorized personnel can deliver them such. You have no authority to be present here. Go back to your sector now or you will be punished."

"Can I at least leave the jug here?" she asked flashing the jug at the shadow guards.

The guard paused for a moment talking amongst the other guards that were with it. The guard turned back to Dayo.

"I'll let you leave it just this once," said the shadow guard. "But next time you better come here with an authorized pass from your taskmaster."

"Of course," said Dayo.

Dayo handed the jug to the shadow guard looking at Tobukwu with pleading eyes. *What I need to tell you is important*, she wanted to tell him. Dayo turned to leave getting to the palace grounds for her work in the garden. She gasped feeling a burn in her chest. Approaching her was Karungu and a few guards with swords drawn.

"This woman has committed treason against Emperor Mercius," said Karungu. "Take her away for interrogation."

The guards approached Dayo. There was nowhere for her to run. Guards were surrounding her. Dayo's only choice was to fight. She kicked one of the guards causing it to stagger. One of the guards behind her clunked her on the back of her neck as she blacked out. Tobukwu hollered, refusing to watch his wife get beaten and dragged away ruthlessly by a traitor. He wacked one of the shadow guards with a shovel while it wasn't paying attention. The men behind him were cheering pausing from their work. Karungu smirked as the guards outnumbered Tobukwu and began beating him with their batons and stomping him consistently.

"That's enough," said Karungu. "Take the girl. Do whatever protocol says for this slime here."

"Yes Lord Ekwenzu," said the shadow guard.

The guards dragged Dayo away accompanying Karungu back to the palace. Tobukwu sat up in tears watching his unconscious wife being dragged away. His vision was blurring. The impact of the beating Tobukwu received left him with bruises and a black eye that couldn't open. Then a boot struck him in the face. A flash beamed through his eyes, then there was darkness.

***

As Moses was taken to the medical chamber, servants of Queen Nadiyya cleaned the mess in the dining room after the gruesome battle against the Shadow Lord. A mixture of blood and food was scattered across the room. Guards were securing the area. The servants separated the bodies into separate piles. The corpses of the guards were to be identified by their loved ones. The remains of the dark warriors were scheduled to be burned.

***

Moses lay in the high-pressure tank. Water was pressuring his body. It's been a few hours since the battle. Ngozi sat along with Uzoma and Imani waiting for their new Chieftain to fully heal. The room was in silence. Queen Nadiyya entered the room along with Makara. Ngozi, Uzoma, and Imani stood to their feet.

"Your highness," said Ngozi.

"I hope you all will forgive me from earlier," said Nadiyya. "The Shadow Lord threatened to harm my people and kill me in the process before you all delivered the message to me the previous day."

"You do not have to apologize your highness. I would've done the same if I was in your position. Regardless of what had happened, we must move forward."

Nadiyya glanced at the high-pressure tank.

"I'm glad he's doing fine," she said. "I heard the battle between him and Mercius was tough."

"He held his ground," said Ngozi. "He reminds me of his father."

Makara stared at a flashing red light on the high-pressure tank. It let out a beep as the light flickered green. She walked towards the tank.

"Looks like the healing process is complete," Makara said. "Good thing he only had minor fractures on his arm. It would've taken all night if he had far more damages."

"We'll be of assistance," said Ngozi referring to him, Uzoma, and Imani.

"That's not necessary. Although you can get a robe for him."

"I'm on it."

Ngozi moved around the chamber searching for a robe for Moses as Makara emptied the high-pressure tank. The water drained from the tank as Moses opened his eyes. A breath mask was on his face. Thoughts were running through his mind. *Where am I? Am I captured? Is it truly over?* He thought of the last thing he could remember, the knee strike. The tank opened letting out steam. He saw Makara appearing in front of him. She pulled the mask from his mouth then helped him out of the tank.

Moses found himself shirtless. He realized he only had on a black undergarment. He was relieved to see Uzoma and Imani. Ngozi stepped in front of him with a robe to cover him.

"It warms my heart to see you in excellent health, your highness," said Ngozi.

"Thank you Ngozi," said Moses. "But what happened? All I can remember is..."

He thought for a moment. The knee strike flashed in his mind once again. Moses nearly slumped as Ngozi placed the robe on him.

"Easy Moses, you have been in the tank for a few hours. You must ease your mind."

Moses' mood was sour. He refused to look in the eyes of his former master. Moses refused to look at anyone.

"I failed Mazị," he said. "The Shadow Lord defeated me."

"There's no need to beat yourself up for this. You held your ground. Your father would be so proud."

A feeling of shame crept onto Moses. If he couldn't beat the Shadow Lord in the last battle, how could he defeat him in the next battle?

"I can't accept what you are telling me Mazị. I'm not strong enough to take the throne. I didn't want the birthright to begin with. The Grand Guardian should've let the birthright stay with Ramses."

Moses stormed away from Ngozi ignoring the others in the room.

"Where are my clothes?" Moses asked Nadiyya.

"I will show you," she said. "Right this way."

Moses followed Nadiyya out of the room. Makara followed behind them.

"So that's it?" questioned Imani. "The best hope for this nation is just going to walk out on us? I might as well go back to merc'ing."

"No," said Ngozi. "Right now he's upset. I will talk to him."

Ngozi walked out of the medical chamber leaving Uzoma and Imani alone.

"So now what?" Imani inquired with her arms crossed.

"We just wait and trust that Ngozi can get through to Moses," said Uzoma. "At the end of the day, he's still a child."

"And that's what bothers me."

***

As Moses roamed about the fortress, the Shadow Lord re-entered the city of Palasera feeling defeated for the first time. The beating wings of his saakuth descended to the palace grounds. His warriors were riding behind him in silence as they made landing towards the side entrance of the palace. The shadow guards bowed, forcing the servants to bow as well to their oppressor. Mercius placed his feet on the palace grounds. His face was grim.

"Welcome back my lord," said one of the shadow guards.

"You may all arise," said Mercius.

The shadow guards and the fearful servants rose to their feet by his command. Ignoring his surroundings, he marched forward towards the palace, the shadow guard walking alongside him.

"Where's my wife?" questioned Mercius.

"She's in the palace with your son," said the shadow guard.

"And what is his condition?"

The shadow guard was hesitant of answering the Shadow Lord's question with fears of his wrath. But it had to follow its master's command, or it would be obsolete regardless.

"The reports show that his condition isn't getting any better. His underlying condition is getting worse."

"Then take me to them immediately."

"Yes my lord. And also, I was given a command by the Empress to inquire about a prisoner captured today for interrogation. We were reported that Lord Karungu Ekwenzu spotted her talking to the former Queen of Nubariah."

"Then let him deal with the prisoner. I have more important matters to deal with."

"Yes my lord."

Mercius trudged inside the palace accompanied by a handful of guards.

***

Amaryllis sat at the bedside of her son in the medical chamber. She rubbed his hand knowing he could not feel her touch. Kulrath was limp, his body was cold. The self-proclaimed Empress of the Bronze Empire squeezed her son's hand, refusing what appeared to be his last few moments.

"You are the heir of Meatis, the second realm of the cosmos," she said. "You cannot pass away. Your father has taught you everything you know in the dark arts to vanquish your enemies. I don't know how you suddenly fell ill, but you must live for the sake of the Shadow League's survival. The Inner Realm of the Shadow Legion must stand victorious so we stand tall as Lord Chashak's champion of all the realms."

She knew Kulrath could not hear her. The sudden disease he had seemed impossible to her. He was in perfect health with a manifestation of power. Amaryllis used her magic, getting in the mind of her son. She had to know what happened. Amaryllis lightly tapped her son's temples, her hands glowing a dark purple aurora.

Her mind tranced Kulrath's. The image of Sahawayda's golden walls appeared in front of her. She saw Kulrath staring at the entrance. Amaryllis stared at a light ahead of her that shined a vivid glow. She gasped as Kulrath coughed up blood and passed out. Amaryllis couldn't stop her gaze at the light. The power within the city was overwhelming. The Grand Guardian stood amid the light. Her nose bled a single stream. Amaryllis screeched, "Mercius, what have you done!"

"Not enough," said a voice.

Amaryllis gasped a long-winded breath. Her mind transferred to her own. She dipped her finger near her nose. She felt a wet sticky substance on the tip of her finger. Amaryllis shivered, staring at the blood on her fingertip. She quivered until she turned and saw her husband entering the chamber.

"Honey, you're back," she said, her voice shaky.

"What's going on here? How's our son?" he questioned.

"I was told his health is declining. The medical drones cannot read his condition."

Mercius clenched his teeth. His fists were pumped, shutting his eyes in sorrow. Wrath was burning inside him.

"Well, who can we find for a second diagnosis?"

"I tried one of the servants who were trained as a healer, but I ended up tormenting her after she couldn't tell me what was wrong. I tried everything in my power to save our son, Mercius, but after I used my magic to enter his mind, I found what's killing him is a torturous light of Sahawayda. You should've stayed away. You caused our son's death with your arrogance."

"I know I made a mistake," said Mercius. "I found out the boy wasn't there. I should've been wiser in my calculations."

Amaryllis stared into the Shadow Lord's eyes. Her demeanor was vengeful.

"Well did you do it? Is the boy captured?"

Mercius shook his head.

"He was near my possession, but somehow he influenced the Oph-Ur army. My warriors were all but decimated and outnumbered."

"So you're telling me that our efforts were for nothing?" questioned Amaryllis. "If the boy begins to influence the rest of Nubariah, our rule will be finished."

"He won't. I still have the Jaguar Clan on my side through the new Ekwenzu. This won't be the last time I do battle with the Chieftain's son. The next time, he will be annihilated by my hand."

"Then you better act fast," said Amaryllis. "I had a vision of a multitude of stars on top of a hill. Crowns were in a valley. The stars came crashing to the valley shattering the crowns."

"Who is the multitude and what are the crowns?"

Amaryllis stared in a state of sorrow.

"The multitude is Nubariah. The crowns... are us."

Mercius dropped his head. He was in near distress.

Amaryllis continued, "With each passing moment, the boy will only get stronger with a rising army."

"Then he must be destroyed."

Amaryllis got up and rubbed his back. Her smile was grim to the curl of her lips.

"We'll destroy him together," she said.

***

Karungu and the shadow guards escorted Dayo down the steps to the prison hall. She walked ahead of Karungu feeling the cold shackles dangling from her wrist. Was this the cost of freedom? Everything her father fought for along with Queen Ashanti was worth the risk. She had a safe home in Dolsa provided with a basic education in aquatic engineering. She led the success of the village's waterpower structure for the use of electricity. She was married to a husband who was talented in agriculture. So this cost of freedom was worth it. Even if it cost her, her life.

Dayo was dragged to a cell that was familiar to her sight.

"Open the cell," commanded Karungu.

A shadow guard followed his command and opened the cell with a press of a button on his metal armored suit. The cell door opened revealing Ramses and Ashanti laying on their cots. Dayo was grieved to see them in the place she was in. She could see the troubled look on Ashanti's face. She could see the anxious look on Ramses'.

The shadow guards ignited their batons. Ramses placed his hands in the air. If he was to attack the guards, the collar on his neck would torment him.

"Alright you two, get out," commanded one of the shadow guards.

The shadow guards grabbed Ramses and his mother that stood beside him. He felt a thud on his back, the stinging vibration of the baton forced him on his knees. He watched his mother shed painful tears as she was forced on her knees. Ramses glared at Karungu feeling a hatred burning within him like a kindled torch.

"It looks like we meet again," said Karungu.

"It looks like it traitor," said Ramses. "I see you're still a loyal mutt to the Shadow Lord."

"Talk as much shit as you can. But I'm the one in control here."

Ramses glanced at the neighboring cell. He could see the woman's curiosity through the steel bars. He could see a bit of sorrow in her expression. Ramses felt a stinging slap across his face. Karungu stared at him menacingly.

"Look at me when I'm talking boy!" he hollered.

Ramses huffed through his nose, pumping his fists.

"Now that I have everyone's attention, you will all tell me what transpired today with your conversation. What are you all planning?"

"Dayo just stopped by to have a friendly conversation," said Ramses.

Karungu frowned and back slapped Ramses across the face. Blood gushed from his mouth.

"This is not a joke!" he yelled. "Now one of you will answer my question or someone within this circle will die! Now, what were you all conversating?"

Ramses was silent, spitting blood on the floor. Karungu scowled, kicking him on the bottom chin causing him to collapse on the hard floor.

"Stop this, please!" cried Ashanti. "My son doesn't deserve this. If you would like to know our discussion, then I'll share it."

Dayo shook her head, pleading with her queen not to say a single word. Ashanti took a deep breath staring at the floor. She gazed into the eyes of Karungu.

"I remember a time when there was honor within our nation," she said. "My husband who was your king fought hard to keep

Nubariah together from the evil spirits of outsiders. There was once peace, order, and justice in our kingdom. Your father once stood by Ouidah faithfully for you and your people's protection. I feel bad for you Karungu. After your father sold his soul out of fear to the Shadow Lord, I knew it was only a matter of time until his corruption rubbed off you."

Karungu glared at Ashanti as she continued.

"You are just a child Karungu. You can turn away from this. Make things right. Correct your father's mistake. Don't go down further of the path of evil. I beg you. This path you have chosen will not work well for you in the end."

Karungu paused for a moment. A part of him knew that she was right. It was that part of him who wanted to restore honor, gain back his humanity. But he couldn't turn back. Ekwenzu's power was too glorious for him. He snorted at the thought of turning back letting loose a scowl across his lips.

"Don't talk to me about honor when your husband failed to bring Nubariah together," he said. "The Shadow Lord has promised me greatness, in a new era of Nubariah. Once you and your sons are dead, I will take the throne as Nubariah's new king. I will accomplish what your husband couldn't. I will unite the territories in a new glorious age!"

Ashanti stared at Karungu. Her gaping eyes were in near sorrow.

"The Shadow Lord is only using you for his own gain. If you choose this path, then you will fall by the sword. I have foreseen a battle coming here to Palasera. You may not survive what will soon transpire."

Karungu smirked pacing back and forth. His pride filled his emotional state of fear.

"So I may not survive huh? That was the conversation? Okay."

Karungu unsheathed his sword and grabbed Dayo. She felt the point of the sword in her back. Her breath was taken away. Blood flowed through her back and her mouth. Ramses watched as the woman he desired fell to her death.

"No!" he hollered.

Ramses rushed to his feet. His only thought was to inflict as much pain as he could to Karungu. A shadow guard pressed a button on its suit causing the collar on his neck to shock.

"Ramses!" he heard his mother crying.

Ramses couldn't breathe. He used his instinct, grabbing the collar. He didn't know how long this torment would last. But he was hoping it would end soon.

"Put them back in the cell," said Karungu. "And dispose of the woman."

"Yes my lord," said the Shadow Guard.

Ramses couldn't take the pain. The shock was killing him as he nearly lost consciousness. He felt the shadow guards drag him into the cell. His pulse was racing. Then his suffering ceased. Ramses gasped for air watching the cell slam behind him.

***

The sun was glistening in the noon sky as Moses rose back to the surface within the old city. The heat caused the atmosphere to sit still. Moses was fully clothed after spending the long few hours in the tank. His body was at a hundred percent, but his spirit felt broken. He couldn't stop thinking of the knee strike that was replaying through his mind. Moses closed his eyes ignoring the heat that was absorbing his melanin. He tried tapping his T'kaf, but there was a mental block. Moses couldn't focus. He felt defeated, lost.

Ngozi approached Moses from behind. There was much concern he had of his former pupil. He stood beside Moses with his hands behind his back.

"I sense you are troubled my former pupil," he said. "Why are you feeling defeated?"

Moses was silent for a moment staring at the ground.

"I failed Mazị," he said. "The Shadow Lord got the best of me."

"So you're allowing one loss to get the best of you? In war, you will never be able to win every battle. But if you can live to fight another day and with every breath that's within your body, there is always hope."

"But how can I defeat him? His power is overwhelming."

Ngozi stared at the dunes rubbing his beard.

"I remember when you and Ramses were babies, I gave the prophecy to your father that one of his offspring will gain the full power of Chukwu to save the entire world from the dark forces. When the Grand Guardian revealed it to me and the council, my curiosity came true. You possess that power, Moses. You are the chosen one Moses to challenge and defeat the Shadow Lords."

Moses felt overwhelmed. He was still unsure of his untapped power. At this point, he couldn't feel it surging within him.

"I don't know how mazị," he said. "I gave it my all, but I still lost. I don't see how you all see this ancient power within me. Perhaps the Grand Guardian was wrong. Perhaps you were wrong."

"You know the reason why you fail? You doubt yourself every time. Look around you Moses. You know the reason why you're gaining allies? Because they believe in you. You are the hope of our nation and that's why the Shadow Lord fears you. Think about it. If you are in disbelief, then what's the point in hope? Death might as well overcome us."

Ngozi walked away getting back to the underground city. Moses thought of what Ngozi said. He closed his eyes in meditation. The dust was brushing the wool in his afro along with sweat. What was the point in hope if he doubted? Was he truly chosen? Moses was able to conquer the demon within before, but how could he defeat the demon that was before him. Then it flickered. He only conquered the demon by clearing his mind and finding his courage. Moses had to believe in himself to unlock his full power. He could feel his T'kaf powering within him. The sun-rays glowed through his skin. His power was no longer locked within his mental box. Moses made up his mind. His power was unlimited.

# Chapter Fourteen

# For the Throne

Moses marched down the hall of the fortress escorted by a few guards. He was empowered filled with a spirit of wholeness. His father was gone; his best friend was killed; his mother and brother were captured; his nation was conquered and colonized. Despite the destruction he witnessed around him, despite Dolsa's destruction, Moses was hopeful. He built an army that believed in him. He defeated the demon from within. He brought fear unto his enemies. His T'kaf became like second nature to him which gave him abilities that an average child couldn't handle.

Moses was led to a door near the end of the hall. One of the guards opened the door revealing a room with a long table with a row of chairs. Within the room, the Queen stood along with Makara who stood beside her. Ngozi was in the room as well along with Uzoma and Imani. The guards escorted Moses into the room. Determination was in his visage. Moses peered at everyone in the room.

"I want to apologize to everyone for my actions earlier," he said. "I was being selfish with self-doubt. I felt defeated after the

Shadow Lord bested me in combat. But I look at all of you in this room. I see the determination within your eyes. You could've easily delivered me to the hands of the Shadow Lord, and it would've all been over."

Moses glanced at Ngozi who smirked giving him a nod. He nodded in a serious tone and continued.

"But you didn't. You continued to fight even though the Shadow Lord defeated me. You fought for what you believe in. The same fight that I believe in. We will take back what's ours. The Shadow Lord will pay for all the blood he shed from our warriors to our innocent. This is our fight. And we will fight to the very finish. As long as you forgive me."

The room was in brief silence.

"We're with you Chief," said Imani.

Everyone in the room agreed with nods and "yeah" replies. Ngozi smiled, his lips curling wider. Uzoma walked up to Moses, his rough hefty hands touching his shoulder.

"You handled the Shadow Lord well," he said. "There is no shame. Even the greatest warrior makes mistakes, including those who are kings. I believe in you Moses. All of us do. And as your general, I will fight for you unto death."

Moses beamed. His confidence rose as if his mind and spirit were levitating in harmony.

"Now that all the warm feelings are in the way," said Nadiyya. "I think it's time for us to negotiate an agreement for Aswan to join your army."

"Yes," said Moses. "Let us begin."

The guards escorted Moses to a chair near Nadiyya who sat at the end of the table. Makara stood beside the Queen.

"Chieftain Ezenwa," Makara said. "On behalf of Queen Nadiyya, we would like to officially welcome you to Aswan. This meeting has officially begun. You may take a seat."

Makara gestured Moses to sit next to Nadiyya. Ngozi, Uzoma, and Imani took a seat at the other side of the table. The guards were surrounding each corner of the room. Moses took his seat next while focusing on the task. No more surprises. No more distractions.

"First off, I would like to apologize from earlier…" said Nadiyya.

Moses waved his hand cutting her off.

"There's no need for apologies," he said. "If you didn't set me up, the Shadow Lord would've killed you. You were under hostage. So were your people. But now I would like to move forward."

"Yes of course. The negotiations. I know you are looking to recruit my army to challenge the Shadow Lord. You can count Aswan as part of your rebellion."

"And I will help command the army," said Makara. "If it's okay with you and General Uzoma."

"Works for me," said Uzoma.

"You will make a great addition to our army Makara," said Moses.

Moses glanced around the room. Everyone had a look of agreement.

"I will also join you in this fight," said Queen Nadiyya.

Moses' eyes were bulged open. Everyone around him was in whispered gasps. Nadiyya was a great ruler, but she was far from a warrior.

"Your highness," said Makara. Her eyes were pleading.

Nadiyya shook her head.

"I brought you in this mess," she said. "And I won't be a victim to this tyrant. I feel like I owe you Chieftain Ezenwa. And like you said, this is our fight."

Moses nodded his head in agreement with what Nadiyya said.

"Then I would like to personally welcome you to the Revolution."

"So when do we begin?"

"We will gather our army now. We will meet at my base in Sahawayda. There we will come up with a strategy on how we can liberate Palasera. If we can defeat Mercius and Amaryllis and take back Palasera, we'll have the leverage of gaining full control of Nubariah."

"I agree," said Nadiyya. "I will gather my warriors and meet you in Sahawayda."

Makara stood to her feet curling a smile.

"It looks like this meeting has officially adjourned," she said.

Ngozi turned to Moses.

"It looks like you have your army," he said. "Now is your time."

Moses nodded. Indeed, this was his time.

***

Hours have passed since the death of Dayo. Ramses sat on the corner of the cell. Streams of tears flowed from the stain in his eyes. The flashes of tainted memories haunted his mind. He thought of Aminnaya's death all those years ago. The images of the shadow bullets piercing through her along with her lifeless stare in a pool of blood was a traumatic memory Ramses could never get away from. Dayo's death made it worse. Now he has to live with the image of the sword being pushed through her back, another lifeless stare. Ramses let out a frustrating roar pounding the cemented floor.

"There's nothing you can do Ramses," said Ashanti. "There's nothing any of us can do. I know you cared for Dayo. I did as well. But she did what she had to do. She knew that death would be the cost of freedom."

Ramses continued sobbing.

"I could've saved her Motha," he said. "But I was too damned weak just like before!"

Ramses punched a crack in the cement. He stared at the floor with thunderous rage. Ramses took rapid breaths, his body quivering.

"I know you are angry Ramses. You have every right to be. But save your strength. You will have your chance to bring young women such as Dayo and Aminnaya to justice. But you must save the strength you will need for the upcoming battle."

"If I ever get my hands on Karungu, I will make him suffer. That bastard will feel my wrath and beg for his life once I'm done with him. And that is a promise."

Ramses's head was continually dropped. Ashanti watched him from her cot. A look of worry was on her face. She fell silent as Ramses bumped the back of his head to the wall. He wiped his tears in aggression.

"Pssst," he heard a voice through the wall.

Ramses stared into space. His mind was discontent.

"Hey you," said the voice of a young woman.

Ramses turned and saw through the crack the young woman from earlier.

"It's you," he said. "I hope you didn't witness what happened earlier..."

"I did," she said. "And I'm sorry about your loss. Was she your admirer?"

"I was hoping. But her heart was with someone else. I'd hate to see how her husband would react when he finds out the news of her death."

"You seemed to have loved her as if she was your betrothed."

Ramses drifted into deep thought.

"I hope I didn't intrude," said the young woman. "I probably came to you rudely. I just wanted to pay my respects."

"Thank you. And you didn't intrude. I did love her, and I feel guilty of her death."

Ramses paused for a moment. Silence was drifting forth for almost thirty seconds.

"I never caught your name," he said.

"My name is Yobanna. My tribe is of the Wolf Clan."

"The Wolf Clan? Your tribe is hard to find within the Walswe Mountains. How was the Shadow Lord able to capture you?"

Yobanna paused.

"The bastard caught me while I went fishing with a few hunters. The dark warriors smoked us out. I'm the only one that survived the ambush."

"He has to be stopped. Some kind of way."

"The Shadow Lord did promise me freedom only if I comply to his favor."

"I am curious. The Shadow Lord always uses our people for his dirty work. This is all but a game to him."

Yobanna glared at Ramses. The look on her face grew intense.

"The deal is for me to be you, your brother, and Queen Ashanti's executor. If I don't comply, I will be executed myself."

Ramses fell silent. He backed away slamming himself on the wall. Again, he felt powerless.

***

The airship hovered over the sky as Moses sat in the airship with the goal in mind of taking back Palasera. Uzoma was flying the ship with Imani co-piloting. Ngozi sat beside him meditating. Imani's voice sounded through the speakers, *"You guys might want to come to the cockpit. There is something you might want to see."*

Ngozi opened his eyes turning to Moses.

"This sounds important," said Ngozi. "We better go to the cockpit to see what's going on."

Moses nodded in agreement and followed Ngozi to the cockpit uniting with Uzoma and Imani. Moses watched their tone. This was serious. Something wasn't right. Imani turned to Moses.

"You might not want to miss this," she said pointing at a monitor above them.

Moses watched the screen in close observation. The Shadow Lord was on the screen with his wife beside him. He was dressed in gold-plated armor with four wings decorated across the breastplate. The helmet on his head matched the gold armor with flaming wave designs. Amaryllis wore a sparkling gold dress. Her mascara matched the darkness within her tainted spirit. Mercius stood behind a podium, the background was familiar to

Moses. Mercius was on the palace grounds, his army standing behind him.

"Citizens of the Empire," he said. "Today marks a significant day for this nation. This is a day where I am giving you all a choice and I will be quite blunt with my message. You have a choice to choose which king you will serve. You can either side with your emperor which I have provided you all with food, shelter, clothing, and labor. Or you can choose the welp and this pointless rebellion against me."

Moses' blood was boiled. He pumped his fists and gazed at the screen as Mercius continued his speech.

"So here is what I will place as law. If you choose me as your emperor, I promise you that I will relinquish the curfew laws and give you the liberty to choose your labor and social status. You will no longer have bonds nor go through any torture methods unless you commit a crime. You will all live as freemen and free women. But if you choose the man child and claim him as your king, then you will be sentenced to death. Starting tomorrow morning, I will set an example for anyone who decides to rebel against my empire by executing your beloved queen and her pathetic first-born son who lost his birthright. And once I kill off your beloved rising king, those who joined him will die. So, choose today the king you will serve! But remember the consequences."

The screen turned blank. Moses curled his lips to a ball. Everyone around him fell silent.

"The bastard," said Imani. "We should've taken him out when we had the chance in Ubana."

"This change everything," said Moses. "We need to prepare our army for Palasera tomorrow."

"Let's not move too hasty Moses," said Ngozi. "The Shadow Lord is using your mother and brother as bait to draw you out. You must make sure that you and your army are moving in one accord."

"But if we don't attack the Shadow Lord's army by tomorrow, he will kill them anyway."

"I never said we should wait. Remember, a great king never goes off to battle unless his army is prepared."

Moses had a thought for a split second.

"When Queen Nadiyya meets with us today, we will plan ahead."

"Now you have the right idea," said Ngozi.

The airship hovered over the land of Sahawayda. Moses and his crew were near the base. All he could think of at this point was how to put an end to the Shadow Lord with compilating thoughts.

*** 

Ramses laid in the cot; his thoughts were spaced out. He heard the cell door zoom open. Ramses got up from his cot in alert. From the corner of his eye, his mother did the same. Two shadow guards appeared in front of him. One of the shadow guards pressed a few buttons on his armor as a holo-screen lit up showing Ramses and his mother's face with foreign inscriptions below that Ramses couldn't make out, *Thanatoó*.

"By orders of Emperor Mercius, Queen Ashanti, and Ramses Ezenwa, you are to be sentenced to death immediately tomorrow morning," the shadow guard said. "The cause of this sentence is due to treason in rebellion against your majesty."

"As if we didn't know," said Ashanti. "Your Shadow Lord wanted us dead anyways."

The shadow guards stared at her with emotionless stares.

"Enjoy your last moments. One of the palace droids will provide you with your last meal momentarily."

The shadow guards walked away closing the cell door behind them.

Ramses slumped his head to his cot.

"We're finished," he said. "It's all over."

"You must have faith Ramses," said Ashanti.

Ramses turned and faced Ashanti. He was seething yet was in melancholy.

"Faith?" he questioned. "What can faith do to save us now? We lost. Karungu betrayed us and have the upper hand. The Shadow Lord and his army destroyed everything we've built in Dolsa. Even if there will be a battle in Palasera, we will probably be dead by then."

Ramses' dropped his head again facing the cell door. Ashanti was sorrowful. She has never seen her son this defeated. Not ever since birth. It was like his spirit was torn from his flesh. Ashanti eyed her son, although he did not do the same.

"If you lack faith, then you lack hope," she said. "You will always lose if you stay in a defeated mindset. You are not my son who was motivated for kingship..."

"Because I lost my birthright! My power has been stripped as well as my dignity when I lost it. Why do I have to lose the kingship? Why am I left with nothing? Why does every woman I love gets killed in front of me? I might as well just die!"

"Enough! I grow tired of your self-pity. So what you lost the fight against Karungu? Either pick yourself up and fight or accept death. But regardless of what you choose, your brother needs you. Our family, our kingdom is on the line. You better decide quickly on what you will do. The morning will be here before you know it."

Ramses soaked in the words his mother told him. They were harsh but true. Ramses' mind was conflicted between defeat and purpose. He slumped himself on the cot curling his body in depression. Ramses knew his mother was right. A battle was approaching. The atmosphere around him began shifting.

The door opened once again. Two androids entered. Ashanti stalked the two droids walking in. Ramses remained in his cot.

"Your last meal before your execution will be one of Nubariah's traditional dishes; rice, fish, and tomato sauce that is flavored with spiced onions, carrots, cabbage, cassava, and peanut oil."

"How pleasant," said Ashanti.

***

Sundown was near as Moses sat around his team within the main chamber of what was the Silent Assault Base. This became his outpost. The mercenaries that stayed came to be his warriors and troops. He was strategizing the whole day since his return from Ubana. Moses focused on how to come up with the attack to save his remaining family. He lost his father already to the Shadow League. He couldn't lose the rest of his family to the enemy in a public execution. The Shadow Lord had to be stopped. His end had to be near. His reign had to be finished.

One of the warriors entered the chamber bowing in honor of Moses.

"Your majesty," he said. "Queen Nadiyya of Aswan is here. Would you like to admit her now?"

"Yes, thank you."

The warrior escorted the Queen into the chamber. Makara walked alongside her. Moses got up and bowed taking her hand. She returned a curtsey to him.

"Hello again your highness," said Makara giving Moses a bow.

"Please, join us," said Moses. "We were strategizing all day on our assault on the Shadow League."

"So tell me. What have you come up with before our arrival?" questioned Nadiyya.

"Since the Shadow Lord will be distracted with his public execution, we could attack him and his warriors at the palace grounds. But we have a few issues concerning this. For one, the Shadow Lord is ruthless, especially when he's desperate. He will kill off our people who are serving him as collateral damage. We can't afford innocent lives being taken during the crossfire. Our efforts would nearly be for nothing if hardly any civilian lives survive the battle."

"And we would try to get them to the underground station," said Ngozi. "But the Shadow Lord will lock everything connected to the palace down."

Nadiyya had an assuring look on her face.

"I will guarantee that my warriors will evacuate the people from the city," she said. "I have enough warriors to aid the civilians and fight in the battle. You can count on Aswan to help lead you to victory."

Moses nodded.

"We still have the matter of how we will form our armies," he said. "I have my warriors and soldiers here in Sahawayda. And Ngozi informed me earlier that the Grand Guardian will spare some warriors. If we are to win this battle, our armies will have to be on one accord. And with our timing, we won't be able to form our units combined."

"I believe I can answer that," said Makara.

Moses turned to her. With her expertise in battle, he knew he could count on her for an answer.

"Me and Uzoma are both generals. Ngozi I'm sure is in second command of your army Chieftain Moses. Plus, we have our queen and chieftain who can collaborate on the attack. It shouldn't be a burden."

"Makara is right," said Nadiyya. "Our armies will move on our command."

"That sounds good your highness," said Ngozi. "But we also need transport. Our warriors cannot travel on foot from Sahawayda to Ouidah."

"That is where we step in," said Nadiyya. "I have warships below my fortress in a hangar near the core. I have prepared for this moment a long time."

Nadiyya locked her eyes on Moses with a smile.

"I can show you myself."

"Yes, you have my attention Queen Nadiyya," Moses said. "I'll go with you to Ubana to check out the warships."

"Well, I'm coming with you just in case things get messy again," said Imani.

Moses waved his hand at her.

"That is not necessary Imani," he said. "I will bring only Ngozi with me. I want you and Uzoma to prepare the army while I'm gone."

"I want you to stay here and assist them, Makara," said Nadiyya. "I will send a transport of warriors here in preparation for the battle."

"Of course your highness," she said.

"We better leave immediately," said Moses. "Time is of the essence."

Queen Nadiyya nodded and left out of the chamber. Moses followed her alongside Ngozi. Moses was headed back to Ubana.

Moses boarded Nadiyya's shuttle with a few of her guards. Ngozi was with him, just like the beginning of the journey. Sunshine drifted to nightfall as the shuttle was led to Ubana. The atmosphere was crisp. The sands laid still. Moses was led back to the underground city, back to the fortress. The city was quiet. The guards were out patrolling in the streets and the airships above. Ubana was secure.

Moses continuously followed Nadiyya through the halls of the fortress. The halls seemed endless, almost like a maze. He saw the same patterned walls and floors surrounding him. Queen Nadiyya stopped at a wall in the middle of the hall. Moses was puzzled as she placed her hands on the textured wall. Moses nearly fell back watching the wall push itself back revealing two metal doors.

"Right this way," said Nadiyya.

The doors had split open leading to a wide elevator. Moses entered the elevator behind Nadiyya. Ngozi and a few guards entered behind him. The metal doors closed behind them in unison with the elevator. Moses could feel the elevator descending. Once the elevator came to a complete stop, the elevator opened revealing a massive hangar. Moses stepped in staring in astonishment at large warships lined in rows. The warships were colossal coated in a fiery-colored chrome. The count of the ships seemed endless. Queen Nadiyya turned and faced Moses.

"So what do you think?" she asked.

Moses was lost for words. The warships were perfect. The Shadow Lord would not know what hit him.

"This is more than enough," said Ngozi. "Our armies will do well in the upcoming battle. Thank you, your highness. This has certainly redeemed you."

"Save it for the battle," said Nadiyya. "We have what we need, now it is time to prepare."

"Indeed," said Moses. "We have all night."

"There is one more thing I need to show you," said Nadiyya.

"What else is it?" wondered Moses.

"It is a battle garment I would like for you to have. It was a design my uncle Chieftain Hullu created before his death. I can get my tailors to fit you and design the outfit."

"Then show me the way."

Nadiyya nodded and led Moses back to the elevator. Ngozi and the guards followed them back to the fortress' surface.

***

It was a restless night for Ramses as he stared at the ceiling. Sleep was in the least of his mind. He was bound for death. It was as if he could taste it. He was beaten not only physically, but mentally. Soon, he was going to get executed by a woman from the hidden tribe. His death would be the cost of her freedom.

The prison door slid open. A force of guards entered the prison doors. Ramses rose to his feet as the guards entered the cell.

"Up on your feet mutts," said the guard. "It's time to get put down."

Ramses was chained once again feeling shackles around his wrist. He looked at his mother who was chained beside him. No words were coming from her. *What faith?* he thought to himself. He and his mother were escorted out of the cell. Ramses glanced behind him. Yobanna was walking behind him in silence. The guards led him and his mother down the prison hall to an elevator. There was the death of silence around him as the elevator shot up to the main floor of the palace.

The elevator door opened revealing the familiar hall where the terror took place when he was a small child. With each step he took, he remembered the screams of captives. Ramses could remember the death of Chieftain Hullu and the grieving of Aminniya before her death. He would soon join her. Death was calling him, so he assumed. The guards opened the front door, the morning sky was dawning before him.

Ramses saw a crowd of servants swarming around the palace. He could tell on the look of many faces that they were fearful to witness the death of their former leaders. It was as if all hope was lost. Shadow Lord Mercius stood alongside his wife at the stairway waiting for his arrival. Karungu stood next to the Shadow Lord as well. A smirk was on his face. Ramses was forced on his knees. The shackles were removed, replaced with a rope that was tied around his wrists behind his back. A cloth was wrapped around his mouth. He could hear his mother whimpering behind him.

"Please," he heard her sobbing. "Please…"

The Shadow Lord raised his hand getting everyone's attention.

"Settle down!" he yelled. "Settle down!"

He peered at the unsettling crowd as they fell in complete silence. He could sense their fear of him.

"Let the execution begin!"

The Shadow Lord backed away retreating to his wife. The shadow guard handed Yobanna an energy sword, its violet flare igniting. She grabbed the sword and aimed it at the back of Ramses' neck. He was tense, she could sense it. Yobanna took a deep breath through her nostrils. She glanced at Ashanti staring at her imploring eyes. She was hesitant lowering the blade. Someone grabbed her arm from behind. Yobanna turned her head slightly glancing at Karungu scowling at her.

"What are you waiting for?" he questioned. "As your future king, I demand you to get this over with. Slice their necks or slit their throats."

Yobanna frowned, feeling Karungu's grip loosening. She took another breath through her nostrils. It was either her freedom or her death. Yobanna raised the energy sword above her head staring at Ramses' neck. If she was to kill the royal family of old, she knew her soul would be lost. If she would die to spare their lives, then she would die a hero, but her efforts could be for nothing, and they would die anyway. Yobanna raised the sword staring at Ramses' neck. She had no choice. She could hear Ashanti whimpering. The sky began to darken. Yobanna looked up and gasped.

A fleet of warships appeared above the city near the palace.

"What?" questioned Karungu.

Ramses peered at the warships wishing he could sigh for relief. He recognized the warships were allies. Moses did it. He gained his army and now he's challenging the Shadow Lord, for the throne. *Well done brother*, he wanted to say. *I guess you've proven me wrong again*.

Mercius gritted his teeth for a moment staring at the warships. Then he smirked.

"So, it looks like I forced the boy's hand," he said to himself. "It looks like I get my chance to end this."

Mercius grimaced at Yobanna.

"Well, what are you waiting for?" he questioned. "If you want your freedom then proceed with the executions!"

"Yes, my lord," she said.

Yobanna pointed the sword at Ramses. She glanced at a shadow guard standing near her and jabbed the point of the energy sword through the guard's armor. Yobanna grabbed the guard's arm and pressed a button on its armor, releasing the collar from her neck. The shadow guard dropped on the marble ground along with the collar. Yobanna pointed the energy sword at Karungu's neck. She glared at the Shadow Lord.

"Let the queen and the prince go," she commanded. "Or I will slit this traitor's throat."

Mercius scowled for a short moment then laughed at her attempt of holding him hostage.

"Go on with it then," said the Shadow Lord. "Kill him. I can always find another proxy king for my empire. But your attempt of freeing the former queen and prince is pathetic."

Karungu glowered gritting his teeth. He could hear Ekwenzu in his head.

*"His death will soon come. Along with Oba's chosen heir."*

The Shadow Lord signaled his warriors to surround Yobanna, Ramses, and Ashanti. He was satisfied watching his guards and warriors surround them. The Shadow Lord smirked gazing at the warships.

"Kill them all. And make it quick. I want the rest of you to secure and lock down the palace. Man the blasters to take out those warships."

A group of shadow guards escorted the Shadow Lord and his wife back to the palace leaving the crowd unsettled.

Yobanna swung the sword at Karungu, but he used his swiftness to dodge the swipe of the blade. He laughed, disappearing through a cloud of dark smoke. Yobanna held her guard. The dark warriors and guards were closing in on her. She slashed a warrior in front of her. Her movement of the blade was like the motion of wind. The warriors and guards were collapsing one by one in flashes.

Ramses used his might trying to pull the rope off of his wrist. He watched the crowd disperse into chaos. If only he was free, he would bring them to order. He turned his head and saw Yobanna walk up to him. The dark warriors and guards were already lifeless around them. He felt her cutting the rope from his wrists. The cloth was removed from his mouth.

"You sure made quick work of them," said Ramses. "Thank you for saving us, I thought for sure that was the end of us."

"You can thank me later once we're out of this mess," she said. "The warships came right on time."

Yobanna cut the ropes from Ashanti's wrists next. Ashanti got up from the ground removing the cloth from her mouth.

"You have chosen the right side Yobanna," said Ashanti. "Ouidah gives you our gratitude. The palace is locked down, so we won't be able to get in. We'll need an alternate route which I remember through the underground station."

Ashanti stared at the dispersed crowd.

"But first, we need to make sure the civilians are secure before they become collateral damage."

"Do you think the warships will assist us?" asked Ramses.

Ashanti gazed at the warships and smiled.

"Yes. My son has done it. Just like Ra'mah showed me in the vision. I believe in you Moses. It's time to end this."

# War

Vengeance was on Moses' mind as he stared at Palasera's surface in the red armor with silver linen that was gifted to him by Nadiyya. It has been years since he departed from his old home. He couldn't stop thinking of the painful memories that haunted him since his father's death. Moses couldn't stop thinking of the deaths he witnessed by the hands of the Shadow League; the nobles, businessmen, businesswomen being rounded up as cattle tied in ropes with electric shackles around their wrists and ankles. He stared at the city from the bridge that was once prosperous and full of life that was lowered to a desolate slum full of ramshackle buildings surrounded by trash heaps in certain sectors of the city. Moses stared at the statues of Mercius being emulated as God. His fists were pumped. War was what he was declaring against his enemies.

"So this is Palasera huh," said Imani. "The Shadow Lord sure turned this place into dung."

"I will ensure his reign ends today," said Moses.

"You will have your revenge but let's focus," said Nadiyya. "I will send my warriors to evacuate the civilians. Including on the palace grounds."

Moses watched the chaos miles away from where the palace grounds stood.

"We better move quickly," he said. "Something doesn't feel right here."

"Moses is right," said Ngozi. "The Shadow League is nowhere to be found. We better stay on our guard."

Nadiyya pressed a button on a comm in front of her.

"Makara," she said. "Get the people out of the palace grounds immediately. Also, ensure the people in the city are not caught in the crossfire."

*"Yes, your highness,"* said Makara through the comm. *"I will pull forward to the palace grounds immediately. The other fleets will stay behind on your command."*

"Uzoma, follow behind Makara," said Moses. "She may need backup."

"I got her back your highness," Uzoma said.

Moses turned to Imani who was skimming through the warship's holo-monitor behind him.

"Imani," he said. "Check the schematics of the palace. I need to know every entrance where the warriors can attack. Also, I need to know if there are any traps."

"Yessir," she said typing on the monitor.

On the monitor, the blueprint of the palace appeared. Moses gazed at the holo-monitor with Ngozi standing beside him. Nadiyya watched across from him.

"It looks like there is a main entrance with four side entries and a back entrance. Also, you have the underground station that hovers around each entrance leading to emergency exits into the city."

Imani gaped into the holo-screen.

"Damn. The Shadow Lord turned the entire station into a prison. Talk about torment. Now taking a look at the live schematics…"

Imani twirled the blueprint on the monitor showing a model of the palace. The model was blinking red on every entrance of the palace.

"You got to be kidding," said Imani.

"What is going on?" questioned Moses.

"The blinking red lights on this model indicates a massive lockdown within the palace. Including the underground station."

"They're making sure we don't get in the palace," said Ngozi. "The Shadow Lord is making this a hard task for us."

"Your majesty," said the pilot. "You might want to take a look at this."

Moses, along with the others, peered outside from the bridge past the pilot's seat. Moses gasped at multiple dark vortexes appearing in the sky.

"It's an ambush," he said.

A fleet of saakuth appeared from the vortexes in multitudes. The dark warriors rode on the roaring beasts with their laser launchers aiming at the warships. The blast of the lasers rattled the warship. Moses nearly lost his balance.

"Bring out the fighters," said Nadiyya on the comm. "We need to take out as many of those beasts as possible."

*"Yes, your majesty,"* said Makara. *"We are launching the fighters immediately."*

Moses watched as the saakuth continued the ambush. The cannons of the warships were able to blast down a few at a time. However, the speed of the saakuth and their evasive tactics were overwhelming. Moses was hoping the fighters would engage quick within the aerial battle. Then the winged fighters emerged from warships with grace. It was almost in a millisecond. Moses could see that the tide of the battle was beginning to even out. Bursts of lasers and atomic bullets scattered across the air. The war beasts were spiraling from the sky. The winged fighters exploded before Moses' eyes. Chaos was in the sky. Despite the turmoil around Moses, he was determined to reach the palace staring at the majestic site.

"Pull forth through the narrow line to the palace," said Moses. "While these war beasts are distracted, we need to get to the palace grounds and figure a way to gain entry through one of those doors."

"Yes, your majesty," said the pilot.

Moses felt the warship pulling forward. The ship was in a constant rattle. However, Moses was focused. He was pursuing his destiny.

***

Pandemonium was around Ashanti, Ramses, and Yobanna as the crowd scattered witnessing the great battle in the sky. There were screams of terror. Ashanti tried reasoning with the scampered people. "Everyone please stay calm!" she yelled. Yet everyone ignored her. Ashanti had the impression that no one in the horde trusted her. She was just as hopeless as anyone else.

Ramses also tried reasoning with the scurrying crowd. "You need to trust us!" he yelled. "The Shadow Lord will kill you all through the crossfire if you don't allow us to get you to safety!"

"How can you protect us, and you couldn't even protect yourselves?" questioned familiar voice.

Tobukwu appeared in front of Ramses. His demeanor was hostile. He had a shovel in his hands gripping it. Ramses didn't have time for this. Why now?

"You didn't even protect my wife when she needed you most. But I forgot, you loved her and couldn't have her. So, you just watched as she died."

"It's not like that at all Tobukwu," said Ramses.

"Lies! Karungu told me everything!"

Tobukwu swung the shovel at Ramses. He ducked with ease from the wild swing.

"Tobukwu, stop this madness!" he yelled. "There isn't much time!"

He ignored Ramses' command and darted rapid swings at Ramses in constant misses. Ramses' frustration took over. He caught the shovel and gripped it. Tobukwu began to struggle.

"Let go Tobukwu, it's over."

"I wish that woman had killed you before the warships arrived. I would've had my satisfaction."

Ramses brow furrowed. His teeth gritted. Enough was enough. Ramses used his strength, snatching the shovel from Tobukwu's hands and snapped it in half. *It's time for me to shut him up*, he thought. Ramses threw the shovel and connected his fist to Tobukwu's jaw. He watched as the man collapsed on the ground. Ramses felt a hand gripping him from behind. He turned with alert finding Yobanna behind him.

"That was unnecessary what you did just now," she said. "Hopefully he's not dead."

"I'm pretty sure he's not dead," said Ramses. "I did have to knock some sense into him."

"You may have outdone yourself."

Ramses peered at two warships descending towards their direction. He was hoping that a rescue came at last since the crowd became more attentive to their allies. Ramses breathed in relief as the warships landed on the palace grounds.

Out of the first warship, Makara rushed out along with a band of Oph-Ur Clan warriors.

"Gather the people and put them on the ship!" she yelled. "We need to get everyone out of here before the Shadow League attacks on ground!"

The warriors obeyed her command and gathered the men, women, and children that were among the turmoil. Makara bowed to Ashanti.

"Your highness," she said. "We tried to get here as soon as possible."

"Well, I'm thankful you're here now," said Ashanti. "You came here just in time."

Ashanti glanced at the second warship. The warriors rushed out of ship. They were a mix of soldiers and warriors of each clan and territory; Ashanti could tell by their weapons and emblems. She was lost for words when she peered at the second ship. Uzoma walked in a stride out of the ship. Ashanti couldn't believe her eyes.

"Uzoma?" she questioned.

He locked eyes with Ashanti and hastened towards her.

"Uzoma!" she yelled rushing to him.

She embraced him with tears flowing through her eyes.

"By the name of the Supreme I thought you were dead," she said.

"I did too at one point," he said. "But I'm here now. Moses is here. We will take Nubariah back."

Ashanti was startled as she watched an explosion in front her. The touch of fire was on her face hearing screams of terror echoing the air. Her pulse thrusted. The innocent lives retrieved were nearly lost. A few of the warriors were taken by the eruption. Ashanti looked at the sky of the battle. A red energy ball the color of flames launched in the sky shattering one of warships.

"No, no, no, no, no," said Ashanti.

"Look!" yelled Ramses.

He pointed at a group of portals that appeared near the palace entrance.

"Everyone prepare yourselves!" screamed Makara.

"On your guard now!" yelled Uzoma.

The warriors followed their command and lined one by one unified for battle.

Ramses stood beside his mother and Uzoma. He gripped the energy sword ready to attack. Yobanna was beside him, holding her guard with the energy sword. Ramses watched as the dark warriors appeared through the portals. Their looks were menacing, weapons drawn with a thirst for flesh. Ramses glared at the dark warriors striding towards them.

"Ready your arms!" yelled Makara.

"Stay close to me Ashanti," said Uzoma.

She nodded focused on the approaching dark army.

"Press on!" yelled Makara. "And make sure every civilian is rushed out of palace grounds!"

The warriors marched forward to her command while others were retrieving the crowd to safety. Their weapons were ready for battle. The two armies began to rush for battle eventually colliding with swords and bullets.

Ramses used his possessed laser sword to block sword strikes and struck a dark warrior on the knee with his foot hearing a *crrrk*. He used his strength using more than the blade to vanquish his enemies. His feet were weapons. His elbows were his backsword. Ramses alone overwhelmed the dark warriors with his might and brute force. Yobanna was swift with her sword giving the warriors leverage in the battle.

Ashanti stayed close to Uzoma defending herself. She watched around her of the dark army getting disintegrated. The Oph-Ur Clan warriors decimated the dark warriors with flaming swords. Lion Clan warriors were demolishing them with their T'kaf. Ashanti haven't seen a unification like this in a long time. Now it was time. It was her time to follow the vision now that the dark army was distracted.

"Ramses!" she yelled.

She rushed towards him as he made quick work of one of the dark warriors.

"Let's go, now while the dark army is distracted," she said.

"Where are we going?" Ramses questioned.

"To the underground station. We need to sabotage those cannons before they cause a lot of damage."

"I'm coming with you," said Yobanna from behind. "I feel the Wolf Clan owes the family of Oba a debt."

"Then we better move quickly before they bring out a garrison."

"Before you go, I have something for you," said Uzoma from behind.

Ashanti turned and saw Uzoma walking towards her.

You will need this just in case."

He grabbed Ashanti by her hand and planted a pistol in her palm. She nodded.

"Now go," he said. "Follow through with your mission your highness. And Ramses, protect your mother at all times."

Ramses smiled.

"It's nice to see that you are alive Uzoma," he said.

"Whatever you do Uzoma, don't die on me this time," said Ashanti.

"Likewise," he said.

Ashanti rushed to get to the back of the palace. Ramses followed suit along with Yobanna as the battle raged on.

***

*Why can't I escape from this?* thought Kulrath. He was entrapped in that very moment he collapsed. The golden gates of the city were locked in his mind. There was a bright light shining before him. The son of the Shadow Lord glared and squinted at a figure within the light. Appearing before him was the Grand Guardian with a radiant glow. The old wise man stepped up to him. His glare was intense. Kulrath stared unto his eyes nearly choking. He felt a clump of vomit shooting up his esophagus trying to hold it. Black fluid spewed from his mouth. His eyes bulged as he collapsed on the dry sand. He wheezed unable to catch his breath. His vision began to blur. The light was growing brighter. He saw the Grand Guardian getting closer in his direction.

"You are dying," he heard the wise old man telling him. "But it is not too late for you to be saved. There is great evil in you. But you are only a child. You can be redeemed, but you have to change your ways and serve me in the temple. You will have life. But you will serve the God of the Universe instead of the god of darkness. Come."

Kulrath saw the Grand Guardian extending his hand towards him. He rasped, trying to let out words in a frown.

"I... I am the son and heir of Shadow Lord Mercius," he said. His voice was hoarse. Black goo oozed from his mouth.

"I will never join nor serve the God who rejects our power."

The Grand Guardian frowned in a pause. His look nearly showed pity for the young boy. He backed away a few steps.

"Then to darkness you will return," he said.

Kulrath gasped a deep breath. His vision blurred in completeness. The light glowed brighter. The sight of the Grand Guardian faded. He could no longer breathe.

***

Mercius watched in dread at the flat line of the heart monitor. His wife sat beside him. Tears flowed down her cheeks. The Shadow Lord watched the limp body of his son on the bed. His fists were balled. He huffed in fury staring at the floor.

"I'm sorry my lord," said the medical android in front of him. "But Lord Kulrath is gone. There is nothing further..."

Mercius threw a flame at the android sawing it in half before it could complete a sentence.

"I already know what's going on!" he hollered in fury. "I don't need a reminder!"

"Honey, what are we going to do?" questioned Amaryllis. "Our son is gone. The Nubarians are rebelling. It's like everything is falling apart."

"The only thing that is left is to spill the blood of our enemies. Oba's chosen son is the perfect opportunity. One life traded for another. An eye for an eye."

Mercius locked his eyes at a nearby android.

"Take the boy's corpse into the throne room. I will perform the ritual in preparation for the battle against Oba's chosen."

"Yes my lord," said the android.

"I will come with you," said Amaryllis. "I want to make sure you're not disturbed."

"We better act swiftly," said Mercius. "The time is drawing near."

***

More corpses of the enemy were laid towards the back of the palace as Ramses and Yobanna gathered their skills and strength together, energy swords clenched in their sweaty palms. Ashanti fought beside them, jabbing the blade through their armor until there were none left to attack them.

The entrance of the underground station was before them. A panel was near the sealed steel door of flashing red lights. Ashanti led Ramses and Yobanna to the door, pointing her attention to the panel.

"Now what?" questioned Ramses. "The doors to the underground station are sealed as well."

"No worries," said Ashanti. "There were plenty of times your father kept forgetting the combination of this panel leading to the underground station. We always had a switch for reset."

Ashanti rubbed her hand on the bottom of the panel, observing the panel. The panel was a smooth touch until she felt a sharp button pressing her skin. *Click*, was the feel of the switch as the buttons stopped flashing.

Yobanna stood next to the door as it flew open.

"It's open!" she said. "Your highness, you did it!"

Ashanti laughed with a squeal.

"It still works," she said.

"Let's go before they seal the door back," said Ramses.

Without hesitance, Ashanti nodded and followed Yobanna and Ramses through the entrance. Behind her, the doors shut. The tunnels of the underground station were just like she remembered. The ceiling matched with the hard cemented ground. The tunnel was dark with dim red lights just like her escape seven years ago.

"I remember the path to get to the palace's interior," she said. "We better act fast before those blasters wipe out our allies."

"We'll follow closely Mother," said Ramses.

Ashanti took the lead and walked through the narrow tunnel leading to the palace's interior. It was the dead of silence. The palace alarm was ringing in the background. She walked through an entranceway and saw a line of prisons lined up on the walls. Standing before her was Karungu.

"I was wondering when you all would show up," said Karungu.

He drew his blade, bloodlust on his mind.

Ramses stepped in front of his mother, Yobanna beside him. Their energy swords were drawn.

"Go ahead of us Mother," said Ramses. "We'll handle this."

"Naw," said Karungu pointing his blade at her. "Why won't you stay here your highness and watch as I dismantle your boy here."

Ramses stepped in front of him. Yobanna stood on the side of Karungu with intensity.

"You better deal with me before you get to her," said Ramses referring to his mother.

Karungu glared at Ramses and peered at Yobanna. Ashanti could see her opportunity to continue forth towards the palace interior. She walked past them with caution.

"Please be cautious my son," Ashanti said. She rushed past the prison cells to get to the interior of the palace.

Ramses and Yobanna circled Karungu. The thought of vengeance was on his mind.

***

Moses stared in horror at the blasters wrecking the warships. The warriors below were blown away in clusters, including the enemies who were in the way. He was hoping that the blasters wouldn't damage the homes of the civilians. They were suffering enough as bondservants.

"We're not going to make it," said Nadiyya. "Those blasters are too powerful."

"We have to get to the palace," said Moses. "This is our only shot."

"You won't be able to make it with those blasters in the way."

Ngozi rubbed his beard nearby in thought.

"We'll need a smaller shuttle where the blasters won't detect us," he said.

"I agree," said Moses.

"So do I," said Nadiyya. "There are pods we usually use for escape. You can outmaneuver the blasts, but you will need an angle from the warship to get there. The pods, however, can only fit two people."

"Me and Moses will go in the pods," said Ngozi. "Aim the pods to the roof. We'll try to shut down the blasters manually."

"Yeah, you guys go without me," said Imani. "Not that I'm scared or anything, but you'll need me to find a way to breach their system while I'm on this ship."

"Sounds like a plan. Come, Moses. We better move quickly."

Moses followed Ngozi out of the bridge to get to the pods. The pods were across the corridor near the hangar. Moses saw six pods on each side of the room. Moses followed Ngozi inside the first pod in front of him that had two seats, just like Nadiyya described. Moses sat next to Ngozi waiting for launch. Ngozi brought out his Optix.

"We're in," said Ngozi. "Ready for launch."

*"We hear you loud and clear,"* said Nadiyya's voice.

She pointed her attention to the pilot.

"Aim the pods at the palace roof."

"Yes, your highness," said the pilot.

Within the pod, Moses closed his eyes. He could sense the evil presence of the Shadow Lord within the palace. Within the pod, he could hear the pilot through the comm. He buckled his seat.

*"Ready for launch in t-minus 50 seconds..."*

Ngozi turned to Moses.

"I can sense him too," he said. "You will have your chance to avenge your father and his legacy."

Moses nodded his head and closed his eyes as the pilot continued the countdown.

*45...44...43...42...41...*

Moses channeled his T'kaf in preparation for his fight for the throne. He could feel the Shadow Lord's dark presence the closer the warship was to the palace.

*20...19...18...17...16...15*

Moses thought of it all. All the pain, the agony, the heartbreak. He could remember their dark presence invading his home. Moses was ready to take the trauma out on the Shadow Lord, the trauma he held onto for seven years.

*10...9...8...7...6...5...4...3...2...1. The pods are ready for launch.*

Moses opened his eyes. He felt the small pod shooting like a rocket. The battle was hovering around him. He saw the saakuth gliding past the pod attacking the fighters. The fighters were counter-attacking the saakuth. Blasters were gliding both in the air and on the ground bringing destruction to anyone who fell in the way.

Ngozi controlled the pod dodging lasers and blasts. Moses could see the roof of the palace. Shadow guards surrounded the perimeter of the rooftop. The pod drew nearer. Moses could see they were on the clear.

"Brace yourself Moses!" warned Ngozi.

Moses' eyes gaped open in a deep breath. The pod made a hard landing skidding across the rooftop. Moses placed his hand on the dashboard keeping his balance. He figured the pod was tearing itself apart the more it slid on the rooftop. Perhaps it would crash on the other side of the palace grounds. Then Moses felt the pod was at a complete stop. He looked out the window and was thankful to be unharmed realizing it was still on the rooftop. The shadow guards hovered around the vessel.

"Check the pod," one of them commanded. "If anyone is alive, set your stun to kill."

"Follow my lead Moses," said Ngozi.

He unsheathed his sword creeping to the door of the pod. Moses followed suit. The pod slid open, Ngozi slit the guard to its death. He rushed his attack cutting through his enemies without harm coming to him. Moses ran out of the pod unsheathing his sword. He slashed through his enemies without hesitance. A shadow guard swung its electric heated stun stick at Moses from the side. He could sense the guard's every move and blocked the attack with his sword. Moses used his T'kaf and slashed the guard's torso in a deep cut and kicked it off the roof. Moses turned and saw a shadow guard from the distance firing laser bullets at Ngozi. He turned and blocked the bullets with his sword. Moses rushed towards the shadow guard clenching his sword. The shadow guard backed away in desperation while releasing laser bullets, but Moses slashed it in half while Ngozi lacerated its neck. The shadow guard collapsed, its head rolling off the drooping corpse.

Moses panted, holding on to his sword.

"The area is clear," said Ngozi. "All the guards are taken care of."

"*Very good,*" said Nadiyya through the Optix. "*You guys need to shut the blasters down fast. I don't know how long our armies will last.*"

"I'm on it now."

Ngozi rushed to one of the turrets. There were six lined in a row at the edge of the rooftop. Moses approached Ngozi.

"We did it Mazi," said Moses. "Our warriors now have the upper hand once these turrets are offline."

"Not quite," said Ngozi. "These turrets are automatic. I can't disable them from out here."

Ngozi placed the Optix over his mouth.

"Your highness," he said. "We have a problem."

*"What's going on down there?"* asked Nadiyya. *"Did you guys figure a way to disable the blasters?"*

"The turrets are automatic. Someone or something is controlling the turrets from within the palace."

"Now what can we do? All palace doors are sealed."

"Actually, they're all unlocked," said Imani.

"But how?" questioned Nadiyya. "That's impossible."

Ngozi smirked.

"That is actually a blessing," he said. "Someone on our side has reset the doors. And I have a clue of who it is."

"Well, whoever opened the doors gave us an opportunity," said Nadiyya. "You guys better move fast."

"We're on our way to the palace's interior," said Ngozi.

"And fellows," said Imani. "Be careful in there."

Ngozi smiled and rushed to the door reaching the palace's interior. Moses followed him closing the door. Moses walked down a fleet of stairs behind Ngozi. There were two flights of stairs below them. Moses rushed step by step down each step. The area was empty in dead silence. Without conflict, Moses reached the bottom of the stairs. Him and Ngozi were on the first floor where they needed to be. Moses and Ngozi walked through a door leading to the palace hall. It was just like Moses remembered when he was a small child.

"I can sense the Shadow Lord's presence," said Ngozi. "Come, you will have your chance to face him. But first, we need to get to the control room to deactivate the turrets before they cause more damage."

Moses nodded and followed Ngozi across the hallway. His blood boiled spotting Amaryllis and Mercius with a few guards across from where he was standing. Their son lied lifeless on the stretcher. There was a sudden pause. Tension rose within the palace walls. Moses positioned his sword at Mercius.

"Your reign ends now Shadow Lord," said Moses.

"Kill them," said Amaryllis to the guards.

The guards charged at Moses and Ngozi. Moses' focus on the Shadow Lord was overwhelming for the shadow guards as he dashed through them with the edge of his sword. Moses pointed his attention to Mercius. The Shadow Lord gave him a blank stare. Moses hollered, his eyes welling aiming his sword at the Shadow Lord.

"Moses wait!" yelled Ngozi.

Amaryllis waved her hand. Moses felt his body frozen in paralysis from his neck to his feet. Ngozi stared in horror at Moses' body being trapped in a crystal.

"Go, perform the ritual," demanded Amaryllis to her husband. "I'll hold them off."

Mercius nodded and moved forward towards the throne room. The stretcher was floating in front of him. Amaryllis lifted her hands. Two daggers appeared, pointing them at Moses.

"You're lucky the Shadow Lord wants your boy himself," she said. "Because I would gut him like a fish right now. But I'll leave that to my hubby. Fortunately for me, my dagger can taste your blood."

"Don't think I'll be an easy match for you shadow witch," said Ngozi.

He unsheathed his sword and swung it at Amaryllis. She blocked it with her daggers holding her ground ready to strike her enemy. Moses watched the battle frozen in place hoping to break free from this spell.

# Chapter Sixteen

# Vengeance

Ramses reeled the laser sword aiming it at Karungu's neck, but he blocked it in an instant. Yobanna aimed her sword at the Chieftain's torso, however, he deflected her swing and kicked Ramses in the chest. Karungu backed away a few feet twirling his sword. He grabbed a hilt from a holster on his side hip as a blade emerged. Ramses gnashed his teeth, clinching hold of the laser blade watching Karungu attach the two blades forming a double sword. Karungu smirked with satisfaction gesturing the two warriors to try and fight him. Ramses rushed an attack towards his enemy, the traitor. Yobanna followed behind in swift motions. *Cling, cling, cling, cling!* sounded the blades in swift motions. Karungu blocked every swing of Ramses and Yobanna's sword returning to them swift strikes. Ramses deflected each assault while Yobanna dodged with retaliation. In unison, Ramses and Yobanna veered their swords, one aiming at Karungu's shoulder blades, the other at his ankles. Karungu backflipped, sivoiding the sharp light of the laser blades. Ramses nearly lost his balance. Yobanna kept her composure lowering the sword. She stared at Karungu with intensity. The Chieftain outstretched his arms in arrogance.

"Is that the best the children of the Chieftains have to offer?" questioned Karungu. His smirk was sickening. Ramses wanted to cut his lips just so he would not curl his lips to another smile.

"Ramses, the first-born son of Oba. Yobanna, the daughter of Chieftain Alpha Akintoye. It's quite a shame that your technique is very sloppy. Even my father taught me better than that."

"We're just getting started," said Ramses.

*"End them,"* said Ekwenzu within Karungu's head. *"Do not waste too much time with these two. The throne is at hand."*

"I will end them quickly," said Karungu.

Karungu channeled the dark energy that was within him as violet flares surrounded his body. His appearance was darker. His visage was grim.

"This is getting serious," said Yobanna. "He's tapping into the power of Ekwenzu."

"That's how he defeated me the first time," said Ramses. "But I won't let it happen again."

"Follow my lead, I have a plan."

Ramses watched Yobanna with amazement. He was impressed by her stature. She was beautiful, fearless. Yobanna was a woman that was rare in the eyes of Ramses.

She dashed towards Karungu. Her laser sword gleamed but her movement was untraceable. Ramses followed suit and charged at Karungu. With the double vision of him and Ekwenzu, the Chieftain sensed Yobanna jabbing the point of the blade behind him. He cut her in the leg with the double sword. Her scream was ferocious. Ramses was ready to plunge the blade through Karungu's breastplate, but he was stopped by the Chieftain's magic. Ramses struggled to break free. The magic that was engulfing him was worse than the last. He could feel his bones crackling. The scream he wanted to let out couldn't come out because the pressure of the magic was in his throat. If death was coming, Ramses was hoping it would come soon.

***

Moses watched helplessly at the fight gatheringing as much of his T'kaf as he could to break out of the spell. The hold of the spell was like a vise grip. Moses grunted trying to ball his frozen fist. He watched as Amaryllis backed down the hall in swift motion from Ngozi. She held her daggers in caution of the warrior's next move. Her hiss was grimacing. Ngozi funneled his T'kaf. His body glowed a golden aurora. Ngozi zoomed towards the Shadow Goddess, his sword aiming at her bosom. She blocked the point of his sword and counterattacked in astonishing swings. Ngozi couldn't feel the weight of her attacks. It was as if he was fighting the air. Amaryllis' speed was tremendous, but Ngozi sensed her every move. Her tricks were not going to work. Ngozi used his weight and clung his sword to her daggers. He pushed her enough for her to lose her balance. Ngozi could see that she was vulnerable. He leaped towards her twirling his blade. Amaryllis clung her daggers together, looking to block his strike with clenched teeth. Ngozi's T'kaf overpowered her with ease as a flare of energy erupted from his sword strike causing his foe to skid across the hallway. He could hear her shrieks.

Ngozi walked towards her, his sword still in hand. Moses watched in continuation powerless of doing anything. He was hoping Ngozi would finish her off soon to break the spell. Ngozi glared at Amaryllis with intensity, pointing his sword at her. She panted holding her stomach.

"That was a warning shot shadow witch," said Ngozi. "The next move will be lethal. So now I'm giving you one fair chance. Remove the spell from Moses then leave Palasera at once crawling back to the filth from where you once came."

Amaryllis glared at him then laughed.

"Oh Ngozi, you think I'll leave my lovely garden behind for some threat? We're just getting started. You are a strong man, but I wonder how powerful you are mentally."

Amaryllis' eyes flashed gold. Ngozi's surroundings faded to a puff of smoke. The area was pitch black. This was an illusion, another trick. Ngozi knew Amaryllis was desperate.

"If you think you can defeat me like this then you're mistaken," he said.

"Oh Ngozi," sounded the voice of Amaryllis. Her presence was nowhere to be found, but Ngozi could sense her nearby.

"I know I cannot defeat you like this, but I am curious to know how the great Lion Clan Master and Spiritual Advisor of the Chieftain became so honored and loved by Ouidah. Or maybe the legacy you created was a lie."

"Give it up," said Ngozi. "I know what you are doing."

"No, I'd rather for you to give in."

Amaryllis walked from behind and pressed her index and middle fingers on Ngozi's forehead creating a flash.

Ngozi saw a blink of light leading to the throne room of old. The event he was witnessing in front of him was Chieftain Oba's coronation 16 years ago. His eyes beamed at the mixture of clans and their custom robes. Even a pack of the Wolf Clan appeared, their leader Alpha Akintoye and his wife walked alongside each other towards the throne. His brown-furred cloak caught the attention of everyone. Akintoye and his clan bowed to Oba placing his fist on his bulked chest.

"The Wolf Clan honors our new High Chief," he said.

He pulled out a glistened reddish-orange gemstone from his pocket.

"As a gift, I would like to personally give you a rare Illirl gemstone, the finest jewel of all Shiveria."

Ngozi watched as Oba smiled and took the gemstone. Amaryllis stood beside him.

"That was the first time our nation ever united," said Ngozi. "Oba was our nation's most powerful Chieftain of our time."

He looked at his younger self standing next to Oba. He wore the custom garments that warriors of Sahawayda wore consisting of a white kaftan with gold linen. He had a white turban draped around his head. A sword was in a hilt on his side.

"And I was appointed as his spiritual advisor. Oba believed in my skills. He knew everything about me. Although we grew up in separate tribes, we grew up as best friends. He knew I was gifted. And that is how we were able to defeat Shadow Lord Khonshu the first time nearly putting an end to the Shadow League. I believe that's why you monsters had to cower in the shadows and wait for a perfect opportunity to strike when our nation weakened and grew apart. And that is why your armies are failing now."

Amaryllis grinned placing her hand over her mouth in a backward sway.

"I have to say that your armies are impressive," she said. "Your little welp formed quite a team. But just like them..."

Amaryllis placed her two fingers on his forehead, flashes of light blinded him. She gripped her dagger. She was inches away from piercing his abdomen. *Pow!* was the sound of a shot. Amaryllis dropped the dagger then looked down and saw a splotch of blood on the side of her stomach. She quivered placing her hand on the blood spot. Amaryllis turned and saw Ashanti pointing a pistol at her. Smoke was steaming from the barrel.

"You remember I told you who had the last laugh?" questioned Ashanti. "It looks like fun, and games are over witch."

***

Ramses couldn't breathe each moment the pressure was applied to his throat and joints. He was beginning to feel bruises all over again. Karungu curled a malignant smirk, glaring into his eyes. Karungu's eyes changed dark violet, his double sword was ready for blood.

"I guess I'll get you out of the way," he said, his voice darker. "This time I'll take you out of your misery."

Yobanna shrieked from behind and rushed another attack on Karungu. Although he was suffering, Ramses watched the two move in swift motion exchanging sword strikes with a *cling*! Yobanna flipped on a wall next to her in an attempt to flip over Karungu. The Chieftain pressed his sword unto her laser blade as she landed on her feet. Karungu used his dark magic to blast Yobanna off her feet, her laser sword sliding yards away from her. Ashes emerged from her unconscious body.

"No...!" roared Ramses. He managed to ball his fists through his anger. The thought of watching another woman die at the hands of Karungu was overbearing no matter if she was a war-rior. Karungu glared at Ramses.

"Now where were we?" he said. "Yeah, tell your father I said salute."

Karungu threw the double sword at Ramses like a spear. Ramses felt a fury in him worse than the day he lost his birthright. Nothing was more disgraceful to him than a traitor mocking his father who gave his life to protect his nation, including Karungu. He felt something fuming inside him like a kindled fire. Ramses hollered staring at the sword that was inches away from his skull. He broke the hold as if chains shattered around him. Ramses caught the double blade and snapped it in half with his knee. Karungu frowned in disbelief. Ramses charged towards his enemy at a speed Karungu thought would never happen. The Chieftain ignited dark energy balls and threw them at Ramses. He deflected each ball causing them to leave wide dents on the walls. Karungu took a step back, trying to crush Ramses' body. However, it had no effect. Ramses used all of his strength and front kicked Karungu in the chest causing him to glide several yards. Yobanna gained consciousness staring at Karungu's body gliding towards her. She looked at the disengaged laser sword a few feet away and dashed towards it. She slid on the ground igniting the sword and plunged it through his backside.

Karungu gasped for air. Blood dripped from his mouth feeling the laser blade pull out of him. He quivered in pain falling to his knees with a pleading look on his face. Ramses walked up to him.

"Now you know how it feels to get stabbed in the back," he said. "And now you want mercy?"

Ramses shook his head and struck Karungu down with his knee. The Chieftain fell to his demise. His blood puddled around his dying body. Death was calling him. Ekwenzu was silent. Karungu took his last breath, then there was silence.

"I think he had enough," said Yobanna.

"Are you okay?" asked Ramses. He stared at her torn prison jacket. The ashes wore off, but she was left with bruises.

"I'm fine," she said. "They are just flesh wounds. We better hurry and get to your mother the queen to get to the blasters."

"Right," he said. "It's time to end this once and for all."

***

Amaryllis turned and faced Ashanti. The blood splotch stained her forest green gown. Amaryllis glared while Ashanti aimed the gun in her direction.

"It's too bad you didn't hit any of my vital organs," said Amaryllis. "Now I have the opportunity of executing you myself."

Amaryllis gripped her daggers. Her glare was vicious. Ashanti shot multiple rounds, but Amaryllis sliced the bullets in half with her dagger. She swiped her daggers looking to cut Ashanti in pieces. She staggered on her feet avoiding Amaryllis' swift blade swings. Ashanti was caught off guard by a kick on her chin. She fell on her back, the pistol sliding. Amaryllis was ready to strike.

"Say goodbye 'your highness'," she said holding the daggers in the air.

Ngozi dashed and blocked Amaryllis' daggers from piercing through Ashanti's skin.

"You will get no victory today," said Ngozi.

"Don't be too sure of yourself," Amaryllis.

She twirled almost in a whirlwind away from Ngozi and Ashanti. It was a moment of a standoff. Ashanti and Ngozi glared across from Amaryllis. The Shadow Goddess curled into a wicked smile. She used her magic causing an illusion around the room of her body multiplying. Echoes of Amaryllis' laughter sounded throughout the room.

Moses watched, helpless of doing anything. The spell was too strong for him to break. The crystal gripped tight on his body.

"Brace yourself, Ashanti," said Ngozi. "This witch is full of tricks."

"I know," said Ashanti.

The multitude of Amaryllis attacked Ngozi and Ashanti, all gripping daggers. Ngozi used his skill to fend off the duplicates. He deflected their strikes and countered with slashes. Ashanti stood close to Ngozi, evading every jab of the daggers, and shot as many atomic bullets as possible of the pistol she could, hitting all her targets. The corpses of the fallen duplicates disappeared the moment they hit the floor.

"How can we know which one of her is real?" questioned Ashanti.

"If you look closely at the wound, the bleeding should get worse," said Ngozi. "These duplicates' wound is fresh."

Ngozi and Ashanti fought through the duplicates without getting a single wound.

Moses watched the carnage from across the hallway. He watched closely at Amaryllis gliding towards Ashanti ready to end her. He could tell that was the real Shadow Queen. The wound was turning black.

"Motha...!" he screamed, but no one could hear him from the concealment of the crystal.

Amaryllis was inches away from what she saw as her first victim. The sword plummeted; Ashanti couldn't see it coming. She turned in a gasp. Her chest was in rapid beats. She was willing to join her husband in the spirit world, but Ashanti wasn't ready to take her last breath. She had too much to live for. She had a purpose and duty as a mother and queen of her nation. She closed her eyes, feeling no pain.

Ashanti opened her eyes. Ngozi stood in front of her. His breathing was heavy in grunts. She saw the dagger plunge through his chest. Ashanti screamed, "Ngozi...!"

Amaryllis took the sword out of Ngozi and used her magic to brush him away as he rolled on the floor a few feet away.

Moses' eyes gaped. He couldn't believe what he was witnessing. Rage fueled inside of him watching his teacher and father figure fall on the floor almost lifeless.

"Well, that was an unexpected turn," said Amaryllis. "But at least I got him out of the way. Now it's your turn."

Amaryllis held the dagger ready for the blade to taste more Nubarian royal blood. Ashanti backed away holding the pistol welling in tears.

Moses shrieked, his voice echoing the palace hall. Ashanti turned her head. Amaryllis was stunned. His voice shouldn't have sounded through the crystal under her spell. It was broken. The T'kaf through Moses fumed through him. Electric sparks ignited through the crystal. The crystal shattered into pieces, the spell was ruptured. Moses stood to his feet. His T'kaf flared around him in a golden color. His glare was set on the Shadow Queen.

Moses dashed at Amaryllis. His sword aimed for a death shot. Amaryllis hissed. She used her dark magic on Ashanti, forcing her body to glide onto a nearby wall. Moses slashed at Amaryllis, but she disappeared in a cloud of smoke. Moses missed. The slash of the blade would've been fatal. Moses closed his eyes, sensing Amaryllis' presence. He took deep breaths. She was close, he could feel her dark energy.

"I have to admit you are a powerful specimen," was the sound of her voice. "But it's too bad you have to die. Once I soften you up for my husband, he will finish you…"

She appeared behind through the smoke.

"And the Shadows will rule forever."

She aimed her dagger at his back. Moses could sense her. She made her move, then she shrieked. It was the harrowing sound of pain. Moses turned around and saw a sword driven from her spine to her chest. Amaryllis turned, her hands quivered foaming blood. Moses could tell that was Ngozi's sword pierced through her. He laid on his side conscious with a smile.

"You're not the only one with tricks," he said.

Amaryllis wheezed. Her thousands of years of conquest were fading. The Bronze Empire in Nubariah was the final empire she would witness.

"This is not supposed to happen," she said in a weak soft tone. "I am a goddess. I am supposed to be immortal."

"I guess even the gods can bleed," said Moses.

Amaryllis gawked. Her delicate skin pruned until her body turned into a hideous skeleton. Her skeleton soon crumbled into a pile of dust. All that remained was her tiara and gown.

Ngozi rolled on his back staring at the ceiling in short breaths. Moses welled in tears. His mother rushed past him kneeling next to Ngozi. She pulled off her white prison jacket applying pressure to his wound.

"C'mon… c'mon… stay with me," she said.

Ngozi shook his head.

"Not this time," he said with a smile.

Moses could sense Ngozi's end was near. First his father, then the man who raised and watched over him. He broke down in tears rushing to his fallen master.

"Master Ngozi no…" he wailed. "Please don't go… please."

Moses held his hand in an overflowing sob.

"Don't weep for me now child," he said in short breaths. "It's not over. Follow your duty. End this. Defeat the Shadow Lord. The throne is for the taking."

Ngozi grunted. The pain worsened. Moses continued sobbing. He felt the hand of his mother on his shoulder. He looked into her sincere eyes.

"You are my precious baby," she wept. "But Ngozi is right. You must go and follow your destiny. Go to the throne room and put an end to Mercius. Do you understand?"

Moses nodded wiping the tears from his cheek. His mother placed her hands on his head and pulled him to a kiss on the forehead.

"Now go, my son. I believe in you, my Chieftain."

Moses rose to his feet in a determined look. This was it, the deciding component of the battle. In Moses' mind, the throne was for the taking. Moses marched towards the throne room while his mother watched.

"Be careful my sweet," she said.

She held Ngozi by her side until he took his final breath.

# Chapter Seventeen

# The Battle of Decision

Moses was close to the throne room. No one was in the way this time as he continued marching forth with his fists pumped and his chest puffed. The door to the throne was at his sight. He could feel a surge of dark energy channeling. The Shadow Lord was present. Moses opened the massive, jeweled doors. There it was. The throne sitting above the flight of steps, just like Moses remembered. He stormed forward. The Shadow Lord was near the steps leading to the throne. He was on his knees speaking a language that Moses could not understand, *"thuó pais skotos…"* Flares of dark red energy flared around Mercius. Moses nearly gasped at the pruned lifeless body of the Shadow Lord's son. He realized Mercius was taking his son's essence through some paganistic ritual. The flare decreased. Moses held his guard prepared for anything.

"You came right on time," said Mercius, his back still turned. "Now that the ritual is complete, I can finally put an end to this."

Mercius stood to his feet and faced Moses. His eyes were bloodshot red. His skin turned dark grey. Flashing white lines appeared from his neck on down.

"I hope you didn't think you would come here to put an end to my empire, the empire I built with the palm of my hands."

"From a land that you stole," said Moses. "You will pay for all the blood you spilled Shadow Lord. Your rule will be at an end."

"I have to admit you are stronger than I anticipated before. But I won't let that same mistake happen again."

Mercius siphoned his dark power. The illusion of his power caused his body to vibrate like an engine. Moses was not phased. He stood in place pumping his fists. Mercius zoomed through supernatural speed. Moses could immediately sense the Shadow Lord's presence in front of him. He placed his hand up catching a heated punch the Shadow Lord threw at him. The Shadow Lord struggled a few moments looking to push the young Chieftain elect backward. Moses kept his balance, using his T'kaf to push the Shadow Lord a few inches away from him. The Shadow Lord scowled, vibrating again before he disappeared with two separate flames dashing towards Moses. He showed no signs of fear. Moses was focused. He could sense the Shadow Lord nearby. Moses looked up throwing his hands to block another punch of the Shadow Lord that aimed for the top of his head. Mercius struggled again but flipped over the boy catching his composure. The Shadow Lord dashed around Moses. Flames of fire swarmed him like a blanket. Mercius stopped in his tracks watching the fire swarm Moses.

Once the fire settled, Mercius' eyes gaped at Moses. The fire didn't damage him. Smoke flared from his clothes as he threw the red turban from his head to the majestic marble floor. The Shadow Lord frowned and stood in place the opposite of where Moses was standing. They were staring eye to eye.

"It looks like you managed to tap into your true power," said Mercius. "But let's see how long you can last before giving out. My power is unlimited. And soon you will die."

Moses was silent, holding his guard. He scowled, focusing on the Shadow Lord's energy. The Shadow Lord tapped into his dark energy. The flare igniting from the Shadow Lord was black and red. Moses focused his T'kaf, the flare around him was gold. Expecting a similar attack, Moses watched as the Shadow Lord spun as the flare formed into a black cloud with red electric sparks. Then he disappeared. Moses closed his eyes sensing his opponent. Moses could sense the Shadow Lord was close. He opened his eyes and flipped in the air. He threw a punch, catching the Shadow Lord off his guard. Mercius appeared blocking the swift punches Moses threw at him. The young chieftain elect spun a sweep kick at the Shadow Lord but missed as he leaped.

Before allowing the Shadow Lord to get on his guard, Moses dashed at a windy speed toward Mercius. The Shadow Lord blocked every combo of jabs and kicks. Moses flipped with each assault he threw at the Shadow Lord. His T'kaf boosted his speed to match Mercius. Moses could tell the Shadow Lord was struggling against him. He found an opening, the possible kill shot. Moses leaped and kicked Mercius on the side of his head, shattering his helmet. The Shadow Lord glided and skid across the throne room ten feet away. The Shadow Lord laid still. Moses saw his opportunity. He unsheathed his sword, ready to take out the murderous tyrant. He pointed the sword at Mercius.

"Your time is at an end Shadow Lord," said Moses.

He raised his sword ready to put an end to the suffrage his nation had to go through, the trauma with which he was living.

"I don't think so," he heard Mercius whisper.

The Shadow Lord rose and threw his hand at Moses. It was as if his breath was taken out as a vortex appeared behind Moses. In an instant, Moses was sucked into the vortex. The throne room disappeared as he hollered for dear life.

***

While the battle for the throne between Moses and Shadow Lord Mercius raged on, Uzoma and Makara continued to lead the armies against the Shadow League. The furor of the battle continued around them. The skirmish in the air was getting crucial. More of the fighters were getting struck out of the air by the saakuth. The blasters were diminishing the count of the warships. Despite fighting side by side holding their ground with combo strikes of the sword, Uzoma and Makara could tell the tide of the battle was working against them. The blasters from the turrets were blowing away their warriors leaving craters in scattered sections of the palace grounds. The number of casualties was increasing. Garrisons of shadow warriors were coming from appearing portals.

"These things are like robots," said Makara defending herself from the shadow warrior attacks.

"Trust me," said Uzoma swinging his sword. "Once they multiply, they're hard to defend off."

"But that's not the biggest issue. These blasters are killing off our armies fast. I don't know how long we can hold from this attack."

"That's why I'm hoping Ashanti or Ngozi will deactivate those things before all hope is lost."

Uzoma and Makara continued their charge towards the garrison of shadow warriors. The armies continued to back them with their united power and abilities.

***

Ramses rode up the elevator to get to the palace's main hallway. Yobanna stood beside him. Ramses turned to face her, breaking the stillness between the two.

"So you are the daughter of Alpha Akintoye?" he asked.

"I am," she said.

"It is no wonder we make good chemistry."

"Don't flatter me. I only did what I had to do for survival."

Ramses' mood turned sour.

"So is that why your father never came to the conference when my father needed him?" he questioned.

Yobanna turned to face him. Her look was in disdain as the elevator continued shooting up to the surface.

"You know nothing," she said.

Her voice fell silent again. There was an awkwardness between the two, a standstill. The elevator was at a complete stop. Ramses immediately walked out of the elevator in front of Yobanna. The gentleman in him ceased. The hallway of the palace was revealed. Ramses could feel the nostalgia of his childhood beaming around him.

He walked down the empty hollow hallway. Ramses expected to fight his way inside the palace and throughout the hallway. Instead, it was empty, dead silence. He cut one of the corners, finding his mother kneeling in sorrow. Ngozi was lying next to her.

"Mother, what's going on?" Ramses asked.

He walked closer to her. Ramses saw the wound on Ngozi's chest. His body was still. His eyes closed. Ramses was filled with emotions of sorrow and rage.

"What happened?" he questioned storming towards her. "What happened?!"

Yobanna placed her hands on Ramses' arms as he squirmed with bitterness. His mother rose to her feet leaving Ngozi's body on the floor.

"There is no time to mourn right now," she said. "Save it until this battle is over."

"No, tell me what happened!" demanded Ramses.

"I can explain after we disable the turrets! Our people need us right now."

"I don't give a damn about all that. What happened to my master?"

"Ramses, you're not thinking straight son. I'm upset too. Amaryllis struck him but he struck back. Ngozi sacrificed himself so we can move forward. Tell me, during your training with Ngozi, what did he teach you about duty?

Ramses thought for a moment.

"I must follow it no matter what."

"Then let us finish this," said his mother. "No one else needs to suffer.

Ramses breathed through his nostrils huffing in frustration.

"Let's finish this."

***

The screams seemed endless as Moses continued descending the vortex. It felt like hours to Moses since he was sucked in the darkness. He was questioning if he was falling to his death. How could he be so careless? Moses should've ended the Shadow Lord when he had the opportunity back in the throne room.

Moses landed on a dirt plain rolling on his back. He realized he was far from home looking at his surroundings. It was a desert without an atmosphere. Stars were in a standstill above him, giving the barren plain its only light. The plain he was standing on was hard. It was as if the dirt was made out of a foreign substance that he wasn't used to. Plateaus and craters stood in the distance from where Moses was standing. The atmosphere was thin. The gravity was lighter.

He saw from the distance a structure. Perhaps there he would find the answer he seeks of where he was. Moses looked around in confusion. This was nothing like the desert. The atmosphere was colder. His T'kaf flaring through him was the only thing that was protecting him from the sparse air. He tried adjusting his body weight but walking on the light surface of this mysterious world was a challenge despite the heavy armor he was wearing. Moses was closer to his destination. The mysterious construct was being more revealing with each step he took.

The construct was a strange place with no walls surrounding it. Moses could see the revealing of a lobby of marble flooring similar to the palace grounds. There was a roof with columns holding it in rows. Moses watched in wonder as he entered the construct. The lobby was empty. There was only a flight of stairs with a back wall in front of him. Moses paused and stared at a glowing ball rotating on a mount. The colors switched in consistency of orange, red, and yellow. Moses realized they were the colors that represented the Shadow Lord.

A red energy ball zipped at Moses' face in an astonishing speed. Moses barely threw his hands up to catch the energy ball. He struggled as the ball pushed him back. The gravity of this world was light, but the energy ball was getting heavier and heavier. The red ball glowed in a hum. Moses eyes gaped as the energy ball exploded causing him to roll backwards. His armor was half torn. His face turned bloody feeling burns on his hands and arms. Moses slowly rose to his feet. He wasn't going to get defeated that easy. Mercius was present, he could sense him. He felt his chin getting clumped before having a chance to hold his guard. Moses flipped backwards glancing at the Shadow Lord's appearance. His arms were in the air with his fist balled. Moses figured Mercius had uppercut him. He fell on his stomach. The Shadow Lord stood over him. A bruise was on the side of his head from the kick Moses planted.

"Get up boy," he said. "I'm just getting started."

Moses grabbed the Shadow Lord's brass boots and lifted himself. The Shadow Lord gave him an icy stare.

"Pathetic," he said.

In a swift motion to where Moses couldn't sense it, Mercius pushed Moses from him and swung a flurry of punches that landed from his face to his stomach. Moses felt helpless. The Shadow Lord was moving in a speed he couldn't keep up with. Moses felt the final impact of the Shadow Lord's boot on the bottom of his chin. Moses gagged, gliding backwards until his body made impact to the back wall leaving a deep dent. Moses fell on the floor. His vision was blurring. This was the end yet he refused to believe in his conscious. Moses had no choice but to follow his instinct. He slowly rose pumping his fists. He had to keep fighting. Moses felt the brass boots stomping his back like a roach. The Shadow Lord pressed his foot on the boy not allowing him to stand. Moses could not move nor breathe.

"Your reign is over before it started boy," said Mercius. "And soon, I will reign supreme. Lord Khonshu was right concerning you. You are the Shadow League's greatest threat. Your power does exceed your fathers. It's a good thing I stomped you out before your power would completely manifest."

The Shadow Lord took his foot off Moses and grabbed him by the throat raising him to his feet. Moses glared unto Mercius' lava eyes. His mouth quivered refusing his death. The Shadow Lord grabbed the chieftain's spear from a back holster, gripping it with a thirst of royal blood.

"And now is my chance to kill you in my own style of extermination. You are in my world where I am untouchable. I, Shadow Lord Mercius of Meatis, the first realm of the cosmos, will become the god of all gods with the death of the Ezenwa family. Like father like son. Long live the chief."

Moses' gawked. The core of his haunted memories flashed before his eyes, the death of his father at the age of four within the spell of the witch Amaryllis. The words of Khonshu rang in his ears, "Long live the chief." The horrific sight of his father's throat crushed was disheartening. Moses' pulse raced in rapid beats. The haunted memories of the suffrage of his people getting chained and beaten like animals who were decent human beings bubbled on the surface of his mind. He could hear the voice of his father in his mind, "You will become Chieftain son. I'm proud of you."

The spear nearly plunged through Moses skin but he grabbed the Shadow Lord's arm, gripping it in astonishing strength. He pushed Mercius' arm away as he dropped the spear. This was the first time Moses could see fear in the eyes of the Shadow Lord. Moses stared at the point of the spear as it glowed a jade color. His T'kaf surged through him in a bright flare matching the spear's. Moses grabbed the spear as the Shadow Lord backed away. He was loss of words staring at the sharp increase of power surrounding Moses. He stared at the Shadow Lord with intensity. Moses pulled his armor from his torso leaving only an elasterell black shirt on his middle and red pants. He walked towards the Shadow Lord. The blood stains on his face began to dry up with the burns on his arm healing. Moses' fists were pumped as he marched towards the Shadow Lord. He felt his T'kaf rising, the flares tingling his body with static sparks.

Mercius clenched his teeth in fury. *I won't be silenced*, he thought. The Shadow Lord dashed at Moses in remarkable speed. Moses vanished in a velocity as fast as warp speed jabbing the hilt of the spear on Mercius's stomach. His bronze armor immediately cracked. The Shadow Lord gagged coughing out spit. Moses planted the spear on the hard ground and threw flashes of punches stinging the Shadow Lord's face. Mercius tried countering, but Moses ducked his swings. The Shadow Lord was struck in the leg by a low kick then he felt his nose crack from a hard punch. Mercius skid from the marbled floor of the structure to the open plain.

Moses walked towards him. This time there was no escape for the Shadow Lord. A spark of energy ignited from the palm of his hand. He was ready to put an end to the Shadow Lord. Mercius rose feeling his nose out of place. He cracked his nose feeling trickles of blood dripping on his breastplate. He scowled at Moses as he finished forming the energy ball.

Vortexes appeared behind Mercius, but Moses refused to miss his opportunity of defeating the Shadow Lord. Anyone in his way would be diminished alongside him. Mercius turned and saw a group of his shadow warriors appearing. He smirked as more of them appeared through vortexes surrounding him and Moses.

Moses scowled forming another energy ball from his other palm. The dark warriors stood in place circling Moses and Mercius. The Shadow Lord scowled picking up on their lack of engagement. His eyes lit up gritting his teeth.

"Well, what are you all waiting for?! he demanded. "Get the welp!"

"Actually, the shadow warriors came as spectators for Lord Khonshu," said a voice from one of the vortexes.

A man of pale skin came from out of the vortex. He was dressed in a black hooded cloak. Moses glared at the man's crow eyes.

"Maur," said Mercius standing to his feet. "What is the meaning to this? Khonshu has no authority of my men in this battle."

"Lord Khonshu wants you to prove your worth as Shadow Lord. If you cannot defeat the boy yourself, then your death will be necessary."

Mercius gritted his teeth. He hollered in rage as Maur and the dark warriors backed away providing enough space for the deciding victor of the battle. A ball of fire swarmed around Mercius.

"When I'm finished with this boy, you tell Khonshu that he will pay for his betrayal!" he shouted. "Soon, I will become lord of all as deserved!"

Mercius glared at Moses.

"Power or not, you will die!"

Mercius charged at Moses, the fire ball swarming him.

"No!" yelled Moses.

He pumped his fists and gripped the spear. As the spear glowed the stars disappeared from the sky only revealing the radiant light. Mercius continued dashing at Moses looking to dish out the final strike. Sparkles of light appeared around Moses and Mercius. The Shadow Lord yelled in a grunt closing in on his prey. Moses spread his arms controlling the multitude of sparkled lights. He threw his arms at the direction of the Shadow Lord as the sparkled lights glided in unity. The Shadow Lord screamed as the lights combusted in his vicinity. The explosion sounded throughout the mysterious plane. The Shadow Lord's cry vanished. His presence faded.

The stars reappeared above. Moses fell on his knees taking a deep breath. It was finally over. Shadow Lord Mercius was no more. He looked at the stars.

"Fatha," he said. "I did it. The throne is finally ours."

***

Ashanti dashed down the hall with caution. The hallway was too silent, too empty. It could've been a trap. Ramses and Yobanna followed behind holding their guard for an unexpected attack from the shadow guards. Each corner they turned, no being was present. Ashanti was close to the place she needed to go, the control room. Yobanna stopped, staring at a generator in a room that was the size to stow away storage or supplies. The generator beamed a blue glow. Ramses turned and stared at Yobanna.

"What are you doing?" he asked.

"You might want to take a look at this," Yobanna said.

Ramses walked towards her. Ashanti followed out of curiosity. He stared in wonder of the generator.

"How did we miss this?" he questioned.

Ashanti observed the generator. It was strange to her.

"This is shadow technology," she said. "I never seen such a thing."

"What do you think it's for?" Ramses asked.

"It can't be for power of the palace. Our palace is run by electricity and the backup generators are located in the underground station."

Yobanna thought for a moment. Then she came to a realization.

"It's the generator that operates the turrets," she said.

"Are you certain?" asked Ashanti.

"I eavesdropped on a few guards a week ago talking about a generator that will give power to their greatest weapon. I'm positive that this is it. We need to destroy it."

Ashanti grabbed her pistol and cocked it reloaded of ammo. Ramses grabbed her hand shaking his head.

"I will destroy it," he said.

Ramses ignited the laser sword and threw it at the generator like a javelin. The point of the sword jabbed the generator. The blue light changed red, glowing brighter with sparks.

"It's going to blow!" yelled Ramses.

Ashanti, Yobanna, and Ramses fled the small room. An explosion sounded. Fire swirled around the area as Ramses leapt out of harm's way. After the explosion ceased, Ramses peeked and saw embers flaring around the small space. The generator was gone. Yobanna and his mother joined him.

"That should do it," said Ramses. "The blasters should be deactivated."

"It's only one way to find out," said Ashanti.

***

Within the air above the city, portals began to appear. Queen Nadiyya watched with worry. The warships and fighters were being blasted out of the sky. There was no way her army was going to last against another wave of shadow warriors. Instead, the saakuth flew to the portals. They only shot at the warships and fighters to defend themselves for retrieval.

"The shadow warriors are retreating," said the pilot.

"I see that," said Queen Nadiyya. "I don't understand."

"Yo!" yelled Imani from behind. "The turrets are deactivated. They did it! That will slow them shadow bastards down."

A smile curled on Nadiyya's face. There was hope after all.

***

On the palace grounds, Makara brought down shadow warriors with the spin of her blade. Uzoma used his T'kaf to push the warriors away. He stomped on a dark warrior laying close to him and plunged his blade through the dark creature.

"Look, the blasters are deactivated!" yelled one of the warriors. "They're not shooting anymore!"

Uzoma watched ahead of him. Portals began appearing behind the army of shadow warriors. He watched as they retreated. Makara stood beside him in confusion.

"They're retreating?" she questioned. "I don't get it."

Uzoma laughed with cheer. Makara scowled at him.

"What is so funny General Uzoma?" she inquired. "Are you this hopeless to laugh while we are all uncertain of their next plot of action?"

"There won't be a next plot of action for them," he said.

"How do you know?"

"The shadow warriors can't function without the control of their lord. Moses did it. Shadow Lord Mercius is no more."

He raised his sword yelling, Victory!"

The warriors around him repeated with their swords raised, "Victory!"

Makara was still confused, but she trusted Uzoma's judgement. She smiled and raised her sword joining the others as they chanted in victory.

***

Moses rose to his feet staring at the deep crater of where the Shadow Lord was destroyed. The shadow warriors appeared along with Maur in the midst of them. Moses turned to face the group of warriors glaring at Maur taking a hold of the spear.

"If you think you have the chance to finish me, then you are mistaken," said Moses. "You will all join the Shadow Lord in your graves."

"That is not necessary," said Maur. "I have not come here to engage in battle. At least not yet. I would like to congratulate you Chieftain Moses on your victory on behalf of Lord Khonshu. But your reign will be short lived once you face the highest lord of the Shadow League. You better prepare yourself because he will soon come to destroy you and end the Ezenwa bloodline once and for all."

Moses' glare was continuous. Tension was in the air. He took a step forward glowering at Maur.

"Tell your lord that I'm coming for him," he said. "My father will be avenged."

Maur let out an abrupt laugh.

"You have no idea what you're up against," he said. "But soon you will find out."

Maur led the dark warriors to a multitude of portals behind him.

"Wait!" called Moses.

Maur paused. He turned staring at Moses.

"How do I get out of here?" asked Moses.

"Yes, an exit," Maur responded.

He threw his hand at Moses. A wave of invisible energy vibrated from his palm. Moses held his guard, but he felt nothing attacking him. Maur stood still for a moment staring at Moses. Then he turned away entering one of the portals. The shadow warriors followed behind leaving Moses. He turned around staring at a portal behind him. That's what the shadow demon was throwing at him. Moses was victorious, but the war was far from over. He was ready to battle Shadow Lord Khonshu to end the Shadow League's tyranny forever, but first, he wanted to celebrate. Palasera became Ouidah's again. The Bronze Empire came at an end. Moses walked through the portal. A light flashed. The world of Meatis was behind him.

# Chapter Eighteen

# Coronation

The throne room was empty as Ashanti entered along with Ramses and Yobanna. It was almost an hour since the battle ended. She walked into the majestic chamber with wonder. She was confused. There was no sign of a battle that has taken place. She wondered what happened. Where was her son? She stared at the throne. Victory meant nothing if he was gone.

"Did they both just disappear?" Ramses wondered from behind.

"I'm uncertain," Ashanti said. "The Shadow League is full of manipulation."

"You guys think he's been abducted, and our victory was a ruse?" questioned Yobanna.

"The Shadow League wouldn't give up their power for anything," said Ashanti. "Something else happened."

"What's going on here?" questioned Uzoma from the doorway.

Ashanti turned and saw the General alongside Makara, Queen Nadiyya, and Imani.

"We're trying to figure out the same," said Ashanti.

Uzoma looked at Ashanti, then turned to see Ramses and Yobanna standing next to her. He was in a confused stare.

"Where is Ngozi?" he questioned.

Ashanti bowed her head. Ramses nearly wailed.

"By saving me, he sacrificed himself," said Ashanti. "Ngozi is no longer with us."

"No," grunted Uzoma shaking his head. "No…!"

Uzoma fell to his knees bawling with a roar. Makara, Nadiyya, and Imani held him in comfort. A portal came in a sudden flash in front of the throne. Ashanti and everyone around her focused their attention on the flashing portal.

"Brace yourselves," she said pointing her gun at the portal.

A figure came out of the portal who was all too familiar to her.

"Moses," she said lowering the gun.

Moses appeared through the portal as it shut behind him. The throne was sitting behind him. He watched below the steps at everyone marveling at him. Yobanna clapped her hands showing signs of respect for the new high chieftain. Everyone else joined in clapping their hands together except Ramses, who had his arms folded. Tears of joy flowed through Ashanti's eyes. She dashed up the steps meeting Moses halfway as he ambled his way down. She wrapped her arms around him.

"My baby," she said. "You did it. You redeemed the throne."

Moses wiped the tears from his eyes. After everything he's been through. After the heartache, the hopelessness, he did it. He became the king he was destined to be. He looked past her mother and watched his brother stare at him. Ramses nodded with approval. Moses returned with a nod of his own.

* * *

The aftermath of the battle led to a festivity of warriors celebrating among the city. The warriors led themselves to the houses of servants telling them that they were free. The people who became former servants rejoiced knowing that the Shadow Lord was gone. The Nubarian people teamed up with ropes, knocking the gold statues of Mercius to the ground shattering them in pieces. The death of their brethren was being collected for proper burials while the shadow warriors and guards were burned in piles. Cheers filled the air, but mourning was amid the casualties of war, both warriors and civilians.

* * *

Moses made his way outside of the palace. He watched around him his kingdom being cleaned from the images of the Shadow League. The damages of war were swarmed around him. It saddened him that people died, but it was the cost of war, the cost of freedom. Moses propped his head up taking in the sun as it was shining bright in the sky. The warm air soothed him. A group of Oph-Ur warriors sauntered towards Moses and the group behind him. The warriors bowed to the new High Chieftain showing respect. Then they pointed their attention to the group.

"My Queen," one of the warriors said to Nadiyya. "Your ship is ready for departure."

"Thank you, corporal," said Nadiyya stepping up.

Makara stood beside her as she turned to Moses.

"Again, I would like to congratulate you on your victory Chieftain Moses," she said. "Aswan and the Oph-Ur Clan will serve you well. May your reign last forever."

"Thank you, Queen Nadiyya," he responded. "I'm looking forward to working with you in a new era of peace and prosperity in Nubariah."

Moses bowed to her. She returned the gesture with a curtsey. Makara and the warriors led Nadiyya to the warship. Moses watched as the remaining warships departed from the city back to the land of Aswan.

***

While Moses adjusted himself as Nubariah's new High Chieftain, the Shadow Demon Maur entered0020a colony on Shiveria's moon through a dark portal. The city was dark made from titanium lit up with shadow technology. Maur entered a dome that covered an entire crater. A hood was on his head. His crow eyes were in a blank stare as droids and drones strolled past. Maur walked in an elevator in silence as it shot up to the top of the dome. He strolled through a corridor and entered a massive room.

Khonshu was on his knees meditating. A dark red flare glowed around him. In front of him was a view of the colony and Shiveria above in the background. Maur walked towards Khonshu and bowed to one knee behind him.

"Lord Khonshu," he said. "I came to report."

"I'm listening," said the Shadow Lord.

"Lord Mercius is dead. The boy out bested him in combat."

Khonshu was silent for a moment. Maur nearly gulped, intimidated by the Shadow Lord's presence.

"I should've known Mercius would fall," he said. "His arrogance and overconfidence led to his destruction. Mercius was a necessary death. I will take on the boy myself. I have foreseen this, and I am preparing as we speak."

"I will prepare the army and inform Shadow Lord Brutus of Yelrara to gather his troops for war."

"No. That is not necessary. The boy will come to me. We will battle on Genies Island. I have foreseen this."

"But my lord, you're going to allow the boy to ambush our army on Genies Island? We can attack Nubariah now while they are vulnerable."

Khonshu fell silent. His dark energy grew in a flare that radiated the room. Maur gulped in hesitance. He placed his hands on the ground pleading with the Shadow Lord.

"My apologies if I misjudged you, my lord," he said. "I trust in your judgment and knowledge. I will follow your every command."

The Shadow Lord remained silent for a moment then spoke.

"Go to Genies Island and wait for my further command. A war is coming."

"Yes, my lord," said Maur.

The shadow demon rose to his feet and sauntered out of the room. Khonshu remained in place, meditating on his inner power. His focus was on his enemy who was now his biggest threat, Moses Ezenwa.

***

Within the throne room of the palace, Moses was sitting in a chair surrounded by the midst of those he was ready to appoint in his ministry. It was a week since the fatal battle took place. The palace was cleaned from the damages of war. The city was at a slow pace of reconstruction. Amid those that were present in the throne room was his mother, who sat near him, his brother, Uzoma, and Imani. The surviving warriors of the Lion Clan were also present ready to hear their new chieftain announce their positions.

"As you may all know I have brought you all here because you all have the capabilities of leadership. For Ouidah to move forward and unite the clans, we must lead by example. My father always had a vision of Nubariah uniting as one nation without any doubt. Without any tyrants and traitors. Without dysfunction. Now is our chance to finally correct the wrongs of our past mistakes. We must learn to trust each other, as well as our judgments. And the first test is to trust my decision of your appointed positions."

Moses looked to his mother.

"Mother, you helped my father rule this nation with grace. Nubariah will always see you as their queen. You did tell me that you will become Nubariah's new ambassador. And for that, as your son and new Chieftain, I grant you that position."

She nodded her head with approval with a smile. Ashanti was proud of what her son has become. Moses turned his attention to Uzoma.

"Uzoma, you have proved countless times of your leadership in commanding an army. And the day is finally here. You served my father then, now you are serving me as my General Commander of the Lion Clan Army."

"I am honored to serve you my Chieftain," said Uzoma.

Moses turned his attention to Imani. She straightened herself up on the chair clearing her throat.

"Imani," he said. "Because you didn't walk away from me when I needed you the most, I decided to reward you with a position here in Ouidah. With your expertise in both the use of war and technology, I am appointing you as the Chief of Security. You will be tasked as the head of all security, patrol, and holo systems of Ouidah."

"Yo…" Imani said. "That is big. Chief, you didn't have to."

Uzoma pressed his hand on Imani.

"Just accept the position," he whispered to her. "It's an honor for someone of your status to take such a high position."

"Oh, I accept it," she responded. "But man, Chief of Security."

Moses smiled and turned his attention to his brother.

"Ramses, my brother. I know you feel like I stripped your birthright from you. If it was up to me, I would've allowed you to be Chieftain. But this is a destiny that none of us can control. Although you do not have the throne, you are still an Ezenwa. You have as much right to rule Nubariah as I do. And that is why I will appoint you as my Second Command. You will be able to take charge of all the ministries alongside me to make sure Nubariah becomes a prosperous nation. Together big brother, we can achieve father's goal and unite Nubariah as one nation."

Ramses gazed at Moses for a moment. He nodded his head with approval.

"I accept the position," said Ramses. "And thank you. I will make sure father's wishes will not be vain."

Moses nodded and turned his attention to the remaining warriors in the room.

"And for the rest of you in the room. I chose you all because you were all once in exile, just like I was. You served in the Silent

Assault along with General Uzoma and Imani. You all were once Lion Clan warriors that only felt like you existed. I felt like that for a long time. But when the calling came, you never turned your back. And for that, I am appointing you all as my new Lion Clan Council. You will all be responsible for training the next generation of warriors and defending Ouidah and all of Nubariah."

"The Council will serve you well your highness!" yelled one of the warriors.

"So, with Ngozi gone, who will be your spiritual advisor?" questioned Ramses.

Moses fell silent. Ashanti glared at him with her lips pinched. *This is not the time for this,* was the look she gave him.

"Ngozi taught me a lot both physically and spiritually. He always knew I had capabilities beyond my father's power. I believe that's why he was so hard on me. My journey with Ngozi had me realize I have my father's physical strength and power, but I have Ngozi's spiritual abilities. So, I really don't need a spiritual advisor."

The room fell silent. Moses rose to his feet.

"You are all dismissed," he said. "This meeting is adjourned. I must retire."

The throne room cleared. Moses turned to face the throne. He began to feel sorrowful, an emptiness. Ashanti stood beside him rubbing his back in comfort.

"What is the matter?" she asked.

"I just wish they were here to see this moment," he said.

"They are here in spirit. Your father is smiling down on your success. And Ngozi wants this for you. His sacrifice was to allow you to become the leader that you are destined for."

Moses turned to his mother.

"I know they are proud," he said. "And they want this for me. But first, I need closure. Ngozi deserves the best burial. That will at least bring me some peace to this."

***

The next morning, Moses sat on the palace grounds beholding Ngozi's grand funeral. Only friends and relatives were allowed in the palace grounds. Millions of people were attending around the city paying their respects for one of the greatest warriors in Nubarian history. Some people traveled from Mombasa, Aswan, including Sahawayda, Ngozi's original home.

Moses sat up front next to his mother and Ramses, who sat on the opposite side. He and his brother were dressed in red and black kaftans with black turbans covering their heads. His mother beside him wore a long black dress with a black head covering. A cape with a red and silver dashiki print covered her backside. Even her glamorous look of jewelry, heels and makeup couldn't heal her sorrowful spirit. Moses was mesmerized at Ngozi's corpse lying in the casket. He was dressed in Nubariah's finest garment of Sahawayda customs of a kaftan and pants of royal blue and gold linen. A gold turban was on his head with black dress shoes. This was still surreal to him. Moses was still in unbelief that his teacher was gone. There were priests and people that were close to Ngozi that said a few words.

Moses barely listened, barely focused on their broken-hearted words of, "you were my brother." He watched his mother speak wailing in tears, "You were our protector. You were like a father to my boys when my husband was brutally murdered. And for that, you forever have my gratitude. I will miss you. My sons will miss you."

She was escorted from the podium bawling her eyes. Tears streamed from Moses' eyes feeling the same despair as his mother. Moses stood to his feet and walked alongside his mother and brother viewing the corpse. They held each other tight bracing themselves for the reality that their father figure and protector was gone. "Rest peacefully my teacher," whispered Moses. Moses gathered the strength to lead his mother and brother away from the corpse, but the pain wouldn't heal. Ramses hollered in a roar while his mother fell on the ground bawling. Moses wept, letting go of his mother's waist nearly falling to the ground. He felt a man in a white turban embracing him.

"Let it all out your highness," he told him.

Moses had to let out all the pain. He knew it was the only way to bring healing, to make him whole.

After his mourning, Moses alongside his mother and brother followed the coffin as it was carried out of the palace grounds into the city. The people swarming the area were dancing celebrating the life of their hero. Drums were beating in a harmonized rhythm. People were chanting in the background. Moses was in silence the entire walk throughout the city. His mother had let go of his hand and kicked off her heels joining in the dance getting rid of all her sorrow. Her cape was waving revealing the dashiki prints. Moses never experienced funerals with the after ceremonies. There was never a burial for his father. Perhaps this was a funeral in honoring his spirit as well. Moses continued walking until Ngozi's coffin was placed on the back of a trailer. A chariot of rhinorses was upfront. The warriors from Sahawayda rode their rhinorses out of the city. Ngozi's body was carried away back to his homeland. Moses watched giving his teacher a final farewell.

***

The day of Moses' coronation arrived the next day. He stood behind the palace door with his purple woven garment of fine gold linen. A round ozo hat covered his fro like a stocking. The sound of a large crowd was awaiting him. His mother stood beside him in a long white dress with blue, gold, and silver patterns. Gold rings were around her neck including a blue head covering.

"Are you nervous son?" she asked.

Moses exhaled breath and looked at the door.

"I would've never thought this moment would come for me," he said. "But I'm ready."

He turned his head smiling at his mother. She returned his smile with a smile of her own. It was time. One of the guards serving the Grand Guardian of Sahawayda opened the throne room doors. The throne was awaiting.

"It is time your highness," said the guard.

Moses nodded and followed the guard inside the throne room. Hundreds of people gathered in the majestic room. Moses could see the nation was looming his coronation as they fell silent. He was accompanied by two guards of Sahawayda alongside his mother. He walked through the open aisle peering through the crowd. He spotted Imani pointing at him moving her lips without making a sound, "You're the man." He saw Queen Nadiyya and Makara within the midst beholding their new High Chieftain. Ramses stood upfront in a gold kaftan. Moses saw the throne. Uzoma stood in the middle of the steps leading to the throne and bowed to his new Chieftain. The Grand Guardian stood on the top of the steps where the throne was sitting.

His mother and the guards stood to the side among the crowd as Moses took step after step until he reached the top. The Grand Guardian stood in front of Moses. In his right hand was the traditional spear. Moses bent his knee honoring the Grand Guardian's majestic presence. The crowd followed suit.

"We are gathered today for the coronation of our new High Chieftain of Nubariah," said the Grand Guardian. "One regime passed from one time to the next. Kings fell like the dawn with the next rising like the morning. Today, we have a new king. A king that will bring our nation to justice and peace among society. A king that will unite all the clans of Nubariah. There will be challenges among the way. We will head into dark times, but we will endure the times together. I just pray for all the souls of Nubariah, including the souls throughout Shiveria."

The Grand Guardian paused for a moment. The crowd was in a continuation of silence. Moses remained on his knee. His head bowed to the floor as the Grand Guardian presented him with the spear. Moses grabbed the spear and rose to his feet.

"And now presenting your new High Chieftain, Moses Ezenwa! May your reign and leadership carry Nubariah in a new era of virtue!"

Moses raised the spear. Drums were roaring in beats. Trumpets were blowing as the crowd cheered, "Hail to our new chieftain! We salute you!"

Ramses snuck from the crowd to make his exit out of the throne room. Moses watched in near sorrow. He had to see what was on his brother's mind.

Ramses made his way up the rooftop. It seemed like thousands of thoughts were flashing through his mind. He watched the overview of the city. He turned his head and saw Yobanna standing near him. This was the first time he saw her in a dress and makeup. He was nearly mesmerized, but his thoughts were outweighing his judgment.

"What brought you here to see me," he said with a smirk.

"I came here to congratulate the new Chieftain," said Yobanna.

"This is the first time seeing you in a dress. I would think you would dress in regular clothing since the Wolf Clan decided not to attend the coronation."

"How you figure none of us attended?"

Ramses smirked. His eyes were glued on the Wolf Clan Chieftain's daughter. He could tell she was flirting through her coy look despite her arms being crossed. Ramses could tell her true purpose of coming. He savored the moment. It was possibly the only moment he had before she would disappear back to her native clan. Ramses responded despite the distraction.

"I looked at the attendance list before the ceremony. No one of the Wolf Clan was on the list. I assume your father declined the invitation. But I know the reason why you came."

Yobanna rolled her eyes curling a smile.

"You think you have me figured out, do you?" she said sauntering towards him.

"One thing my master once taught me was to read your target."

"I came here to personally thank you. You truly had my back when we fought Karungu."

"I did what I had to do. But I'm grateful you spared me and my mother's life."

Yobanna leaned towards Ramses and pecked his cheek with a kiss. He felt warm from the touch of her lips. Ramses let out a faint smile hoping to not ruin the moment of cheesing too big. Yobanna took a step back.

"The Wolf Clan supports our new High Chieftain," said Yobanna. "My father just needs time to gain his trust of how your clan will deal with Khonshu and the Shadow League."

Ramses nodded his head with assurance.

"Tell your father we will handle Shadow Lord Khonshu and his army when the time comes."

"My father is a hard man to convince. But you have my trust. Until we meet again."

"Until we meet again."

Yobanna walked away leaving Ramses back to his thoughts. He continued gazing at the city. Rays of the sun descended on the buildings and the city streets. He could see the sign in the sky. The dawn of a new kingdom.

"I know it is upsetting that the crown was given to me," said a voice Ramses didn't expect. "But none of us couldn't control destiny."

Ramses replied without turning to face Moses who stood a few feet away from him.

"We all have the power to control our destiny," he said. "Tell me, brother. After how I treated you these past few weeks, why are you not condemning me?"

"Because you are my brother, and I love you. Even though I always thought you were a bully, which you were, I always looked up to you. That is why I chose you to be my second command."

Ramses smiled.

"I do appreciate it, Moses. You didn't have to do it. You could've just made me into some clown for entertainment."

The two brothers laughed. Moses got closer standing next to his brother.

"Naw, I would've used you as a champion gladiator or something," Moses said.

"But all jokes aside. I am ready to make amends with you Moses. You did defeat the Shadow Lord. Something I know I was too powerless to do. All I care about at this point is avenging our father with Khonshu's blood smeared on our swords."

"We will avenge him Ramses. That I promise you."

"We will bring a new era to Nubariah brother. Together, we will bring peace and justice to our nation."

"I'm looking forward to it big brother. I know Father would be proud."

Moses and Ramses stood together staring at the city. The future of Nubariah was in their control. Perhaps it was their destiny after all, two brothers ruling side by side rebuilding a nation that was lost to them. One brother had the throne as high chieftain, the other ruling as the chief prince.

Epilogue

While Chieftain Moses planned his war strategy against Shadow Lord Khonshu, members of the Hawk Clan within the country of Atlantica across the sea sat in the Chieftain's cabin outside of the metropolitan city of Stoney Pine. The men sat with hawk feathers on their headbands and clothing staring at the monitor in front of them. It was a concoction of young men, boys, and elders in caramel and mocha colored skin. Their hair were straight, braided, and curly. Some of the men held their wives while the Chieftain in his golden years sat on his comforting chair.

A woman's voice was reporting on the monitor. Images of the battle was gruesome. The Clan around the room watched the Nubarian people run for cover as laser blasts launched in every corner of the atmosphere. Bodies were on top of bodies. The images of the news clip were graphic. The headline read Nubariah and Bronze Empire Conflict.

"As you can see this is the cost for independent freedom after seven years of slavery and oppression," said the woman.

Shadow Lord Mercius was shown on the screen. His posture of pride tainted the screen as the woman's voice continued to sound on the screen.

"Emperor Mercius, ruler of the Bronze Empire, was pronounced dead after the grueling battle. His alleged death was reported by Ouidah General and Nubariah's new Principal Advisor Uzoma right after the smoke cleared from the battle."

The image changed from Mercius to Moses, the new High Chieftain making his way to the throne.

"Now Nubariah has a new High Chieftain, Moses, the youngest Chieftain to ever rule Nubariah at only the age of 11. He is the 120th ruler within the Ezenwa Dynasty that ruled Nubariah for almost six millennia."

The image of a man with pale skin drenched in a red and gold robe appeared on the screen. He was in his elderly stage, but his posture was youthful. A gold crown was around his head. Men dressed in black suits were swarming them as they were treading down a corridor.

"Czar Godfrid of Sierra congratulated the young Chieftain indicating that he was not going to interfere with in the Nubarian Uprising against the Bronze Empire. Furthermore, the Czar announced that he would like to meet with Nubariah's new Chieftain and discuss negotiations of diplomatic solutions to prevent war from spreading among the two kingdoms."

The monitor was shut off. The men in the room were in stares. The Chieftain had a blank look. The room was in silence. One of the men stood to his feet breaking the silence.

"It amazes me how the Nubarians fought for their freedom," he said. "Shouldn't that motivate us!"

The men in the room agreed, their voices echoing the room. The Chieftain rose to his feet silencing the men around the room. His hand was raised. His silver hair radiated from the light flaring in the ceiling.

"That boy you see on the screen is chosen," he said. "Moses Ezenwa is following his purpose. To unite Nubariah, and hopefully bring back the lost of Sahawayda."

"So you think that a boy is gonna save us from the Sierrans?" questioned a young man of brown skin with the look of fifteen.

The Chieftain glared at him staring at his graphic t-shirt that read the word "Respect". A man past his youth stared menacingly at the young man. The young man looked back at the man and fell silent. The Chieftain shook his head answering the young man's question.

"We are dealing with more than oppression from our enemies," he said. "Our issues are deeper than two kingdoms battling for a right to rule and to judge. Before figuring out how to fight for independence, we must first figure out how to defeat the corruption within our very own."

Welcome my fellow readers. If you're reading this book, it means you're embarking beyond a single world and into a **multiworld**—a genre I created from my own desire to explore what lies beyond the traditional confines of a narrative in literature.

As a writer, I've always been fascinated by the idea of interconnectedness, the silent threads that bind people together across great distances. I initially discovered the multiworld after my wife and sister in-law critiqued me of creating a white character, Peter Tucker. They both asked me a question that had my subconscious mind bubbling, "Why not create a black character?" That is when I eventually discovered the Moses and Ramses character parallel to Peter Tucker and his brother Jason. At first, I thought of eliminating the white character and keep the black character, but I didn't want to limit my story to one narrative. So, I thought back of me reading and viewing both Marvel and DC comics and film, which introduced the ideology of multiple worlds, universes, and heroes. I studied those distances that weren't just geographical, but cosmic. Think of the multiverse in the MCU spanning entirely separate realities, with different laws of physics, different histories, and different definitions of what it means to be alive.

That thought was the seed that grew into this story. I didn't want a single hero's journey; I wanted to tell the story of a shared destiny woven from separate threads. To do that, I needed guides, and that's when the pieces of the missing puzzle where my characters, **Moses Ezenwa**, **Peter Tucker**, and **Donavon Ahoka**, came in to play. They aren't just characters in a book; they are young heroes in their adolescence, heirs to leaders, and resilient warriors. They are your anchors in each of their unique, vibrant realities.

This narrative is an invitation to you. You are about to witness not just one story, but a symphony of them, each one a universe unto itself. My hope is that by following Moses, Peter, and Donavon on their separate paths, you will see how their individual struggles, victories, and very existences are all part of a single, breathtaking tapestry.

Thank you for joining me on this journey. I can't wait for you to see what's on the other side.

# ABOUT THE AUTHOR

K.T. Brown is a self-published author and educator from South Carolina, born in Greenwood and raised in Columbia. From an early age, he developed a passion for storytelling, fueled by a vivid imagination and a deep love for writing.

He earned his Bachelor of Arts in English from Allen University and went on to receive his MFA in Creative Writing from Converse University. His academic background informs his work, blending literary depth with compelling, character-driven narratives.

K.T. Brown currently resides in Columbia, South Carolina, with his wife, Desiree, and their three children, Hezekiah, Kyleah, and Selah.

To stay updated on new releases and events, visit his Substack at ktbro.substack.com or follow him on Facebook, Instagram (@kt_brown77), TikTok (@ktbrown25), and YouTube (@ktbrown).

While Moses prepares for war, Peter Tucker and Donavon Ahoka prepares for the opportunity of a lifetime but is faced with a conflict that hits home. Find out what happens in

# Peter Tucker and the Hawk Warrior

## Tree of Souls

## Coming Soon

## CANON

**Path of the Lion Rising Kingdom Pt. I The Birthright**

## NON-CANON

**The Adventures of Peter Tucker: Introduction of the Tiger**